Haunted Nights

Supernatural Noir

Swan Sister (with Terri Windling)

*Tails of Wonder and
Imagination: Cat Stories*

Teeth: Vampire Tales
(with Terri Windling)

*Telling Tales: The Clarion
West 30th Anniversary Anthology*

*Troll's-Eye View: A Book of
Villainous Tales* (with Terri Windling)

Twists of the Tale

Vanishing Acts

A Whisper of Blood

A Wolf at the Door (with Terri
Windling)

The Year's Best Fantasy and Horror,
Volumes 1–21 (with Terri Windling,
Gavin J. Grant, and Kelly Link)

ALSO BY LISA MORTON

By Insanity of Reason
(with John R. Little)

The Castle of Los Angeles

Cemetery Dance Select: Lisa Morton

The Devil's Birthday

The Free Way

Hell Manor

The Lucid Dreaming

Malediction

Midnight Walk (as editor)

Monsters of L.A.

Netherworld

The Samhanach

Smog

Summer's End

Wild Girls

*Zombie Apocalypse!:
Washington Deceased*

Nonfiction Books

The Cinema of Tsui Hark

Ghosts: A Haunted History

*A Hallowe'en Anthology: Literary and
Historical Sources Over the Centuries*

The Halloween Encyclopedia

*Savage Detours: The Life and Work of
Ann Savage* (with Kent Adamson)

Trick or Treat: A History of Halloween

*Witch Hunts: A Graphic History of the
Burning Times* (with Rocky Wood and
Greg Chapman)

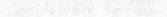

Haunted Nights

A Horror Writers Association Anthology

Edited by

Ellen Datlow and Lisa Morton

BLUMHOUSE BOOKS | ANCHOR BOOKS
A Division of Penguin Random House LLC
New York

A BLUMHOUSE BOOKS/ANCHOR BOOKS ORIGINAL, OCTOBER 2017

Library of Congress Cataloging-in-Publication Data
Names: Datlow, Ellen. | Morton, Lisa, 1958– editor.
Title: Haunted Nights : a Horror Writers Association anthology /
edited by Ellen Datlow and Lisa Morton.
Description: First edition. | New York : Anchor, 2017.
Identifiers: LCCN 2017001402 (print) | LCCN 2017020359 (ebook) |
ISBN 9781101973837 (paperback) | ISBN 9781101973844 (ebook)
Subjects: LCSH: Halloween—Fiction. | Horror tales, American. |
BISAC: FICTION / Horror. | FICTION / Anthologies (multiple authors). |
FICTION / Occult & Supernatural.
Classification: LCC PS648.H22 H366 2017 (print) | LCC PS648.H22 (ebook) |
DDC 813/.0873808—dc23
LC record available at https://lccn.loc.gov/2017001402

Anchor Books Trade Paperback ISBN: 978-1-101-97383-7
eBook ISBN: 978-1-101-97384-4

Book design by Anna B. Knighton

www.anchorbooks.com

Printed in the United States of America
10 9 8 7 6 5 4 3

Contents

Introduction

Lisa Morton

WHEN WE THINK of Halloween—especially if we're Americans, where the holiday was really (re-)created in its modern, still-recognizable form—we probably go first to memories of costumes and masks, trick or treat, jack-o'-lanterns and haunted houses, horror movies on television, and autumn in the air. Those of us who persist in revering the printed word may revisit beloved books like Ray Bradbury's *The Halloween Tree,* Norman Partridge's *Dark Harvest,* or Washington Irving's "The Legend of Sleepy Hollow" (contrary to popular belief, that classic work never actually mentions Halloween). The more knowledgeable among us might know of Robert Burns's 1785 poem "Hallowe'en," a lovely and playful description of a Scottish celebration at which (mostly) young people engage in fortune-telling games, even going so far as to call on the devil in their various efforts to divine the future.

But the first literary mentions of Halloween precede Burns by two centuries; they describe a holiday drenched in deliciously spooky superstition. Take, for example, these two lines from Alexander Montgomerie's 1584 poem "Flyting Against Polwart":

> *In the hinder end of harvest, on Allhallow even,*
> *When our good neighbors do ride . . .*

Montgomerie goes on to describe those "good neighbors" in more detail, and he could easily be ticking off the characters in any modern haunted attraction: there are the King of Faerie and the Elf Queen, "many elrich Incubus," witches ("the Weird Sisters"), ghosts, spiders, owls, ravens, and werewolves. The fact that "Flyting Against Polwart" is actually a satirical attack on one of Montgomerie's rivals doesn't lessen the strange and whimsical portrait it paints of Halloween night.

Looking back further into the past, we find that Halloween's ancestor, the Celtic New Year's festival Samhain, probably gave birth to the holiday's macabre side (although some scholars believe that the Catholic All Saints' Day, on November 1, and All Souls' Day, on November 2, were more responsible for Halloween's obsessions with death, spirits, and all things hellish). We really know very little about how the Celts honored Samhain—they kept no written records, and so we have nothing more than the reports of early Christian missionaries and scant archaeological evidence to rely on—but it does seem to have been a night of mystery and power for them. As the time when an old Celtic year gave way to a new one, it was also a time when the border between our world and the next was thin enough to allow both dead spirits and malevolent *sidh,* or fairies, to cross over. The Celtic legends are packed with fearful doings on Samhain: female werewolves that lay waste to flocks of sheep, corpses that return to life and speak, *sidh* warriors who venture out of the otherworld to burn down palaces, and humans who cross into the otherworld and spend whole lifetimes in a single year. These stories were passed down through the centuries, eventually becoming Irish and Scottish folktales about men who were lured by fairies into dancing themselves to death, encounters with hordes of ghosts, and deals with diabolical tricksters.

Samhain may have provided Halloween with the raw grist for its dark mill, the Irish and Scots may have kept it alive through the centuries (while the British condemned it as a relic of a religion they no longer accepted), but it really took the Americans to produce the Halloween we know today. When the Irish fled famine in the mid-nineteenth century and brought their celebrations with them, they found an American upper-middle class hungry for ways to party. The explosive growth of magazines introduced American matrons to the quaint October festival, with its games and costuming and glimpses into the world beyond. The New World provided a native squash called the pumpkin, which proved perfect for carving ghoulish faces into (in their native land, Irish pranksters had been content to light up turnips), and by the twentieth century, manufacturing companies had found ways to profit from candy, costumes, and decorations.

Now, in the twenty-first century, Halloween has overcome religious objections, emigration, destructive pranking (at the height of the Great Depression), unfounded urban legends of poisoned candy and razor blades in apples, co-opting by counterculture groups, acts of terrorism, and (in a curious full circle) religious objections to not merely survive, but thrive. It has overtaken other holidays in sales of sweets and booze, its influence has spilled into areas of pop culture as diverse as tattooing and "escape rooms," and Halloween literature has experienced a renaissance.

The stories in *Haunted Nights* showcase why Halloween is such an effective theme in fiction. Halloween, with its roots in a night that lifts the veil between our world and the next, is broad enough to hold horror tropes like ghosts, witches, and shape-shifters, but it also has its own specific icons, like "Stingy Jack," the blacksmith who outwits the devil but is finally forced to wander the earth forever with his way lit only by a glowing hell ember carried in a carved pumpkin (or turnip), the jack-o'-lantern, in other words. Halloween's universal appeal—we are all interested in death, aren't we?—makes it work in both isolated, rural settings and densely packed urban locales. It has a rich history and seems poised to extend into a long and interesting future. And it has given rise to related holidays—Devil's Night, held on October 30, the night to which pranking was banished; All Souls' Day, when souls trapped in purgatory can receive our offerings; the Welsh Nos Galan Gaeaf, with its bonfires and particularly vicious fortune-telling games; and Dia de los Muertos, which merges Catholicism's somber devotions to the dead with the far more colorful celebrations of Mesoamerica's Aztec and Mayan peoples. There are stories here about witches and fairies, the devil and his foe Jack, madness and art and revenge and birth and death and veils between worlds.

I think the Celts would have recognized these stories, traded them around a Samhain fire, and shivered in delight at them. When you read them, I hope you'll think of the grand, millennia-old tradition you're participating in.

Happy Halloween.

Haunted Nights

With Graveyard Weeds and Wolfsbane Seeds

Seanan McGuire

I t's halloween," Mary told Cook while Cook boiled caramel and dipped apples and laid them on the table to dry, buttery and glistening in their new candy shells. Cook smiled indulgently and gave Mary a ball of caramel to play between her fingers and shooed her out of the kitchen.

"It's Halloween," Mary told Mr. Evans the gardener while he stuffed old clothes with hay and sticks and raised his new-formed scarecrows onto their stands, propping them around the grounds like watchful sentinels. Mr. Evans smiled, not quite as indulgently as Cook, and gave Mary a stick and some string to tie around it and shooed her out of the garden.

"It's Halloween," Mary told Mr. Blake the coachman while he oiled the hinges on the front gate so they would creak like *such* and not like *so* when the trick-or-treaters came to call. Mr. Blake smiled coolly and gave Mary an old horseshoe, heavy and red with streaks of rust like drying blood, and shooed her away from the gate, back toward the house.

"It's Halloween," Mary told herself, caramel and rust streaking her fingers, the stick shoved lengthwise into her hair so her ponytail held it in place, high and bobbing bright in the autumn wind. Atop the house, crows cawed their delighted caws into the air, and a curtain swayed, pulled aside and let go by an unseen hand. Delighted with herself, with the world around her, Mary tucked the horseshoe into her pocket and raced on.

GROWING UP IN the shadow of the Holston house means growing up understanding why people believe in ghosts.

Believing in the ghosts yourself is optional, which is a good thing, because screw that: nobody's going to convince me that some peeping Casper is hanging around to watch me get my titties out at the end of the school day. Dead is dead. Dead moves on. But the Holston house ... it makes you understand why people *would* believe. Why they might even *want* to believe.

It should have fallen down a long damn time ago, for one thing. It's older than any other house in town, built when this was nothing but pastoral fields, evergreen woods, and horse farms for rich people. The Holstons had a butt-load of money by old-timey standards, and to hear people who knew them before they died out, it was a lot of money by modern standards, too. The kind of money that sees a pretty field and says "I should build a giant-ass mansion there for no good reason, just because I want to."

I shouldn't be too hard on them, dead old rich people that they are. This town exists because they built here—in case the name wasn't clue enough. Holston, Oregon: A Nice Place to Live. The motto's not wrong. It's *nice* here. No crime, no drugs, nothing beyond a little teenage mischief that never seems to out-last high school. It's so nice it makes me sick sometimes, like it doesn't leave room for anything else. Guess old man Holston got what he wished for when he chose that motto. It's the rest of us who didn't have a choice.

When rich people decide they need to build a house, they also decide they need to buy food, and clothes, and entertainment, and all sorts of other good things that make a house a home. So people followed them, one after the other, and then those people built shops to sell their shit out of, and they built houses to keep their shit in, and eventually they turned around and went "shit, I guess I live here now." And the Holstons loomed above it all in their ridiculous nightmare house, with its black iron grillwork and its redbrick facades, and when they started dying, everyone sort of shrugged and figured they'd brought it on themselves, what with building a house that looked like it belonged in a gothic romance.

The last member of the family died long before I was born, but I still know them. Everyone knows them. You can't grow up here and not know them, because dying wasn't enough to make them *leave*. See, they died too fast, some sort of disease that started with the youngest daughter and swept through the rest of them like a wildfire. They didn't change their wills, and they didn't dissolve the trusts that were supposed to make sure that hard times for any specific member of the family wouldn't deprive the rest of them of their precious ancestral home.

No one can buy it. No one can sell it. No one can demolish it. When it falls down—which it will, someday; everything falls down someday—we'll be able to clear the land and reclaim it for city use, but so far, the annual inspections have failed to find anything, not even water subsidence in the foundation. The place is in perfect shape, especially when you consider that it's been standing empty and unattended for seventy years. Deer crop the grass so short that it looks mowed. Rain washes the windows, and wind blows the debris out of the gutters.

It's enough to make you understand why people believe in ghosts. Which, supposedly, the house has: Mary Holston, the youngest girl, the one who got sick first. They say she still walks the halls, lonely, looking for someone to play with her. Forever.

It's also enough to make the place a beacon for bored teenagers on Halloween night, like the lone candle lit in the middle of a swarm of moths. We don't have anything else to do out here in the sticks, and the adults have made it clear that while vandalism is a no-no, they don't patrol the grounds of the Holston house. If they leave it to our devices for long enough, we might be able to bring the whole thing down.

Probably not, though. It's going to outlast me. It's going to outlast us all. Except for maybe little Mary Holston, with her ghostly garden growing in the shadows of the house where she died.

WE GATHERED OUTSIDE the gates, a motley gang of bored kids who wanted the opportunity to smash things without anyone catching on. There was Elisa, with her spray paint and her bubble gum and her yellow hair and her tight black jeans, which always seemed like an invitation to stare and then feel bad about it later; Chuck, whose backpack bristled with eggs and jars of liquid that I could smell from where I stood, viscous and obscene; Aiko, with her baseball bat and her scowl that dared any of us to say a damn thing about it; Tyler, who always had bruises on his face and arms, and who never wanted to talk about them, but who could chuck a chunk of masonry with an artist's skill, taking out windows from twenty feet away. We greeted one another with nods and gruff insults, trying to seem cool, trying to seem casual, trying to seem like our hearts weren't pounding and our skins weren't too tight, like costumes we'd already outgrown.

Or maybe that was just me. Elisa had never given any sign that she cared what people thought of her. Chuck's father actually *liked* bailing him out of trouble, like he was reliving his own chaotic teen years one crushed mailbox and one egged house at a time. Aiko hated everyone, including her best friends, and Tyler . . .

Sometimes I thought Tyler was hoping we'd get into the kind of trouble that ended with us being sent to juvie for a nice long stretch. Not hoping hard enough that he was willing to go out and start something on his own, but hoping anyway. He'd probably get beaten to a pulp in juvie. Any of us would. At least there, we wouldn't be related to the people doing the hitting.

"Emily," said Aiko, in a voice like a razor blade. "You're late."

"I was getting supplies." I held up my backpack. She looked at it with dull disinterest. "Matches. A glass cutter. The good stuff."

"Why would we need a glass cutter?" asked Tyler.

"Because if we can get into the house before someone calls the cops on us, we could find better shit," I said.

He thought about it for a moment. Then he nodded. "Cool."

That the cops *would* be called was a foregone conclusion. Even with the adults turning a blind eye to our nocturnal activities—as long as we were just participating in the town tradition of trying to trash the Holston place—someone would eventually hear glass shattering or smell smoke and decide we needed to be curtailed, lest we get so excited that we started trashing a house people actually cared about. Teenagers were wild animals, at least in the eyes of the adults who pretended to give a damn about us. We had to be controlled, or else we would run rampant.

Elisa popped her gum. "How are we getting in?"

"Bolt cutters," said Chuck, pulling them out of his backpack and brandishing them like a sword.

Elisa clapped her hands. Even Tyler smiled. Aiko turned to frown at the chained gates, brow furrowing.

"You see that?" she asked.

"See what?"

"Someone . . ." She paused and shook her head. "Nothing. Just a trick of the light. Come on. Let's get this party started."

The end of the world is probably going to begin with those five words. Let's get this party started. Just once, I wish someone would say "let's not."

Just once.

IT'S HALLOWEEN, whispered the wind through the eaves, blowing against the pressing dark of the October night. It carried dust and fallen leaves, and as it blew, it left them tangled in the cobwebs, knocking the spiders from their holes, sending them tumbling down into the tangled overgrowth of the flower beds like fat black raindrops.

It's Halloween, hooted the owl in the trees at the back of the property, wings mantled and yellow eyes wide, alert, staring at the house. It flexed its talons against the branch that bore it, splintering wood and bark alike, and when it launched itself into the air, it made no sound, but soared as soundlessly as a shadow.

"It's Halloween," breathed Mary, nose pressed to the glass of her bedroom window, eyes fixed on the figures coming through the gate. Five of them this year, five trick-or-treaters coming to play with her, to be her friends, and maybe even—if she was very, very good, and very, very lucky, and if they were very, very clever—to stay for a while.

Oh, how she hoped they would stay for a while.

"It's Halloween," she repeated, and hugged herself tight, watching her new friends come.

. . .

THIS WAS THE closest any of us had ever been to the Holston house. We were silent for a long while before Tyler finally put voice to what we'd all been feeling:

"There's some bullshit going on here, and I don't like it."

Aiko, wary as a kicked cat, stopped and looked at him. "What do you mean?" she asked.

Tyler gave her a challenging look. "You can't tell me you don't see it too."

"I didn't say I didn't see it," she replied. "I want to know what *you* see."

"The house," he said, and pointed. "This fucking thing is, what, a million years old? Older than my house, anyway, and my house has peeling paint on the corners, and the gutters always have half a ton of leaves in them. This place . . . there isn't a broken window. There isn't even any graffiti. How can this place be in such good shape when nobody takes care of it? And when this shit happens every year?"

"Language," drawled Elisa, popping another bubble.

"He's got a point," I said slowly, and tried not to squirm as their eyes turned toward me. Their combined gaze seemed to have a palpable weight, like a shroud. "Did any of you come out here last year?"

One by one, my friends answered in the negative. Tyler had been running with a different crew then, and had spent the night egging cars from the overpass. Elisa had been out of town following a little "incident" with the girl across the street. Aiko had been in New York visiting family. Chuck had been in some unspecified "somewhere else," and refused to say more than that. I frowned.

"Okay, so . . . how do we know that anyone has actually done this before?"

"What do you mean?" asked Chuck.

"Maybe they were lying to make themselves sound braver." It was a believable theory. Most of the kids who claimed to have thrown a rock or taken a swing at the Holston house were milquetoasts, the kind of people who cared more about homework than hooliganism. The real troublemakers always seemed to find something else to do when Halloween rolled around.

If the real troublemakers actually existed. I frowned, trying to find a face to put to that label. I could summon the vague image of a skulking gang of older teens in ripped jeans and leather jackets, hanging out behind the school and trying to look tough enough to take on the entire world, but it seemed like I'd never really *seen* them, only sketched the shadow cast by the things they had supposedly done. It was weird.

Maybe they skipped class a lot. I shook my head to chase my lingering unease away and turned to Chuck.

"Cut it," I said.

"Who died and put you in charge?" he asked—but he clipped the chain. It fell to the driveway with a muffled clink, metal striking stone, and the gates, freed from the tension that had been holding them in place, swung majestically open.

The hinges didn't creak so much as sigh, soft and distant and weary. It was like this was a place where rust had never dared to grow, where time itself played by different rules. We moved closer together without discussing it, taking a little thin comfort from the proximity of people we were sure of. These weren't the distant shadows of the bad kids we were trying so hard to emulate, to grow up to become. These were my *friends,* assuming I could honestly claim to have anything of the sort. These were the people I had chosen to have my back while I rode off to become a Halloween legend.

"It's open," Elisa said, and popped another bubble. The sound was sharp and bright and somehow pink, gooey around the edges. Only Elisa's gum could sound like that. "Who goes in first?"

"What, are you scared?" Tyler swaggered forward, passing through the gate and only stopping when he was easily ten feet onto Holston property. He turned to look over his shoulder, smirking—more for Elisa's benefit than for the rest of us put together, I was sure. Everyone knew Tyler was sweet on Elisa, just like everyone knew Elisa would never do a thing to encourage him. Near as anyone could tell, Elisa was attracted to bubble gum, spray paint, and Elisa.

Which at least put her in a category with me and Tyler, so hey. She had good taste.

Slowly the rest of us followed Tyler through. Elisa paused to produce a can of red paint from her bag and shake it to life, eyeing the wall around the gate with hungry eyes.

"You go on ahead," she said. "I'm going to make sure anybody else who comes looking for a little Halloween fun knows that they didn't get here first."

"You want a lookout?" asked Tyler eagerly.

Too eagerly. Elisa treated him to a withering look. "Go play, little boy," she said. "Maybe if you're fast, you can trick-or-treat at the big house before the candy runs out." She turned back to her wall, giving the can another shake, eyes far away, already picturing the masterpiece she was going to put there.

Tyler muttered something nasty under his breath as he slogged down the driveway toward the rest of us. Chuck gave him a sympathetic look. Aiko did nothing of the kind. Her attention was reserved for the house, taking in the undented wood and undamaged windows with an artist's eye. And she *was* an artist, as were we all. Only our mediums differed. Elisa was a painter. Chuck was a performance artist, of a kind. Tyler was a dancer. Me, I liked to play the changes, a jazz musician with a hammer—or any blunt instrument—in my hand. Aiko?

Aiko was a sculptor, and to her, the house might as well have been an untouched block of marble, ready for the chisel.

"Let's go," she said, and her grin was a jack-o'-lantern carved out of the twilight, eerie and bright and flickering with unholy fire.

SOMETIMES THE TRICK-OR-TREATERS didn't reach the door. They got scared, was what Cook said. They couldn't handle the majesty of the grounds, or the way the windows seemed to watch them. They didn't understand that the house only ever wanted to make friends, like Mary only ever wanted to make friends. Friends were *important*.

"It's Halloween," Mary whispered, shivering with delight, and stepped out of her room, space bending around her until she emerged through the wall to the side of the gate, passing easily through the brick and mortar. The trick-or-treater who hadn't been able to make it to the house was standing at the wall, a canister in each hand, painting something *wonderful* over the brick.

It was big, and red, and white, and swirled like a peppermint candy cane, sweetness and sharpness, waiting to cut the roof of the mouth when bitten into wrong. Mary clapped her hands.

"What the fu—" The trick-or-treater spun around, eyes wide, mouth hanging open. A wad of something pink fell out, landing on the driveway with a splat.

Mary frowned. "Littering is bad," she said. "You should pick that up. Mr. Evans says I'm not to litter the grounds ever."

"Who the hell are you?" demanded the trick-or-treater.

Mary was beginning to suspect this wasn't a good friend for keeping. "My name is Mary. I live here. What's your name?"

"No one lives here, kid. This is the Holston house."

"Yes," said Mary patiently. "This is my house."

The trick-or-treater stared at her, still not picking up the pink thing from the driveway. "No fucking way," she breathed. "You're dressed as Mary Holston? Your parents let you do that? Where are they? Is this some viral video bullshit?"

"You shouldn't use that sort of language," said Mary. "It's not nice."

"Yeah, well, neither is dressing up like a dead kid who—"

The trick-or-treater kept talking, but Mary wasn't listening to the words anymore. They were bad words, *wrong* words, big lying words that people weren't supposed to use around her. She needed to make the trick-or-treater stop using them.

So she did.

When she was done, when the screaming stopped and the trick-or-treater wasn't saying things anymore, Mary looked at the picture on the wall again. The candy cane swirls were gone. Now it was pink and yellow and sad, like a memento mori for something that should never have died here.

Mary sighed, stepping back into the wall. Maybe the others would be more fun.

After a moment, the thing that had been Elisa climbed to its feet. It left the paint cans where they were as it stood there silently, waiting for the others to return.

We all heard the scream, but when we turned to look, it was just Elisa by the wall, which already bore the outline of another of her grandiose grotesqueries. I waved hesitantly. She waved back.

"Bitch," muttered Tyler.

"Yeah, yeah," said Aiko, and eyed the door. "Emily? You have the lock picks. You want to let us in, or you want me to start bashing?"

That was one of the most polite things she'd ever said to me. I stepped into position, pulling the picks from my pocket and getting to work. The Holstons had been rich enough to afford good locks, but technology marches on; I was expecting something tricky but not impossible to pick, just hard enough to make me look cool in front of my friends. They might never be impressed by me—I was too plump, too slow, too reluctant to smash things when I thought we might get caught—but I could get into places, and so they'd keep on keeping me around. As long as I was willing to open doors, I was part of the crew.

Even here. The picks moved, and the tumblers clicked, and in half the time I'd been aiming for, the door was swinging open, revealing a hallway as clean as it was old-fashioned. I held my crouch for a moment, unable to shake the feeling that something about this was very, very wrong. We knew the quirks of architecture and geography that allowed the Holston house to look so well maintained even when no one was actually taking care of it. They taught those in school, using them as examples of outliers. But here . . .

Were we supposed to believe that ravens flew down the chimney and swept the cobwebs away with their wings, or that raccoons wandered the halls accidentally dusting things with their tails, somehow not doing any damage in the process?

Chuck whistled, long and low. "It's like a fucking museum in here."

I had to swallow the sudden urge to tell him not to talk like that, not where the ghostly shadows cast by the moonlight flowing through the stained glass windows could hear us. Luckily, Tyler saved me the trouble, elbowing Chuck casually in the side. The bottles in Chuck's backpack jangled.

"Someone's trying to screw with us," he said. "They came and cleaned the place up, and now they're going to jump out at us. Let's screw with them first."

"You do what you want," said Aiko. Her eyes were on the great stained glass circle of the window at the top of the stairs. She'd be able to reach that easily with her bat if she climbed up to meet it.

"What if the stairs are rotten?" I asked.

Aiko looked at me coolly, dismissively, the way she looked at everything. "I'll still get to smash something," she said. "The house or myself, it doesn't matter."

She walked away from us. Tyler whistled.

"Okay, forget Elisa," he said. "I'm in love."

"She's out of your league," said Chuck.

"She's out of everyone's league," said Tyler.

"I can hear you," said Aiko, and climbed the stairs to the sound of laughter.

Chuck hooked a thumb toward the nearby hall. Tyler nodded, and the two of them skulked that way. I looked toward Aiko, silhouetted against that big round window, and followed them away from the door, deeper into the house.

THE SECOND TRICK-OR-TREATER was in front of the star window with a stick in her hand when Mary stepped out of the wallpaper. Mary frowned. These weren't good friends. They weren't even good trick-or-treaters. It was Halloween, and not one of them had said the words. It was like they didn't *care*.

If they didn't care, Mary was going to make them care.

"Breaking things is bad," she said primly.

Aiko shrieked and whirled, bat held defensively in front of her. She blinked when she saw Mary, a frown spreading across her face, wiping her terror away. "You're just a kid."

"This is my house," said Mary. "It's Halloween, and that means you don't need to be invited to come for trick or treat, but even uninvited, you're still supposed to act like a guest. Guests don't break things. Guests are *polite*."

She took a step forward. Aiko took a step back. The menace radiating off the child was like smoke, intangible but filling the air until her lungs ached and her head spun.

"Why do you want to break my things?" Mary asked. "It's *Halloween*. We're supposed to trick, and treat, not break things that aren't ours."

"Kid, this window isn't yours. No one owns this house."

"I do," said Mary.

Unlike Elisa, Aiko didn't scream. Her baseball bat made a clunking sound when it fell from her fingers and rolled down the stairs. Her body was quieter when it hit the floor.

Anyone looking closely at the great starscape of the stained glass window might have found the outline of a teenage girl, sketched out by distant points of light, screaming forever. But they might not. It could easily be a trick of the shadows, after all.

THERE WAS NO single sound that caught my attention as Chuck and Tyler were setting up their bizarre Rube Goldberg machine of jarred smells and pilfered antique kitchenware, clearly intending to bring the whole thing crashing down as soon as they had it stacked to their satisfaction. My role in this construction project was simple: I was the one who picked the locks on the china cabinets and eased open the ancient cupboards, keeping the boys safe from spiders.

For a couple of guys fixated on projecting their own version of aggressive, unrelenting masculinity, they sure were freaked out by spiders.

But something was different. Some small, indefinable quality of the air around us had changed between one breath and the next, becoming raw and wrong and unwelcoming. I turned away from the boys, frowning, trying to decide what was bothering me.

Tyler noticed, of course. Tyler paid too much attention to the wrong things, and always had. "What's the matter, Emily?" he jeered. "You scared?"

"Suck my ass," I replied genially. "Just because Elisa doesn't want anything to do with you, that doesn't mean you have to be a jerk to me."

"Elisa doesn't want anything to do with you either, dyke," he said. There was a darkness in his tone that matched the darkness in the house.

"Don't say that shit," said Chuck.

"Thank you," I said.

"Whatever," Chuck said, and added another jar to his stack.

I turned to look back at the pair of them, frowning. These were my friends? These were the people, out of the entire school, who I had decided were worth impressing, worth spending time with?

Sometimes I think most relationships are nothing more than a matter of stumbling from loneliness to loneliness until we find someone whose company is better than being alone, and then putting up with their jackass associates until we realize it's not worth it after all. Elisa was hot and funny and could even be sweet, when no one else was around to see her doing it. Sure, sometimes I'd wondered whether she was like that with all of us—gentle and kind in private, flirty and rude in public—but I'd never wanted to think about it too hard, because if I did, I would need to decide how I felt about it.

I wanted to have friends. I wanted to have people who'd have my back if things went south. But somehow, "having friends" always seemed to mean getting stuck with people who didn't really like me, and who I didn't really like either, while Elisa did her own thing and told us about how sick it was later.

"I'm going to check on Aiko," I said.

"Dyke," said Tyler again.

I whirled. "I will shove one of Chuck's chemistry projects so far up your ass that you'll be burping stink bomb until you turn thirty-five," I snarled. "There are words you don't use. They're not yours."

"Nobody owns a word," said Tyler, looking at me coolly. "I'm just saying it like I see it."

"You see it like an asshole."

His laughter followed me out of the kitchen and back down the hall toward where we had left Aiko. She wasn't my friend either, but at least she didn't go out of her way to insult me. Actually, she didn't go out of her way to do anything, good or bad, where I was concerned. Mostly, she looked at me like she was trying to figure out my deal, like once she understood me, she could decide what she wanted to do about me. There was nothing cruel in her gaze. Cold, sure, but not cruel.

Aiko's bat was lying at the bottom of the stairs.

I stopped when I saw it, blinking, unable to quite process what I was seeing. Aiko carried that bat everywhere. She took it to class with her, and when new teachers objected, she'd go home and come back with a note from her parents explaining that her mental health was directly tied to her possession of the bat. Our school had a zero-tolerance policy for weapons, which meant if anyone came right out and said "but she could beat someone with that," they ran the risk of doing away with the entire baseball team in the process. Aiko was clever. She knew where the cracks in the rules were, and she knew how to exploit them.

So why was her bat on the floor? Slowly I bent and picked it up. I'd never actually touched it before, and on some level, I was surprised when I was able to. It should have been like Thor's hammer, too heavy for a mere mortal to lift. It should have burned my hand. Instead, it was just an ordinary bat, with an ordinary weight, worn smooth by Aiko's skin.

"Aiko?" I asked, in a small voice.

There was no reply.

Step by step, I climbed the stairs, moving toward the stained glass window—which wasn't broken, wasn't smashed, wasn't even cracked. It showed a vast field of stars, silver and gold against a background of blue, and must have turned this hall into an eternal twilight when the sun was up. There was something strange about the way the stars were placed, like they made some sort of picture I could almost but not quite see.

When I saw what was on the floor, I stopped looking at the window.

Aiko was crumpled there, folded in on herself like a discarded doll, her face hidden behind the careless tangle of her hair. I ran to her side, dropping to my knees and shaking her.

"Aiko? *Aiko!*"

She was utterly unresponsive, recalling and strengthening my first impression: that she was a child's plaything that had somehow displeased and been cast aside, to be reclaimed later when the offense had faded. I rolled her onto her back. Her open eyes stared up at the ceiling, the black strands of her hair crossing her irises like cobwebs. I brushed them aside, unable to stand her fractured, unblinking gaze.

But she wasn't dead. She was breathing shallowly, and her skin was soft and warm. She *wasn't* dead. She couldn't be dead. I had come here tonight looking for a little good, old-fashioned mayhem, the sort of Halloween pranks that would make us gods at school and maybe—just maybe—bridge the differences between us, making us the sort of gang that stuck together through thick and thin, and not only when it was easy and convenient. I wanted that. I wanted it so badly I could almost taste it, like sugar on my tongue.

There was a sound from the kitchen, short and sharp, the beginning and ending of screams compressed into a space too small to hold them. I didn't move. I closed my eyes, and cradled Aiko close, and wished I were strong enough to lift her up and carry her out of here, away from whatever haunted this place where the gutters never clogged and the floors never mildewed.

Something was wrong with the Holston house. Something had always been wrong with the Holston house.

For the first time, it occurred to me that there was a name for something shiny and untouched and perfect: lure. Or trap. Either would do. The adults we trusted, who were supposed to take care of and protect us, they'd sent us here, hadn't they? They'd talked about what a wonderful target this house was, how no one cared about it, how we could wreak whatever havoc we wanted without getting into trouble. They'd set the bait and we had snapped it up like animals, rushing out without stopping to wonder why generations of teens hadn't gotten here before us.

There was a footstep behind me.

THE LAST TRICK-OR-TREATER had found one of her friends and was holding her, rocking her, the way Mama used to rock Mary, before Mama had to go away. Mary paused. She didn't like remembering Mama, not really. Mama had gone outside the house before things ... before things changed, and when they'd changed, Mama hadn't been able to find a way back in. Cook said it was because Mama had been outside the gates, and outside the gates was a different world.

Mr. Evans said it hadn't always been that way.

Mr. Blake said Mama had Done Something when she realized things were going to change one way or the other, and that whatever she had Done was the biggest trick and the biggest treat ever, because it was why they were able to stay here, Halloween after Halloween, no matter how much the world changed outside the gates. The Holston house would stand forever, because Mama had known her little girl was dying, and Mama had wanted to give Mary a house to haunt.

"It's Halloween," said Mary finally, to the last trick-or-treater.

The girl raised her head and turned, spitting words over her shoulder like an angry cat. "So do whatever you're going to do. Get it over with."

Mary cocked her head to the side.

This trick-or-treater didn't have anything that she could use to hurt the house or break things. She'd opened the doors, but she had done it gently, kindly, doing no damage, leaving no mark behind. It was Halloween. It didn't matter that she didn't have an invitation. What mattered was that she had come, and Mary had been so very lonely.

"It's Halloween," she said again. "Do you want a trick, or do you want a treat?"

The girl looked at her and said nothing, but there was hope in her eyes. Mary smiled.

Mary took it.

SHE SAYS SHE'S my sister now, and I guess she's going to keep saying it until I forget it isn't true. This is the Holston house, after all. There's nothing here but time.

We stood by the bay window, watching as the people who'd been my friends walked toward the gate where the girl who'd been Elisa was waiting. They looked small and strangely naked without the paraphernalia of their mock wickedness. The house had swallowed it entire, along with whatever it had taken from them. Less, according to Mary, than it would have taken if I hadn't agreed to stay; more than it would have taken if they'd listened to the things no one was saying and chosen to stay away.

They would be good now. Good like the older teens, the ones we'd always been puzzled by, the ones who should have destroyed the Holston house long before we'd had the chance to go there. The ones who'd met Mary, who'd become her treats when she saw the tricks they were trying to play.

Maybe this is the last time. Maybe next year, when Halloween comes, I'll be able to warn the naughty ones away, be able to tell them to go and throw eggs at some other, lesser house, one that's a little less protected, a little less . . . aware. Maybe I can save them.

Or maybe they'll find my body, the only thing allowed to decay in this haunted, hallowed place, dissolving into dust at the top of the stairs. Maybe they'll meet Mary, enjoying the holiday highlight of her year, trading tricks for treats for the whole town to enjoy.

Holston, Oregon, is a nice place to live. Its founders—what remains of them—make sure of that.

"It's Halloween," whispered Mary, and she slipped her insubstantial hand into mine, and held me tight.

She says she's my sister now. Give us enough time, and it will be true.

"Mary, Mary, quite contrary, how does your garden grow?" I didn't mean to ask the question. I asked it anyway.

She looked up at me and smiled. "With graveyard weeds and wolfsbane seeds, and empty graves all in a row," she said. "It's Halloween."

"Yes," I said, and the night went on around us, and the night would never end.

Dirtmouth

Stephen Graham Jones

First you need to know that my children, Zoe and Keithan, the only memory of their mother they ever had a chance at, it was through that television movie. You've seen it, haven't you? All of Colorado tuned in that night, for the story they already had from the news: "Woman Battling Postpartum Depression Attempts 'Mountain Cure.'" It's a tragedy any way you look at it. A success as well, yes, a "triumph of the human will," all that clickbait, but, for us, more than a year ago already, a tragedy. I don't blame Marion for it, though, Officer—Detective, sorry— and neither could I blame her depression or, of course, the twins. Especially not Zoe and Keithan. If there are to be victims here, then it's them.

The second thing you need to know, probably, is that it was Halloween. So it's been two weeks, I know. If I could have hiked down, braved the chest-high drifts, I would have, believe me. And please also believe me that I was beating the drifts those first few days. Just, not downhill from the cabin, so much.

I'll get to that.

The reason I mention it was Halloween is that, sure, it's like Valentine's and Mother's Day and Christmas and the rest, commercialized to the point of death. But, unlike those other holidays, there's still something we instinctually respond to with that holiday, something more than the stimulus-response we've had conditioned into us by an avalanche of marketing.

Halloween's always been the night where the rules don't hold, hasn't it? It's like the world's night off. And we still kind of can get glimpses of that in the masks some of the older kids wear. In the movies that get recycled in October. Taken singly, it's all harmless, but considered en masse . . . I think it congeals into something darker, Detective. I think the impulse we feel to lower our face into a mask for that one night of the year, it's our instinctual need to hide the true self we feel might surface, on accident.

But, to get back to the cabin. It's two weeks ago now, and I'm taking my own version of the mountain cure, I suppose. What I've got planned is a whole month in Marion's parents' cabin with the kids, just me and them for once, with promises from her parents and sisters that there'll be minimal contact. You maybe have a handle on this kind of thing already, doing what you do and all, but after a mom dies, her whole family is right there every time you turn a corner. Casseroles and babysitting, that's pretty much what it comes down to. Because no way could any *guy* keep himself and his kids fed and washed and safe, right?

Those first couple weeks after the funeral, okay, this was maybe the case. Not because I'm male, just because I'm human. I was down, I was despondent, I was pulling my hair. I was looking ahead to the next seventeen years. I was seeing Zoe and Keithan walking the stage of their graduation, me out in the crowd carrying Marion's framed portrait or something.

I know, I know, realistically I'd probably be remarried by

then, but, too, I think it's kind of natural to key on the most painful image we can conjure and then just stare at it until there's nothing else in the world.

But, I finally managed to tear my eyes away from that, to take it a day at a time like all the books and sites and groups say, and, now, two weeks ago, I'd made the announcement to Marion's sisters and to her parents that I wanted some alone time with the kids. To get to know them again. To start over.

The keys to the cabin were already hanging by our fridge. They were Marion's parents' wedding gift to all their daughters, kind of a family time-share we don't have to pay into, just schedule.

I scheduled most of November, right up until Thanksgiving— on the laughing provision to Marion's mom that, yes, I would dress the kids up, then video-call so the grandparents could see their cute costumes. What kind of cabin has a satellite with enough of an uplink for video? The answer is: any kind of cabin Marion's dad, the retired-but-still-consulting CFO, would build.

It was a deal. I stopped on the way out of town to stock up on the kids' favorite crackers, on milk and eggs and microwave waffles, and I bought two all-in-one costumes for them: an inchworm and a happy devil. If you knew Zoe and Keithan, I wouldn't have to tell you which was which.

They fell asleep on the drive up the mountain, of course, which I was so grateful for. Since they'd never been up that winding road—up to ten thousand feet—I didn't know if one or both of them would get carsick or not. And, single-parenting it, I had zero clue what I'd do with two puking kids in the backseat, facing the other way from me.

Anyway, I bundled them one at a time into the cabin, started the fire crackling, ate a cold waffle—I should tell you the why of that, I guess. It's Marion. The whole time we were dating, probably a third of our dates were in tents. And she always brought a single waffle in a hard plastic bin there was never any actual space for in her pack. It was her prize, kind of. For pushing up this slope, for weathering that storm, for wearing wet socks all day.

When she went up for the last time, she had a waffle with her, even though every ounce counts when you're on a rock face like she was.

As for where she got the idea that pushing herself like that would battle the hormones left over from pregnancy—or coming on just then—that was completely her. No guru, no mystic, no books. Like her dad, she was fiercely self-sufficient. Had a book said that the best thing to battle postpartum depression with was life-risking physical exertion, she probably would have joined a knitting circle instead.

But it was her idea, and she prepped for it the right way, got back in climbing shape ahead of what the doctors said she could do, then she buddied up with Sheila from the rock gym, and, just like the movie says, one day they drove up that twisting road to conquer a mountain, one toehold at a time. And only one of them came home.

That last image of Marion—of the actor playing her—is from that split instant after her fingerhold crumbles, when she's floating back into all that open space behind her, when you think that the mist from the creek, in full-on spring-melt mode, can maybe cushion her, catch her, deliver her safely to the ground.

Instead, as all of Colorado knows, it just did what nature does, what the mountain's been doing for the whole history of our species: it swallowed her.

Worse?

Though bodies lost to the creek up in the canyon usually wash up down in Boulder, to great dismay and consternation, this time the waters didn't surrender what they held.

But I'm not telling you anything you don't know. The search continues, all that.

I don't keep track anymore, honestly.

And after Halloween night, well—I guess this is where you're going to start doubting me. Where you're going to start thinking that there are paternal or spousal grief hormones that can pull a left-behind dad down as well.

I'll agree with you, too. At least that far.

And I appreciate the . . . I guess we can call it irony? Of this not happening until I ventured back up into the mountain that ate my wife? And I guess that must have been lodged somewhere in my head?

But, if you're thinking I just imagined all this, I beg you to reconsider. And if you think I'm making it all up to cover something else, then I guess I'm not surprised.

I trust you, though.

I came in here myself, didn't I? Not because you sleuthed me up, not because evidence was pointing to me and only me, and not because Marion's parents were nudging you.

I'm here to tell you what happened Halloween night, two weeks ago.

I had just taken the first cold bite of the one waffle I was allowing myself, for having made it this far past Marion's death—it was a made-up communion, I admit, something I was definitely doing in remembrance of her—when a shuffling on the porch presented itself.

Because I'm a dad, the first place I looked wasn't the frosted window, but to the two car seats Zoe and Keithan were still sleeping in. When you're a dad, you make sure your kids are safe, and *then* you check on the rest of the world.

Sure they were all right, I edged over to the window, saying it singsong in my head: "Trick or treat?"

Not that there would be any trick-or-treaters at our altitude, at the door of a cabin only lit up maybe once a weekend, a cabin I'd needed four-wheel-drive low to get up.

There was nothing on the porch. No little goblins or super-folk, of course, but no black bear snuffling at the base of the door, no lion eyeing the love-seat swing, daring it to creak just one more time.

"Raccoons," I told myself, not really sure if raccoons hibernated.

Because raccoons have hands, though, I twisted the dead bolt, and that was just enough sound to stir Zoe, who stirred Keithan. That's how kids are, right? You can play the song in your SUV at full tilt, sing along and cry with the memories associated with that particular song, and the kids just sleep. Then lock a well-oiled dead bolt and they're sitting up, wondering what that cacophony was.

I didn't mind. If they weren't up now, then they'd be up all night. So I fed them and changed Keithan and then, feeling ambitious—also wanting to keep all the hesitant "just wondering if you made it" phone calls from coming in—I suited them up, the inchworm and the little devil, and booted my laptop awake. It grabbed the network right off.

That Marion's mom answered on the first ring told me that she'd been sitting there waiting.

Marion's sister Denora was over too, and they crowded the monitor to see the kids. I held them up one by one and turned the little devil around, to show her tail, and I made sure my smile wasn't too forced.

"Sure you're all right?" Denora asked when Marion's mom had traipsed off to help arrange suitcases for their annual November "jaunt" to Paris—video calls are always fun for the first minute, then a chore for the rest of the conversation—and, with a kid on each knee, I told her we were fine, we were great.

We were becoming a family again. And Marion was still part of it.

This was enough for Denora.

"I'll pretend the connection failed," she said, looking down to manipulate the mouse. "You wanted some alone time, I know."

I nodded thanks, keeping my lips together, and she whispered bye and terminated the call, leaving me blissfully alone for what was supposed to have been the whole month.

I disconnected from the Wi-Fi as well, just to be sure nobody would be ringing in. Feel free to scavenge logs or anything from my laptop, but I can tell you now: as far as I know, the network was up. I just wasn't hooking into it.

Does it look guilty to disconnect like that? Like you're trying to hide?

I hope not. I hadn't even considered that.

But I'm telling you now, anyway, so you can believe me.

So, because it was Halloween, I let the inchworm and the little devil keep their costumes on, not that they really understood, and I took my usual inventory of the food and alcohol left behind by whichever sister had stayed here last, and then there were the three back-to-back viewings of that cartoon that zones them out, that I always promise myself I'm not going to use, and then came the crying that means they're tired again.

Thirty minutes after that, it was snoozeville, like always.

Because we'd never considered it, there was no bassinet or crib up here. And definitely not two of each. My solution was to tuck Zoe and Keithan back into their car seats, and strap them in for good measure.

I imagined an avalanche scouring down the face of the mountain for us and two kids riding its crest in their car seats, their mother's children, for sure.

My first glass of wine, I lifted it in memory of Marion.

My second glass, there was a single knock on the door. Like a hand barely closed into a fist, then reaching across to lean on the door more than actually knock.

I stared across the living room, trying to convince myself I hadn't heard what I knew I'd heard.

Had Marion's mom hustled everyone up through the storm, because I wasn't answering a call?

But I'd have seen headlights. I'd have heard snow crunching under all-terrain tires.

It wouldn't be a lost hunter, either, unless that hunter was really lost; rifle season had closed ten days earlier. I'd read about it in the paper.

Game warden, maybe?

Just knocking once?

You're being stupid, I told myself, and hustled my *own* self across the rug, hauled the door open all at once, to prove how stupid I was being.

Standing there was Marion.

I know, I know. But you've got to believe me.

Marion Graves, who had fallen from a face of rock into roiling waters fourteen months ago and likely been shattered on rocks, ground up by thousands of gallons of spring melt, was supposed to be lodged in debris somewhere in miles of underwater, only to surface this season or next, she was standing there before me in a ski outfit that was still in the garage down in town, a blank white mask pulled over her face, surely scavenged from some trailhead trash can.

I think her eyes are what I recognized first. How she was using them to implore—how she needed me to recognize her, after all these months.

If you're going to ask why I let her in, my first response would be simply that it was cold out there. The snow was swirling and skirling, nearly had my SUV drifted over already. My second response would be that her snow boots—moon boots, she'd called them when she'd first bought them—they were glittery wet, meaning she'd physically walked through some snow to get here, which I don't think I would have had the imagination to remember to do, were I making all this up. But my third response is really the only one that matters: she was my wife. And she was back.

"Marion," I said, exactly like a word I'd been holding back for too long now.

When she opened her mouth under her mask, her whole face shifted, and instead of my name, there was only a creak. Had the mask not been there, I may, yes, have been privy to a cloud of moths unfurling past her lips or to a vomit of black dirt, or even the cold water that would have made sense.

But: the mask.

It was Halloween, after all, wasn't it?

She draped herself around my neck, and I held her in return, my hands gentle, probing not so much for familiarity but for materiality—to see was she solid, was she real.

She was. Even down to the smell I knew.

She creaked broken words into my chest that I took to be her saying she'd missed me.

"I missed you too," I told her back, guiding us into the living room.

What I was already spinning in my head was the explanation for this, the one the mask was cueing up: that it was Halloween, when things can happen, when borders can be stepped across; that this high on the mountain, nobody would be watching, so what harm could this one trespass do, really; that even the kids were sleeping, meaning I could just be making this all up, right? Dreaming it real.

Except then, in a flurry of what I guess I would just call joy,

Marion was off my neck, was leaned over the kids. When a drop of melted snow descended from her blank white mask to Zoe's cheek, Zoe squirmed away from it.

This was really happening.

"Where have you been?" I asked. "We thought—we all thought—"

I didn't finish, couldn't, and she couldn't answer anyway.

How do you explain death to someone who hasn't been there, right? The vocabulary surely doesn't exist, and to have that description in my head, anyway, it would surely turn malignant, send its dark tendrils through the rest of what I called my life, and it would then pull me down, or across. Somewhere else.

I'm thankful to her for sparing me that.

Or, of course, it could be that she just wasn't listening to me.

She hadn't seen her two little darlings for more than a year, after all.

"They're walking," I told her, and when she turned to show me she'd registered this, I saw the impossible bulge under her ski jacket.

At first I couldn't process what I was seeing, what this bulge meant. And even when I did, it didn't make sense. Either the gases of decay had swelled her midsection up, or she was carrying. She was pregnant.

It was the latter. The way I knew was that the sway of her back, it was the same as it had been when she'd been carrying the twins inside her.

She saw me see and looked down herself, as if shy.

I took her hand, led her to the couch, to sit down by me, but at the last moment she peeled left, sat on the cowhide chair across the coffee table, the one we all knew was her dad's.

"Are you—are you going to be able to do this every year?" I asked.

Already I was looking to the future. Imagining it into place.

I would reserve the cabin for every Halloween. Marion wouldn't age under that mask, in that already-outdated ski suit, but I would. She'd get to see the children grow into versions of her, into some version of me. More important, they'd come to know her.

One day of the year, it isn't much. But it's so much more than no days at all.

She didn't answer me. Her hands were clutching one another between her knees. It suggested a demureness I wouldn't have ascribed to the Marion I'd always known. Not that she was ever vulgar or anything, but she had always been insistently bold, sometimes even reckless. Thus the plunge off the rock face, right?

But I have to think it was that same boldness that was giving her nerve now, for this return.

"Is that part of it, then?" I said, nodding down to her stomach in what I hoped wasn't a rude way.

She was watching my eyes. Was this a confirmation of sorts?

"You can't—you can't talk about it, can you?" I said for her. "That's one of the rules."

Her not looking down meant yes. I have no doubt that's what she was saying.

I leaned forward, staring into her face, nodding with the pieces coming together in my head. Of the two of us, I'd always been the believer, in bigfoot, in aliens, in ghosts, in whatever the next thing was, so long as it was really and truly out there, while she'd always been the contrarian, the skeptic, the one who claimed that my insistence upon all this, it was just the religious impulse rising in an avowed atheist—that, deep down, I *needed* to believe in something.

In life, I'd always resisted this, didn't want to be that shallow, that transparent.

After her fall, though, I'd started to wonder. Or, no, what I'd been doing, it was kind of making true everything she'd ever suspected of me, so as to preserve her. To preserve a Marion I could believe in, one who was always right, who was persistently smarter than her stupid husband.

If she'd have been around and somehow outside this scene, this living room, she'd have said I was just finding a different object for my need-to-believe—*her*. All the belief I'd been storing up, that I'd been too timid to use, as it might look like bargaining for her return, I could spend it now, here.

And? I probably would have jumped on that bandwagon as well. When you've lost your wife, you jump on any wagon you think might take you somewhere else, because you know where you are, it pretty much sucks.

In the living room with her now, though, when she was definitely throwing a blurry shadow in the firelight, when the snow was definitely melting off her onto the hardwood floor, when she was definitely blinking regularly behind that mask, I could believe in the old way again, the way I knew: she was a . . . a ghost, an apparition, a vision-given-form, a memory-made-solid. She was returning not so much to tie up loose ends—if that was why people came back as ghosts, then the world would be bursting with ghosts—but because she wanted to see us one more time.

Only, there were conditions. It makes sense there would be.

It's what you tell your kids when they're old enough to go to the park by themselves, right? Okay, I'll let you go this one time, but only if you're back before dark, only if you stay out of the trees, only if you leave if you see the same car drive by twice, and on and on.

It's how you preserve the world.

One of the conditions Marion was having to work under, here, it was that she couldn't impart any new information to me—she couldn't speak at all. Probably something about balance: if there was X much on this side and Y much on the other side, then her saying YYYY to me, it would throw existence out of whack.

"I understand," I said to her.

At which point, in a way only a husband would recognize, she lightly touched her pregnant belly.

"I'm so glad you're here," I said to her, instead of a response to what she'd just so obviously told me: that I wasn't to mention her pregnancy.

This was the Marion I knew. She was someone who would dare a mountain, only two months after giving birth.

That's the kind of woman who will nod yes to whatever conditions are necessary in order to return, see her family again. But what only her husband would cue into, it's a certain glitter in her eyes. That she's now getting away with something.

That something? It was in her belly, I knew.

She wasn't pregnant when she died, of course, so that she was *now,* it meant either that there was sex on the other side and she'd been having it with someone, which begged the question why come back to show that to her husband, or it meant that this pregnancy, it wasn't what it seemed, which made more sense—I can't imagine biology and reproduction have the same mechanisms on the other side.

I ask you, Detective, if your dead wife came back one last time, would you accuse her of adultery-after-death, or would you allow her something better than that?

"Keithan looks more like you every day," I said, to fill the room with patter. Who knew what other conditions applied here? Were there invisible forces massed at the window, listening in? Could the fire itself be a conduit? But of course those were just bad guesses, constrained by my own lack of imagination. More likely, if there were any active eavesdropping, then it was in some manner I couldn't even conceive. As it should be.

Meaning, we should behave ourselves.

Not that Marion ever cared about proper behavior. Here, after my mentioning Keithan, she forced a croak that held two distinct syllables. The two of Zoe's name, I was certain. What Marion was telling me, it was that Zoe was resembling me more and more every day, bless her.

When Marion saw that I was hearing this as she said it, as she meant it, she—as if to prove she was still herself—threaded a loose bang back along the side of her head. This had been one of the mannerisms she was always chiding herself for, as it smeared hair oil onto her fingers, which she would then transfer to her face the next time she touched it without thinking.

Only, this time, her hair stayed with her fingers.

She held the loose strands on her knees and considered them.

I said nothing about it.

This meant that this visit was on a timer, of course.

She could incorporate herself for only so long. And then she would begin to decay all over again.

Already I could see the nail bed of her index finger, bruising into black.

Would she, as I watched, suffer again all the indignities of her fall?

"It doesn't matter," I told her, almost forcefully, as I considered it a declaration of my undying love.

I would sit with her until she was bones, if need be.

"They made a movie about you," I said, smiling so she would get my estimation of that whole situation.

She smiled, and looked into the fire.

"It'll pay for their college," I said, nodding over to the kids.

She nodded that that was okay, then. My guess is that the things that are important to us in life, they lose some of their importance in death.

"Can you eat?" I asked, holding the rest of the waffle up.

As if she was having to marshal things inside her so massive I couldn't even guess at them, she stared at this once-bitten waffle, considering it and everything it could mean, perhaps. But finally she reached an unsteady hand forward and took it with trembling fingertips, lifted it in thanks, and turned away, as she had to raise her mask for access to her mouth. Here I could have glimpsed her profile, seen the face I'd known for so many years, but, too, I had to think she wouldn't want me to remember her like that. So I looked away. Into the open door of the kitchen. Into nowhere.

But I heard.

The mask didn't just lift, it peeled, it clung. Moistly.

When I saw in peripheral that she was facing me again, the mask back in place, I then had to watch her try to swallow that small bite of cold waffle. Maybe swallowing's something you forget, when you haven't had to for so long. Or maybe it reminded her of the creek's waters.

She set the rest of the waffle onto the table beside her father's chair.

Neither of us said anything, but I knew: we didn't have much longer.

Meaning—meaning whatever it was she was smuggling across in her belly for us, for me, or just for the kids, she needed to deliver it soon, in the next few minutes.

My dream, of course, spawned just while sitting there watching her decompose in front of me, it was that what she was bringing back, in infant form, it was herself. She was going to deliver the baby she'd been, thirty-two years ago, and then that baby was going to mature at an accelerated rate, in wide-eyed wonder, hidden away in this cabin, until, two or four or six years later, we could dress Marion up in weathered rags and "find" her back in the woods, where she'd been lost for so long, living on berries and grubs.

Coloradans love a good survival story, and this one, it would be the best.

Still, what kind of birth would this be, I wondered.

Would Marion, momentarily, use her blackened index finger to slice the top of her belly skin open, and then pull a struggling, still-dead infant up from it, for me to breathe life into?

Because I would.

Was this to be a more natural birth, one that would literally split her in two, leaving me to sweep up what was left so the kids didn't crawl through their mother later? And, if so, would I be the one to bite through the umbilical cord, and perhaps hold it to the navel of either Zoe or Keithan, siphoning a breath or two of their life, for their mother's?

Because I might.

Now Marion was darting her eyes around the room, at first lighting on the fireplace tools, perhaps gauging the sharpness of the ash shovel's edge, the fineness of the poker's point, but then moving on, to the next possibility, and the next, almost desperate.

The cesarean, then.

She needed to be able to open herself up to deliver herself, and could already tell that the nail on her index finger would only fold stickily back, were she to try to use it like that.

"Just, just—" I told her, and rose, not wanting to leave her for an instant, since each moment was one moment more with her, but knowing she needed an actual knife, too. From the kitchen.

Crossing past her, I let my fingertips brush the skin of her forearm. I shouldn't say this, I should leave this between me and her, but since I'm telling you everything, I'll include this: that one slight brush, that single contact, it explained to me why she'd sat alone in her father's chair, and not by me. Her skin tore like the most delicate tissue, and underneath was the dark wet soil and undulating, shiny worm shapes I'd expected to spill from her mouth the first time her lips parted.

I pretended not to have seen. I pretended this was nothing.

It was Marion, I mean, worms and all. I would take her any way she presented herself.

Any husband would.

In the kitchen, I of course found myself instantly entrenched in the same battle that had been being waged ever since Denora had her first son: child-safety locks. They were on all the cabinets, all the drawers. They were why there were no sharp implements in the living room.

And, because Zoe and Keithan were just starting to explore on their own two feet, my fingers were still too dumb to bend these locks to my will. So, in order to open the stupid knife drawer, what I had to do was come down to its level like always, to get a mental picture of the mechanism at play, which in turn reminded me how I had always been just such a mechanism to Marion.

Bear with me for this, Detective. I'm not just making it up.

Of me and Marion, she had always been the smarter. I didn't mind, but I was appreciative that, when she needed to manipulate me to this work party, to that weekend with friends, she could always set things up such that she was playing on beliefs I already held, or could be prompted into, such that, in the end, when I agreed to go, it was more that I was convincing myself than that she was talking me into anything.

To her I was as simple as this child lock.

And, the thing was, she was usually right. The party *did* turn out to be important to attend. That weekend *did* turn out to be a good time.

I pushed the button in the unintuitive way that opened the silverware drawer—there was no knife block, of course, as

Denora's oldest son was a climber—and the instant the drawer sighed open on its plastic rollers, I realized that that soil-and-worm interior I'd glimpsed inside Marion . . . wasn't that just what I'd been *expecting*?

And—and had she, by saying nothing, by just directing her eyes around the room here and there, by wearing a mask that would focus all my attention on where and how she looked, had she allowed me to fill all the empty or dead places in the conversation with wish fulfillment? With my own fantasies?

Or, or: I mean, initially, and without hesitation, I'd accepted her presence, her return, but did that then crack the door open on everything I wanted to be true, such that it all came spilling out, past my ability to effectively herd it?

Conditions indeed.

Wasn't it just like me to ascribe rules on the return of a dead wife?

And, is it not pure unadulterated wishful thinking that would allow me not just to believe that my wife is smuggling her own self out of the realm of death in her own stomach, but that I needed to assist her by coming into the kitchen to retrieve her a *knife*?

My throat dropped into my stomach. That's what it felt like.

"Marion?" I said, loud enough to risk waking the kids.

Instead of a reply, a lone pine needle dislodged from the baseboard under the cabinet the sink was sitting in.

It was dislodging because of a slight draft. The slightest of drafts.

Still holding the knife, I rushed into the living room, saw only black-and-white cowhide where Marion had been, and the mask upon it, its backside unspeakable, and even then the story I was already spinning in my stupid, idiot head, it was that she'd known she was going to dissipate, and, not wanting to make me see that, had tricked me into the kitchen in her way, such that she could leave unseen.

I was partly right.

The front door *was* open.

And the table the kids' car seats had been resting safely on, it was empty.

I fell to my knees but was up just as fast, crashing through the front door, immediately miring in the snow already up to my waist.

There were no tracks to follow, Detective.

What I did find, finally?

In the bank of snow on the north side of the porch, where it had crested against the railing, there was a hole of sorts. A burrow. A tunnel.

The two car seats were there, because they would have been too awkward in such a confined space. Because mothers, they like to hold their babies close to them. The way I knew she'd taken them into that snowbank was that a mound of wormy soil had sheared off when she forced herself in. It was crumbled, of course, but it was the same as I'd seen wriggling inside her forearm, just under the tissue-thin skin. Go up there, Detective, you'll find a pile of dirt on the porch, I promise. That's how you'll know for sure. That and that waffle.

In short, here's what happened, if this fits better on your form there: my wife Marion, a new mother, she died fourteen months ago, and then this Halloween, she came back not for me, but for her children.

As for where she took them? That's got to be the next question. That's the only question.

From summer hikes around that cabin—guided hikes, I should say, the guide being a woman who had grown up spending her summers there—I can tell you with assurance that there are fissures in the rock for miles around that cabin. What you'll think, what I can see you're already thinking, it's that any one of those fissures, they could hold a small body long enough for it to disappear. Not even a year, right, the bones still being so soft?

You're wrong, Detective.

You want the version of the story where the father succumbs to the same cycle of grief the mother did, so goes to the mountain for his cure, and, when he can't find it, he forces it, he makes an offering on that most holy of nights, to try to conjure his wife up from the rocks.

Better you should think I slathered my own two children in strawberry jelly and left them just past the porch for the raccoons to find, and gnaw into. Better you should think that I watched.

As for what Marion's family will think when they all get back from Paris, that's a foregone conclusion: I did it. As evidence, they'll probably offer that it had always been Marion who was paranoid about accidentally leaving the kids in the car after arriving at the bank or the grocery store. Or, in this case, the cabin.

Granted, for fourteen months, I hadn't had to be the one to keep track of who was where, car-wise. And, for the few months before that, Marion had been on the job.

But what kind of father would I be?

Would I not, at some point in the snowy night, get off email at last and spy the shopping bag on the counter, an inchworm and a little devil peeking out of their cardboard there?

I never logged in to email from the cabin, that's the thing. Check the logs.

If I did anything, it was use Marion's father's precious bandwidth to watch through her movie one last time and pause it at exactly that moment she falls back, into space.

She's looking right at me, I can tell.

She's telling me that the kids, the kids—

What she's telling me, what I know, it's that Zoe and Keithan, they're all right now. They're with their mother.

She died hanging on to one side of a rock face. She now lives on the other. And, on one night when the membrane was more permeable than it is all the other nights of the year, she crawled back for her babies.

You'll never find Zoe. You'll never find Keithan.

I'm sorry, this doesn't make your job any easier, but it's true.

I can see you're already drawing your own conclusions, too.

That's fine, really. I understand.

In your shoes, in your uniform, I might too, right?

We're rational people here.

But, what I want you to do here, Officer—Detective, I'm sorry, it was a long trudge through the snow—what I want you to do mainly here, it's hold on to your position for as many years as you can. Or, if you hire away, or retire, then keep a line of communication open back to here.

Why?

Before too many years have passed, I'm pretty sure reports are going to start trickling down the mountain, see. Reports of a large blind grub moving through the shale. Reports of a squat red demon watching from an abutment, its eyes bored with humankind.

There will even be, at some point, word of a woman with matted hair and hollow eyes, running barefoot through the trees alongside a mountain biker.

And then you'll know, Detective.

That will be the sequel to the television movie, only, you'll be the only one piecing it all together, as I'll be long gone by then, dispatched by the law, eaten by the media, driven into hiding, suicided in a closet with a twice-bitten waffle that should have proved everything, it doesn't matter.

What will matter, it's that woman running through the trees, her eyes locked with this mountain biker's.

What she's saying, it's not stay away, this is my mountain.

What she's saying, it's wait until October.

Come back this way when there's snow on the ground, and I can pull you close, my long fingers to the base of your skull, my dry lips covering yours, so my dirtmouth can vomit across into yours, and it's like that we never really die.

My wife should have washed up on a creek bank this spring, and the spring before that, too.

Ask yourself why she hasn't, sir.

See what you believe.

A Small Taste of the Old Country

Jonathan Maberry

I

Campan Deutschargentinierrio Cantina
El Chaltén Village
Santa Cruz, Argentina

October 31, 1948

WOULD YOU GENTLEMEN like something fresh from the oven?"

The two men seated at a small table by the window looked up with wary eyes. The question had been asked by a very old man with a face that seemed to be composed entirely of nose and wrinkles from which small, bright blue eyes twinkled. He held a wicker basket with a red cloth folded over the heaped contents.

"No," said the older of the two seated men. He was about forty and had very black hair. His mouth was a hard horizontal slash bracketed by curved lines. Laugh lines, perhaps, though he was not smiling at the moment. "We did not order anything." His Spanish was rough and awkward, fitted badly around a thick foreign accent he had difficulty trying to disguise.

"I'm sure you will both enjoy what I have." The intruder nudged the basket an inch closer.

The rest of the cantina was quiet; a few clusters of men bent close for discreet conversation over tall glasses of beer. There was no laughter in the place. No music. No one who entered did so with a happy laugh or with a boisterous call to a friend. There was a large fire in the hearth because the temperature had dipped during the cloudy day, and stiff winds blew inland across the Falkland Current.

The second man at the table was a young bull with blond hair and huge shoulders. "Does the landlord know that you're peddling your crap here?"

"Sir," said the old man, "I am a baker, and the landlord is a regular customer."

The black-haired man leaned a couple of inches toward the basket, then cut a look at his friend. "Did you smell this?"

"Smell what?" said the younger man, whose chair was set on the far corner of the small table.

Encouraged by the expression on the black-haired man's face, the baker said, "I have something here that you might enjoy, my friends."

"I doubt that."

"May I show you?" asked the baker, his smile obsequious but earnest. "I can guarantee you both that this is something you cannot get here. Not even in the houses of your friends who understand such things. Alas, no. The recipe is an old family one and is, perhaps, too regional and specific to be popular among the locals here. It is something that you probably thought you would never smell or see again, and certainly never taste again. Not truly. Not, if I may be allowed a liberty, *authentically*."

"Oh, very well," grumbled the blond. "Show us and be done with it."

The intruder bowed, plucked a corner of the cloth, and folded it back with great ceremony to reveal small loaves of dark bread. Steam rose in soft curls, and a delicious aroma filled the air. The black-haired man smiled and let out a long, soft breath. His friend's eyes widened.

"*Schwarzbrot . . . ?*"

"Indeed, my friends," said the baker. "I'm delighted you've heard of it, even here in Argentina. Yes, *schwarzbrot* it is. And it is a German recipe for it, handed down from my grandmother's grandmother. With some Austrian touches, of course. The very best wheat and rye blended with caraway, anise, fennel, just a little coriander. And, of course, a touch here and there of all-spice, fenugreek, sweet trefoil, celery seeds, and cardamom. I grind each of the spices by hand and then grind them again together and mix them into the dough. Everything is done the old way. Everything is done right, because such things deserve precision, do you agree?"

The men nodded absently, their eyes fixed on the hot bread. They both swallowed over and over again as their mouths watered.

"Baking is a tradition as worthy as any other," continued the baker. "In Austria and Germany each family of bakers guards its own recipes for making *schwarzbrot* jealously. Go on, my friends, try them."

The men exchanged a brief look and a briefer shared nod, and then they each took a loaf of the black bread. They sniffed and then took tentative bites. The baker watched their eyes, saw the eyelids flutter, and he smiled as the men chewed, swallowed, and took larger bites.

"Mein Gott," murmured the black-haired man. "This is heaven. This is pure heaven. I'd never thought . . ." He stopped, shook his head, and took a third bite, leaving only a nub pinched between his thumb and forefinger.

The young blond man ate the entire loaf without comment and then eyed the basket. "How much for another?"

The baker smiled and placed it on the table. "Consider these a gift. It is a great pleasure to know that you not only enjoy them but also truly *appreciate* them. So, please, enjoy a small taste of the old country."

Each man snatched seconds from the basket and bit into them. After a few moments of undisguised gustatory lust, the black-haired man looked up, his jaw muscles bunching and flexing as he chewed. "Which *old* country would that be, exactly? We are Argentinians. Santa Cruz is our home. We are from here."

"Of course," agreed the baker, returning the nod and adding a small wink. "We are all clearly Argentinian."

"Yes," said the black-haired man.

"Yes," said the blond. "I have never been out of the country. Born and bred here."

"Of course," agreed the baker.

They all smiled at one another. When the two younger men finished their loaves and explored the basket, they found it empty, and their faces fell.

"I have more in my shop," the baker said quickly. "It's near here, on a side street off the square. Becker's Breads and Baked Goods."

"And you are Becker?"

"Josef Becker, sir," said the old man. "And you gentlemen are . . . ?"

The black-haired man said, "I'm Roberto Santiago, and this is Eduardo Gomez."

Becker looked amused. "Santiago and Gomez? Of course."

Santiago eyed him. "Your name is not Spanish. Are you Deutschargentinier?"

"No," said Becker, "I am not a descendant of immigrants, as I imagine you are."

"Sure," said Gomez without conviction. "That is what we are."

"My great-grandmother was born in Berlin but married an Austrian, and I was born in Hallstatt, which is in Austria," said Becker. "Perhaps you have heard of it? Such a lovely place in the Salzkammergut, located on the southwestern shore of a lake. Those of us from Hallstatt, there is great pride in who we are, and what we are, and what we have endured."

"I have never heard of Hallstatt," said Gomez in a guarded tone.

"Have you not?" said Becker, looking sad.

"We are Argentinian," insisted Santiago. His eyes were hooded.

"Of course, of course," Becker soothed. "As are so many here in Santa Cruz, and in Buenos Aires, Misiones, La Pampa, Chubut, and a hundred small villages."

The men said nothing.

"We are all Argentinians because it is such a lovely place," continued Becker amiably. "A lovely and very safe place to be. The brisk and breezy nights, the tequila . . ."

Santiago and Gomez sat very tense, very attentive, and their eyes were hard as fists. Becker gave them an understanding nod and the slightest suggestion of a wink. "It is a very large world, my friends, and even here in lovely Santa Cruz we can all sometimes feel very far from home. I know I do."

"You talk a lot," said Santiago.

"I'm old," said the baker with a shrug, "and old men like to talk. It reminds us that we are still alive. And . . . well, the world has emptied itself of so many people that I knew that I often have only my own voice for company. So, yes, I talk. I rattle and prattle and I can see that I try your patience. Why, after all, would men as young and healthy as you, my friends, care to waste time listening to the babblings of an old man?"

"That question has occurred to me," said Santiago. "I am utterly fascinated to know why you feel that it is appropriate to interrupt a private conversation."

Gomez turned away to hide a smile.

The little baker was unperturbed. "I take such a liberty, my friends, because tonight is the second day of Seelenwoche. All Souls' Week. Do you know of it?"

Gomez began to answer, but Santiago stopped him with a light touch on the arm.

"No," said Santiago, "we don't know what that is."

"Of course not. It is an Austrian holiday, and you have never been to my country, as you have said. Let me explain. In Austria we do not celebrate Halloween, as the Americans and Irish do. For us, this holiday is about reflection, about praying for those who have been taken from us, for making offerings to the spirits of our beloved dead. And we all lost so many people during the war."

Gomez kept his gaze locked on Becker, but Santiago looked down at his hands.

"The war is over," said Santiago softly.

"Is a war ever truly over if people are alive who remember it?" asked Becker mildly. "Can it be over if people are alive who remember the world before the war and can count the number of people and things they have lost? Family members, cities, friends, dreams, promises . . ."

The corner of the room was very quiet now.

Becker pulled out a chair and perched on it. "Seelenwoche was never a time of celebration, and now that the war has run its course we are left to tally the costs. We honor our dead not only by remembering them but by recalling what they stood for, and what they died for."

Santiago nodded and lifted his beer glass. He stared moodily into it, nodded again, took a long swallow, and placed it very carefully back on the table.

"Why do you talk of such things?" asked Santiago.

"Because it was always a custom of my family to celebrate Seelenwoche. My family was very . . . ah . . . dedicated to custom and tradition."

" 'Was'?" asked Gomez.

"Was."

The two younger men looked at him, and although they did not ask specific questions, Becker nodded as if they had. Answering in the way that many of the pale-skinned residents of Santa Cruz did these last few years.

Becker touched the curved handle of his wicker basket. "We love our dead. Their having died does not make them less a part of our family. We can see the holes carved in the world in the shapes of each one of them. You understand this?"

The men nodded.

"We believe that during Seelenwoche," said Becker, "the spirits of our loved ones come and sit beside us at our lonely tables. We know that the dead suffer. We know that they linger in the world between worlds, because the church tells us that all souls are in purgatory awaiting judgment. The priests tell us that only the perfectly pure are then raised to heaven, but the rest must wait for their sins to be judged and their fates decided. It is what all souls must endure, for—after all—was anyone ever without sin? Jesus, perhaps, but who else? No one, according to the priests with whom I have spoken."

The men offered no comment, nor did they chase Becker away.

"The priests say that when Judgment Day comes, then the souls of all the dead will be either raised up or cast into the pit. Until then, they linger and linger. So it is up to those of us here on Earth to care for them, to remember them, to pray that their sins be forgiven, to offer what comforts we can. That is why we have this holiday. It reminds us to remember them. And to remember that they *remember* being alive. They may be dead and may have no earthly bodies that we can see except when the veils between worlds are thin—as they are this week—but they *feel* everything. Hunger and thirst, joy and despair, ecstasy and pain. And fear. Yes, my friends, they know fear very well. During Seelenwoche we leave bread to ease their hunger and water to soothe their thirst. We light lanterns so that the dead know they are welcome in our homes and, for a week at least, not be so alone, and so that they will not be afraid of the dark. These are good customs because they remind us of our own compassion, and of our better qualities, mercy among the rest. And that is why we have traditions, is it not? So that we remember what is *important* to remember? That is why we go to church so often during that week. We go to pray for the dead and to beg God to call them home to heaven."

Santiago began to speak, but Gomez touched his arm. The young blond man gave Becker a fierce and ugly look. "Perhaps it is in your best interest to go away now."

"No, please, a moment more," begged the baker. "I did not come here to tell ghost stories and spoil your evening."

"Yet that is what you are doing," growled Gomez.

"I said all of that in order to say this," Becker said brightly. "I opened my little bakery here in order to preserve more than the recipes of my family. I opened it to celebrate who I am and where I come from. After all, I may live the life of an exile here, but I am Austrian, now and forever. Surely you can appreciate that, even though there are tensions growing between my country and yours now that the war is over. For a while there it seemed as if we would become *one* country, one people, our old differences forgotten as we all marched together under a shared flag." He paused and laughed. "Of course I say this as if you are German, which of course you are not. Forgive me. It's just that I feel that men of the world such as you would understand that when I speak of the 'old country,' I mean the land I left behind and the one from which your, ah . . . *ancestors* must surely have come. For although you are clearly not European, you could pass for Germans quite easily."

Santiago said, "It's possible there is German blood somewhere in our family trees."

Gomez said nothing.

"So," said Becker, "in the unlikely event that you might be interested in tasting more of my family's recipes, why not come by my shop tomorrow night? I would be happy to make you a traditional dinner with all of the delicacies for which we Beckers are—or rather *were*—famous."

Gomez cocked his head to one side. "Like what? I mean . . . I have, ah, *heard* of your cuisine because of the number of Austrian and German expats living here, but have never tasted any."

"How sad," said Becker, then he brightened. "Well, my friends, I would be delighted, indeed honored, to introduce you to *tafelspitz,* which is lean beef broiled in broth and served with a sauce of apples, horseradish, and chives. Or, if you prefer, there is *gulasch,* which is a lovely hot pot that should best be eaten with *semmelknödel*—a dumpling of which my mother was rightly proud."

Gomez closed his eyes for a moment and breathed slowly through his nose. Santiago must have kicked him under the table because the younger man's eyes snapped open and he cleared his throat. "You describe it so well," he said awkwardly, "that I can almost taste it ... even though I am completely unfamiliar with them."

"Of course, of course, these names must be quite *foreign* to you," said Becker, giving him a small wink. "Let me enchant you further. If you come to dinner, you can try *selchfleisch* with sauerkraut and dumplings. And for after you can try my aunt's recipe for *marillenknödel,* a pastry filled with apricots and mirabelle plums. The dumplings are boiled in lightly salted water, then covered in crisply fried bread crumbs and powdered sugar, and baked in a potato dough."

"Gott im himmel," murmured Gomez, and again Santiago kicked him under the table. This time, however, Gomez shook his head, and to Becker he said, "You're killing me."

"Will you come?" asked Becker eagerly. "Will you allow me the great honor of making such a meal for men who, I have no doubt at all, will truly appreciate it? Here, in this town, I am a simple baker. Most of my day is spent making local goods. *Aljafor* and *chocotorta* and—God help me—*tortas fritas.* That's what my customers want, and because I need to make a living, it is what I sell. But it is not who I am. It is not the food that I understand, and I cannot sell Austrian goods to the public. Not even here. Not openly, anyway. That would present so many problems, and, unlike you gentlemen, I have no papers that say I was born here. Everyone knows that I am Austrian, although to hostile and suspicious eyes, I am German, and these days everyone hates the Germans."

Gomez turned and spat onto the floor.

"Argentina is a haven in name but not in fact," said Becker, lowering his voice. "People are *looking* for Germans. For certain kinds of Germans. No, you do not need to say anything because I know you are men of the world and understand such things. My point—and I admit that like all old men, I wander around before I approach the kernel of what I mean to say—is that I need to be a *good* German if I am to live safely. That means letting go of so much of my culture. To abandon it and forswear it and pretend that it never mattered to me at all."

Becker paused and dabbed at the corner of his eye, studied the moisture on his fingertips, and wiped it off on his shirt.

"I have had to become a stranger to the man I used to be," he said. "So much so that my family, were any of them still alive, would not know me were it not for the things I prepare in secret. For me. For them. That is why I ask you fine gentlemen to come to my shop after it is closed and share a feast in celebration of Seelenwoche . . . to remember all of those who we loved and who died in the war. Will you grant me that kindness? Will you tolerate further the company of a talkative and sad old man who wants nothing more than to offer that taste of home? Of . . . my homeland? Can I entice you? Will you taste what I so eagerly want to prepare for you?"

It took a long time for either of the men across the table from him to answer. Eventually, though, Santiago croaked a single word.

"Yes."

2

Becker's Famosa Panadería
El Chaltén Village
Santa Cruz, Argentina

November 1, 1948

THE KNOCK WAS DISCREET, and Josef Becker answered it at once.

He opened the door, stepped past the two tall men, and looked quickly up and down the crooked street. There were no streetlights, but cold moonlight painted the cobblestones in shades of silver and blue. A dog barked off in the distance, and a toucan—very far from his jungle home—sat on the eave of the shuttered jeweler's across the street. There were no people at all, though the chilly breeze brought the sound of laughter from some distant party in a house around the corner.

"Come in, my friends," said Becker, and he patted the backs of the men as they passed through into the bakery. When they were all inside, Becker pulled the door shut and locked it with a double turn of a heavy key.

The shop was small, but the space had been used with care. There was a long glass-fronted counter in which were set square platters of baked goods. There were small cakes dusted with powdered sugar, round chocolate double-wafer cakes, corn-starch biscuits covered with coconut, glistening cubes of quince, vanilla sponge cake ladyfingers, and many other delicacies particular to Argentina. There were French and Italian cakes and sweets, too, and even some pastries of American invention.

But what dominated the store were the breads. So many of them. *Aajdov kruh,* the Slovenia bread made from buckwheat flour and potato, dark Russian sourdough and crisp Japanese *melonpan* made from dough covered in a thin layer of crispy cookie dough, *michetta* from Italy and *taftan* from Iran, and dozens of others from dozens of places, including a whole tray of sugary *pan de muerto.* And, of course, central to all were the breads from Austria and Germany. The light *brötchen* wheat rolls; whole grain rye *vollkornbrot; dreikornbrot* rich in wheat, oats, and rye; five-seed *fünfkornbrot.* Even thick, dark salted *brezels.*

The two guests stood staring through the glass, eyes wide, lips parted with obvious hunger.

"Gentlemen," said Becker, beaming with pride, "I can say without fear of contradiction that there is no finer selection of baked goods to be found anywhere in Santa Cruz."

"Anywhere in this entire godforsaken country," breathed Santiago.

Becker chuckled. "Pride is a sin, they say, but if so, I will accept whatever punishment is awarded me, for I am very proud."

Gomez kept licking his lips like a child. "May I . . . ?" he began, then stopped and gave Becker a quick look. "Are these for sale?"

"Nothing here is for sale," said Becker, then laughed aloud at the crestfallen looks on his guests' faces. "I am only teasing! Nothing is for sale to you because you are my guests. Which means that everything you see is yours for the asking. Come, come, we will eat dinner and then have some wine and conversation, and when you go, I will overburden you with bags and bundles of goodies to take back to your home. Come, gentlemen, come into the parlor and let us sit."

Still chuckling, Becker passed between the folds of a drapery hung over a doorway and waved for the two men to follow. They did, and within minutes they were all seated at a large wooden table set near a crackling fire. A fine linen cloth had been placed upon the table, and places set at each chair. Santiago frowned across the table at three additional settings.

"Are we expecting others?" he asked.

"Hmm?" murmured Becker, then he smiled. "Ah, remember that this is Seelenwoche, my friend. I have set an extra place for each of us so that we can offer food and drink for those we have lost and perhaps bring them here to share our feast and be warmed by the fire and by our company."

Santiago looked uneasy, but he nodded. Gomez briefly looked down at his empty place.

"Would you gentlemen prefer a local red wine or something from *my* country?" Becker leaned on the word "my," and it brought the two men to attention.

"What do you have?" asked Gomez.

"Yes," agreed Santiago, "if it is from your country, I would be interested to take a taste and judge it."

"How delightful," said Becker, springing up and fetching a heavy bottle from a large terra-cotta wine cooler. He uncorked it and filled all six of the glasses on the table, then uncorked a second and third bottle and set them close by. "This is a Riesling from the Wachau region of Austria. You will notice, perhaps, just a hint of white pepper."

"This will do very well," said the black-haired man after a sip.

"What shall we toast?" asked the baker. "Or, may I suggest something?"

"It's your house," said Santiago. "The first toast is yours."

"Most gracious," said Becker. He raised his glass and said, *"Genieße das Leben ständig! Du bist länger tot als lebendig!"*

Always enjoy life! You are dead longer than you are alive!

His guests paused for a moment, then they nodded and drank.

After the glasses had been refilled, Becker vanished into the kitchen and returned with the first of what proved to be many courses. Not only had he prepared the delicacies with which he had tempted the men to join him, but he had gone further and set dish after dish on the table. More than any three men could hope to eat. More than a dozen men could manage. With each course, the baker served his guests first and then placed small portions of every dish on the plates set aside in honor of the dead. Soon those untouched plates were heaped high with slices of rare meats, with strong cheeses and steaming vegetables; and bowls of soups and stews were set in place beside the plates.

Gomez picked up his fork and then frowned. "Excuse me, but I do not have a knife."

"Do you not know the custom?" asked Becker, raising his eyebrows. "On Seelenwoche many people hide their knives so as not to tempt evil spirits to acts of mischief. Granted that is usually only done on Halloween night, but in my town we hid the knives all week." He sighed. "Strange, though, how mischief found us regardless."

After only a brief pause the guests attacked their food, and soon thoughts of knives were gone. As promised, the slices of roast beef and boiled pork and baked chicken were so rich and tender that their forks easily cut through the flesh. The men devoured the food, often in long periods where there was no conversation and the only sounds were that of chewing and crunching, swallowing and sipping, of forks sliding along plates and spoons scraping along the rims of soup bowls. And throughout there were gasps of delight and sighs of contentment. Bottles of wine were opened and emptied. The faces of the three men grew flushed, and their eyes took on a glaze as bright as that on the cooked hams.

It was only when the feast began slowing that conversation began. At first it was questions about ingredients and origins of the recipes. Becker told them about how one aunt would prepare a dish and how a cousin would do it differently but equally well. He spoke of town fairs and Christmas feasts and wedding banquets and funeral luncheons and the menus appropriate to each. Then, as he refilled their glasses once more, he sat back and said more wistfully, "But that is all what was, not what is, my friends. We speak of ghosts, do we not?"

"Ghosts?" inquired Gomez, his mouth filled with a large bite of a schnitzel that was so spicy that sweat beaded his upper lip and forehead and glistened along his hairline.

"Surely," said Becker. "The ghosts of everyone who created the recipes on which we dine. None of them are my own, of course, but were crafted by members of my family. Sisters and aunts, cousins and nephews, and my dear mother and grandmother. Even my father was a veritable demon in the kitchen.

The *schweineschnitzel* you seem to be enjoying so much was his personal recipe. It was as if he stood beside me in spirit as I prepared it, as if the ghosts of everyone I loved were with me in my kitchen, guiding my hand. I often feel them with me, though perhaps because of the holiday, I feel them more acutely this week. And I have no doubt they each added a touch of this and that when I was not looking."

Gomez swallowed and picked up his glass, sloshing a little of the wine as he did so. "Then let us drink."

"Ja," said Santiago, *"Zum wohl!"*

"Zum wohl," growled Gomez, and Becker echoed it as they all raised their glasses in the direction of the empty side of the table, and downed the wine to the last drop. Becker filled the glasses again.

Santiago stared at the plates of uneaten food across from him, and he slouched back in his chair, chin down on his chest. "What happened to them?" he asked. "To your family, I mean."

The baker sighed. "They died during the war."

Gomez frowned. "In Hallstatt? I did not know that city had been bombed."

"Oh, none of them died from bombs," said Becker as he pushed back his chair and stood. "Let me clear away."

Gomez looked down in dismay at his plate and seemed surprised that the heap of food was gone.

"Time for something very special," said Becker as he stacked the plates and set them on a sideboard. "I hope you saved room. A little room, at least."

Santiago discreetly unbuttoned the top of his trousers to ease the pressure on his swollen stomach, while Gomez looked eager to start the whole feast again. Becker vanished into the kitchen and returned a few moments later bearing a small silver tray on which was a pyramid of small cakes. They were each round and about a quarter-inch thick. Pale, with a hint of gold baked in around the edges, and each was marked by the indentation of a cross cut across their surface. Steam rose from them as if they had come straight from the oven, and the smell was wonderful, enchanting, hinting at nutmeg and cinnamon and allspice.

"Every village has its own recipes for soul cakes or soul bread," said Becker as he placed the tray in the exact center of the table. "Some prefer to bake loaves of it, while others make cookies. My mother's recipe was for little cakes like these. Crisp at the edges but soft as butter in the middle and light as a whisper on the tongue."

The two guests stared hungrily at the pile of cakes.

"I remember so many times helping my mother as she baked a hundred-weight of soul cakes to give to the poor children who came knocking at our door all through Seelenwoche. You see the crosses on each? That means they are alms, and are therefore righteous gifts given freely to any who ask. That was so like my mother—she would open the door at anyone's knock and welcome them inside. She could not bear the thought of turning someone away hungry, especially when we—as bakers and cooks—always had enough."

Becker placed his fingertips on his chest over his heart the way some people did when touching crosses, but he wore no jewelry of any kind.

"We were luckier than most, for we never knew hunger. We knew *of* it, of course. We were all aware of the horrors of hunger, of want, of unbearable need. Of having no place and being unwelcome and having doors closed to us. So when my ancestors settled in Hallstatt and opened the doors of our bakery, how could any of us turn away someone who came to us asking for something to eat? A crust of bread is nothing to those who have so much, but it can feed a starving child or keep a man alive to work another day in hopes of providing for those he loves. These cakes? They might be all that a starving child might eat that day. How could anyone with a beating heart turn a deaf ear to the knock, however weak and tentative?"

"Good for you," said Santiago.

"No, not good for me," said Becker. "Good for my mother. She was the kind heart of my family. She was like her mother, and her sisters were like her. Kind and generous, in part because it was their nature and in part because they remembered hunger and want."

"These cakes smell delicious," said Gomez.

"Do they? My mother would be pleased that you think so."

"Then let us each have one in honor of her," suggested the big blond man.

"Of course, my friend, of course." Becker leaned across the table and picked up a cake, careful not to crumble the delicate crust between his fingers. He set it on a small plate and placed it in front of Gomez. He repeated the action for Santiago. Then he took one for himself and sat down.

Santiago nodded toward the empty side of the table. "Aren't you forgetting something?"

Becker glanced at the untouched plates of food. "Ah. So courteous. But, no, my friend, soul cakes are for the living."

"Oh," said Santiago, clearly not following.

"One more thing," said Becker as the other men began reaching for their cakes. "A last bit of seasonal ceremony, if you'll indulge me. I like to follow the traditions in form as well as spirit." He crossed to a cabinet and removed a small lantern, checked that it was filled with oil, and brought it to the table. "Do either of you have a match?"

Gomez produced a lucifer match from a pocket, scraped it alight on the heel of his shoe, and leaned the flame across to Becker. The old man's eyes twinkled with blue fire as he guided Gomez's hand toward the lantern wick. The flame seemed to leap from match to wick, and at the same moment Gomez twitched with a deep shiver.

"What's wrong with you?" asked Santiago.

"I . . . nothing," said Gomez. "Just a chill. It's gone now."

Becker adjusted the flame and placed the lantern on the table close to the untouched plates of food. "So the souls of the dead can find their way here to join our feast."

"Forgive me, Herr Becker," said Santiago, his faux Spanish fading in favor of cosmopolitan German, "but isn't that a bit ghoulish?"

"Do you think so?" asked Becker, looking surprised. "How perceptive."

"What?"

"Nothing. A joke." Becker refilled their glasses with the last of the final bottle of Riesling. He placed his palms flat on the table and let out a long, satisfied sigh. "Now, my friends," he said, also speaking German. "Before we partake, let me tell you something of these cakes. There is magic in baking. A special sorcery that can transport us to other places and times with a single bite. That is why I invited you both here."

"What do you mean?" asked Santiago. "Why us?"

"Because you are no more Argentinian than I am, nor even Deutschargentinier.

"You are sons of Germany, as I am a son of Austria. No, please don't deny it. We are all friends here. We are safe and alone here, and we may be who we are. There are no spies here. No Americans or British. No hunters from the new state of Israel. We have nothing to fear from each other, and that allows us to take a breath, to be real, to be ourselves."

"And what if we are German?" asked Santiago, his tone dangerous, his eyes cold.

"Then I am among countrymen," said Becker. "I invited you

here to share my holiday feast because I knew—I *knew*—that you would appreciate it as only sons of the fatherland could."

"How do we know you are not a Jew?" demanded Gomez.

"Because I have eaten pork with you," said Becker. "And beef with cream sauce. Because I say that I am not a Jew. Because if I was a Jew, there would have been a dozen armed men waiting for you in here and not a feast and good wine and hospitality."

"He's not a Jew," said Santiago.

"No," agreed Becker. "I am a baker from Austria, and my family has lived in Hallstatt for generations." He touched the surface of the soul cake on his plate. "I asked you here to share in this special and sacred celebration. To break bread with me, to feast with me and the spirits of my family because I am alone and lonely, and I knew you would understand. Neither of you has families here, either."

"No," said Santiago. "Mine were killed in Dresden."

"Um Gottes willen," blurted Gomez, but Santiago shook his head.

"Enough, Erhardt," said Santiago. "He is right. We are alone here. We are safe here, if nowhere else."

"I . . . I . . ."

Santiago turned to Becker. "My name is Heinrich Gebbler, and this is Erhardt Böhm, and we are happy to share this table with you. God! How good it is to be myself, even for a moment."

Gomez—Böhm—cursed and slapped the table hard enough to make the wine in all of the glasses dance. "Then be damned to all of us. Yes, yes, I am Erhardt Böhm. There, I said it. Are we all happy now?"

"Very happy," said Becker. "And I thank you for your trust. Believe me when I say that it is a secret that I will take with me to the grave."

"You had better," warned Gebbler. "We are taking a great risk."

"Now, can we eat these damned cakes?" asked Böhm.

"Wait, wait," pleaded Becker. "Everything must be done exactly right, as I have said. To eat a soul cake is a very serious matter, especially in such a moment as this. After all, we have each seen our world burn. We have each lost so many of those we loved during the war, have we not?"

The two Germans nodded.

"Then should we not honor the dead by inviting them to join us at this table?"

"Sure, sure," said Böhm, "invite Hitler and Himmler and Göring, for all that I care. The dead are dead and I am hungry."

"The dead are dead but they are hungry, too, Herr Böhm," said Becker. "I have lit the lantern so that they can find us, and I have prepared food for them, because the dead are always hungry. Always."

"You're being ghoulish again," muttered Gebbler.

"Perhaps." He gestured to the cakes. "Did you know that the moment grain is milled it's possessed of its greatest life-giving potential? The dough for the soul cakes must be made when the flour is fresh and alive. It must contain life in order to be worth consuming."

"I don't follow," said Böhm.

"You will," said Becker. "Now, please, try the soul cakes."

The Germans shared another glance, then shrugged and picked up the cakes. They each took small tentative bites.

"This is delicious," said Böhm.

"I've never tasted anything so good," said Gebbler.

"How delightful!" cried Becker, clapping his hands. "Have another. Have as many as you like."

Böhm pulled the tray over and pawed four more of the cakes onto his plate, then offered what was left to Gebbler. Despite the heavy meal, they ate with relish, their faces dusted with sugar and crumbs falling onto their shirts. While they ate, Becker spoke quietly of the holiday.

"During Seelenwoche," he said, "the souls are released from their graves, and they wander the earth as hungry ghosts. Lanterns like this invite them to dine with us in the hopes that they can feast well enough to ease their hunger and gain a measure of peace."

"So you keep saying," said Gebbler, pausing with a fresh cake an inch from his mouth, "but quite frankly, Herr Becker, I am not a very good Catholic. I never was, and less so since the world fell apart. Everything that I cared about burned down. The damned Russians and British and Americans have taken it all from us. Our hopes and dreams and every single thing of worth that we owned. *We* are the ghosts haunting a world in which we no longer truly live."

Becker nodded. "To be equally frank, Herr Gebbler, I am not a very good Catholic, either."

"But not a Jew?" asked Böhm, his cheeks bulging with soul cake.

"Not a Jew."

"Then if you're not Catholic," asked Gebbler, "why do you go to such lengths to follow these rituals?"

"Because I am a *kind* of Catholic," said Becker. "My people tend to adopt the customs of wherever we live. It is how we survived all these years. Well . . . how we once survived. Clearly, we did not blend in well enough. They still came for us and rounded us up and took us away. It's not really something that can be blamed on the war, though. My sisters and brothers, uncles and aunts, cousins . . . they all died far from the battlefields. I doubt they ever heard a shot fired or saw a bomb fall."

The two Germans suddenly paused in the act of chewing and looked at him with sudden suspicion.

"What does that mean?" demanded Gebbler quietly.

"It means that I am not a Jew or a homosexual or a Pole or a Slav or any of those groups, nor were any of my family, and yet they all died in the camps. In Bergen-Belsen and Sachsenhausen, in Buchenwald and Dachau, in Mauthausen and Ravensbrück." He leaned slightly forward and smiled a sad little smile. "I am Romany."

"A damn gypsy!" Böhm spat the half-chewed cake onto the table. "This is a trap. He's poisoned us."

Both Germans shot to their feet.

"No, no, no," said Becker, holding his hands palms out. "I would never pollute my family's recipes with poison. There is nothing hidden in the meat or bread or anything else. Did I not eat it along with you?"

"You didn't eat the cakes," snarled Gebbler. He took a threatening step toward the baker.

"No, but not because they are poisoned, which they are not," protested Becker, still seated, "but because they were made specially for you. For tonight. They were made in celebration of Seelenwoche."

"This is a trap, Heinrich," said Böhm. "Let's see how much of him we need to cut off before he tells us who else knows about us and—"

"No," said Becker. "You will not need to do that, Oberscharführer Böhm. Oh, don't look so surprised. Do you think I picked you at random? I came here to this town to find you and Obersturmführer Gebbler. I came looking for both of you because you were at Mauthausen, where my mother and grandmother were taken. You took the gold from their teeth and cut the rings from their fingers. You worked for the commandant, Franz Ziereis, and under his direction you worked them and starved them until they dropped, and you buried what was left of them in mass graves. My brothers and sisters, too. And my father. All of them. Starved to death and buried like trash."

Becker's voice was soft, quiet, unhurried.

"So they died," sneered Gebbler. "So what? You Romany

are trash and you have always been trash and the world is better off without you. You're worse even than the Jews. At least they never renounced their faith even when we held their children above the flames of a bonfire. You gypsies would forswear anyone and anything to try to survive. Your mother probably offered to spread her legs for us and maybe did."

"Maybe she did," said Becker. "Maybe she begged and maybe she said that she renounced her faith, her culture, her people. What else could she say? Why would she—or any of them— not try anything in order to survive? What is a proclamation of renouncement except words? How is that more ignoble than slaughtering innocent people by the hundreds of thousands? By the millions?"

His tone never rose beyond that of mild conversation, and he wore a constant smile of contentment.

"We'll see what you are willing to promise," said Böhm, reaching for a serving fork with two long tines.

"No," said Becker. "We won't. Or, rather, it won't matter. Nothing you can do to me will matter at all. Not now. Not anymore."

Böhm and Gebbler glanced toward the windows and doors.

"Don't worry," said Becker, "no authorities are coming. Argentina doesn't care who or what you are or what you did. That's why so many Nazis came here. It was a safe haven. However, 'safety' is a funny word. It is conditional on assumptions about how the world works."

"You're babbling," said Gebbler.

"No," said Becker, "I'm explaining. The assumption is that you are politically safe, and you are. The assumption is that you cannot be extradited, and you can't be. The assumption is that no earthly power is likely to harm you here, and that is almost certainly correct."

"Then what the hell is this all about?" demanded Gebbler.

"The fault in the assumption," said Becker, "is that I have any interest in relying on earthly powers to punish you. I don't. I have no faith at all in governments and agencies and courts."

Böhm pointed the fork at him. "Talk plain or—",

"Shhh," said Becker. "Stop for a moment and think about where you are and what I have said. Think about the time of year."

The Germans stared at him.

"My lantern is not very bright," said Becker, "but it is bright enough. Oh yes, it is bright enough for the spirits of my beloved dead to follow, even though their bones are buried on the other side of the world. What is distance to ghosts?"

The lantern flame suddenly danced as if whipped by a breeze, but all the windows were closed. It threw strange shadows on the wall. Becker smiled.

"I have been a good host," said the baker. "I have prepared the very best dishes from the recipes of my family, and you have fed well. Very well. Some celebrations require fatted calves, but I think fatted pigs will do nicely."

Böhm shivered again, and now Gebbler did, too. Their breaths plumed the air of the dining room. The flickering shadows on the wall looked strangely like silhouettes of people. Many people. Old and young, short and tall, male and female. Everywhere, all around the table.

"The dead are always hungry," said Becker. "And you will be, for them, a small taste of the old country."

He sat back, still smiling, and watched as the shadows fell upon the two German officers. It was a quiet street and the windows were shuttered and if anyone heard the screams they did not come to investigate.

Wick's End

Joanna Parypinski

BITTER COLD, it was, as I entered the roadside tavern—a mutinously archaic structure, rudely built, whose splintered wood shrieked with each passing gust of wind and whose hostile atmosphere attracted only the least savory of patrons. I had taken a liking to the place, to the world-weary travelers who occupied its rickety stools and the brand of smoky darkness one finds in such a highway hovel. It was, perhaps, my favorite haunt on October 31, this night of mischief.

And the night was a cold one, indeed, as the heat within the tavern failed to thaw that arctic hollow within my chest. I could feel my very bones creaking and grinding. 'Tis a pity, to be so old yet trapped upon this earth, to have suffered these many years and all these many Octobers without making an end of it. How I can hardly recall, now, the stony cliffs and crumbling castles of old Ireland, where I had spent my youth as a ragged boy whose knack for deception outweighed his innately limited sense of caution. My memories do begin to fail me, though, as the passage of time whittles them away. The uncanny turning of the years blurs vivid details into a streak of gray.

The prevailing spirit of the New England roadside is one of ineffable solitude and mystery. I find great pleasure in the superstition these wandering souls still cling to even in a modern and, I suppose, more scientific time. I may sit, particularly on a Halloween evening, and please myself listening to wondrous tales of ghosts and haunted roads, haunted taverns, haunted schools, haunted train tracks—all a kind of gloomy fancy.

Tonight I came into the tavern seeking these chilling delights, for it was yet another Halloween, and my light was growing dim. The flame had faded to the dull red glow of exhausted coals. I needed a new flame, and I needed a mark for this evening—one best chosen from among the scarred and forgotten barflies who dwelled in seedy motels and lived nomadic lives upon trucks and motorcycles. Here there were no families, no trick-or-treating children, no one in costume, and they all sat in the dusky light and drank as if it were any other evening of the year, but for the pervasive atmosphere of ghoulish enchantment.

I sat myself at the unvarnished bar and set my dying lantern beside me, ordered a whiskey, and proceeded in my second-favorite pastime of getting drunk. I listened to the men behind me betting on a game of pool, and the Hells Angels telling favorite ghost stories of nameless abandoned roads and old stone bridges across America. I saw truckers typing on their cell phones and pulling baseball hats low over their foreheads for a snooze.

The door swept open again, and a night wind beat its way inside with the woman who brought it through the threshold. She wore a leather jacket and black boots, her wild hair was threaded with gray, and her eyes were black as pits within a face carved as if from wood. She sat down at the bar, alone, two stools from mine, and she smiled when she ordered, a kind of toothy and devilish smile that revealed several gold fillings.

She drank some murky liquid clinking with ice, and she held the glass with a gnarled, suntanned hand that looked as if it were made of leather. "You gonna stare at me all night, honey, or you gonna pay for this drink?" she said with a smoker's rasp, without turning her head toward me.

"That depends," I said.

"On what?"

"Your answer." I took a sip. "Trick . . . or treat?"

Her laugh was like the wind huffing through dead leaves. She tossed a few bills onto the bar, which the barkeep snapped up and made disappear. "On second thought, I'm not taking no treats from you."

I smiled. "Very well."

"Tell me a good one, old man," she said. She swilled her drink and finally turned to face me. Her irises were as black as her pupils. "A ghost story. That's the real currency around here on Halloween."

The clack of balls striking one another on the pool table sounded like a crack of thunder, although the night outside was clear and cloudless, with only the thinnest drape of mist. I had found my mark; thus did I decide to play my game with her. I sipped my whiskey in contemplation and replied, "I'll have to think on it, but I'll make a wager with you. Whoever's story proves the more frightening pays for the next round of drinks."

She laughed again, a grim sound. "And if nobody wins?"

"If neither concedes to the other, we'll simply tell another."

She eyed me up and down as if I had said something terribly amusing to her. "All right. Who goes first?"

From an inner pocket of my overcoat, I produced an aged and faded coin, the images in relief smoothed and worn down but still visible enough. On one side, the St. Patrick's farthing depicted the noted saint carrying a staff and driving the snakes from Ireland, and on the other, King David playing a harp. I held up each side to show her. "Let's call this one heads, and this tails."

"Tails," she said. "Where'd you get that old thing?"

I flipped the coin, and it landed with a spinning rattle atop the bar. When at last it settled, we both leaned in to see which side faced up.

"Well, that's me, then," she said. After swigging the remainder of her drink, she pushed the empty glass away from her, swiveled toward me, crossed her legs, and leaned an elbow casually on the bar. At last, she spoke:

"Hear the one about the lonely traveler on the highway? On this highway, matter of fact. The traveler sees a light in the woods, and because he's cold and hungry, and no cars've been by, so he can't hitch, he sets off into the trees. All's he can hear's the crickets singing to the moon, and that strange unquiet you get alone in the forest with a darkness so thick you feel it. But he's heading toward the light, which he sees now is coming from the windows of a little shack. Now, this is Halloween-time, and some years ago, so he don't have a phone to call someone—but he's just a lonely hitchhiker, who's he gonna call anyway? As he's coming to the house, he senses he's being watched, and then he sees something that stops him dead: there's faces all around that house, watching him. Faces with glowing eyes and mouths. And he thinks these here are ghouls, this place is haunted, and he should head back for the road—but then the door of the house creaks open, and a woman steps up, and she's just an old woman, not a ghost or goblin or other fantastic creature of the night, so the man laughs and says he thought there was something sinister going on, pointing to the faces. 'Those are just my jack-o'-lanterns,' says the woman, and the man don't know how he could've been so foolish. He comes closer, knowing now they're just lit pumpkins, hoping to ask the kind woman for some food and drink, only when he gets up to the doorway, she says, 'I think you will make a fine jack-o'-lantern,' and he looks again and sees those lanterns aren't pumpkins at all but human heads, hollowed out and filled with candles so their empty sockets and gaping mouths glow. He turns to run away, but he's no match for the witch. She has her way, and damned if his headless body don't walk a few steps before it dies."

The barkeep appeared as if from nowhere, just then, and refilled her drink. She lifted it to him in cheers and threw it back.

"Very good," said I.

She looked me over, gauging my reaction, but then her eyes lit on my lantern. "That a turnip?"

"Why, yes," I said, lifting it by the handle and bringing it closer for her to see. The turnip had taken on the mummified guise of a dead man's face, with a sharp gash carved in for a mouth and two slashes for eyes. Within that hollowed vegetable, the coals smoldered low and red, burned down almost to nothing.

"Who exactly are you, mystery man?"

"Would you like to hear about me, or would you like to hear my ghost story?"

She removed a cigarette from her pocket and lit it, filling the bar with a heady smoke; yes, this place was a revolt against modern norms and laws. No one seemed to mind. It was a last refuge of those who lived in the past. Her smoke drifted into my face, and she motioned for me to tell my story.

"In the twilight of a century long past, there lived a miserable drunk—a wretched thief and swindler, an insufferable and despised man. Each night, from dusk until dawn, he sat in the town pub and drank himself into oblivion.

"On his way to the pub one night, a fog-riddled late October night with sea salt in the air, he happened upon a grotesque and rotten corpse lying in the road. The polite thing, in this case, might be to notify the authorities of the body's presence, but this man met the body with indifference and continued on his way. He was not far past the place where the body lay when he heard a rustle from behind him; he turned and in the full enchanted moonlight observed the corpse rise up to its feet. Horror! His own feet were rooted to the ground, and thus he could not dash away in fright.

"The corpse approached and proclaimed himself the devil, here to take the man's soul to hell. One could not help but believe the walking corpse, for its eyes gleamed a feverish red, and its black lips split in a terrible grin.

"The man had only one request before he agreed to go with the devil: one last drink. Thereupon the devil did transform his appearance to disguise himself, and they went to the pub so the man could have his final drink. When they finished their ale, this man, so full of gall, dared to ask the devil to pay the bar tab; certainly, he would swindle his final drink for free. The devil, secretly impressed by the man's audacity, transmogrified himself into a sixpence. Pleased with himself, the man snatched up the coin, but instead of paying the bartender, he placed the coin in his pocket where he was also carrying a crucifix. With this powerful symbol beside him, the devil could not escape from his present form.

"There is a reason this man had made it through his life on his skills of trickery and deceit, and thus he made a deal: he would set the devil free, but only if he would be spared his life another ten years. Naturally, the devil agreed, and the man enjoyed ten more years without disturbance."

I took a sip of whiskey to quench my parched throat and waited for her assessment.

"Fair," she said, "but no scarier than mine."

"I disagree."

We both drank.

"Well," I said. "I suppose it's a draw."

We both paid for our drinks and grew quiet with rumination while a game of cards erupted in fierce betting behind us; I recalled my youthful days spent cheating at such games and very much would have liked to join them, but alas, I had begun my duty for the night and it must be completed by morning, or the consequences, I feared, would be intolerable.

"So, next round?" said the woman, referring not to the empty drinks that sat before us.

"Let us venture outside to give our next stories the proper atmosphere," I suggested. She looked at me, then at the door, turning over the idea—there is great reason to fear strangers in these lonely parts of the country—and nodded. We took our leave into the brisk night, pervaded with that chill silver mist that cast a kind of apparition over the distance. My lantern had diminished considerably and now gave off only the merest light, which hardly was able to filter through the thick, dried flesh of the turnip, and only its eyes and mouth now offered their failing glow. Despite the whiskey, I grew cold again, and with the lantern so near dead, my confidence soon doused itself as well. I had perhaps chosen a challenge with the woman this Halloween, having grown bored with spineless marks in the past, but now in the occluded moonlight I grew concerned that things would not go in my favor this evening. But no, such thoughts could never suit me; I always got what I needed in the end.

Beyond the dejected tavern lay a vast tract of black forest, rising gently in the distance into a gradual hill beyond which the horizon vanished in darkness and mist. Only the moon revealed the sharp contours of tall trees and wasted branches reaching their crooked limbs to the heavens as in desperate prayer. Dead brown leaves crackled where we tread as the woman and I slowly approached this wood, both seeming to lead the other closer and closer to its shadowed depths.

"Well, honey, I need time to think of another story—you go first this time," she said, her voice brimful of smoke and a kind of self-satisfied and secret knowledge. She drew toward the wood, and I . . . Did I lead her there, or did I follow? Which of us was leading the other, I wondered, into those ominous trees?

"The tale of the stingy man who bested the devil is not yet over," I said. "Ten years later, the man was out walking alone through an apple orchard." We reached the barrier of trees and continued creeping, together, into their dark embrace. "Once more, he found a putrescent corpse upon the ground, exposed to the sun and its dead flesh writhing with scavenging insects. He knew at once that this was no ordinary corpse, but the man did not attempt to run—he knew his time had come. The devil had returned, as promised, to collect the man's soul, but never had it been in the man's nature to capitulate without a final request: this time, one last apple.

"At first, the devil attempted to refuse him, but the man persisted. Thinking there could be no harm in granting him this particular request, the devil grudgingly climbed the nearest tree to retrieve an apple, and while he was within the branches the man carved a cross into the bark of the trunk, thus trapping the devil up the tree. And so he made another bargain; this time, he would release the devil only if the devil would agree never to take his soul to hell—and he agreed."

We had ventured deeper into the dense wood now so that the light of the tavern had vanished behind us. Woodland sounds of owls, crying animals, and insects echoed through the quiet; these I did not fear, but the woman beside me, too, seemed unafraid, and this ignited my concern once more that somehow I had chosen wrong. No, no—confound these blasted thoughts—let her enjoy a final walk in the woods, for I would kill her yet!

The woman laughed with that voice like grinding tree bark and told me this story was even less frightening than the last. "Old age has made you mild," she suggested.

"That isn't quite the end," I said, hurrying to the conclusion. "After a long life, the stingy man died alone, of old age. His soul was turned away from the light, and turned away, of course, from that seething pit of terror known as hell, as the devil kept his promise. Alas—the man would be condemned to roam in darkness for eternity, but that the devil offered him a burning coal to light his way."

Ahead, through the gloaming, I perceived a distant light, as that of a will-o'-the-wisp floating incorporeally on the wings of shadow. We trod on leaves and brush, and ducked beneath low-hanging branches, each still leading the other, now, ever closer to that mysterious light.

"And lemme guess: he wanders still, undead, so watch out? Honey, there's scarier things out here than that. Urban legend says there's a killer in these woods. I heard tell each Halloween they find a burned-out body around here, like its insides spontaneously combusted. What do you think of that?" Her mouth curled into a terrible grin, and I wondered if she knew that she would be this year's victim, and if so, how she could smile that infernal smile.

The blasted woman shook her head and hiked more swiftly now, directly toward that light, which beckoned like a gleaming beacon, and I hastened to keep pace. My lantern swung on its handle, emitting only the barest semblance of light now. Time was running out. It was rare that I ever let it get so low, and I knew I played a dangerous game in waiting until the very last moment—yet I had grown bored over the years, and I very much wanted to see the fear in this woman's eyes before I killed her. I wanted to see the horror of her recognition when she discovered that I'd bested her. My pride, as always, prevailed over my sense of caution.

The light ahead of us, I saw, was coming from a house ensconced within the trees. It was a ramshackle construction of stone and wood whose planks were stained and rotting with fungus, the discoloration reaching up to the sharply peaked roof, and whose tall windows emitted their light. A harsh light, too white to be fire, filtered through the soft curtain of the fog.

Ahead of that ominous house, which seemed to repel me with a metaphysical force, I slowed my pace, and the woman did likewise. When she turned to look curiously at me, I fixed her with a terrible grin.

"Look upon this, here," I said, holding aloft my lantern, which was perilously close to dying. "I require a new flame. It goes out each Halloween, you see, and I must relight it just before it dies or I shall be left in darkness." I reached out for the woman—"The only way to light these coals is with the burning flame of a human soul."

Now is when, in each of these many long years I have been playing this game, terror commonly flashes before the eyes of my mark. This woman, though, this maddening woman, simply laughed: an eerie, unnerving, and echoic sound that scraped the eardrums as with sandpaper or rough bark—a horrid, unbearable laugh of some terrible substance I can hardly describe.

"I know," she said. "I know just who you are, Jack. Don't you recognize me?"

We had arrived, now, at the house that emitted the white light into the forest from its tall and prominent windows, and around this woodland cottage did lay a dozen or more glowing faces, which startled me to see—but they were only jack-o'-lanterns, of course. My mind conjured up the witch from the woman's story, and it was then that I noticed the jack-o'-lanterns were not, indeed, carved from pumpkins but from human heads, hollowed out, their eyes burned from their skulls, and shining internally with candlelight, which glowed a hellish orange from their sockets and their gaping mouths.

Worse still, I discovered with absolute horror, were the identities of these severed heads—for I recognized in each one a mark from Halloweens gone by, a person whose soul I had harvested for my lantern and whose burned-out husk of a body I had inevitably left behind in these very woods, to be found or devoured by animals. It was not possible! It was some magic the likes of which I had not seen in many years, to have preserved each head so well as my own lantern, which I have carried these many centuries of undeath.

There was, however, one pumpkin among the ghastly heads, and its carven face very much did mirror that borne by my turnip lantern—the selfsame horrid gash for a mouth, shrieking in terror, and the hasty slits for eyes.

"What is this?" I could only stammer. "What is this?"

"That one I have carved specially for you," she said.

I looked down upon my own lantern—alack! It was going out! The coal was turning black, and soon I would be unable to relight it and forced to spend the rest of my days, years, centuries, millennia, in perpetual darkness. Here it is, going out within a moment, out, out!—and my panic drove forward my hand to grasp the woman, whose neck I seized in my aged and clawed appendage. As I grasped her, yes, she began to light up with flame from within—her eyes and laughing mouth began to glow with her burning soul—but why, why was she laughing? Just now my mark should be screaming with torture as her insides are incinerated—but she was laughing, laughing while she burned!

And then she said at last—"You fool. I am the devil; I have no soul!"

I had only a moment to experience this shock, and she had only a moment to witness and relish in my horror, before my own trick backfired upon me, and all at once the flame was quenched from her and rushed, instead, into me, for I did still have a soul, the only thing keeping me here on this earth. My soul ignited into flame, and I felt, then, the growing heat, and the wretched burn inside that cold and blasted hollow where my heart should be, and the flames growing within my ancient, creaking body as they charred my skeleton to ash. You cannot fathom the agony of being burned alive from the inside out, of feeling your soul devour the body you inhabit—oh, it is torture, a torture I have inflicted upon innumerable individuals! I opened my mouth to scream and knew the flames leaped out between my rotten teeth, and my vision danced and flickered with those flames so that the woman grinned at me as through a film of fire.

"I have been waiting a long, long time to seek my revenge on thee, Stingy Jack."

As I watched, her face began to rot; her eyeballs bulged from swollen, putrid sockets; her lips turned black with gore; her flesh bubbled, contorted, turned green with putrefaction; thus did she transform into an awful, laughing corpse.

"The devil does not like to be tricked," she said with glee.

My body crumbled as I was transformed into a flame.

The devil took this flame and placed it within that jack-o'-lantern that she had carved specially for me. I was a strange sort of mless consciousness within the orange gourd, and I wondere then, with mounting dread, whether the souls I took for my lantern remained somehow alive while I carried them in my lantern—if they were forced to experience all that I did, and live in anguish as a flame, alive, somehow, alive.

I did not have long to wonder upon this awful possibility, for the devil bent forward then and blew out my light.

And now, snuffed out but still existing, still existing, I am in a primeval and purgatorial darkness for all eternity—not dead, not alive, but a bodiless consciousness. Pity me, mortal souls, for though ye will die, and some will go to that wretched pit of despair that is known as hell, you will never face the terror and the endless madness of eternity as I will—I, Jack of the Lantern!

The Seventeen-Year Itch

Garth Nix

Six Weeks Before Halloween

"WHAT IS THIS?"

The new hospital administrator was peering through the peculiarly curved door, into the interior of the twelve-foot-diameter sphere of heavy steel that sat in the middle of the otherwise empty room. The curious object looked like a bathyscaphe or diving bell somehow lost far from the sea. Further compounding the mystery, the interior was completely lined with some sort of rubber or foamlike material, heavily impregnated with the stale smell of ancient piss and shit, hosed out but not forgotten.

"It says here 'Special Restraint Sphere: Broward' on the floor plan," replied her assistant, a young man called Robert Kenneth, a failed MD who was hoping to make a new career in hospital administration. He'd only been at the place—an institution for restraining and forgetting the criminally insane—for two months longer than Dr. Orando, the administrator, who'd arrived the previous Friday and was now looking into every nook and cranny of the place, which had been built in three great surges, in 1887, 1952, and 1978.

"What does that mean?"

"Uh, I don't know," said Kenneth. "Um, we do have a patient called Broward. I think."

"What can *you* tell me about this?" asked Orando, turning to the third member of their tour-of-inspection party. Templar McIndoe, senior orderly, was by far the oldest employee in the hospital, almost seventy and working on past retirement age by special permission and his own dire financial need. He knew everything there was to know about the hospital, though he didn't always share this information.

"Stephen Broward," said the old man. "They built this for him, special, back in forty-nine. That's when he came here, after what he did."

"Nineteen forty-nine? How old is this prisoner?"

"Oh, he's old," said McIndoe. "Older'n me. Must be ninety-five, ninety-seven, something like that. You've seen him, Mr. Kenneth. Guards call him Stubbsy."

"Oh, him," said Kenneth, trying and failing to contain a twist of his mouth, a visceral sign of distaste. "The one with no fingers or toes."

"He's got fingers, sort of," said McIndoe stolidly. "He only cut 'em off from the middle knuckle. But you're right about the toes."

"A self-mutilator?" asked Orando with clinical interest. "Why do we have him? And why has he been held so long?"

"Murder," replied McIndoe laconically. "Multiple murders. Back in sixty-five he killed near everyone in the place he was at then, an asylum down at Wickshaw. Twenty, thirty people."

"What?" asked Orando. She frowned. "He can't have. I'd

know about something like that. My second doctorate was on the psychology of mass murderers. I covered everyone who killed more than a dozen."

"Just what I was told," said McIndoe with what he hoped came across as an apologetic shrug. He already knew not to argue with this new administrator, and he needed to keep the job. Just for a few more years . . .

"And this sphere?"

"Somewhere to put him over Halloween," said McIndoe. "That's when he's particularly . . . upset."

"You put a patient in there?" asked Orando. She had drawn up to her full, impressive height and was looking at McIndoe like he was some sort of vicious animal.

"Nope," said McIndoe. "He puts himself in there. Morning before Halloween, he asks nice as pie to go in his special room and to not be let out till after the following dawn. Every Halloween; though it's the seventeenth he's always particularly wound up about."

"It looks airtight," said Kenneth. "He'd asphyxiate if he was in any longer than overnight. And there's no facilities . . ."

"Nothing to scratch with, neither," said McIndoe softly.

"What was that?" asked Orando. "And what's this seventeenth Halloween business?"

"He has this terrible itch," explained McIndoe. "It builds up over time, and it's always worse at Halloween, and it gets worse every year. The peak comes every seventeen years. After that, it ebbs away, builds up again slowly. Nothing to scratch himself on, inside that sphere."

"That's why he cut off his fingers and toes?" asked Kenneth, the twist in his mouth coming back, but fascination in his eyes.

"Reckon so," said McIndoe. "Pulled all his teeth out, too. He hands over his false ones before he goes in."

"What a ludicrous waste of space, not to mention the original investment to build this ... this sphere," said Orando with decision. "What were my predecessors thinking to pander to a patient's delusion in such a way? Well. He's not going in that sphere anymore. A ninety-year-old patient in such a restraint? Not in my hospital. We'll sedate him if necessary, but it's still six weeks to Halloween. A course of therapy—under my direction—should ameliorate or even remove the problem. You said something, McIndoe?"

"Yes, ma'am," replied McIndoe. "This Halloween is a seventeenth year. Broward will be real, I mean real bad—"

"I've already mentioned pandering to delusions!" snapped Orando. "I trust I will not have to deal with psychoses from staff members as well as the patients?"

"No, ma'am," said McIndoe. Already he was thinking ahead to be sure he was rostered off over Halloween. Him and the few friends he still had among the staff.

McIndoe had seen Broward in 2001, and seventeen years before that in 1984, and even seventeen years before that, when he'd first started at the hospital. On each of these three past occasions, he had been greatly relieved there *was* a sphere to put him in.

Ten Days Before Halloween

"HOW YA DOING, Mr. Broward?" asked McIndoe, stopping by the tall but stooped old man who was slowly refilling his paper cup from the watercooler in the recreation room.

"Bad," said Broward, grimacing. "That new doctor, the boss one, she keeps giving me different tablets, trying out stuff, and she talks to me during rest period. It's called rest period! I want to sleep then, like I'm supposed to."

"How's the . . . how's the itch?" asked McIndoe carefully.

Broward looked down at his chest and his stubby, shorn hands in their leather gloves began to close on his sternum before he visibly willed them back to his sides.

"It's bad," he said gloomily. "That doctor reckons she's hypnotized me so I don't want to scratch. But I *do*. Ten days to go . . . This is going to be a terrible one, I can tell. Even for the full seventeen."

"Seventeen years," whispered McIndoe, looking carefully around the room. He didn't want any of the other staff reporting him as insane.

"Yeah," said Broward. "If old Doc Gutierrez hadn't got me that sphere, I'd be really worried right now."

His hands moved again, remnant fingers heading for his chest, stumps reaching to scratch whatever lay beneath his blue patient's smock. Broward grimaced, baring his beautifully white false teeth as he forced his arms to his sides, his hands turned inward like claws.

"So . . . so all that talking and hypnotizing and the new drugs, they aren't working?" asked McIndoe.

"Nope," replied Broward. "It's itching fierce. But I can hold It off, Mac. I can hold It off until Halloween. And in the sphere . . . nothing to scratch with. It'll be okay. My great-great-granma, she carried It for more than a hundred years, I reckon. I've been okay more 'en fifty years, haven't I?"

His voice was pleading, eyes wet.

"Yeah, yeah," mumbled McIndoe. He gripped Broward's shoulder, offering him support. There wasn't much muscle there; it was all bone. The old man wasn't much more than skin and bone.

"You're a good man," mumbled Broward. "Hell, you're like family to me. . . ."

His voice tapered off as he said that, and he suddenly looked at McIndoe as if seeing him in a new light.

"Family . . . ," he whispered.

"Yeah, we've known each other long enough," said McIndoe. "Hell, I've known you longer than almost anyone."

He tried to smile, but inside McIndoe felt cold, and old, and frightened. He'd already arranged to be rostered off over Halloween. There was nothing he could do. If he helped Broward get in the sphere, Dr. Orando would just let him out, and McIndoe would lose his job, and if he lost his job, he lost the house, and he was raising three grandchildren, still four years to get the youngest through high school. There was nothing he could do.

"Shit," said McIndoe bitterly.

"What?" asked Broward. He'd rallied, was standing straighter, taking sips of his water. "Don't worry about what I said. . . . I can hold It off. I can. Don't you worry, Mac. I'll get in that sphere, hold It off another seventeen years! I'll beat my great-great-granma yet!"

"Yeah," said McIndoe. He tried to smile at the near centenarian being impossibly brave and failed. "Yeah. Keep up the good work."

He walked away, leaving the old man sipping his water. While he waited for the orderly on the other side to open the door, McIndoe glanced back. Broward was holding the cup between the palms of his hands. The stubs of his fingers were twitching, curling and uncurling.

Making scratching motions in the air.

McIndoe fled, heart hammering, all the way back to his special refuge, the cleaning cupboard on level two of the oldest building. He took the Scotch from behind the loose bricks and took four swallows in quick succession, following it up with a gargle of mint-flavoured mouthwash, also from a bottle hidden behind the bricks.

The Day Before Halloween

"MR. KENNETH. I got to talk to you."

"What is it, McIndoe?"

"Broward. He has *got* to go in the sphere tomorrow."

Kenneth slid out from behind his desk and went to the door, looking to make sure Dr. Orando was not in sight. He shut the door and returned to his desk.

"You've got to help him get in the sphere," repeated McIndoe.

Kenneth fumbled with a pencil, picked it up, drew some doodles on his desk blotter.

"The boss made it clear he's not to go in that thing," he said. "Broward is restrained in Ward Three, and heavily sedated."

"He's still trying to scratch, though, isn't he?" asked McIndoe. "Should be out deeper than deep, and he's *still* trying to scratch that itch, right?"

"Uh, yes," said Kenneth. He swallowed several times. "Look . . . look, McIndoe, were you here in 1966?"

"Yep," said McIndoe. "Nineteen years old, invalided out of the army—I took some shrapnel at Ia Drang—and looking for steady work. It was this or the Down's bakery. I should've gone with the bakery."

"Dr. Gutierrez, the old administrator . . . she left specific instructions for her successor, confirming what you said about Broward going into the sphere. Kind of odd . . . a personal letter, as well as the file instruction . . . she underlined a lot of it."

"She was the best person I ever knew," said McIndoe. "She worked out what would help people, made it happen. Not someone you expect to find in charge, well, you know what we got here. No one wants to know what happens to the people who come here. They get written off, whether they're murderers or just plain don't fit in."

"But Broward *is* a murderer," said Kenneth. "Isn't he? His file isn't clear on that point. He was committed for something to that place in Wickshaw, but its records went when it burned down in forty-nine. A lot of people died in the fire, and he was implicated in those deaths. Murder by arson. But was he already a murderer?"

"They burned it themselves," said McIndoe. He was staring over Kenneth's shoulder, looking back, seeing something long past. "Broward said they thought he was inside; that's why they did it. But he'd already got out."

"*Who* burned it?" asked Kenneth. He was doodling faster now, strange, grinning faces with lots of teeth, which he hastily drew over, scribbling heavy, thick lines.

"The staff who were left," said McIndoe. "Least, that's what Broward told me. I looked it up too, you know. Back in the day. They blamed him for the fire, but he didn't do that."

"What did he do?"

"He scratched an itch," said McIndoe. "And you can't let him. He has to go in the sphere."

Kenneth drew a straight line on the paper, then underlined it, three times.

"We can't," he said slowly. "Orando will be here. She wants to observe him. But . . ."

He hesitated, pencil stabbing down in a sharp, black dot.

"But, you know . . . tonight, maybe. He's an old man. He might die . . . with a little bit of—"

"No!" exclaimed McIndoe. "No! Don't you think anyone thought of that before? *He's* thought of it before. We can't kill him. He can't kill himself. And I think . . . I think he can't even die."

"Why . . . why not?"

McIndoe didn't answer at once. Kenneth stared at the older

man, the pencil broken in his hand. He hadn't even noticed his hands clenching, snapping it in two.

"He wants to scratch that itch. . . . He needs to scratch it," said McIndoe. "There's something inside him. Something that grows real slow, irritating the flesh, getting itchier and itchier. And when it gets to seventeen years old, it's just unbearable and he's got to scratch away and on Halloween it's . . . I don't know . . . ripe. . . ."

"What?" asked Kenneth. "What?"

"He has to scratch that itch, he has to scratch all the way through skin and all," whispered McIndoe. "So it can come out."

Kenneth stared, still not understanding.

"But he *must* be able to die, and if we—"

"You don't get it!" snapped McIndoe. "If he dies, where does whatever is inside him go?"

The two men sat in silence for a long, long minute. Finally Kenneth stood up and dropped the broken halves of the pencil in the trash bin by his desk.

"I . . . I can't go against Orando," said Kenneth. "I need this job."

"Yeah, so do I," said McIndoe. "But you're young, you can get another—"

"I didn't just fail my medical degree," interrupted Kenneth. "I was struck off. Stealing drugs. I'm lucky not to be in jail. Orando's a friend of my dad's; she said she'd give me a chance."

"If we don't do anything . . . people will die."

"Yeah, well, not me," said Kenneth. He wiped his eyes. "I'm calling in sick. You do whatever you got to do, old man. I'm not going to be here."

"I'm not working tomorrow," said McIndoe. "None of the old crew are. And I reckon some of the young ones too, they've felt the vibe. Lot of people'll be sick tomorrow."

"What about the ones that come in?"

"Shit, I don't know!" exploded McIndoe. "Some of the staff at Wickshaw survived. Some of them. I mean, they'll have a chance. The inmates in the newer buildings, they might be all right."

"Maybe it's nothing," said Kenneth. "We're just scaring ourselves. Projection. Lot of crazy people here, right?"

"Sure," said McIndoe bitterly. "But I'm not working tomorrow, and I bet you're still calling in sick."

"Yeah," said Kenneth. "I *am* sick. I got to go home *now*."

Halloween

"THIS IS REALLY very interesting," said Dr. Orando. "I've never seen anything like it. There is nothing in his records to indicate how he could be so resistant to anaesthesia."

"No, ma'am," replied the nurse, even though Orando had really been talking to herself. "Uh, he broke a strap before, ma'am. That's not supposed to be possible. We've got six tight on him now, and he's still moving against them."

"Hysterical strength," said Orando. She tilted the video camera on its tripod down a little, making sure it captured Broward's wriggling movements under the restraints. His arms were rippling like a snake pinned down by a shovel at the head, and the stubs of his fingers were trying to tear at the sides of the bed.

Scratching, Orando realised. Broward was trying to reach his chest. That was the target for his scratching. His own heart.

"Nurse, I'd like you to cut the patient's robe down from the neck to reveal the sternum, please."

"Doctor? Cut his robe?"

"Yes, that's what I said. This psychosomatic scratching is so developed I am wondering if it's capable of producing a physical effect. I saw some signs of a rash yesterday. A reddening of the skin, though it was transient. I want to see if it has developed further."

The nurse nodded, picked up a pair of scissors, and approached the bed. As he did so, Broward's struggles intensified. The IV tube in his arm shivered, constant small movements of Broward's arm making it vibrate. The restraining straps creaked and groaned, the clips screeching as they were slid back and forth against the metal frame of the bed.

The nurse got the scissors in position and started to cut, but he'd hardly slit a few inches when the fire alarm went off, a siren out in the corridor echoed by many others throughout the three buildings. A quick, strobing *whoop-whoop-whoop*.

All the lights went out. When the red-framed emergency lighting came flickering back, the nurse was by the door. He'd dropped the scissors in his hasty retreat.

"Go to your fire station in the main ward," snapped Orando. She snatched up the phone by the bed and dialled the hospital control centre. No one answered. After six rings she hung up and redialled, stabbing the buttons with her penlight. This time her call was answered by a breathy, clearly discomfited guard. There should have been two on duty, but a lot of the staff had called in sick that day, something Orando was going to investigate. Probably people wanting time off to be with their kids for Halloween, but they were going to have to pay for it out of their regular holiday entitlements when they got back tomorrow.

"This is Orando. What's going on?"

"Uh, two heat-detector trips in Building Three, and the main power and CCTV is out across the complex, which is weird because they should be independent. . . . I can't see what's going on," gasped the guard. "The board says all the inter-building automatic fire doors are closed, and City Fire and the police have been automatically notified. I was just . . . uh . . . Now there's another detector trip, also in Building Three—"

"Make an announcement: Building Three is to be evacuated according to the plan, all other buildings to lock down, staff to their fire-emergency positions," said Orando. "Get the closest orderly in to help you go through the checklist and then get them to call in all the off-duty staff. Patients are to be corralled on the south lawn as per the contingency. I'm on my way over."

She put the phone down and looked back at Broward, eyes running over the monitors to make sure he was still stable. He continued to writhe against the restraints, the clanging of the buckles a counterpoint to the *whoop-whoop* of the fire siren. For a moment, Orando considered whether she should order this building evacuated too, but with the automatic fire doors closed and the relatively new sprinkler system in Building Three, she considered there would be time enough to evaluate whether that was necessary, and it would be far better to keep everyone inside if they were not actually at risk from fire or smoke.

Certainly, she considered that Broward should not be moved while he was still being infused with anaesthetics, and though he seemed stable enough, intervention might be required, which could not be done on the lawn.

"I will be back shortly, Mr. Broward," she said. Orando often spoke to patients, even ones apparently far more deeply sedated than the old man jerking and struggling on the hospital bed in front of her. "Remember. You are not itchy. You do not need to scratch. Relax. Let yourself fall into a deep, healing sleep. All is—"

At that moment one of the straps broke, just broke, with a sound like a gunshot. Orando flinched but calmed herself. She approached the bed, glancing over at the video camera to be sure it was recording what was happening. Broward had got one arm free, and his mangled hand had gone instantly to his chest, stubby remnant fingers digging deep into his flesh.

Orando blinked. There was an odd, fuzzy glint of red under

those desperately scratching fingers. A reflection from the emergency lighting, no doubt.

She came closer, careful to keep to the end of the bed, out of reach of that scratching, scrabbling hand. Orando had worked with the dangerously insane for many years and would not risk getting too close. But she had never had such a fascinating patient, and she couldn't help but lean forward. . . . The fuzzy, red glint was clearer now, almost as if a kind of tendril of suspended desert-red dust was rising between the mutilated joints of the man's hand. . . .

Orando didn't realise she'd been holding her breath, in the excitement of observing a case that would give her not only a great leap in her professional career but probably a popular nonfiction book as well.

She breathed in.

A few moments later, her fingers twitched. Unlike Broward, her fingers were long and she had nails. Sensibly varnished, well-trimmed nails. But nails, nevertheless.

There was an itch on her chest. A really annoying, deep-seated itch along her sternum. She started to scratch, just with one hand. But the itch could not be assuaged.

"Help," groaned Orando. Broward was forgotten. There was only the itch. "I need . . . I need help!"

She ran out of the room. Scratching with both hands, nails digging deep into her own flesh, long streaks of blood spreading across her blouse, the pearls in her necklace washed red before her frantic scrabbling broke the string and they fell to go rolling across the floor.

A puff of ochre dust went with Orando, twining in and out of her mouth and nose with every inhalation and exhalation, as she ran sobbing and scratching, out to the lawn where all the patients and staff from Building Three were beginning to gather. . . .

· · ·

THREE MINUTES LATER, McIndoe appeared out of breath and trembling in Broward's room. He was not in his orderly's uniform. The hood of his tracksuit was up, pulled over an unusually long–billed cap, completely hiding his face. He had a bag of tools in his left hand, the end of the kitchen blowtorch he'd used to spoof the fire detectors just visible.

He stopped when he saw Broward sitting up on the bed, all the straps broken or undone, trailing by the sides. The old inmate was hunched over, cradling himself.

Broward's stubby, remnant fingers were finally still. Not twitching, not scratching. At rest.

But they were red, the old man's hands were red, soaked to the wrists with his own blood.

McIndoe froze in the doorway. The fire alarm was still whooping, rising and falling, but in the moments between its wails he realised the sound he'd unconsciously been hearing for a few minutes was now identifiable.

Screaming.

Screams, coming from outside the double-glazed security windows, coming from the lawn between the buildings. The designated evacuation area.

There was often screaming in the hospital, but this was different. McIndoe had never heard such screams, never heard so many people screaming, all at once.

"I couldn't . . . ," muttered Broward. "I couldn't hold it in. Seventeen years, and It knows, It knows. Halloween."

He looked up at McIndoe, his gaze older and more defeated than anyone's the warder had ever seen.

"The itch . . . the itch . . . I just had to scratch."

"What . . . what is *It?*" asked McIndoe. He didn't even really know what he was saying, what good it would do to know. He'd hated himself for staying away, and he hated himself for coming back and trying to do something, and most of all he hated himself for being too late. He should have got Broward into the sphere earlier, no matter what it took.

"I don't know," whispered Broward. "I've never known. Something ancient, something terrible. People knew it before, but we've forgotten. All Hallows' Eve. Old Scratch. You'll see. I'm sorry, McIndoe. I'm sorry, sorry . . ."

"You tried," said McIndoe. "Hell, whatever's happening isn't your fault."

"Not that," whispered Broward. "I'm sorry for *you*. *It* will be back here soon."

"Yeah," said McIndoe. He shrugged wearily, knowing that this time he'd irretrievably fucked everything up. His life insurance was paid. The grandkids would make it, maybe they'd even do better without him along to try and guide them. "Don't worry. Like I said, you tried. I saw that, every time. You fought. I'm almost seventy, I could drop dead any moment. Not your fault."

"*It* comes back when it's had enough. Looking to be reborn again, to hide and grow," whispered Broward. "*It* likes a familiar place. Familiar. *It* was called that, sometimes. In my family . . ."

He leaned over as if in great pain, and when he straightened up, there was a pair of sharp surgical scissors clutched between his palms, stubby fingers folded over to keep it tight. "I'm so sorry, McIndoe, but I . . . I can't do it anymore. *It* has to go to family, and you're the closest I got. The itch . . . oh, the itch—"

McIndoe lunged, but he was too late. Broward had shoved the scissors as hard as he could into that itchy spot, right under his sternum. He was already good as dead. All the warder could do was help him lie back as the blood blackened the old man's chest and his eyes became dull. Curiously, his face continued to hold an expression McIndoe had never seen before. The attendant had seen plenty of men die. He'd never seen one look relieved before.

The orderly sat down in the chair next to the bed. The screaming was fainter. He could hardly hear it now. Just isolated, fading wails and cries under the constant up-and-down whooping of the fire alarm, and the sharp, frantic beeping of the monitors that had detected the absence of Broward's pulse and blood pressure.

Air moved in the corridor outside, a wind whistling through, though there were never windows open here, no way for a breeze to get in. The door creaked and moved a few inches. McIndoe tensed, trying to remember the words of a prayer he hadn't said since he was a very young man, lying wounded in the mud. It had been hot and very humid then. Now it was cold, air-conditioned cold, but he was sweating, and he wanted to move but he couldn't.

There was a red glint in the air, the hint of dust carried on the wind, or a flight of tiny red insects flying all together like a little cloud, coming straight at McIndoe, straight at his chest—

McIndoe screamed as a white-hot wire thrust through his heart and out his back. He clutched at his chest, frantically lifted his tracksuit top and the T-shirt beneath. But there was no wound, and the pain was gone as quickly as it had come.

He stared at his breastbone. It looked no different from before. His skin was wrinkled and old, a few remaining hairs wiry and white. McIndoe thought it looked like someone else's chest, but he'd always thought that, at least since he was sixty.

Now it didn't just look different. His skin *felt* different. Like there was something there, something just under the skin, though it was not visible.

It *was* a little itchy. Just in the middle. Only a little bit now, but it was bad enough. Hard to imagine how much worse it would be in seventeen years. . . .

McIndoe automatically moved to scratch but stopped himself. His face set hard, and he sat for a while, thinking. Then he got up and found the tool bag where he'd dropped it on the floor.

There was a big screwdriver in there that would serve as a chisel, broad enough to sever a finger at the joint. And he had a hammer. The floor would be his workbench, and there were plenty of bandages close by he could use to stem the blood.

Painkillers too, but he didn't think he'd use them.

The pain would be a good distraction.

A distraction from the itch.

A Flicker of Light on Devil's Night

Kate Jonez

I SUPPOSE I SHOULD CARE MORE, but little by little all the ordinary cares I had before got chipped away.

The girl's teddy bear is wedged in the corner of the floral sofa that was the least ugly one at the thrift store. She's rearranged the cotton cover that's supposed to hide the hideous thing. I'd wanted furniture that would be as pretty and elegant as the old house had been before it had been cut up into apartments. When I first moved in, it seemed possible.

A beam of October light that seems transported from a Crate and Barrel catalog makes the earth tones I've been trying to decorate with look like they've been rolled around in actual earth. I guess you have to be rich to successfully dye fabric with tea and have it look good. I'm about as broke and beyond glamour as the old turn-of-the-century house, I guess.

The bear is wearing the only good pair of earrings I ever owned, will probably ever own if I'm honest about it. They are gaudy and haven't been in style for years. For a minute, I think I can hear the Pink song that was playing the night my ex gave them to me. That night his eyes glittered hard as the little stones with his excitement about all his big plans, all the crazy wild things we were going to do.

Nostalgia is stupid. It makes me physically sick. I never listen to old music anymore. I should probably sell the earrings. I forgot I even had them. I've got more important things to care about.

The living room windows vibrate like a bomb just created a concussion. Construction-paper Halloween bats the girl made twirl on their fishing line. Their wings cast long shadows across the braided rag rug. I can almost hear wings flapping announcing the arrival of the dark angel of the cold times. I imagine the whole neighborhood dropping to the pockmarked ground with hands over their bleeding ears. I guess I'm not in a festive mood. There's no reason to look out the window. There's not a chance the angel dropped a bomb. Nothing as definitive as that. It's only kids fighting. They're stomping and thumping around hard enough to rattle the windows. Why can't they be happy for ten consecutive minutes?

I stomp through the living room and yank open the door to the attic. "What are you doing?" I try to modulate my voice so the situation, if it *is* a situation, and it probably is, doesn't escalate.

The girl's siren howl barrels down the stairs. It's not the worst kind of scream, the kind that evokes a pool of blood or a bone poking through skin, but it's alarming enough.

"Shut up, you fat-ass cockhole," the boy yells. The attic is his room now because he's too old to share with a kid, and he doesn't care about the spiders. That's the least of what he doesn't care about. "Get out of my room."

"I don't have to. Mommm!" the girl wails.

I march up the stairs. They are hardwood and still shiny at the edges where no one walks on them, remnants of the days when the whole house was a showplace for robber barons or shipping magnates and no expense had been spared, even in the attic. They'd be nice if I sanded and refinished them.

"What is the problem?" I demand as I squint into the gloom.

The floor is rougher up here. It would take a lot to make it nice. A lot more than I could justify spending on a rental. Like fixing a floor is even one of my options.

The October sun barely squeezes in through the dormer window. Outside, across the street, a fire burns in a green plastic trash can. The Devil's Night ceremonies are starting before the sun even goes down. I listen for sirens but hear nothing. One little fire is hardly the worst of it. The trash can is one the city owns, heavy and durable. It won't melt right away. Maybe someone will put it out soon. Maybe someone will catch it in time.

"He's going to cut my arm off," the girl says, her voice hitching with her sobs. "He's got a knife."

"How's she supposed to be Furiosa for Halloween if she's got two arms?" The boy pulls his dreadlocks, dyed white even though his hair is naturally blond, forward and strokes them. The gesture reminds me of the baby blanket he'd always insisted on draping over his head when he was little. He's shirtless even though the attic is chilly. His lack of concern for personal comfort troubles me. But that's the least of the things that trouble me. He grins at me with that cocky smile he uses when he's sure he's winning an argument. "It'll grow back, anyway." He lounges back on the filthy black-and-white-checked futon he dragged in from the eviction trash heap next door in spite of my warning about bedbugs and slides the tip of a folding knife under his fingernail.

"I don't want my arm cut off," the girl cries. "Even if it's going to grow back." She hugs herself but doesn't run away.

"Arms don't grow back," I say. "You can be whatever you want for Halloween."

Her crying escalates.

"Give me that." I reach for the knife.

The boy snatches it away. His hair swings back revealing an angry "X" carved over where most people think their heart is. The lines of the symbol are crusted black as though he's rubbed dirt in the wound. The ridges are raised and puffy looking.

I am concerned, but it isn't serious enough for an emergency-room visit. Antiseptic will fix this. And he's got an appointment with a counselor. It's not all that bad. It can't be. The appointment is in January, so the doctor must think it's okay to wait three months. He wouldn't make him wait if the boy was really sick, if this self-harm was a symptom of something bad.

"What happened to you?"

"The angel Ariel came down and cut out my heart. She said I'd be better prepared to do my work without it." He lifts his chin and stares at me as if daring me to contradict him. His voice is as deep as his father's. When did that happen?

"He's cutting himself other places too, Mom. I saw him do it."

"Shut up, buttwipe, or I'll cut you too." He sounds like a boy again. The curtain that momentarily lifted to expose a glimpse of the future has fallen.

"He poops in a jar, Mom." The girl smirks until a pillow whacks her on the head.

I breathe in and in and in. There is not enough air left in the world.

Should I tell him he's confused the name of Gabriel the angel with the name of Ariel the little mermaid? Is this the kind of thing other teenagers say? I'm afraid to ask other parents. I'm afraid to ask. I'm afraid—

"Little snitching bitches get stitches." The boy pounces on her and knocks her onto the disgusting futon.

The girl giggles instead of cries for once. They really do like each other in spite of the evidence.

"That's enough. Stop using language like that." This is hardly the worst of it, but there are so many things I need to say and to put a stop to, I don't know where to start.

The attic smells of dirty socks and something fermented. I let my eyes crawl across the magpie tangle of clothes, game cards, buttons, dice, shoes, bags, cups, comics, bits of string, feathers, candles, cigarette butts he says were here all along and shiny unidentifiable detritus. They fall on a two-quart mayonnaise jar. I can't deal with this right now. I can't deal with this. I can't deal—

I don't even know what to say to a kid who poops in a jar.

"Come downstairs. It's time for dinner."

"I want hamburgers," the girl says. She sprints to the stairs. "Hamburgers and french fries."

The boy rolls over on the mattress and closes his eyes.

Somewhere in the gloom of the rafters the dark angel Ariel flaps her wings to warn of the coming cold times, or perhaps it's a bat. Most likely it's a bat.

"You too. Put on a shirt but don't button it. I want to put medicine on that cut."

"I'm not hungry." He opens one eye and looks at me. Even lying down, his chin has that defiant tilt.

"Get up and go downstairs." I reach to grab his arm and help him along, but he rolls away onto his feet. His head grazes the rafters. He's tall for fourteen. He takes after the men on my side of the family. Before long he'll have a beard he can braid like his Viking ancestors.

I'd send him out to tramp through the woods on his first hunt if I could track down any of those cousins or uncles who were everywhere when I was growing up. It would be good for him.

"What are we having, anyway?"

"Toast."

He raises an eyebrow and makes a face.

"With apricot jam," I say definitively before he can get his complaint out.

I watch as he digs a shirt from the pile and shuffles down the stairs. As I bring up the rear, I glance through the dormer window and notice the trash fire has grown. Thick black smoke billows from the bin.

As I round the landing, there's a knock on the front door.

Little feet scurry.

"Tigis!" the girl cries. The doorknob slams into the wall. A sprinkle of plaster from the hole I need to repair ticks to the wooden floor.

"Don't slam—" I don't even bother finishing my sentence as I hurry across the room and reach for the door to pull it away from the wall. Words circle around and back. They've lost all meaning through repetition. I need a new language.

Tigis steps inside and pushes a pot into my hands. She is the type of woman I would take care never to stand by when I used to go to the club, petite, fragile. Next to her I look hulking. She just barely looks me in the eye, not giving me enough time to decline or be embarrassed. I wish we could be better friends than we are because she completely understands food stamps don't come for another five days.

She says something I don't understand. I'm not sure what language she speaks. Is Ethiopian a language? I always mean to look it up and check out a dictionary from the library. I'm going to get her something with the tips I earn on my shift tonight. I can't imagine what she might like, though.

"Take me with you." The girl clings to Tigis's arm. "I don't want to stay here. Please!" Tigis smiles and strokes my daughter's hair.

"Stop that." I get a bad feeling in the pit of my stomach when the girl says things like this. Nothing is so terribly wrong at our house. The angel isn't a real harbinger of cold to come. The angel isn't real. The angel—

I want to hug the girl and let her know everything is okay, but I have the pot in my hands. There are bits of chicken, and the sauce smells exotically spicy. "Come and eat now."

Tigis says something in her language.

The girl grins like she understands and lets go of the woman's arm. "She says I can come over later."

"We'll see."

I say, "Thank you," to Tigis with a smile. I don't like this secret code she and my daughter share, but I don't want to be rude. The girl is mine. I've given up all of my dreams and possessions to keep her happy.

Tigis turns and walks down the stairs that were probably once the centerpiece of the grand old house, a stage for debutantes to descend, but are now only a path from one section-eight apartment to another. There's a man huddled into a puffy coat like he doesn't want anyone to see him waiting at her door.

The last time the girl went downstairs she came home with ten dollars and fingers smelling like cat pee. Tigis's husband gave it to her for helping put weed in little Ziploc bags. It's just weed, but still. And people I don't like the looks of, like that man in the puffy coat, come and go all the time. It's no place for a kid, a girl. Bad things can happen to girls in the blink of an eye, things they won't ever fully recover from. Maybe there's a chance I can keep her safe just a little longer. At least here there aren't cousins and uncles on the safe side of the locked door.

"Close the door now. Lock it," I say. "Go and sit down."

I follow the girl to the kitchen and place the pot in the center of the Formica table that came with the apartment. It's cool and vintage looking. When I first saw it, I could imagine how my new china would look on it as we all sat around it and talked about our day. We haven't done that yet.

The girl throws herself in the chair by the window.

The windows of the house next door glitter behind her head. Another old grand dame of a house carved up to shelter people it was never built for. The orange and yellow flickering in the glass is the exact shade as the Halloween pumpkin on the refrigerator. The fires have taken the place of the blazing sunset. There won't be any dark tonight as the devils cavort.

I place a plastic bowl in front of the girl and ladle chicken stew into it. I haven't been able to get the new china yet.

There's another fire. This one looks like a pile of leaves in the alley. There are a bunch of teenagers gathered around it throwing trash on to make it blaze higher. Even through the closed window, I hear a crash and the chime of glass sprinkling the ground. I hope this will all be over before the little kids go out tomorrow night. Where are the police anyway?

"I'm not eating this." The girl pushes her bowl away. "It stinks."

"Tigis made that just for you."

"I don't care."

"Then you can just go hungry and take yourself to bed now." Anger surges in me, filling my mouth with words as sharp as broken glass. Why won't she just eat? It's a miracle we have chicken tonight.

"I'm never going to bed again." Her face is screwed up like she's going to cry. Her pigtail has come unbraided, and a strand of it trails into the bowl. "There's a monster in the mattress. He has a knife."

"You *are* going to bed." I tip her out of the chair because I don't trust myself to grab her. The sharpness inside me might hurt her.

The girl screams. It's not her best work. She reserves the worst of her screaming for three a.m. The shrill siren of her five-year-old voice conjures up mayhem and murder and rips me from sleep nightly. The boy told her the monsters aren't under the bed or in the closet. They are in the mattress, and there is no way to escape them.

If it wasn't for the screaming, I'd admire the brilliance of this little twist to the tale. He has conjured the ultimate horror. No squeezing eyes tight or covering every inch of skin will keep a kid safe from a monster in a mattress.

"Quiet, now. Go get ready for bed."

"No!"

For a second I think about slapping her. . . . She earned it. But that will only make things worse.

The pediatrician says she needs consistent discipline, and time-outs are the way to go. It makes sense in theory. I can pick her up and put her in bed. She won't stay. I'll have to hold her there. How is that different from hitting?

"Do you want some toast?" I say instead. I suppose this is about as consistent as I'm going to get tonight.

She bobs her head with much more enthusiasm than heated bread deserves. I put two slices in the toaster and push the lever. "Where is your brother?"

A shadow flickers by the kitchen door. I think I hear a flap of wings. I hesitate only a second until the front door creaks.

I catch the boy with his hand on the doorknob. "Where do you think you're going?" I sound exactly as ineffectual as my own mother did.

"Out," he says.

"No you are not. Not tonight. Especially not tonight." I don't have time for this argument. I have to be at the restaurant for my shift in an hour and my gas tank is close to empty. "You have homework."

The boy makes a sound like a serpent and stomps down the stairs.

If he goes through the main door out into the night, he'll be lost. He'll become one of the devils of the night starting fires and smashing windows. I can't let it happen.

"Get back here—now." I run after him and grab his arm.

"Get off me." He shakes his arm and gives me a shove.

The sole of my shoe glances off the edge of a stair. I teeter. An inevitable gravity grabs me. I'm falling. It's a loss of control I haven't felt since I was a kid. My knee, my hip, my shoulder hits the face of the stairs. I land in a heap in the foyer right in front of Tigis's door, which in olden times must have been the door to the parlor or salon. I'm not hurt. I don't think.

The boy stomps down the rest of the stairs and steps over me. His face is expressionless. He jerks the front door open and steps out.

The boy is mine. The teenaged brain isn't fully formed. He's made a mistake, an error in judgment. Or is something truly coming unwired and crossed?

"Is that the kind of man you are going to be?" I had heard my mother say these words a hundred times to my uncles and cousins. She never did find the language that would deliver the message. She never once was able to shame them or cause them to change their behavior. I feel my words decaying like I've rung the same old bell.

The boy's shoes hit the porch steps. I don't get up right away; instead I stare through the door into the deep violet sky. The air smells of burning plastic, but under it all there's a hint of snow. I'm going to have to find the box with the mittens in it soon. It's somewhere in the attic with the knife and the spiders and the poop in a jar. I'll have to beat back wings to get into the darkest corners because the cold times are coming.

What am I going to do now? If one wheel falls off, the whole cart collapses. Who's going to take care of the girl tonight? The boy is trouble. Is troubled. The boy—I should find a better place for him with someone who knows what to do. There might still be a chance to save the girl. I doubt I have the recourse to do this. I doubt I can. I doubt—I don't get to throw one kid under the bus to save the other. It has to be both or neither. That's the rule of mothering, isn't it? That's the only justifiable decision.

I swear I hear a flurry of fluttering wings outside the front door.

The boy peeks his head in, then steps inside. He holds out his hand to help me up. "Sorry, okay?"

"Okay," I reply. I take his hand. It's exactly as cold as the night.

"I . . ." His face is flushed like he has a fever.

"I said okay." Things are far away from okay, but the word means something specific only to me in the language I speak. "Can you put your sister to bed? I've got to get gas for tonight."

The boy looks at me longer than he has for a while. I think he's disappointed that I didn't hand out a grand punishment. He's just done the worst thing he's done so far. I've been unveiled, revealed as a fraud and a coward. I'm powerless to keep anything intact. I can't stop him from breaking things. I can't stop him from breaking. I can't stop him—

I step out into the night, gas can and plastic tubing I stash in the foyer in hand. Fires are blazing. It's much worse than it looked from inside. The flames from the eviction heap lick high into the sky. Higher than the second story where the items in the pile once furnished a home.

Devils skulk on stoops or duck into the alley. They carry liquor bottles pre-stuffed with oily rags. They are kids by daylight but something else entirely tonight.

It's too late to sneak into the neighbor's backyard and siphon gas from his old RV with the flat tires. I'll never make it to work on time. Not a chance. It's too bright for that in the firelight, anyway. It's too late to continue on this half-baked ill-conceived plan. It's too late to continue. It's too late—

I stick the hose into the gas tank of my car, and it hits some sort of obstacle. This works just fine on the old RV around back. I guess my old beater isn't old and beaten enough. I slump against the hood and stare into the blazing heap of trash next door. I'm out of energy and ideas about what to do next. I'm out of energy. I'm out—

A shadowy figure emerges from the flames. Black wings beat the thick gray smoke until it swirls.

"Shouldn't be out here on a night like tonight," Colonel Carpenter says, "devils will get you." He doffs his hat at me and leans on his cane.

I shrug at him. "I guess," I say. He probably thinks I'm rude. I'm pretty sure he knows I've been stealing the gas from his camper, so rude is the least of it.

"Your boy . . ."

"What about him?"

"He's running the streets. Making all kinds of noise." The old man's eyes are obscured by the brim of his hat. "I'm going to call the police."

"He's inside." I glance up at the attic window. It's mostly dark, but I'm pretty sure I see the outline of the angel Ariel's wings and the glitter of her eyes as she watches me.

"Last night," the colonel says. A wisp of his Old Spice cuts through the smell of burning plastic, and then it's gone. "Ripping and running with his boys, then up there." He cocks his thumb to the balcony off my living room.

We don't go out on the balcony much because the railing isn't sturdy.

"Blasting that damn rap music and throwing their empties at cars passing by. Had your little one up there with them knuckleheads."

Of course that happened. Of course it did. Why would I think otherwise?

"I'll talk to him about it," I say. "It won't happen again."

But it will. I can't stop events from unfolding. I can't stop them. I can't—

"You need gas?" the colonel asks with a nod at my gas can.

"I do." Now more than ever.

"There's a can over there on the side by my mower." He pushes his hat down. "Welcome to it."

"Thank you," I say as he hobbles off to shake his cane at the rest of the neighborhood.

I find the colonel's mower at the side of his house, and just like he said, there's a gas can. As I grab it, a rag snags on the lawn mower gear shift and pulls loose. Gasoline dribbles from a rusty hole in the can. I'll have to move fast if I'm going to move at all.

Seconds flutter by like years unfurling. The cold times are coming. Worse times. Much worse.

I sprint up the porch steps, then the flight to my apartment. The doorknob slams into the wall and plaster ticks to the floor. One more thing I will never repair. I dash through the living room and even step up on the ugly sofa.

The girl's teddy bear still wearing my gaudy earrings gives me a glassy-eyed look of disapproval. I run down the hall for good measure, past the girl's room with the knife-wielding monster in the mattress, and back again through the kitchen. The pot of chicken stew is congealing into something inedible. I won't forget to return the pot this time.

The pan of cloves and cinnamon sticks has boiled dry again. No need to fill it or worry about it tonight. No spice can mask this smell.

I climb up the flight of stairs to the attic. I stand at the top and gaze into the shadowy depths. Gasoline drips on my shoes. I didn't think I was gone that long, but I guess I was. The boy and the girl are sleeping. I place the gas can gently on the floor so I won't wake them. It's not so full anymore.

I lie down with them on the filthy black-and-white-checkered futon, as the devil light flickers along the trail I have made.

The girl snuggles up.

"It's hot in here, Mom," the boy murmurs, not fully awake.

The boy and the girl are mine, forever and always. They are mine to care for and love.

I lie still gazing up into the rafters watching the firelight flicker and the shadow wings beat. I try to recall something pithy my mother might say at moments like this, but language is inadequate to describe how something so hot can be the harbinger of something so cold.

As the air grows thin, I wait for the angel Ariel to descend and cut out my heart because I can better do my job without it. As the air grows hot, I wait for the angel Ariel. As the air grows hot, I wait—

Witch Hazel

Jeffrey Ford

BACK IN THE DAY, in the Pine Barrens of South Jersey, from October 31 to November 2, All Souls' Day, people who lived in the woods or close to them would pin to their coats, their blouses, the lapels of their jackets a flowering sprig of witch hazel. It's a shrub that grows naturally in the barrens and blossoms right around Halloween. The flower looks like a creature from a deep-sea trench, yellow tentacles instead of petals radiating from a dark brown center that holds a single seed.

The name of the plant could have something to do with real witches and witching but not necessarily. The word "witch" is derived from Middle English "wicche," and all it means is *pliable* or *bendable*. It's a reference to the use of the branches of the witch hazel shrub in the art of dowsing by early homesteaders to the barrens. Dowsing is the practice of locating things underground with and through the vibrations of a Y-shaped tree branch. One thing's for sure, the "hazel" part of the word comes from the fact that in England the branches from the hazel tree supposedly made the best dowsing rods. That tree didn't grow in the barrens, though, and so the settlers found a substitute that was equally pliant—a shrub with crazy flowers that blossoms in the season of jack-o'-lanterns.

The practice was fairly prevalent until well after World War II, but most of those who still don witch hazel for the holiday don't know its symbolism, and only do so because they remember a parent or grandparent wearing it. In this manner the tradition might limp a little further into the future before completely disappearing. There's a tale, though, that is now rarely repeated save around the kitchen tables and fireplaces of real old-timers. It begins in the year 1853, in the barrens village of Cadalbog, a place that presently exists as only one crumbling chimney and the foundation of a vanished glass factory lost among the pines. The loose-knit community of glassmakers, blueberry harvesters, colliers, and moss rakers had been there since 1845. By 1857, the village was deserted.

A reminiscence of the place that has survived in the diary of one Fate Shaw, the wife of the factory owner, describes Cadalbog as "an idyllic place of silence and sugar sand as soft and white as a cloud. The local cedar ponds are the color of strong tea, and along lower Sleepy Creek there always seems to be a breeze shifting through the pines, even in the heart of August." Supposedly Mrs. Shaw did everything within her power to provide for her husband's workers and their families. She was well liked and well respected, as was Mr. Shaw. One of the events she put on every year was a Halloween celebration.

Unlike the citizenry of most of the other settlements of the barrens, either Swedish or Puritans from Long Island, Cadalbog was founded by Irish immigrants fleeing the potato famine back home. Their Halloween antics were brought with them from the Old World. There was disguise, not as monsters or ghouls, but people would dress up and pretend to be dead relatives. Turnips were carved instead of pumpkins. There was always a huge bonfire, dancing, fiddle and tin whistle music. Out in the middle of a million and a quarter acres of pine forest, in the spooky autumn night, it didn't seem so outlandish that those who'd passed on might return to beg for prayers to shorten their stays in purgatory. In that setting, even these pragmatic people, who'd survived much, could believe for a few nights that spirits were afoot.

In 1853, Halloween fell on a Monday, and the celebration could not be held on the night of a workday. Likewise, Sunday was out of the question, as it was given over to the Lord. So it was Friday, October 29, that the incident occurred. There was a cold breeze out of the north. A roaring bonfire licked the three-quarter moon with a snapping flame, and the music reeled. A strong fermented brew called *heignith,* concocted from crab apples, wild blueberries, cranberries, and raw honey, among other ingredients (its full recipe is lost), was consumed by the barrelful.

Attending the celebration that night was Miss Mavis Kane and her sister, Gillany. These two women, identical twins, were well-known even though they lived on the outskirts of the village. Gillany had been married at one time, but her husband, Peter, a Quaker collier who'd been born in those woods, succumbed to a rattlesnake bite, leaving the sisters to fend for themselves. By the account of Fate Shaw, they managed quite well. To quote from her diary, "The Kane sisters are a stoic pair—dour and pale and of few words. They move silently like ghosts around their property, chopping wood, repairing the steps to the front door, throwing a stick for that black dog of theirs, Brogan."

As reported by Fate, their sole uniforms were ankle-length black dresses of a sateen weave. Even in summer, out in the forest, hunting the yellow shelf fungus that grows on the sides of trees (they made a good profit drying it, crumbling it up, and curing it with honey to make a kind of sweet brittle), they wore light corsets and high collars. Their long black hair was gathered into one large knot and left to lay upon the spine. To the Halloween celebration they brought a basket of Kane's Crumbs, as the local treat had come to be known. The sisters, though both handsome women, weren't asked to dance. They didn't drink or eat but sat and simply stared at the fire and the goings-on. Their fixed expressions were the only masks they needed.

Sometime after the drunken singing had turned to whispered laughter a small meat cleaver appeared, as if from nowhere, in Gillany's left hand. Its blade glistened in the glow of the dying fire as it sliced the air, struck, and split the backbone of Ray Walton, the foreman at the glass factory. As he screamed, blood immediately issuing from his mouth, Mavis put a knife through the throat of the Ahearn girl, who folded to the ground like a paper doll. They each went on hacking out their own private trails of horror: fingers flying, blood and bowels falling, eyes skewered, ribs cracked, wrists hacked. A storm of screams broke the stillness of the barrens.

It took some time for a group of factory laborers—male and female—to subdue the sisters. The Kanes fought, it seemed, without awareness—as if they were under a spell. By the time the two murderers were tied up and being led away, there were six dead and twenty wounded. That's a lot of people to dispatch in a relatively short time with only sharp kitchen utensils. The Burlington County sheriff in Mount Holly was sent for, and the twins were incarcerated in separate storerooms in the glass factory. Old Dr. Boyle, once of Atsion and since run away to the woods after accusations of malpractice, was already on hand, drunk, pronouncing death and treating the wounded. He agreed with Mr. Shaw's assessment that the attack was too random and mindless to have carried an intention of murder. Most everyone who witnessed it firsthand agreed.

When his duty to those injured at the celebration was finished, Boyle went to the factory to inspect the Kanes. By then the sun was coming up, and the breeze dropped yellow oak leaves in his path. The smoke from the bonfire pervaded the air, and bottles lay strewn about the clearing behind the factory and down the path into the deep pines. He entered the brick structure and was greeted by Shaw, who showed him down a back hallway to a small door hidden by shadow. Boyle, a careful man, put his ear to the door and listened. The factory was empty and unusually silent.

"Who can tell the difference, but I think someone who would know said this was Gillany," said Shaw.

"Is she tied up?" asked Boyle.

"Oh, yes, quite securely."

"Did she say anything when you got her in here?"

"Nothing. She foamed at the mouth and spit. Growled some."

"Okay," said Boyle, and nodded.

Shaw moved forward and inserted a long iron key into the door's lock. He turned it, there was a vicious squeal from the hinges, and they entered. The room was small, with a low ceiling and one window at eye level looking out across an expanse of reed grass toward the pond. The only light in the dim room came from that source. Boyle felt claustrophobic. He set down his bag, took off his hat and coat, and hung them on the back of a chair. The only sound was that of the woman's breathing, steady and strong. She was asleep on the floor, her hands bound behind her back, feet tied. Her black hair was unknotted and covered her face. Blood soaked the sleeves and skirt of her dress.

The doctor had Shaw fetch him a lantern, and by that, he examined her. When he rolled her onto her back, he discovered her eyes were wide open as she slept. "Most unusual," he said, bringing the light closer and closer to them, unable to make the dilated pupils constrict. As he wrote in his personal report of the case (held, along with surviving files of his other cases, at the Joseph Truncer Memorial Library at Batsto Village), "There were a number of odd signs upon the first of the Kane women I examined, not the least of which was a high fever. The eyes were like saucers, the skin around the sites of her lymph nodes had gone a vague green, her eyelashes had fallen out, and there was a silvery substance dribbling from her left ear. All of these struck me as potent signs of disease. When I inspected her lower body, I found her legs covered with insect bites, which I knew were chiggers from that feel of sand when I brushed my open palm against her shins."

According to the story, it's then that Shaw, standing by for support along with his wife, who had since joined him and Boyle in the storeroom, took a small jump backward and gave a grunt, pointing at something white wriggling out from beneath Gillany Kane's undergarments. Boyle swung the lantern to give a better view. There wasn't just one bloodless worm inching down her legs, but it was clear there were a dozen or more. Fate Shaw put her hand to her mouth and gagged. The doctor got to his feet and moved away as fast as a man of seventy-five with a bad liver and bad knees could. He went to his bag, hands shaking, and removed his tools to extract a blood sample. As he leaned over the body again, he called over his shoulder for Shaw and his wife to get out. "No one is to enter this room or the one in which the sister is being kept until I return. Make sure to lock them both as soon as I'm gone."

Back in his home halfway between Cadalbog and Harrisville, Boyle brewed himself a pot of coffee and brought out the brass microscope a wealthy Dutch patient of his had gifted him early in his career for saving a favorite son. Still not having slept from the previous night's festivities and mayhem, he peered bleary-eyed into the tube of the mechanism at a slide holding Gillany's blood. What he wrote in response to what he witnessed through the eyepiece was only this—"A strange pathogen, blossoming, from the woman's blood cells—many armed, like the wild witch-hazel flower. I've never seen the like." He stood from his table on which the microscope rested and stumbled to bed. There he slept for a brief interval before heading back to Cadalbog.

He arrived at the factory in late afternoon to find a commotion. It seems that the woman who was hot with fever and in a trance, sleeping with eyes open, somehow revived enough to smash through the small window that looked out upon the cedar pond. As Fate Shaw put it, "We were novices as prison guards. No one ever suspected she'd break out. It was beyond possibility to us. A search party has been sent out after her."

Boyle told the Shaws and a few of the workers not home grieving for murdered loved ones or caring for those wounded, "Gillany's got a disease I've not ever heard of or seen before. Something that has crawled out of the dark heart of the barrens, no doubt centuries old. She's got the telltale signs of a bad chigger infestation on her legs. I believe she spends a good deal of time in the woods? She and her sister are mushroom gatherers, if I'm not mistaken."

Fate Shaw nodded.

"I'm guessing the chiggers carry the bacterium. She's infected. We've got to find her and treat her, or if she's discovered already dead, burn her."

"Not to mention, she's diabolical with a meat cleaver," said Fate.

"Whatever it is, it's like typhus, a parasite that affects the brain."

"What about her sister?" asked Shaw.

"Take me to her," said the doctor.

The factory owner handed Boyle a rusty Colt revolver. "In case she becomes murderous. It's loaded."

"You hold on to that. I'll end up shooting myself in the foot," he said.

On the opposite side of the factory, they came to another door cast in shadow. This one opened into a storeroom with no window, but larger than the first. In the middle of it, surrounded by shelves holding various bottles and tools, was Mavis Kane, bound to a straight-backed chair with her arms joined behind her. Boyle noticed immediately that she was awake and alert. She too had blood on her black dress, but her hair was still in a single knot. He found another chair in the corner of the room and moved it around so he could sit facing her. He found the resemblance to her sister distracting. As he set his bag on the floor, he said, "Miss Kane, how are you feeling?" She was placid, expressionless. She stared straight through him. Her lips moved, though, and she answered.

"I've a fever," she said. "An infernal itching down below."

"Your sister is also ill. When did she begin not feeling well?"

"After we met the woman out by the salt marshes."

"Who would that be?"

"An old woman, Mother Ignod, the color of oak leaves in spring. She wore rags and told us she was a witch who had been put to death by settlers almost a century before because she spoke to the deer and they listened. She found magical power in the lonesome, remote nature of the barrens."

"How did they dispatch her?"

"Drowned her in a bog."

"And now she's back?"

"'For revenge,' she told us."

"Upon whom?"

Mavis remained silent.

"Do you recall your sister being afflicted by a bad case of chiggers?"

"Yes."

"What about you? Did you also have them on your legs?"

"Yes."

Boyle retrieved from his bag at his feet a blue bottle with a cork in the top. "I'm going to give you something to drink. It's going to cure you," he told her.

Mavis didn't say a word, didn't look at him when he stood from his chair and came toward her, pulling the stopper from the blue bottle. "Drink this," he said, and handed it to her. He was a little surprised when she took it, put it to her lips, and did as he commanded without a question, without spilling a drop, without grimacing at the bitter taste. What he'd given her was a tea made from the witch-hazel blossom, toadleaf, and ghost sedge. She drank till her mouth filled and overflowed and dribbled down her bloody dress. He let her finish the entire bottle. She handed it back to him; he put the cork in it and returned it to his bag. As he sat in his chair, he reached back into the bag and took out a different bottle, this one brown. Black Dirt Bourbon, Boyle's self-prescribed cure-all. He sipped and mused while he waited for his elixir to work.

In his notes on the case, the doctor stated that he believed the invading parasite had caused swelling of the women's brains, which caused their psychotic behavior. The witch hazel was an anti-inflammatory, and the other two ingredients had what today would be called antibiotic properties. Although he'd been trained at the University of Pennsylvania's medical school, a few years living in the barrens and he'd combined his formal knowledge with the teachings of folk medicine. He writes, "The two of them must have been under the influence of the disease for weeks as it slowly grew within them. Gillany was further along for some reason, and I had lost hope for her—feverish, catatonic, birthing worms, wandering through a labyrinthine wilderness."

Shaw woke Boyle from a sound sleep. Though there was no window in the room, immediately the doctor could tell it was night. The factory owner held a lantern. Mavis was sleeping peacefully, her eyes closed, her bosom heaving slowly up and down at regular intervals. Boyle got out of his chair and walked across to her. Lightly slapping her face, he spoke her name, rousing her. Before long her eyelids fluttered, and she made a soft moaning noise.

"She looks better," he said to Shaw.

"Remarkable."

"Her sister?"

"The search party just returned without her. They combed the woods, twenty men and Chandra O'Neal, the tracker, and not a trace of her."

"Even if you could find her, and I could administer my cure, she's no doubt too far gone," said Boyle.

Shaw was about to admit defeat as well when Mavis opened her eyes and murmured something. Boyle put his ear down to her lips. "What was that?" he asked. She mumbled some more, and Shaw asked, "Is she speaking?" The doctor nodded.

Boyle went back to his bag and pulled out another blue bottle full of the witch-hazel elixir. He slipped it into the pocket of his coat.

"What did she say?" asked Shaw.

"She said to get the dog, Brogan. The dog will track Gillany if you speak her name to him."

Heading out into the Pine Barrens at night, even with a torch and a gun, was daunting. People who knew how unpredictable the wilderness could be usually stayed close to home at night. Still, the doctor, the factory owner, Fate, and three other work-ers most loyal to the Shaws headed out with guns loaded. There were two shotguns and two pistols among the party. Fate car-ried an over-under, double-barreled pistol, and the doctor went armed only with his elixir.

The night was cold as the world moved toward winter. There

was a strong breeze, and the leaves from scarlet and blackjack oak to maple and tupelo showered down around them. The moon was a sight brighter than on Halloween, and in the clearings it reflected off the sugar sand, glowing against the dark. They found the black dog, Brogan, a powerful beast with a thick neck and broad chest, chained up next to the outhouse beside the sisters' home. He was happy to see them, having gone unfed since the morning of the day prior. Fate thought to bring a cut of salted venison from her kitchen for the beast. This made her and the dog fast friends. Shaw undid the collar from Brogan's neck while he devoured the meat.

"Find Gillany," said Fate in her most soothing voice. "Find Gillany."

The dog looked from one member of the party gathered around him to another. Mrs. Shaw repeated her order one more time. Brogan barked twice and padded down the path into the pines.

"Stick together," said Boyle, and they were off at a slow jog trying to keep up with the dog. The torches crackled and threw light but also made it difficult to see anything near the intensity of the flame. They passed down a sandy trail all of them were familiar with and then the dog dove into the brush and all followed him winding among the pitch pine and cedar. Luckily, there were no chiggers or mosquitos still active. The doctor heaved for breath as they moved quickly along, wishing he'd brought another bottle of bourbon. An owl called far off to the west. He knew from the direction they were heading that the dog was leading them toward the marsh.

It wasn't long before the doctor found himself alone in a meadow of marsh fern gone red with the season. He'd lost the others a good twenty minutes earlier but could hear the dog barking not too far ahead. The ground was soggy, and he moved slowly, knowing that in a moment he could be in water up to his neck. At first he intended to call out, but on second thought he realized that Gillany might be somewhere close by with a sharp weapon of some kind. He thought silence a better strategy. It's then that he heard the dog yelp and whimper in a manner that could crack ice. A gun went off. There was a human scream followed hard by a splash.

A brief moment of silence and then more screaming, more shots. The din of the commotion sparked Boyle's adrenaline, and he so wanted to run away. Finally, he called out, "Shaw!" at the top of his voice, and then stood still, listening to the night over the pounding of his heart. He shivered in the breeze for a long while, and then he heard the crack of brittle twigs and the crunch of dry leaves. "Shaw? Is that you?" he called. But it wasn't Shaw. A pale figure staggered through the marsh ferns toward him. He backed up into a clearing of sand, wanting to flee but unable to, as fear robbed his energy.

She came toward him in the moonlight, her hair loose in the wind like the tail of a black comet. She wore nothing but carried a hatchet stained with blood. He swept the torch in front of him as a means of warding her off. As she approached, he could see a gunshot wound to the hip, the bloody hole writhing with white worms. "That's it," said Boyle. He turned and ran as best he could, which wasn't all that good. With no idea which direction he was headed, he stumbled forward through the marsh ferns toward where the moonlight showed him a tree line. Not even a hundred yards, and he'd slowed to a hobble, out of breath and caught in the grip of a coughing fit.

It was work to get control of his breathing, but he finally managed. Behind him he heard or thought he heard, even above the sound of the wind, the tread of Gillany. He turned and saw her only yards away. Her breathing was like a whistle, and she limped stiffly. She lifted the weapon when she saw him looking, and he groaned, knowing there'd be no more running. His heart was pounding. She came for him and he crouched away from her. She lifted the hatchet, and from above his head, he saw an arm descend from behind him. At the end of that arm there was a hand aiming a derringer. The finger pulled the trigger just as Gillany was upon him. The pistol exploded with a dull thud, smoke and sparks, and the two balls of shot ripped off her face. There was blood and flesh, and just below the skin there was a tangled layer of worms. She fell on him and he screamed.

Fate Shaw and the doctor made it back to the village at daybreak. Once there, she turned doctor and prescribed a bottle of bourbon for Boyle. When he was comfortable, she called the village together by ringing the bell outside the factory. She told those who gathered how they'd tracked Gillany Kane into the marshes and how she'd attacked Mr. Shaw and the others. A dozen men volunteered to go and search for survivors in the daylight. Fate decided to accompany them as did two of the wives whose husbands had been part of the posse. They uncovered the remains of Brogan's mangled body, but no sign of any of the men. They searched every day for the better part of a week. Nothing. They followed the creeks and streams in case the bodies had been deposited in the water and swept along with the tranquil current. Nothing.

Finally, the sheriff from Mount Holly arrived and was told the tale just as it happened. Fate and Boyle gave much of the testimony, and the other half was supplied by Mavis, who had made a full recovery from the disease that gripped her sister. She referred to the illness as the suspicions, for the paranoia it engendered with a fury that took over the mind. The sheriff couldn't make heads nor tails of it and eventually slunk back to Mount Holly to file five missing persons reports. Somewhere in the middle of that very harsh winter, Mavis Kane disappeared. No one was sure exactly when it happened, but everyone was certain it was after the snow came and before it left. She could have slipped away from Cadalbog, but there were also many who weren't willing to forgive her part of the Halloween mayhem. Maybe the barrens took her, but after that most forgot, leaving only Fate and Boyle to wonder what actually had happened.

Three years later, in spring, Fate Shaw reported in her diary on the passing of Dr. Boyle. "I'd go to see him out there at his place on the way to Harrisville. He'd drink and talk, and I'd listen. He was the one individual who didn't mind hashing over the enigma of the Kane sisters' disease. He was convinced it was a matter of biology and chemistry, the psychosis of a fevered mind. I, on the other hand, knew better, because I was privy to the end of the story. The helper I'd hired to look after the doctor reported to me that the day the old man died he'd had a visitor, an old woman in tattered clothes with a strange green-tinged complexion. She was accompanied by a black dog. The helper didn't know how long the old woman had been there, but when he returned the next morning to make a fire and cook breakfast for the doctor, he found Boyle in a chair, head flung back and white worms crawling from his nose and ears, squirming out through his tear ducts.

"The last thing he told me on my final visit to him was, as he put it, 'His confession.' It so happened that the reason he'd come to the Pine Barrens in the first place was due to a botched delivery. It was a breech birth, and he was pie-eyed drunk. 'Twin sisters with the cord wrapped round their necks,' he said. 'As they struggled for their freedom, they strangled each other. I was passed out on the floor. Unsettling that the tragedy occurred on All Souls' Day. The parents wanted to put me in jail, and I fled like a thief in the night.' I didn't have the heart to wonder aloud about the twin connection and neither did he. The strangeness we'd been part of was already too complicated.

"Before I left him that day, he gave me, written out in a shaky hand, the recipe for his elixir against *the suspicion*. 'Sooner or later, it'll be back,' he told me. Twenty years have passed since then, and I've long ago misplaced that scrap of paper. But every year at Halloween, I wear a blossom of the witch hazel in honor of Boyle, and oddly enough, it's beginning to catch on."

Nos Galan Gaeaf

———◦•◦———

Kelley Armstrong

Adre, adre, am y cynta',
Hwch ddu gwta a gipio'r ola'

Home, home, on the double,
The tailless black sow shall snatch the last.

Cainsville, October 31, 1979

SEANNA WALSH WAS NOT PRETTY. Not bright. Not charming or witty. Not good or kind. Yet Lance could not get her out of his head. She'd wormed her way in, that insidious thought he couldn't escape. He had to, though. Had to pry her out before he went mad. Which meant she needed to die on Nos Galan Gaeaf.

Lance would not actually kill her. That is, he would not wrap his hands around her scrawny neck, nor fire a bullet through her flat chest, nor slit her pale throat and watch her strange blue eyes bug as her lifeblood soaked the ground. He thought about that.

He thought about all of it, late at night, replaying the fantasies until he lay shivering and sweat soaked. But then he imagined the reality of it, and the fantasy became a nightmare, handcuffs clamping around his wrists, his mother sobbing, his father staring, wordless for perhaps the first time in his life.

No. Lance would not kill Seanna Walsh himself. But he would bring about her death on Nos Galan Gaeaf . . . by removing her stone from the bonfire.

WHEN THE MORNING of Nos Galan Gaeaf arrived, Lance asked the gargoyles if he should give Seanna one last chance. He counted them on his way to the school bus stop. If they came up with an even number, that would mean yes. Yes, he should give Seanna another chance.

Of course, it was easy to game the system. He walked the long way to the bus stop, knowing that route would give him five gargoyles, meaning no, he did not need to give her another chance. He just had to get the right answer. Like he had to check the door four times after he locked it, to be absolutely sure his father wouldn't come home and find it open. Check the door four times. Check the gas stove six. Check the lights twice.

Even numbers were good omens. They were safe. The number of times to check depended on the severity of the transgression if he made a mistake. Leave on a light, and he'd only get a snarl from his father. An unlocked door would lead to a smack. Leave the gas on? Lance didn't even want to think what would happen if he did that.

Check, check, and check again, so his whirling mind could rest easy. The same went for any question of importance. It had to be checked against the gargoyles.

In cases like this, Lance would walk a route where he knew how many gargoyles he should see. Yet that was no guarantee in Cainsville, where he could walk past the bank four days in a row and clearly see the gargoyle perched there . . . and the next day there would be no sign of it. Two days later it would reappear, sneering at him as if to say it'd been there all along and he was a fool if he thought otherwise.

Today, all five of the gargoyles he expected to see were there, and on counting the last, he shuddered in relief. The question had been answered. He did not need to give Seanna another chance. Then, as he approached the bus stop, he heard Seanna's smug voice say, "I spy with my little eye, one hidden gargoyle."

"Where?" Keith said as he peered around. "I don't see anything."

"For ten bucks, you will."

"Fuck you, Seanna."

"You wish, zit face."

The other kids laughed. They always did, no matter how unimaginative her insults, no matter how many times they'd been the targets of them. It was as if she held them all under her sway. But none so much as Lance.

"Give you five for it, Seanna," Abby said.

"Make it six plus your Twinkies."

Abby handed over the bills and the snack, and Seanna whispered instructions. Abby gave a slow look around, careful not to tip off the others. Then she chortled. "Got it! One more for my May Day list."

Lance tried not to look for the gargoyle. He desperately tried. But his heart started to pound, his mouth going dry, and he knew if he didn't look, he'd spend the day obsessing over it. He would give a quick glance, and if he didn't immediately see—

He spotted it peeking from under a roof edge, its color blending with the stonework, and he could tell himself that's why he'd never seen it before. It was the comfortable answer. It was not, however, the truth. As for what was the truth? He didn't know. No one did. No one cared. To them, it was no different than a rainbow, a glimpse of everyday magic. To him, it was an uncomfortable reminder of factors he could not control, could not predict. The odd boy out, as always.

That unexpected sixth gargoyle meant he had to give Seanna one last chance. He spent the next five minutes frantically searching for another gargoyle to change the answer. When the bus came, he reluctantly followed the other kids on, still gaping about.

No gargoyles were coming to save him. They'd given their answer. One last chance.

He went to slide into the seat with Seanna. She thumped her backpack down on it and gave him a sneer.

"As if," she said. "Back of the bus, loser Lance."

He took the seat behind her. A couple of kids chortled. Abby jerked her chin, warning him to abandon his course.

"Excuse me," Seanna said. "The restraining order says fifty feet."

"You got a restraining order?" Keith said.

"I *wrote* a restraining order. Either this loser leaves me alone or I kick his ass. Again."

More chortles.

"I'll move," Lance said. "As soon as you give me back my money."

The chortles turned to open guffaws.

"You'd have more luck getting blood from a gargoyle," Keith said. "If Seanna conned you out of your pocket money, consider it payment for a lesson learned: don't mess with a Walsh."

Seanna settled into her seat with that smug smile. A few other kids high-fived each other. Walshes, all of them. One of the oldest families in Cainsville. And not an upstanding citizen in the lot of them.

Seanna and her kin proudly claimed an ancestry of con artists, pirates, and thieves, and in Cainsville, Walshes were treated with as much respect as doctors, lawyers, and priests. Don't mess with them, and they wouldn't mess with you. It was the barest whiff of a moral code, and somehow, that was good enough.

"She didn't con me," Lance said. "She picked my pocket."

"Because you were stalking me again," Seanna said. "Violating the terms of my restraining order. Consider it a fine. If you don't want to pay, don't get close enough."

Even Abby nodded at that, giving Lance a look of mingled sympathy and exasperation. The boy who kept sticking his finger in the electrical outlet and expecting a different result.

"So you won't return the money?" he said.

"Hell and no. Now get your skinny ass to the back of the bus before I kick it there."

Lance slid from the seat and walked to the back. Only once he'd passed all the other kids did he allow himself a tiny smile of satisfaction.

He'd given her a chance, as the gargoyles decreed. And she'd blown it.

Tonight, he would take her stone from the bonfire.

FOR THE OTHER KIDS, tonight was Halloween. It was for some in Cainsville, too. Some of those who wished to celebrate October 31 that way piled into cars to visit family in Chicago and go trick-or-treating. For others, the town elders hired a bus to take them to a nearby town that had agreed to welcome any children of Cainsville who wished to celebrate the more common holiday. The bus left before dinner, filled with kids in costumes, their chaperones bringing bags full of candy to donate to the host town.

Lance watched the bus pull away, and he did not wish for one moment to be on it. Even when he was a little kid, he'd never wanted that. In this, he was *not* the odd boy out. He wanted to stay and celebrate Nos Galan Gaeaf. If he felt anything watching the bus leave, it was pity for the children on it, noses pressed to the glass, mournfully watching the town fade as the bus carried them away.

Every family was welcome to stay, but Lance had heard it whispered that the newer families were not encouraged to join Nos Galan Gaeaf. Few wanted to—the adults, anyway. What made Cainsville delightfully eccentric most of the year changed at the holidays. Pagan holidays, outsiders whispered. May Day. Solstice. And the most discomfiting of all: Nos Galan Gaeaf. No, they were happy to stick to their modern Halloween, ignore *its* pagan roots, and pretend it was all about princess dresses and candy corn.

The first of November was Calan Gaeaf. The beginning of winter. Marking the boundary was Nos Galan Gaeaf, or Spirit Night, when the veil between the human world and the other-world was thinnest. A night to be indoors. But before that, when the evening was still young, it was a time for celebration.

It began with the harvest feast. Tables were set up all along Main Street, right in the road. Everyone ate for hours, and then the children played *twco fala,* bobbing for marked apples that would earn them prizes. The teens hung around acting bored, but when the elders came by with "extra" candy and trinkets, all apathy evaporated, everyone partaking with, "Thank you, ma'am," and, "Thank you, sir."

When the apples were done, the bonfire began. Lance could feel the heat from the massive fire three doors down. Seanna stood less than ten feet away from him, having apparently decided not to enforce her restraining order. He watched the light of the bonfire lick her pale face and imagined it was real flames instead. Imagined her bound to a stake, the fire burning at her feet.

Burned as a witch. An apt punishment. That's what she

was—a witch transformed into a foul, poisonous mist that had insidiously crept through an open window one night to be inhaled in his sleep. Until then, she'd been just another kid, brattier than most, braver than most, but not special. Certainly not special. Then last summer she went away to visit relatives, and when she came back, he saw her as if for the first time, and he could not look away, however hard he tried.

She'd bewitched him. That was the only answer. And so burning would be apt. Unlikely, but he could hope.

As the bonfire roared and one elder told a story, another brought around a basket of smooth stones. Lance held his breath as he watched Seanna. She was thirteen, which made this her first time participating in the rite of Coelcerth. She could abstain. Then he'd have to think of another way to rid himself of the witch.

Seanna took a stone without hesitation. She plucked the felt-tip marker from Abby's hand. Abby only sighed and waited as Seanna wrote her name on the stone and then took the marker back to finish her own. When it was Lance's turn, he wrote his name in careful block letters.

Once all of the rocks had been distributed, the town elders proceeded to the bonfire, one by one, and laid their stones around it. Then the townspeople lined up. It was a solemn procession, a silent one, but with an air of hope. Come morning, when they found their rock still in place, they'd breathe a sigh of relief and hug their family and celebrate, as if life had handed them a guarantee. *You will live another year.*

Lance waited until all the other kids had set down their stones. He made a mental note of where Seanna put hers. Then he laid his a few feet away. He tapped it to the ground twice first. Two for yes. Two for a positive result. If he fumbled, he'd do four. He didn't fumble. Two taps and down it went, nestled among the others.

When all the rocks had been placed, one of the elders stood before the fire, raised her wrinkled arms, and shouted,

"*Adre, adre, am y cynta', Hwch ddu gwta a gipio'r ola'.*"

It was Welsh, like Nos Galan Gaeaf and Calan Gaeaf and Coelcerth and everything else about Cainsville. Founded by Welsh immigrants, it held on to that identity like the towns-people clutched those rocks—a talisman against the uncertainty of the world.

The old ways always worked for them, so they would continue with them long after others had forgotten their roots.

Adre, adre, am y cynta', Hwch ddu gwta a gipio'r ola'.

Home, home, on the double, The tailless black sow shall snatch the last.

The elder shouted that, and the children squealed with the giddy delight of feigned terrors. An excuse to run as fast as they could. A better excuse waited at home—a bag of candy—and if you had siblings, you'd best hurry because not all bags were created equal.

Off the children ran, shouting and bumping into each other like pool balls. The adults urged them on, laughing and yelling, "Watch out for the sow," and, "Last one gone will be eaten!"

When Lance was a child, it hadn't mattered that he had no siblings, that there was no reason to run to claim the best bag of candy. He'd done it for the thrill, to be part of the excitement, part of the crowd. Now he watched as the children raced down the passage beside the bank, and he crowded in to see them reach the end, where a figure dressed in black flew out, waving his arms, a painted hog's skull on his head. The children shrieked and squealed as if this didn't happen—in this exact spot—every year.

Lance couldn't see the children, but he knew the path the brave ones would take. They'd veer to the playground. Then over to the bushes on the left. Past the massive oak. Finally down the east passage back to the street. All places that hid *Hwch Ddu Gwta*—another black sow, leaping from behind bushes or jumping from a tree.

Lance tracked their progress by the shouts. Then he looked over to see Seanna watching them, too, a rare smile on her thin face.

He saw that smile, and he hated it worse than her smirks and sneers. That smile said there was more there, something worth saving.

The smile was a lie.

He escaped down Main Street, stopped in an alcove, and studied the bonfire for later, when he'd return to take Seanna's stone. As he turned, he found bright blue eyes laser-beamed to his, and he gave a start, as if those beams probed right into his thoughts. Which they might have, given who it was.

Rose Walsh might be Seanna's aunt, but when Lance was little, he'd thought of her as Seanna's big sister. An easy mistake to make—the families were so close they shared yards, kids running from one house to the next. "Like some kind of commune," his mother would sniff, and if Lance noticed Seanna at all in those days, it was with envy for that life she had, that family.

Rose was about eighteen, built sturdy like most Walshes, with the kind of chest that magnetized his gaze if he wasn't careful. He stood in no danger of that now. He could only stare at her eyes, desperate for a sign that she didn't actually know what he had planned for Seanna.

Rose Walsh had the sight. That's what they called it in Cainsville, and they said it no differently than they'd say someone had a knack for baking pies or playing piano.

"Too old to run home?" Rose said.

He started at the sound of her voice. Her lips curved in just the faintest smile as she wished him a good Nos Galan Gaeaf. Rose Walsh wasn't given to smiles, but she had always been kind to him, steady and unflappable, and her expression bore no sign that she'd foreseen his plan.

"Too old to run home?" she repeated.

"A bit."

"But old enough to join the *Mari Lwyd*. I bet if you asked, they'd let you go along." That faint curve of her lips again. "It's a fine excuse for underage drinking."

He smiled at that, and at the thought of joining the revelers, but he shook his head, saying, "I'll wait. Thank you, though," and then slipped off. He felt the weight of Rose's gaze following him.

Lance poked around Main Street, scoping out the area for his return. He kept an eye on the dwindling crowds, not wanting to be noted as among the last to leave.

He was walking past the fire when one of the elders fell in beside him. He didn't know her name. To him, they were just "the elders." Old people. Gray haired and wrinkle faced. A homogeneous lot of senior citizens.

This one was a woman with long, graying hair. Short and stout, like the teapot in the rhyme. Despite her obvious age, she fell in at a perfect pace with him. He slowed, though, out of respect. Even Seanna treated the elders with respect.

"Rose tells me you might like to join the *Mari Lwyd*," the woman said.

Lance shook his head. "Not this year. Thank you."

"Are you sure? I can make a place for you. I think you'd enjoy it."

"No, thank you, ma'am."

"Well, then, best run along home. Before *Hwch Ddu Gwta* comes out to play."

She patted his back, and he felt the weight of her gaze, too, watching as he headed for the side street.

.   .   .

ON THE WALK home, Lance heard the *Mari Lwyd* making the rounds from house to house. The gray mare.

He heard the chatter and laughter grow louder, and he turned onto his street just as the *Mari Lwyd* left a house. He saw it, and for one split second, he was a child again, getting his first look.

After his parents thought Lance had gone to bed, he'd snuck out to see the *Mari Lwyd*. One glimpse, and he'd run home so fast his lungs burned, and he'd lain in bed for hours, reciting multiplication tables, his talisman against the night and its horrors.

He shook his head at his younger self. Sure, it was a spooky sight. A hooded figure wearing a mare's skull, white garments flowing, an equine specter. But the men and women with the fearsome creature were laughing, halfway to drunk, jostling like kids as they made their way up the steps to the next house with its light on.

One of the men rapped at the door. It opened immediately and someone inside let out a cry of feigned terror. The group shouldered their way inside, where they would tell a story in exchange for a "tipple" of whiskey and then bless the house against the coming winter.

The front windows were open, and through them Lance heard the story start, and his steps slowed. He thought of Rose and the elder and their invitation.

Join the procession of the *Mari Lwyd*. You don't need to be the odd boy out. It's Cainsville, where gargoyles appear and disappear, where a teenage girl can see the future, where the *Mari Lwyd* bestows her blessings for the winter ahead.

Come and join us.

He wanted to. He desperately wanted to.

Next year.

Tonight he needed to kill Seanna Walsh.

. . .

SNEAKING FROM THE HOUSE was easy. His parents barely noticed he'd come in. The hardest part was going out his window. That was not difficult in itself—it opened easily. The problem was it was bad luck to exit through a different door than the one you'd entered. He gritted his teeth and went out his window. Then he checked it four times to be sure it was closed.

Lance counted steps to Main Street. Another talisman. Get an even number, and everything would go well. Of course, it was easy to get an even number—just take an extra step if it came up odd—but it was the mindfulness that mattered. It also helped quell his anxiety over not exiting through the proper door.

As for any anxiety over what he was about to do? He was afraid of getting caught. That was all. Seanna Walsh had earned her fate the day she'd bewitched him. He could not rest while she lived, so she could not live.

Main Street was dark and deserted, leaving only the embers of the bonfire to guide him. It was enough. He went straight to Seanna's stone. He snatched it up and put it into his pocket. Resisting the urge to run, he backed against the brick wall of the bank. Then he pushed one trembling hand into his pocket and found the smooth stone. As his fingers caressed it, he smiled.

Come morning, the townsfolk would gather early, stomachs too knotted to drink their morning coffee. One of the elders would go around the dead fire, collecting stones, one by one, and calling out the names. If any were missing . . . well, they all knew what that meant. At next year's Nos Galan Gaeaf, that person would not lay a stone at the fire. They'd be dead under one, rotting in their grave.

Or that was the story. But there was a trick, and Lance knew it. When Cainsville children were young, no one told them exactly what the rite of Coelcerth meant. That would be cruel—

ruining the night for them as they lay in their beds, terrified that a parent or other loved one might not hear their name read out the next morning. Lance had been twelve when he overheard older kids talking, and the very thought of it had been a shock wave through his brain. It was as if all of his personal talismans and rituals had coalesced into simple perfection: a ward against the ultimate uncertainty. Would he survive another year? This rite would tell him. Every year, he could answer that question.

Last year, having passed his thirteenth birthday, he'd laid down his stone . . . and plummeted from the heights of absolute control to the depths of darkest doubt as he realized he had to wait until dawn to find out if he would live.

He couldn't wait.

He'd snuck back to the bonfire and found his stone. Then he'd hidden in the shadows, waited and watched the spot where his stone lay. Several times, he thought he saw a flicker in that ring of stones. Thought he saw one disappear. He'd been about to check when he'd heard footsteps.

As he'd hid, a figure had appeared. Hooded and dressed in black.

The reaper. Death. Come to claim his due.

In terror, Lance had watched as the figure circled the bonfire. It crouched, reached into a pocket of those voluminous black robes, and pulled out a rock.

Next it pulled out a felt-tip marker, wrote something on the stone, and laid it in one of the empty places. Twice more the dark figure did that. Then it stood and under that hood, he'd seen the wizened face of one of the elders.

Lance had held himself still until the woman left. Then he'd fled all the way home.

Over the next year, Lance realized what he'd seen. The trick of Coelcerth. The truth about fate and certainty.

The elders didn't take stones. They replaced them. Some of

them, at least. Every Calan Gaeaf morning, a few *would* still be missing. When the rite finished, the elders would speak. They would warn.

If you did not hear your name, the die has been cast. But remember this: there is no fate you cannot undo. Take heed. Watch your health. Examine your life. Find out why your stone has vanished, and correct it while you can.

And those whose stones were missing? The absence rarely surprised anyone. They were people who ate too much, worked too hard, exercised too little, drank to excess, or had otherwise entered into a life too dangerous to survive.

The elders used Coelcerth not to frighten people, but to shake them out of their complacency.

Death is on your doorstep. Do something about it.

Some heeded that advice; some did not.

As for the stones the elders replaced, those were the deaths that could not be prevented. Accidents and tragedies. No one ever wondered why the rite of Coelcerth did not foresee these. It was presumed they were unforeseeable, that the rite did not guarantee you another year but merely suggested you were on the right path.

Lance knew the elders would replace Seanna's stone. She would think she had another year. But she did not.

He smiled again. Then anxiety began gnawing at his gut, the one that insisted he had to be sure he hadn't made any mistakes. He took out the stone and held it up in the moonlight.

Seanna W.

This stone was her grave marker. Seanna Walsh, R.I.P.

Lance snickered. Never had the epitaph been more accurate. *He* would rest in peace once Seanna Walsh was dead and gone.

He pocketed the stone again, making sure it nestled deep in

his pocket where it couldn't fall out. Then he headed down the passageway beside the bank. As he reached the end, his steps hitched, as if *Hwch Ddu Gwta* would leap out at him like it had for the fleeing children.

He smiled at the thought. The adults who played the role were long gone, the passage silent and empty, the park equally quiet. He took another step and—

A shadow slid over him.

Lance looked up to see an owl gliding over his head. The raptor landed on the playground fence. It perched on one of the cast-iron chimera head posts. He kept walking. The owl's unblinking gaze followed him into the square.

Lance reached into his pocket to clutch the stone. The owl's head swiveled, still following him. He had to circle the playground to get to the passageway that would take him home, and as the raptor's head kept turning, his did, too, watching the bird, ready to bolt if it flew at him.

He knew that was silly. There were always owls in Cainsville. At night, he'd see them perched beside gargoyles, as if joining them in silent vigil. Spotting them always vanquished any fear he had of being out past dark. The owls and the gargoyles stood watch, so he was safe.

Tonight, he did not feel safe.

When a rustle sounded in the bushes behind the playground, Lance stopped so fast he stumbled. His hand flew from his pocket to stop his fall. The stone sailed free and thumped to the ground.

The rustling stopped.

Lance straightened and held himself still as he peered into the darkness. After a moment, he could see a figure half-hidden behind the bushes. A black shape on all fours.

Hwch Ddu Gwta. The tailless black sow.

Lance shook his head sharply, ashamed by the very thought. Really? Whatever magic there was on Nos Galan Gaeaf, no one even really pretended there was such a thing.

The tailless black sow will snatch the last.

It'd been years since a child had died in Cainsville, and never on Nos Galan Gaeaf. He was imagining things.

He took a step toward Seanna's dropped stone. As he bent to pick it up, a snort from the bushes startled him, and he rose, stone forgotten. A black, misshapen figure rose from behind the bushes, low and hunched, making him think of the headless woman who accompanied the black sow.

As the figure stepped around the bushes, Lance scrambled backward, his hands rising to ward off . . .

"You have got to be kidding me," Seanna said. "What the hell are you doing here?"

He opened his mouth.

She beat him to it, saying, "Dumb question. You're following me. *Stalking* me. Again."

"I—"

"You just don't take a hint, do you?" she said as she strode toward him. "I'm not interested, Lance Miller. You think this will get my attention? It only pisses me off, and you really don't want to piss—"

Her foot kicked the stone. She stopped moving. They both did. Silence.

Lance's heart pounded, every fiber of his being screaming for him to lunge, to grab that stone. But he couldn't move. Absolutely could not move.

Seanna reached down and picked up the polished stone. "This is . . ." Color bled from her pale face. "You stole my Coelcerth stone?"

"No, I—"

"I tell you I'm not interested, and you steal my stone to punish me? Let me spend a year thinking I'm going to *die*?"

She closed the gap between them in an angry stalk.

"You cowardly little *prick*. You don't even have the balls to threaten me to my face. That's it. I'm taking this to the elders. No more dealing with your bullshit. Let the town council handle it."

She turned away, stone in hand, and that's when his paralysis broke. He lunged. Knocked her flat on her ugly face. Grabbed her hair and yanked it back to slam that ugly face into the ground.

Bash it until it was bloody. Bash it until she never opened her foul mouth again. Bash it until he dashed her brains out. Until he was free.

As he slammed her face into the dirt, he waited for her scream. For her pain. For her fear.

Seanna didn't make a sound.

He yanked her hair back again and—

Seanna ripped from his grasp. She rolled over, blood flying from her nose. As she raised her hand, he saw something clutched in it. A rock. A large one. She swung it against the side of his head, and everything went black.

LANCE OPENED HIS EYES to see the full moon overhead.

How was he seeing the moon from his bed?

And why did it feel as if he were lying . . . ?

the ground. He bolted upright as he remembered Seanna with her Coelcerth stone. Seanna with the rough-edged rock. Swinging it at his head.

He leaped to his feet and looked around, his head pounding.

He was alone beside the playground.

Damn it, no. No, no, no. He couldn't let her tell the elders.

Seanna might have thought he was only trying to frighten her, but the elders would know the truth, and if they did not, Rose would tell them.

This whole thing was a trap. Seanna had *made* him take her stone, and then she'd lain in wait to catch him. Why else would she have been out here?

Her fault. All hers.

He heard a noise from the street. The slap of shoes on pavement.

Seanna, returning her stone to the bonfire.

He still had time to stop her. Stop her and make her pay for her trick. He wouldn't rely on old magic to get rid of her. She was right—that was the coward's way. He would do this himself. He looked down at the rock she'd hit him with.

Justice.

Lance scooped it up and started for the passageway back to Main Street. He was just about to step into it when a shadow passed overhead. He looked up, ready to glower at the owl. Instead, he caught a flash of what looked like . . .

No, it was an owl. It must be. The yellow talons and feathered tail of an owl. Not stone-gray talons. Not the flick of a stone-gray tail.

Just an owl.

He picked up his pace as he crept between the buildings, his footsteps silent on the well-worn path. Shadows swallowed the moonlight, and he had to reach out with his free hand, fingertips grazing the brick wall as he used it to guide him.

When a figure stepped into the passageway, he gave a start. Then he shook himself. It was just Seanna. He could tell by her thin body and height, though she'd tried to trick him by donning one of the *Hwch Ddu Gwta* cloaks, the oversize black robe trailing behind her, hood up over her face.

Lance hid the rock behind his back and walked right up to her and said, "Is that supposed to scare me?"

Seanna just stood there. He couldn't see her face in the shadows under the hood. A tickling chill ran up his spine, but he forced it away and reached up to knock her hood back.

The hood fell. There was nothing under it.

Lance staggered back. Pale hands appeared from the sleeves of the robe. Bony fingers unfastened the cloak. As the flowing fabric pooled to the ground, he saw a neck. A bloodied, raw neck, the severed spine poking through.

He spun so fast he pitched forward but came out running, tearing down the passage. When a shadow filled the other end, he knew what it was. Knew and told himself he was wrong.

A trick. Just a trick.

The black sow curled back its lips, dagger-sharp tusks flashing. Lance wheeled, rock still in his hand, back to the wall, gaze swinging between the two, ready to bash whichever came at him first.

But they just stood there, one at either end of the passage, blocking his escape.

The headless woman.

The tailless black sow.

Silent.

Motionless.

Waiting.

SEANNA CROUCHED BEFORE the glowing embers of the bonfire. She'd found the place where she'd laid her stone. Empty now. She cursed Lance. Nasty tricks were fine, but this was outright cruelty.

She reached into her pocket for the stone. When she pulled out snips of ivy instead, her temper sparked anew. *Goddamn* him. When he'd shown up, she'd been cutting ivy for the rite of Eiddiorwg Dalen.

Snip ten pieces of ivy on Nos Galan Gaeaf, throw away nine, and sleep with the tenth under her pillow. That would grant Seanna the gift of prophetic dreams. The gift of the sight. Rose might claim that wasn't how she got hers, but her aunt had to be lying. Trying to keep her gift all to herself.

Seanna threw the ivy aside. Too late now. She'd have to wait for next year. All because of Lance.

She returned her stone to its place and settled back on her haunches to survey the ring of rocks. She had to squint to make out names, and she was about to give up when the clouds veiling the moon thinned and its glow lit the street.

Another scan of the stones. Then a smile as her fingertips touched down on the one marked with Lance's name.

To her left, she heard what sounded like a sudden gasp. She squinted toward the sound. It seemed to come from the walkway by the bank, but she couldn't see anything.

She reached again for Lance's stone. Her fingers wrapped around it. A shriek rent the air, and she stumbled, falling flat on her ass. Then a screech, this one cut short, the cry of some animal seized by a predator.

Seanna peered toward the walkway. She'd seen an owl earlier by the playground. As she caught the faint but sickening crunch of bone, she shuddered. Definitely the owl.

She rose, pocketing Lance's stone. Then she set out for home, taking the long way around, letting the crunching of bone and ripping of flesh fade behind her.

We're Never Inviting Amber Again

S. P. Miskowski

I STAND ON the lawn staring at the October night sky. I'm trying not to shiver from the damp and cold. Clouds are etched like a black-lace veil over the moonlight. The street is alive with shadows. And at this moment I'm certain of only one thing: all of this is Amber's fault. My sister-in-law ruins everything. There's something wrong with Amber, even if no one else wants to admit it. Tonight is a perfect example. We go out of our way to be nice to her, and this is how she repays us. So, that's it. We're never inviting Amber again, not after tonight, not ever.

I was wrong to let my wife invite her crazy sister. I only caved because it's Halloween. I thought our friends—Meredith and Connor, Steven and Jeff—might get a kick out of Amber's palm-reading mumbo jumbo and predictions. The way she stares with those raccoon eyes, or blanks in the middle of a sentence and has to be coaxed back into conversation. Or the way she tries to run a simple errand and winds up stranded in the middle of nowhere. It's the kind of thing I've been describing to Meredith and Jeff, at the office, for ages.

"Guess where my sister-in-law called from, last night?" This would be a typical prompt of mine at lunch, followed by sly grins and guesses all around.

"Fiji?"

"Reykjavik?"

"Nope," I would say. "Abu Dhabi."

"How did she end up *there*?" my wide-eyed friends would ask. "No broomsticks involved?"

Then I would smile and spend the next half hour reconstructing my wife, Cecily's, story of her sister's Uber ride to a downtown hair salon. The trip somehow morphed into a global adventure inspired by one of Amber's "visions." Along the way a suitcase was stolen, foreign currency was exchanged for precious gems, a tourist was suspected of launching a curse, and someone was stranded with a goat in New Zealand. None of it made sense. Probably all of it was invented. Of course I added a few details of my own, and this was part of the fun.

"Your sister-in-law is *so crazy*," a coworker would say, after one of my stories. The way you might describe a reality-show star, or a pop singer who shaves her head and knocks out the windows on her husband's car with a baseball bat.

"Crazy doesn't *begin* to do her justice," I would reply, and we would all laugh.

"I hate to tell you, but Amber doesn't want to do palm readings tonight," Cecily informed me after we'd finished lighting the jack-o'-lanterns along the patio in the backyard.

We were arranging the table in the dining room so our guests would have a pleasant view of the glowing pumpkins on the other side of the sliding glass door. My wife insisted on the jack-o'-lanterns because Amber said they kept something away—I honestly don't remember what, maybe evil spirits, or bad karma, or misfortune.

Indoors we placed these tiny, spiderlike skeletons everywhere. On the table the skeletons leered with skulls tilted back, proffering toothpicks clutched in both hands. In the center of the table we set up platters with three kinds of cheese and deli meat, crackers, chips and dip.

"I don't understand what she means by that," I said.

"She doesn't want to do it," Cecily told me again. My sensuous wife with the long neck and amazing legs has a terrible weakness when it comes to her family.

"What *does* she want to do?" I asked more gruffly than I intended. The pre-guest whiskey was kicking in. "I mean, what does she *feel* like doing?" Consciously not grinding my teeth. Affecting the nonchalance my Cecily finds so appealing. Trying to adopt the easygoing manner she once mistook for my nature.

"I don't know what she wants to do next, but she definitely quit telling fortunes. No palm reading, no tarot. Said she's never going to do it again."

All of this was news to me. It was typical of Cecily to keep quiet until the last minute, to avoid the "discussion" for as long as possible. It was typical of Amber to screw up our plans. I can't count the number of times we've rescued her from a nightclub or a freeway ramp or a stranger's apartment in the middle of the night. She couldn't give us *one* evening of free entertainment in return?

"When?" I asked. "When did this happen?" Thinking maybe it was something Amber had dreamed up after she was invited.

"I'm not sure, but I think she said it was a couple of weeks ago," Cecily explained.

"But why?" I asked, controlling my voice for my wife's sake. "Why *now*? We invited her because she could do this *one thing* she's done for years, and suddenly she's quitting?" Prompting a thin sigh of indulgence, a sound I've come to dread.

"Drew, she didn't quit because she wanted to ruin our party, if that's what you're implying. She said she *scared* herself."

"Ooooooo . . . ," I said in what I hoped was a playfully teasing voice. "Did she accidentally see her own future as a parking lot attendant with an apartment full of rescue cats?"

Cecily pinched my arm gently. She slid away from me, opened the mini-fridge we keep in the dining room, retrieved a chilled bottle of Chardonnay, and poured a glass.

"You know, we shouldn't make fun of her," she reminded me. "Not after all she's been through. It isn't fair, not really."

Every conversation about my wife's family leads eventually to Amber's misfortunes. "All she's been through" is a way of alluding to the stupid things she's done, like flunking out of two colleges, accidentally setting a dorm room on fire, crashing her car and blaming it on a "vision" of dead people at a bus stop in the rain, or getting fired from her job as a receptionist after telling a client the advertising firm might be a portal to another dimension.

"You always defend her," I said as calmly as possible. "I love your loyalty," I lied. "But I reserve the right to point out that we're discussing an adult—someone our own age—with no sense of accountability. Why did we ask her to come, if she won't do one of her routines?"

"I told her we want to see her anyway, and we love her company."

I groaned a little. I couldn't stop myself.

"Cheer up, Drew. She promised to bring her Ouija board thing. Well, sort of promised."

"Are you serious? I haven't seen a Ouija board since college. Why don't we just download spooky sound effects online?" I asked. "Creaking doors and cackling witches. I mean, if we want to put everybody to sleep."

"Drew, if you're mean when she gets here . . ."

"I won't be," I lied. "But really, honey, what were you thinking?"

"She said no more palm readings, never again. I couldn't un-invite her. She seemed very upset. I guess she met this guy at a party—"

"Here we go." At least I'd have another story to pass around.

"No, he was nice. He was this sweet, handsome guy named Hamish, and he said he really liked her."

"Hamish?" I said.

A cheer went up in a backyard down the street. More parties for grouchy grown-ups like us, I imagined. Drunks bobbing for apples and flirting, neighbors in black corsets and fishnet stockings, all the people who hate their jobs or their spouses or both drowning their blues and acting like horny teenagers. I wished I could join them.

This is a quiet neighborhood. People keep to themselves, even on Halloween. We've lived on the same street for six years, three blocks from an elementary school, yet we've never seen one actual child trick-or-treating. Every year Cecily and I come up with a new explanation—alien abduction, urban coyotes . . . This year we finally chalked it up to the abnormal fears of fretful young parents. "Ninnies with babies," we call them. Every time we say it we toast our fortuitous lack of children. Lately I've noticed a hint of something besides mirth in my beautiful wife's hazel eyes.

"Okay, tell me what happened with this Hamish guy," I said. Not riveted by Amber's problems but trying to convince my wife otherwise.

"It's pretty bad," she said. Her slender fingers held the wine-glass beneath her gaze like a Magic 8 Ball with an answer she was trying to decipher. Behind her, beyond the sliding glass door, the sky was dark as slate.

"You mean she took him home and he didn't call her again?"

Cecily shook her head.

"Come on. What?" I asked. "Did he go all psycho on her?"

"No. It wasn't like that."

"Did he hit her?" I asked, maybe with too much excitement.

"No," she said. "It was nothing like that. He was wonderful. They spent the night together. And he died."

This took a moment to sink in. I didn't like any of the images it conjured.

"With Amber?" I asked. "At her place, like, in bed?"

Cecily shook her head again and sipped her Chardonnay. I studied the delicate curve of her scarlet lips. Add to my frayed nerves the fetching little set of leopard ears she wore as casually as barrettes. While we talked I was making after-party plans for my feline Cecily. It had been a while.

"No, he wasn't with her," my wife said. "It happened the following night, on his way home."

"Did he wreck his car?"

"Not a traffic accident," she said. "The details didn't seem clear to me, but she said he was attacked."

"Attacked?"

"Yes, in his car. He was driving. Well, he was waiting at a red light. I guess he'd left the doors unlocked, and he was attacked and killed."

"Wait a minute," I said, and helped myself to a Corona from the mini-fridge because another whiskey would have taken me over the line. To the place my wife calls Drewville, where she stops talking and averts her eyes, and her magnificent red lips freeze in a pinch of disapproval. I was determined not to go to Drewville, not again.

"Is this what she predicted," I said, "when she read the guy's palm, or told his fortune or whatever?"

"I guess so."

"Then why didn't she, you know, do something? Didn't she tell the guy to watch out for red lights, or lock his car, or anything?"

"She wanted to," said Cecily. "But she was trying not to scare him away."

"So, you see," I pointed out. "She just uses this stuff to get attention. If she believed in it, she would have warned the guy. Right?"

"I don't know, Drew."

"Do you see what I mean? Right? You get what I'm saying, right?"

The doorbell interrupted. Playing good host and hostess, we put on our best smiles and made our way to the front door.

Steven slouched on our doorstep in his usual costume, the wool slacks and gray pullover of a civil servant off the clock. Beside him, Jeff wore jeans with a black T-shirt and a werewolf mask.

"Where's your getup, Steven?" Cecily asked.

"We're before and after," Jeff mumbled beneath the layer of latex and fur.

"Before and after what?" she asked. "You're not even wearing matching outfits."

"It doesn't work," I told them. "No treats. Fuck you both. Good night."

Jeff pulled off the mask and threw it away, across the lawn. Steven shook his head in mock disgust. "I told him it wasn't a costume party, but he never listens. Let us inside, it's getting frosty out here."

We had barely settled into a round of drinks when Meredith and Connor arrived. No masks for the Harrisons. "Were we supposed to wear costumes?" Meredith asked, delicately pinching one of Cecily's leopard ears. "It just occurred to me, this minute!"

"God, no," I said. "Jeff wore some half-assed thing, but we made him take it off."

"Give me another cocktail before you talk about me, you office drone," said Jeff.

The volume of chatter increased to a ridiculous degree now that there were six of us. We gathered around the dining table, and our guests made polite "ooh" and "aah" sounds of appreciation at the sight of the glowing jack-o'-lanterns on the other side of the glass. I noticed a few seemed to be sputtering but decided to ignore it.

We ate and shared stories about the traffic, the perilous construction downtown, the gradual loss of all our favorite shops and cafés, and our baseball team's rotten record. We smoked a joint and drank another round before Amber's name came up in conversation.

"She might not even show up." I hoped this was true. I considered Cecily's mood and said, more lightly, "You never know with Amber."

This elicited a few chuckles and nods. I refreshed all the drinks, hoping no one would repeat one of my sister-in-law stories in front of my wife. Fortunately, Connor announced his and Meredith's plan to move to a larger house, and the conversation turned to real estate.

Cecily heard the knock first. She lifted her chin and adopted a listening expression. "Do you think that's Amber?"

"Well, I don't think it's our first trick-or-treater in six years," I said, and then checked my tone. "Don't get up, honey. I'll let her in." The others resumed conversation while I answered the door.

How do I explain the effect Amber has? Every time I see the woman it's a shock to the senses. Not the way it hit me all those years ago at a nightclub near campus, a wild strain of animal desire mixed with alcohol and revulsion. The uncanny shiver she induces nowadays isn't entirely due to her lack of grooming and maintenance. It's the underlying, ever fading, yet vaguely familiar resemblance to my wife.

In college, for a very brief time, they almost looked like twins. When Cecily began her freshman year, Amber moved out of the dorm. They shared an apartment near campus and swapped clothing, makeup, and (in our case, for a strange semester) boyfriends. Then I broke up with Amber and the drift began. She moved back to the dorm, pretended to study, but then flunked most of her exams.

Cecily and I graduated early, with honors, and married soon after. Amber changed her major for the seventh or eighth time, failed at a second university, hinted at travel plans, and was fired from a series of jobs. This is when I recognized Amber's inability to stay on track without her younger sister's constant advice and attention. Honestly, she must have called us ten times a day until I gave her a warning.

"Well, *there* you are," I said, standing in the doorframe, unable to summon a more enthusiastic greeting.

I motioned for her to come in. As I closed the door I saw an Uber car pulling away from the curb. No trick-or-treaters in sight, of course. Only a couple of adult vampires heading toward another party down the block, velvet capes gently swaying as they walked.

"Hey, Drew," said Amber, her voice husky from smoking. "Thanks for letting me come over. I mean, thanks for inviting me."

Even her breath and the voluminous dress she wore reeked of candles and spice. When she put her arms around my neck and pulled me close for a mushy kiss on the side of my face, I felt the mass of her body trying to surround and envelop me.

"No problem," I said, gritting my teeth and disengaging myself from her awful embrace. I noted the circles under her eyes and the nocturnal heaviness of her mascara, wondering for the millionth time what I had once seen in her. I chalk it up to youthful ignorance. She was a sample, a trial relationship, before

I gave myself over to Cecily, sanity, the suburbs, and investment portfolios. My wife appreciates these things, and she's willing to work for them. So am I.

"Hey, Amber!" Cecily called out from the other room.

"Hey, babe!"

"Come and join us!"

As we wandered back to the dining room, I noticed our final guest wasn't carrying the promised Ouija board. Two houses over, a soundtrack rose up with musical shrieks and creepy haunted house noises, and then went silent. I was comforted by the thought that at least our neighbors were having less fun than we were.

Cecily embraced Amber and offered her a glass of wine. There was the briefest dip in energy. We all felt it. The "Amber Chill" is what I like to call it, but this never fails to make my wife look sad, so I kept the observation to myself. Meredith covered the awkwardness by tidying up and topping off her husband's drink.

"I understand you're going to guide us through a séance, is that right?" Connor asked with a smirk.

"What?" Amber asked. "No, I've never performed a séance, no."

"That's right," said Meredith. "You read palms. Yes?"

"Change of plans," I said. "Or a change of heart. Apparently."

Amber's face lost its final trace of color. She sat there in her chair at the dining table like an adult who's suddenly deflated to child-size, arranging the folds of her dress around her. When she was done, she looked as pasty as before but also on the verge of collapse. I had a fleeting image of her being sucked down inside the dress that pooled around her, swallowed up and digested by her garment. It made me smile imagining her screams.

"I thought Cecily would explain," she said. Leaving our guests to stare vacantly.

"Yes," Cecily jumped in. Ever the social one, the slender and gracious proof that Amber wasn't a genetic aberration but a self-made monster, an experimental version of Cecily gone wrong.

"Amber suffered a terrifying experience recently. After all she's been through, she needs a break from—"

Here my nimble Cecily fumbled for words. What the hell was it her sister actually *did*? From what dire circumstances did she need a break? Here was Amber, too weird to behave like a normal person and hold down a job. Yet too high-strung to make money telling fake fortunes. Her flaw was always her belief in things any sane person would call BS—spirits, auras, premonitions, tarot, you name it.

"I see you didn't bring a Ouija board," I said. I knew point-blank observations made her nervous.

"No worries," said Meredith. "As long as the wine and cheese last, I'm good."

"Yeah," said Jeff. "No pressure."

"Come on, Amber," I said. Trying to sound sporty and not mean. "It's Halloween. We're all excited about hearing our fortune told, or trying to contact the dead, or something. Maybe you could just . . ."

"If she doesn't want to, it's fine. Really." Steven said this so good-naturedly I wanted to throw a slice of smoked chicken at him.

From somewhere in the gloom outdoors came a high-pitched howl. We were silent for a second. Then we burst into laughter. All except Amber, who seemed so wrung out and pathetic, Meredith reached over and took her hand.

"Hey, what was this experience you mentioned?" Meredith asked. "Do you want to talk about it?"

I think I made a snorting sound when I laughed. Cecily gave

me a glance, and I shut up. For the moment I couldn't stop the runaway train, which is how I thought of Amber's need for attention. My coworkers and their spouses were falling for Amber's routine and there was nothing I could do about it.

"It's happened a few times in my life, this kind of thing," she said. Her voice was pitched low enough to draw the others in. They pulled up their chairs and huddled around the table like kids at camp. Cecily even dimmed the overhead lights and lit a couple of candles. In this natural spotlight, Amber went on. "There was a terrible night years ago when I was in college—"

"Why didn't you just bring the Ouija board?" I interrupted. "We could figure it out by ourselves, even if you didn't want to play."

This time I got a look from *all* of them—Cecily, Meredith, even the guys. I took this as a sign I was edging toward Drewville, so I decided to pull back. I popped the cap on another Corona and took a seat.

"It's all right. Take your time," Cecily said to Amber. "Do you want to repeat what you told me? I mean, about why you stopped doing readings?"

"It's such a long story," Amber said. "Probably boring to most people."

"No," said Steven. "Go on."

"All of my life," she said, "since I was a little girl I wanted someone to love, someone to be my very own. You know what I mean, someone devoted to me and only me. And once I thought I almost had this glimmer of love . . ." I caught the glance she gave me and felt a shiver at the base of my spine. "But it never came true. Not for me. Not for me . . ."

"Everybody wants to be loved," said Meredith.

"It's universal," said Jeff.

"Jesus." I really didn't mean to say this. It just popped out.

Cecily gave me a withering sigh.

"Okay," I said as gently as possible. "Tell you what. It's a party. Let's make our own Ouija board."

"Drew, please," said Cecily. "She's telling us what happened."

Amber stared at me like I'd kicked a puppy. "It's a Ouija, *not* a Ouija board," she told me. Those dark, messy eyebrows were all knotted up and crazy; her overdrawn mouth was as sloppy as I remembered it from those nights in her dorm room, long ago.

Cecily sighed and turned her gaze toward the patio. From where we sat, we could see the stupid jack-o'-lanterns along the edge of the cement, angling past the barbecue pit and around the side of the house to the driveway. The candles had sputtered out but the effect was still there, snarling faces glowing orange in the intermittent shadows and moonlight. It crossed my mind that I should relight them.

Not that I believed any of that spirit world Halloween stuff. I've always felt an interest in the occult is an excuse for being childish and strange. Years ago, the night I made up my mind to ditch Amber, we were at a frat party in full swing. The upstairs rooms were occupied, all pumps downstairs were spewing ale into plastic cups, music was throbbing, and the people who were still dancing started to shed pieces of clothing.

Amber claimed she had a "vision" of a young woman sprawled across the floor, her skirt torn and stained with blood and beer. Amber ruined that night for me with her loony performance, stumbling through the crowd, pointing and shrieking while onlookers laughed at us. We left the party early. So much for schmoozing the best and brightest guys on campus, guys who would go on to start their own companies and could have offered me a job someday. Forget all of that. Amber had a "vision." Jesus.

I read the newspaper account a few days later. The party we

left had turned ugly at some point. The photo of a dead girl in her ruined party outfit confirmed what I suspected. Not that Amber was psychic. How could she be? There was nothing special about her, and there was no such thing as a "vision." It seemed as though she triggered bad events, just by being there. Like the time she warned a bus driver to quit his route early to avoid a catastrophe; two hours later the guy slammed his bus into a utility pole and injured six passengers. Some people would call it a premonition, but not me.

Maybe she gave people ideas they didn't have before. Maybe she just freaked people out or set them on edge, and this had a sort of ripple effect. She was tuned into something nasty, something I didn't like and didn't want living under my roof or sleeping in my bed. The news story about the dead girl proved me right. It was wise to break things off with Amber and give my full attention to Cecily.

"Come on," I said to our party guests. "This will be fun. We'll use the salt-and-pepper shakers for 'yes' or 'no' and then we'll only ask questions the ghosties don't have to spell out. Look at me! I'm a psychic!"

"Never make fun of the dead," Amber said. Her voice was low and gravelly, and for a second I was afraid she might go into one of those trancelike states, where she sort of resembles a dog having a spasm.

"Jesus, Amber," I told her. "Lighten up."

I set up the shakers like goalposts on the table. The tiny skeletons stood guard, holding up their remaining toothpicks like weapons. The lights were still dim, and on the table the candle flames wavered.

I sat before the shakers. I placed my hand over an empty paper plate. I smiled, really beamed for the first time all night.

"This is no joke," said Amber.

"Sure it is," I said amiably. Then I turned my attention to the paper plate. "Is anyone here with us?" I asked.

Cecily sighed and shook her head. Meredith forced a polite grin. The others only stared at me as I continued.

"O spirits!" I intoned. "Are you *with us* tonight?"

At this point I slid the paper plate toward the saltshaker, indicating "yes." At the same time I raised my eyebrows in mock surprise and prepared to ask another question, but I was interrupted.

"No!" Amber screamed, standing and grasping the folds of her dress with one hand. A second later her chair hit the floor, tipped backward behind her. *"No!"*

Steven and Jeff were staring wide-eyed at me from their end of the dining table, no doubt making plans to escape. Meredith was pale, and Connor held her hands.

"No *what*?" I yelled. "Are you kidding me, Amber? Are you *kidding*?"

Amber pointed at the patio beyond the glass. "You let the lights go out!"

"What?" I said. "Are you *nuts*?"

"Drew!" Cecily hissed. She stood and took a step toward the sliding glass door.

"No," I said, trying to calm my voice and my thoughts. "Forget it, honey, I'm not letting you make excuses this time. She's ruined every party we ever invited her to, and I'm fed up. Hear me? I'm sick of it!"

"Drew, for God's sake!" Cecily had an edge of hysteria I'd never heard before. "Drew! *Look!*"

I turned toward my wife. Her face was pale and her hands were clasped beneath her chin. At the table our guests rose to their feet simultaneously. I stood and followed Cecily's gaze.

On the other side of the sliding glass door a tall figure was shambling toward the house. Not swaying exactly but struggling to find purchase with each step, crushing dead jack-o'-lanterns along the way. It loomed, a shadow stretching beyond that of any ordinary person, well over seven feet tall.

I put a hand on Cecily's shoulder and nudged her to one side. The instinct welling inside me was natural enough, but I wasn't protecting my wife. I had a quick, deep, overwhelming desire to see this thing stumbling into the light.

"What the hell?" I asked. Once the words were out of my mouth I realized I needed to direct them at Amber. "What the hell have you done this time?" I shouted at her. "Tell me or I'm calling the cops!"

My righteous anger was interrupted by a thump. Cecily let out a yelp and headed toward the other guests. They clustered like children behind me.

We watched while the figure outside—broad shouldered and muscular—bumped against the patio door, causing the glass to shiver in its frame. It was hard to judge the figure's true height because Jeff's werewolf mask was stuck on its head at a jaunty angle, revealing a zigzag of scar tissue below its mouth and disappearing into the V of a torn shirt.

"No!" Amber screamed again.

This time we all jumped. But before we could answer, she went striding across the room. She stopped at the glass door, staring out while the figure seemed to stare in (although it was hard to tell through that mask).

The figure grew agitated when Amber pressed her hands against the door. It bumped the glass again and again, catching one shoulder on the metal frame each time.

"Hamish!" Amber screamed with her face close to the glass, her breath fogging its surface with every word. "Hamish, I'm sorry!"

I could have slapped her. I could have killed her. I don't know why she's always called out the worst in me, the most despicable parts of my nature, but it was so even when I found her appealing all those years ago. Even when we made love, I found myself possessed by a desperate urge to crush her face with my hands. Taking in the spectacle of Amber and the figure wearing the werewolf mask made me nauseated—the overweight woman in her sloppy dress and runny makeup and the pitiful creature out there whose only desire was to reach her, the horrible object of its pathetic affection.

"Hamish! Go back!" she shouted.

At this the figure stopped bumping against the glass. It leaned there for a moment with its head tilted, looming a good two feet taller than Amber. It made a doglike sound, a whimper or a whisper, I couldn't tell which. Then it turned and went lurching off across the patio, its clumsy steps knocking the remaining jack-o'-lanterns out of its path.

"Jesus Christ!" Meredith said. "Who was *that*?" She collapsed into Connor's arms. He held her and began to steer her out of the dining room, in the direction of the front door.

The others stood watching me. I guess they wondered what I would do, but I didn't do anything except almost wet my pants when I heard a howl from the side of the house. The sound broke us. Cecily ran to her sister, who was shouting nonsense about ghosts and dead pumpkins. Jeff and Steven started for the front door, and I followed them.

"What the heck was that all about, Drew?" Jeff asked me. "Was that thing real? It wasn't real, was it? It's a joke, right?"

Meredith was crying. Connor held her tight and steered her outside, toward their car.

"Oh no," I said. "Come on. Do you have to go?"

Connor shouted at me over the hood of the car. "What the hell is wrong with you, Drew? You're not funny, okay? Not funny!" Then he glanced around, and his gaze locked onto the figure now struggling to break free of the shrubbery along the side of our house. "You too," he yelled at it. "Not funny!" Connor climbed into the driver's seat and burned rubber out of there.

Jeff and Steven stood in the foyer, whispering, arguing. Jeff shook his head.

"Look," he said. "Whatever that is under the mask, it's very convincing. That sound it made . . . ? Yeah. Good one."

"Jeff," I said. "I didn't set this up. I have no idea . . ."

"Too much," he said with a tight smile. "Okay, well, it's late."

"Jeff," I said again.

He didn't answer. They headed to their car and once they were inside I could hear the thump of the auto-lock, followed by a few expletives as they continued their argument. I heard my name shouted just before they drove off.

"Amber!" I heard my wife shriek from the dining room. By the time I reached her, Cecily was alone. The sliding glass door stood open, and the chill night air wafted in.

"Amber!" Cecily shouted again. "She's gone, Drew. I couldn't stop her. She ran after that guy, whoever he is."

"Hamish?"

"I don't know who it is, or what it is," she said. "Go find her, Drew!"

"She left on her own. She's an adult."

My expression told her everything. All the disgust and contempt I usually took pains to conceal. Cecily read all of it and began to cry.

"Great," I said. "Perfect."

"You blame my sister for this, too?"

"She's the lunatic, isn't she?" I asked. I tried to put my arms around her, but she pulled away. Aroused, I reached for her again, and she slapped my hand away.

"Unbelievable. I can't . . . Just unbelievable!"

"And who insists on inviting Amber every time we have a get-together?" I asked.

"Who can't stop making fun of her in front of everybody? Who can't leave well enough alone? Tell me," she said, her voice climbing.

"You chose me!" I screamed. "I didn't ruin your sister's stupid life. I chose you, and *you chose me*! Remember?"

She stopped crying. She snapped off the outdoor lights, closed and locked the patio door, and walked away. I heard her footsteps as she stomped upstairs to our bedroom.

I thought about braving the chill night, playing the hero, searching for Amber. But I couldn't do it. I went as far as opening the front door and stepping out onto the walk. The figure, Hamish, whatever it was, had disengaged from the shrubbery and escaped.

I checked the spot where Jeff had tossed the werewolf mask earlier. It was gone. I thought I heard children singing on the next street over, but I couldn't be sure. Suddenly, across the street, where the trees cast spindly shadows like trembling fingers, I spotted movement.

If my life ever depends on it, for some reason, I'll swear I saw nothing in the shadows. I'll never admit I saw the figure in the werewolf mask shambling around the corner with a group of people, some walking and some floating with their feet off the ground. A few steps behind the group Amber followed, and I could hear her voice, fading. "Hamish! Hamish!"

No matter what version of the story I'll tell at the office, I won't describe how I looked back over my shoulder just a moment before and saw my beautiful, unhappy wife upstairs, at the bedroom window, watching. I won't say we both stared into the dark for a long time, neither of us daring to move or call out, not knowing what to do next.

In conversation with people at work, I'll blame my sister-in-law. I always do. I'll say she ruined the party and left with a friend. I'll explain how one of Amber's creepy dates must have stalked her, and followed her to our house. I'll say I have no idea why Amber did it, but we're never inviting her to our house again.

Sisters

Brian Evenson

WE HAD JUST moved in, hadn't even done anything to our neighbors yet. We were all alone at the end of the block, and already Millie was complaining. Was this going to be another of those stays where we hardly ever left the house? Couldn't we at least join in celebrating the holidays?

"They're not our holidays," Mother explained. "We're not like them."

Millie just stamped her foot. "I *am* from around here," she said. "I am. Now."

Father just rolled his eyes and left the room. I could hear him in the other room, the creak of the liquor cabinet as he opened the door, the glug of his pour. It was a big pour. Tonight we would probably leave him to sleep on the floor.

"No," said Mother. "You're not. At least they wouldn't think so."

Millie turned to me. "I mean, you know what they do?" she asked. She said it as if she were addressing me, but she was really saying it for Mother, so I didn't bother to nod. "It's crazy. One holiday involves brightly wrapped gifts. A laughing man climbs up on the roof and throws them down the chimney. If there's a fire in the fireplace, the gifts burn up in the fire. Doesn't that sound fun?"

Well, yes, to me, it did. To Mother too, I knew, but she just shook her head. "Where did you hear about this?" she asked.

"I hear things," Millie said. "I make an effort to stay informed. And another," she said, her gaze inching back toward me, "they take a large candle and they knead it and prod it until it becomes nine candles, and then they light them all without touching a flame to them."

"I don't think you have that quite right," murmured Mother.

"And there's another one, where you look at yourself in the mirror and keep looking until you can see through your skin, and then you draw your own heart and send the drawing in a letter to someone else."

"Why would you do that?" I couldn't stop myself from saying.

"So that they can control you," she said. "You are saying 'I do not want myself and so I am giving you the gift of me.' Or something like that."

"It's very strange here," I said.

"Yes," said Millie. "Very strange. And another one where you dig up a tree in one place and then carry it to a different place and then plant it there. A sort of tree-stealing day."

"It's a tree-planting day," said Mother. "And most of them around here don't even know it's a holiday. Almost nobody celebrates it."

"But you have to get a tree from somewhere," Millie insisted. "If you're going to plant it, don't you have to dig it up from somewhere first? It seems to me that it's more a tree-stealing day than a tree-planting day."

Mother shrugged.

"Can we at least steal a tree?" said Millie.

"Absolutely not," said Mother.

"Why not?" she whined. When Mother didn't answer, she sighed and went on.

"And then there's the one where we put on a face not our own and go from one door to the next and take things, and—"

But Mother had reached out and grabbed her arm. "Where did you hear about this?"

"I," said Millie. "The immature specimens down the street. I was listening to them as they walked to the instructional center. They were talking about it."

"Did they see you?"

"No, of course not," said Millie. "I would never—"

"And what did they say this day was called?"

"Halloween," said Millie.

"Hallows' Eve?"

Millie considered, shrugged. "Maybe."

Mother let go of her arm. "Now, that," said Mother, "that is something we can celebrate. That's not their holiday: it's ours."

THAT, FOR MILLIE, was permission enough. For the next several weeks Halloween was all she could speak about. Any moment she heard voices outside she was out there stalking them, hidden, listening. She was out there so much that people began to sense her. Not see her, exactly, but they began looking over their shoulders more often, increasingly sure they were missing something.

"Don't get caught, Millie," I warned her, "or you'll end up like Aunt Agnes."

"What happened to Aunt Agnes?" she asked, seemingly innocently. But when she saw my expression, she said, "Joking. Don't worry. I won't get caught."

· · ·

MILLIE WAS OUTSIDE the house more often than not, gathering facts about the holiday, getting the local take on the thing. Father didn't like it and retreated more and more often to the liquor cabinet, which, perhaps because he had created it, proved surprisingly endless. Before long, he was spending so much time passed out on the floor that the walls of the house began to run and grow furzed around the edges. Mother had to kick him awake and walk him into semi-sobriety, or else we would have been off to the next place, or maybe to no place at all.

About two weeks in, Millie gathered the family together to report what she had learned. She had been, as it turned out, to an instructional center, and had benefitted, from her vantage in the coat closet, from a series of short sermons related to the "true" nature of "Halloween." These included the carving of pumpkins into the shapes of those rejected by both heaven and hell, the donning of costumes (by which she meant a sort of substitute skin affixed over the real skin, though in this locale they used an artificial rather than, as we were prone to do, an actual skin), and the "doorstep challenge." This latter, she said, was accompanied by slapping the face of the respondent with a glove, and then saying something such as: "Shall you accept a trick from my hand, or shall you satisfy the aggression of that same hand by soothing it with a treat?"

"That was how it was phrased?" asked Mother.

Millie shrugged. "No, not exactly. I'm improving it."

"And the glove slap?"

"Also an improvement," she admitted.

But improving it, Mother told us, was not something we were meant to do with the holiday. If we were to practice this holiday, we should do our best to practice it just as it was done locally. We needed to fit in.

"Even the artificial skin?" asked Millie.

Mother hesitated. "You have a particular skin in mind?" she asked. "Other than the one you currently wear?"

"Oh yes," said Millie, "very much so."

Mother thought for a while, hesitating. Then Father slurred from the adjacent room, "Hell, let the girls have their fun." And so she shrugged and acquiesced.

THE PLAN WAS for me to tie Millie's current skin to a chair and then for her to tie mine to a chair, and then she would lead us to the new artificial skin she had in mind. "You'll like it," she said. "Once you've tried this new skin, you won't want to come back."

"But you will come back," Mother warned.

"Of course," said Millie. Though from the way she said it, I knew it would be reluctantly.

The tying down of Millie's current skin went smoothly, particularly since she waited to extrude herself until the skin was firmly restrained. I watched her ooze out through the nostrils and become once again just Millie plain and simple. The skin was for a moment inert, and then it came to itself, beginning to scream, then screaming full-throated until Mother gagged it.

"What do you suppose it remembers?" asked Millie, her voice papery and whisper-thin beside me, a kind of light flutter against my eardrum. "Does it know how I've made use of it?"

"It must know something," I said. "Otherwise it wouldn't be screaming."

What we hadn't considered was that now, out of her skin, Millie couldn't tie my skin to its own chair. And I could hardly tie myself up. "Shall I go borrow a skin," whispered Millie, "and bring it back to do the job?"

Mother sighed. "I'll handle it," she said.

She tied me tight—she had had the most practice—and also pushed a cloth deep into my mouth while I was still in the skin: easier that way. And then I wriggled about inside the flesh and slowly detached myself and, panting, dragged myself out.

MILLIE LED ME, a flitting form. Still panting, I tried to keep up. Mother was there at the door, arms crossed, watching us go. It felt good to be out, good to be able to stretch. *Why even bother with a new skin?* I wondered. But when I voiced this to Millie, she scolded me.

"This is important," she said. "We're getting to know them, seeing how they celebrate. Once we understand that, we'll understand much more, and soon we won't have to move so often and may even start to feel like we're them."

"Why would we want to feel like that?" I asked, but she ignored me.

She led me to a telephone pole, one without climbing pegs on the side, and then sped up it. I followed. A moment later we were beside the wire, the buzzing loud, and louder of course because we were there. And then she slipped into the current and flowed away.

I followed. I could barely keep up and nearly lost track of her in the flow. Too late, I saw her clamber out. I had to force myself back hard against the current and just managed to reach the step-down. By the time I pulled myself out, Millie was already across a lawn and headed toward the porch of a house. It wasn't a *true* house, like ours was. You had the sense, even from a single glance, that it was made of nothing but brick and wood and mortar, not likely to last more than a few dozen years, and was rooted stolidly to one spot. What good, really, was a house like that? Why she was interested in it at all was impossible for me to say.

"Look," she said.

And there it was: on the porch, half-hidden behind the bushes, a mannequin of some kind, a black tattered dress, face made to look old, long white hair, a dark peaked hat, eyes like burning coals. We approached with care, but something about it saw us in a way that the locals had not, and it began cackling at our approach, its eyes strobing.

"What is it?" I asked. "Some kind of moving statue?"

"You can get inside," she said. "Go ahead, climb in."

And so I did. Not climb so much as flow quickly in. It was a different sensation from the fleshy skins I usually occupied, and decidedly stiff. The arms moved just a little, constrained as they were. The head swiveled a few inches in each direction. The legs wouldn't move much at all. A moment later my sister had forced her way in as well.

"Hey," I said, "it's tight in here."

"Stop grumbling," Millie said. "There's plenty of room."

She was right, mainly. But still, it was awkward with both of us operating the artificial skin from the inside. Slowly we got used to it. Working together, we could force the joints of the arms farther. We could make the fingers snap open and closed. Together, with effort, we could even make the legs creak and move.

"Now what?" I asked.

"Now, we wait," she said.

WE STAYED THERE as night got deeper. A person resembling our father who was perhaps a father himself came out of the house that the porch was attached to and peered at us through thick glasses. He went and fiddled with the cord that was attached to our artificial skin, unplugging it from the wall and plugging it back in again.

"What do you suppose he wants?" I whispered.

"Hush," my sister said.

Eventually, seeming to grow frustrated, he unplugged the cord and went back inside. Once she was sure he wasn't coming back out, Millie said, "The skin must have been made to do something that it's not doing now that we're inside."

"It was doing something when we arrived," I said. "Eyes glowing, sounds of some sort. Cackling maybe, or screams."

"Eyes glowing, cackling, screams," said my sister. "I can manage that." And she started rummaging around within the thing until the porch was bathed in a deep red glow and a speaker embedded within the artificial skin was making sounds like a giant being strangled.

"Too loud," I shouted. "Too much light!" She let it all go at once, the porch suddenly dark and silent.

A moment later the man burst through the door and back onto the porch, looking frantically around. He regarded the unplugged cord a long moment and then, mumbling and shaking his head, went back inside.

"What was that all about?" Millie asked.

"How should I know?" I asked.

WE SETTLED IN. We waited until the lights inside the house went off, and then we waited as the stars whirled lazily above us. We were good at waiting. The night began to fade and still we waited.

"What are we waiting for?" I asked Millie.

"Shh," she said. "For the right day. For Halloween to start."

The sun rose and it became warm inside the skin. I stretched and tangled with Millie and then elbowed her until she gave me space. The day slowly crept by. A family came out of the house attached to our porch, a father like the one we had seen last night first, then two immature specimens, then what we guessed was a mother. The sun rose and passed above us—not directly overhead but clinging more to one-half of the sky. Eventually the family, bit by bit, returned. Or some family, anyway—I couldn't be exactly sure they were the same ones.

The sun was just beginning to set when I realized there was someone else inside the skin with us, someone of such presence that she was pushing me up against the walls of the skin, making me start to ooze through.

"Hi, Mom," I managed.

"I tell you girls that you can celebrate one holiday, and you think that gives you permission to stay out all night."

"No," I said, "I'm just . . . Sorry, Mom."

"Not even a note," she said. "What have I done to deserve this?"

"We weren't doing any harm," said Millie. "We hadn't even gone far."

Mom turned to her. "And, you: Do you want to end up like Aunt Agnes?" she asked.

"No, Mother," she managed.

For a long time she was silent. I thought she was going to drag us home, that the holiday would be over for us before it even began. And then she sighed. "We'll deal with this tomorrow. Home by midnight," she said, "and straight from here to the wires and then home. No stops!"

"Yes, Mom," I said.

"Millie?"

"Yes, Mom," she said.

"Good," said Mother, and as abruptly as she had arrived, she was gone.

IT WAS JUST DARK, the streetlights buzzing on, when they began to come. Small groups of them, two or three, wearing peculiar false skins tightened over their own skins. They were immature specimens, a dozen years along or less. Invariably, they were accompanied by one or two mature local specimens, who did not wear false skins but instead stood with folded arms at the sidewalk's end, far away from the porch.

"Are they not allowed to come onto the porch unless they are wearing a false skin?" I wondered.

"I don't know," whispered Millie. "If that's the case, why would they come at all if they didn't have one?"

Of the ones that came onto the porch, there were those that wore skins resembling animals and those that wore skins resembling the dead. Others chose skins that resembled nothing I had ever seen—strange shining figures with buglike eyes, figures with veiled faces with symbols emblazoned on their chests. There were even a few that adopted the terrifying species designated the clown.

"They don't all take the same sorts of skins?" I asked.

"No," said Millie. "Apparently not. They take skins of all kinds."

"What good is that?" I asked, but to this she had no answer.

They stepped onto the porch, walked past us, and approached the door. They rang the doorbell. When the door was open, they cried out the ritual phrase *Trick or treat.* But yet, there was no trick to be had, only the rapid distribution of fistfuls of sweets followed by the shooing of these double-skinned creatures away.

"So, if they don't produce the sweets rapidly enough, that's when the trick comes?" I asked.

"That's my understanding," said Millie. "Then they will soap a window or throw rotten fruit at a façade or kill the primary member of the household."

It seemed to me that there was a large gap between the first two tricks she had mentioned and the third. Surely, I suggested, there must be some tricks in between. Such as the severing of a finger, say, or the slow torture of one of the secondary members of the household—an immature specimen, say, or a pet. Even killing someone *other than* the primary member of the household struck me as a viable intermediary step.

But my sister claimed to have her information from a combination of overheard talk and television viewed through the window of the local bar and grill, two sources of authority, which, taken in tandem, were difficult to dispute.

NEVERTHELESS, WE MIGHT have continued to argue had we not both simultaneously become aware that one of the doubly skinned specimens on the porch was regarding not the man with the bowl of sweets at the door, but us.

"Hush," said my sister to me.

But the specimen came closer, then closer still, peering quizzically at the fabric and metal and rubber armature that contained us. The specimen's false skin was colored all orange and black. It sported black boots and an orange skirt. It had a tall black hat, floppy and crimped, impractical in every respect, and carried a black broom. Meant to represent some sort of ancient and inefficient cleaning woman, perhaps.

It came very close indeed, looking right into the eyes of the armature, and then its vision slid down and to one side. I could see that it was looking through the armature and right at my sister.

"What are you doing in there?" it said to her.

IN RETROSPECT, I think my sister, so long undetected, so long unseen, was not prepared to be seen. Before I could stop her, she'd taken control of the armature's hands and locked them around the small creature's neck.

There was a commotion on the porch; someone was screaming. The bowl of sweets dropped and shattered, and the man who had been holding it was prying at the artificial hands, trying to free the child.

I had a choice. Either I could save the child or I could support my sister. I could add my will to her own and between the two of us we could easily snap the creature's neck. Or else I could loosen her fingers.

In the end I did nothing. Instead, I left. In just a moment, I was out of the artificial skin and had fled back down the sidewalk and up the pole and into the wire itself. A moment later I was back at home, coming conscious within the skin I had occupied before.

Mother was standing there, patiently waiting, wearing her traveling clothes. When she saw I was back, she cut the ropes, quickly freeing me.

"Where's your sister?" she asked.

"She was seen," I said.

She just nodded, her skin's lips a thin line. I got up and massaged my wrists. My father was standing there beside her, an ice pack pressed to his head. "She may still come back," he said.

I sat there, nervously waiting. In the end, yes, she did come, with a deep gasping breath, and in a state of panic. She looked at me with fury.

"You left me," she accused.

I shrugged. "You were seen," I said.

She looked to Mother and Father for support, but they remained impassive. She had been seen. She knew the rules. She was lucky we had waited for her at all.

"It can't see me anymore," she said. "No need to worry."

"You blinded it?" asked Father.

"Killed it," she said. "Strangled it." She looked at me again. "No thanks to you," she whispered.

"Don't be snippy," Mother said to her. She belted her coat around her. "Come on," she said, "let's go."

BUT WE HAD barely thrown open the door when the specimen appeared. It looked just as it had before, same orange and black, same unfortunate hat, except for the black marks on its neck. And the fact that, in places, you could see right through it.

"Hello," Mother said.

"Trick or treat," it said.

"Can I help you?" Mother asked. "Are you lost?"

"I . . . don't know," it said.

"Yes," Mother said. "I can help you."

For a long time it was immobile, silent. "Who are you?" it finally offered.

"Me?" asked Mother, bringing her hand to her neck in a way that brought back memories for me. "Why, I'm your mother. Don't you recognize me?"

And that was how our family grew from four to five, and I came to have a new sister. Millie did not seem excited, but I most certainly was. *A new sister,* I thought, imagining all I would be able to teach her, *a new sister!* And teach her I did, and loved her too, for the whole remainder of the evening. Up until the very moment when, as the clock struck midnight and the holiday came to an end, we ate her.

All Through the Night

Elise Forier Edie

W HEN THEY SHOWED Maggie her husband's body, it was
Granny O'Neill she mourned, not him. To be sure, she
had loved Aiden once. But New York had hardened her heart
into cobblestone, and the sight of his snapped neck, and poor
dirty drawers, only twisted her mouth in disgust. Every finger
in his right hand was broken. He had died in the streets like
a dog.

She said to the men who had probably killed him, "See that
he's properly buried." In autumn, they sent her some money.
Maggie set it aside. By then she knew she was pregnant, and her
troubles were only just beginning.

But first, she thought of Granny O'Neill, and the rain-washed
fields of Kerry. How, even when they were both starving, light
and fragile inside as spiderwebs, Granny's bewhiskered face had
been smiling.

"See how hunger makes the world like a veil," she had said.
"How another Place hides behind it."

And wee Maggie, just a child then, with her bony side pressed to Granny's, had seen: how the grass hid a greener field beyond, how the hedges were full of slim doors and slit windows, how the fields glittered with a thousand faceted eyes. She looked and never forgot the World-Behind-the-World, the one you could see only if your belly was empty.

But if such a World-Behind existed in Five Points, Maggie imagined it a wretched place. For New York pressed in on all sides, and instead of clean, green hills and bog ponies, there were crowds of people, cramming like hogs at feeding time. Their first few days in America, Maggie white-knuckled Aiden's sleeves like a child, and when he laughed and tried to peel her off, she whined and clutched him more. Everywhere they went, they banged into horrors. Pits of shit steaming behind tenement houses. Fireworks exploding over a river of fish corpses. A pack of ragged children cooking rats on a fire.

They shared a room with ten other immigrants, curled on a straw-strewn floor. She wept. "What if we die here?"

"Die?" he laughed. "But of course we will. And here. This is our home now. But don't fret, my love. We'll be on to something better."

But weeks passed and she saw nothing better in the whole New World. Not mist-bathed fields, or warblers, or wych elms, not mushroom circles, or hills furred with green. Just sights so strange, she didn't know what to make of them: A Syrian lad with a ragged pet monkey. A long braid snaking down a Chinaman's back. A peddler holding a tray of tomatoes, the fruit's smell and color so foreign and alarming, she almost yelled at the sight.

And poor Aiden breathed his last in the gutter, lips and blue eyes beaten to jelly. Maggie cursed herself thrice over. For it had been she who asked to come to this stone-cold country, an impossible ocean away from everything they'd ever known.

For a time, she felt safe at a grocery on Orange Street. She would linger there, after sewing pieces for a Jew down the road. Cheerful apples tumbled in bins; fragrant hams hung from the rafters. Mrs. Docker, the proprietress, was like an apple herself, crisply round and red cheeked. Her boy Jack would sing the old songs betimes, in a tenor clear as church bells. Maggie could cozy up to the counter and almost feel she was back in Ireland. Granny would be alive again; this mistake called New York would be but a fading nightmare, ere Maggie blinked her sleep-filled eyes.

One evening in October, walking home from Rosenbaum's, she saw a big fire burning in the middle of Paradise Square. A pack of ragged boys, sticks clamped in their fists, sang and chanted as they pelted down the crowded lane. Maggie didn't think on it at first; she was weary, and her neck ached from bending over stitching. But when she stepped in Mrs. Docker's door and saw the merriment in every corner, she cottoned it was All Hallows' Eve.

At the stove, wee Jack roasted nuts. Nearby, a gaggle of girls took turns peeling apples. They tossed the parings over their shoulders and blushed to the shouts and whistles of young men looking on. "I fling yon paring over me head," they sang. "My sweetheart's letter on the ground is read."

"'Tis in the shape of a 'P,' so it's Peter she'll be marrying," proclaimed a tall lass, squatting in the sawdust, pointing from a pile of apple skins to a lad, who hunched brawny shoulders and grinned at the floor.

"Nay! 'Tis a 'D,'" a dark-haired girl shouted. "And Damien's the lucky one who will have our Nell."

"'Tis a 'P' and that's final!"

"La! You couldn't read the nose on my face!"

And Maggie watched as a laughing argument broke out, which had no real resolution, until everyone determined blushing Nell must pare down another apple, so as a final reading about her intended's initials could be made.

At the bar, Mrs. Docker presided over an enormous barm brack. It was a thick cake, into which trinkets had been baked, along with apples and raisins. For a penny, Maggie could buy a piece, and the cake would tell her fortune. If her slice had money in it, she'd find wealth in the coming year; if her teeth clamped on a bit of wadded rag, bad luck would follow.

She bought a wedge and a glass of ale. But once the cake lay in front of her, she hesitated to eat it. She was hungry, but she also feared her fortune, as she did everything these days.

"Afraid of breaking a tooth on your penny?" Maggie felt a bump, and a warm hand cupping her elbow. She turned and gazed into bright, slanted eyes. The man's skin was pretty, foreign tinged. A blue coat wrapped his shoulders, and a big, blue hat toppled on his hair. "You can poke it to crumbs first," he said. "Shall I show you? Here," he called out to Mrs. Docker. "Give us a spoon. We've a shy one."

Maggie's face heated as Mrs. Docker handed over a dented utensil. The blue-clad man whistled, a cheerful sound like a kettle. "I like a fresh Irish lass. You're all dappled like turkey eggs and innocent as daylight. Am I right?" He smashed at Maggie's poor slice with the back of the spoon, crushing it flat as he talked. "Do you speak, darling? Or only stare?"

"I can speak. And I didn't ask you to ruin my cake." The crumbled remains reminded Maggie of poor Aiden's face.

"Ach, it'll taste the same, I promise." The Blue Man winked. "And I can't help wanting to ruin things. You, especially." He leaned forward, his lips inches from her own. "Your hair's like a flaming phoenix, love. Tell me, does it burn the same downstairs?"

Everyone in the grocery laughed. Maggie snatched at the spoon. "That's for my husband to know, not the likes of you."

"Oh ho!" said the Blue Man while the crowd hooted. "Hot and fiery and slick as an eel's tail, I'll warrant. But married, alas. Where's your husband, then? Drinking? Fighting?" He cocked his head. "I hope he'll at least come home to help you with the baby. Do you want a boy or a girl?"

Maggie was scarcely sure of the pregnancy herself and didn't know how the Blue Man could have guessed. A knowing whisper spread through the room. She bit back the words trembling on her lips: I don't want the baby. I don't know how I'm going to feed it.

Something like pity shone in the Blue Man's eyes. He had flecks of gold in them, and his hair was dark as a forest floor. "Ach, I meant no harm. But here. What's this?" He bent over the flattened cake. "Ah, yes. A pretty for the pretty, unless I'm mistaken." He brushed his long fingers in the crumbs and plucked out something shiny. Maggie gasped. It wasn't the expected coin, or rag, but a jewel, red as a flower. It caught the light as he rolled it in his fingers. "Why, Mrs. Docker!" he called over the counter. "Are you so rich as to be baking rubies in your cake?"

"Enough of your games, Blai Orrit," Mrs. Docker said. "You pulled that thing from your very own pocket."

"I never!" the Blue Man said. "'Twas baked in this Irish girl's barm brack, I swear it, and a fine fortune it foretells." He twirled the stone. It was pretty as fire. "What say you, Irish? A year of riches, and girl baby, fresh and fair as her mother? Is that a fortune fit for your beauty?" He smiled and dropped the stone in her hand.

Holding it, Maggie felt cold and hot all at once. She'd never seen anything so lovely. It looked alive, shimmering on her palm. "I don't know," she said.

"Don't you? Well, mayhap you'll sell the babe to me, if you don't want her." The Blue Man had leaned in close again, voice so soft, she hardly heard it.

"What?"

He grinned. His canine teeth were long and sharp looking. "If she's a lass, your child, you can sell her to me. I'd treat her well. Put her to work only when she's ready. Would you like that, love?"

The heat in Maggie's face had become a cold chill. He had discerned the worst wish of her heart, like a traveler reading tea leaves. She took in his slant eyes and bright blue clothes, the pearl-and-gold sheen of his skin. With a start, she realized he wasn't human. Why, he must be a strutting sidh lad, come on All Hallows' Eve to tempt and trick her. And he was a Five Points Fae too, as wicked and dangerous as the city they stood in. The spit in her mouth dried up.

Another chuckle rippled through the market, but Maggie paid it no mind. She let the red bauble drop and backed away.

"Come now, lass," the sidh lad called. He stooped and plucked the jewel from the floor. "Don't forget your fortune. It's bad luck not to take it." He clawed at her arm again.

"For the love of God, stop teasing the poor child. She's too green to even know it's glass." A woman slid herself between Maggie and the Blue Man. "Buy me a drink, damn your eyes, Blai Orrit. Leave the poor child to her beer."

"If I must." The sidh lad tipped his hat. "But her beauty puts me in her debt. And I always pay my debts. Do you, Irish?"

At that, Maggie stumbled out the door, leaving her cake and her beer and the laughing crowd behind.

All the way home, she startled at shadows, for it was perilous to be alone and abroad on All Hallows' Eve. She had been foolish to linger in Mrs. Docker's. Revelers danced in the street; firelight glimmered on every corner. But she did not gaze at or join in the merriment. Instead, she kept her eyes to the ground. She was afraid she might glimpse Aiden's corpse, lurching through the streets, looking for her. Or she might see the sidh lad's blue coat as he came to tempt her more. Only when she was home safe in her tenement room did Maggie heave a sigh of relief.

The feeling was short-lived. For when she reached in her apron pocket, her fingers closed on something hard. With a gasp, she pulled forth the shining, red stone, the one the sidh lad had dandled. Somehow it had found its way back to her—unasked for and uninvited.

When it rolled to the floor, one of her flatmates snatched it up. "Gods, where did you get this?"

"Pulled it from my fortune cake at Mrs. Docker's." Maggie had backed into a corner.

"That's a piece of good luck."

"I don't think so, Lynn. I'm afraid one of the Good Folk put it there."

Lynn smirked. She was a sharp-faced girl, with a mouth full of chipped teeth. "Bosh. There's no such things. Don't be a bumpkin, Maggie."

"I tell you, he looked passing strange. And he knew I'm with child, though I'm not yet showing."

"Then he'd a sharp eye, that's all." Lynn turned the jewel in the lantern light. It sparkled in her grimy fingers. "When are you due?"

"Spring, I suppose."

"Hard, with your man gone."

"Yes." Maggie swallowed, thinking of the sidh lad's offer. Had he paid for her baby with this jewel? Would he come for the child after Maggie bore it? Did she want that?

"Shall I sell this for you?" Lynn asked. "I'd get a fair price, I promise."

"No." Maggie snatched back the stone.

Lynn sniffed. "You'd do well to be nice, now you're on your own. You'll need friends."

"Don't want them." Maggie didn't want to know anyone from this foul place.

She lay down in the straw on the floor and turned her face to the wall, clutching the stone with one hand and her belly with the other. Could she bear to leave her child with the Good Folk and buy a ticket back to Kerry? Could she stand to stay in Five Points and raise it on her own? Either choice seemed bad, the same way every street in New York led to heartbreak and ugliness.

In the end she kept the jewel, though Maggie knew it was wrong. Still, she liked to hold it up to the light. Red and bright, it made her think of flowers and tales. She rolled it in her fingers as she walked and warmed it in her palm. She had never had anything so pretty. And she told herself she'd return it soon, for certain before her child came. But she made no effort to find the Blue Man. Instead, she avoided Mrs. Docker's altogether and bought her ale at an oyster bar instead.

The child inside her grew fast. First, it felt like a butterfly, with shivering wings in her belly. Then it bubbled and roiled like a stew. Finally it came, swift and on a tide of pain so strong, Maggie shook and shrieked and forgot everything. There were two days of weeping and straining and screaming, then the babe was delivered, and the midwife pronounced her healthy.

Maggie stared, dumbfounded at a golden-haired girl. She looked like Aiden, and when the child opened her mouth and gave a cry, everything in Maggie's chest thrummed. It was like a factory switch churning giant machinery. Her heart flooded, her eyes filled. Look at the cunning creature, she thought, with her fingers curled like new leaves, and tiny spikes of eyelashes shadowing her cheeks.

With plunging terror, she remembered the ruby. Oh, she must return it, and right away! She'd been foolish to keep the thing for so long. She didn't want to sell her baby.

She searched her apron, the straw, the sills, the sashes, and even the grime-filled cracks in the floorboards. But no glowing little jewel was to be found. And when she went to ask Lynn about it, Lynn was gone, and Maggie knew her for a thief.

"Now Blai Orrit will come for my child," she thought, more scared than ever in her life, more terrified than the day Granny breathed her last, or Aiden took her hand and they boarded a ship. She screamed and swore and gazed at her baby and screamed and stomped and swore some more. For two days her heart galloped as she nursed and waited for the sidh lad to claim what was owed. But he didn't come. So Maggie scrounged a bent nail from the gutter. Cold iron would protect them both from the Fae. Then she tied the child to her bosom and named her Bride.

Maggie returned to the Rosenbaums' flat, where she worked sewing pieces six days a week. Cloth and trim clogged their dank apartment. She sat there with six other girls and sewed the same things over and over. But when Maggie crouched in her wooden chair, with Bride bundled to her breast, bearded Rosenbaum tutted and told her that she must leave the child with someone else while she worked.

"But the cost—"

"What of the cost to me?" he asked. "If your breast milk leaks on my piecings? If the baby ruins your work with her chewing and meddling?"

Mrs. Rosenbaum cooed and clucked at the child. "Don't worry," she said, wren-brown eyes twinkling. "Find a girl to watch her. Buy her good, fresh milk, and she'll grow up strong. All the advertisements say cow's milk is better. She'll be fine, love. This isn't Ireland, after all."

Maggie heeded the woman. After all, Mrs. Rosenbaum could read newspapers and add up sums. So she found a babysitter, two rooms down from her own. The girl was smooth-haired, twelve years old, and simple, but Maggie knew she would treat Bride with gentleness. Half of Maggie's pennies went to the babysitter. With the other half, she bought fresh milk. She would tote a tin cup to the street each day, where peddlers ladled milk out of buckets. Some wagons were grimy, others buzzed with flies, but Maggie always looked for the thickest, creamiest product, milk that hissed and foamed from containers and poured like silk into wee Bride's mouth. Instead of buying new shoes, Maggie wrapped rags around her feet. Every day she sewed until her hands cramped and her eyes burned.

All seemed well, as frail spring gave way to fetid summer. To be sure, there were days Maggie reeled from hunger and the whole world ran like candle wax. She thought of her last days at Lansdowne then, when she and Aiden were so weak from starvation, they clung together just to stay upright. They took refuge in the workhouse, where Maggie boiled grass for their supper. They'd lain entwined, weak as kittens, waiting to pass to a better world. Then the marquis offered free passage to New York, for any tenant who wanted. It was cheaper for him to send his people to America than to attempt to feed them all.

"Here's our chance," she told Aiden, "to find something better."

What had she known? For there was no grass to eat in Five Points, either. Maggie gobbled clay and sucked on small stones. At night, she brushed straw from the tenement floor and chewed it. When her gums began to bleed, she relished the iron flavor. And whenever Bride smiled, her heart turned over. At least the girl would have it better, Maggie thought. At least she will have a chance.

The air grew brittle. Wind off the river bit hard as a wolf's teeth. It was autumn again, drear and damp, when Maggie stumped home from a twelve-hour shift at Rosenbaum's to find Bride pale as a corpse, purple shadows ringing her eyes. Her little neck had swelled, and her breathing was labored.

"She won't eat. She won't smile," said the girl who watched her, pale eyes watering with tears.

The only doctor Maggie could afford worked out of a damp room off an alleyway. He reeked of gin, and his wool coat billowed on a sticklike frame. But his voice was steady enough as he said, "I suppose you've been feeding her milk?"

"To be sure. Cow's milk, as it's better."

"Right." He sighed.

He lit a flickering lantern and wiped a table with his sleeve. He poked and prodded Bride's small body, grunting at the blue and purple swellings behind her ears, listening to the rasping wheeze of her breath. The baby didn't cry or smile or kick. She lay limp, her blond curls plastered on her forehead.

The doctor said the milk sold in Five Points came from sick cows and looked thick and creamy only with the addition of paint and chalk. "Your girl would have been better off at the breast, my dear. I'm afraid you've been feeding her poison."

"But what do I do?" The tears on Maggie's cheeks were warm, though everything else about her had frozen.

"You hope the dear thing can fight it," he said. "Get some clean water down her, if you can. Though I daresay what comes from the pumps is hardly that. Maybe if you buy some beer?" He shook his head. "I'm sorry. There's nothing I can do."

Beer Maggie tried, and gruel and bread, but the baby just turned her face away. So she walked back and forth in her room, picking her way between the huddled bodies of her flatmates, trying to sing the poison out of the child. When her flatmates complained that they couldn't sleep, Maggie took to the alleyway and walked until the rags around her feet unwound and dragged in dirty twists behind. Night turned to day, and still she rocked and sang, for what else could she do? Maggie walked until her feet were like the bricks on the sidewalk, red and numb and swollen to blocks. Then she sank to the ground, and propped against a wall she slept. All the strangers in the world passed by and paid her no mind at all.

When Maggie woke, it was night again. Flames flickered in the distance, and fireworks snapped. She realized All Hallows' Eve had come round again, and her heart seized. The spirits were abroad. Maggie fumbled in her pockets for her bit of cold iron. The baby rolled stiff in her arms, like a log.

She shouted when she saw what Bride had become: a child no longer, but a beast with black skin and white eyes. It croaked like a crow and, when Maggie turned it, she saw a tail sprouted from its bottom, one that whipped and lashed like an angry cat's.

She screamed again. A pack of boys across the street laughed in reply. They sang and smacked sticks against the brick buildings, making loud clacks and clatters. Maggie shook as the creature in her arms spoke, in a voice like fire crackling.

"Esuriens!" it said. *"Tua ossua manducabo!"*

Blai Orrit had fetched his due, while she slept, a year to the day of his bargain. He had taken Bride and left a changeling in her place. Maggie shut her eyes and steadied her breathing. I can fix this, she thought. The night is not over. If I am brave and smart, I can find Blai Orrit and fetch my Bride back. No price in this world—or his—is too high. Whatever the cost, I'll pay.

She scrambled upright and, clutching the monster, tottered down the street.

Mrs. Docker's door was flung wide open. The smell of holiday cakes and beer wafted. Jack was a year taller, and broader, but he roasted hazelnuts the same as before. A lass by his side, with ribbons in her hair, sang to the roasting nuts, "If you hate me, spit and fly! If you love me burn away."

"Blai Orrit!" Maggie shrieked above the calls of the crowd. "Blai Orrit, damn him, where is he tonight?"

The merriment died as one by one, people turned to look.

Stevedores and laborers, lasses and wee ones, all with firelit faces, stared. Maggie stood in the doorway, wild and wet.

"What's Blai done now?" someone asked.

"He took my child. He took my girl." Maggie's voice was hoarse with tears and terror. She stomped her foot to keep from shattering to pieces in the doorway.

"Why, you're scarce a child yourself." Mrs. Docker came from around the counter, wiping her hands on her apron. Maggie hated the kindness in her face. "What's this about Blai Orrit, dear? Did he hurt you?"

"He left me this." The changeling brayed like a donkey, and everyone but Mrs. Docker drew back. Maggie's voice rang in silence but for the hazelnuts bursting on the hearth. "I let him . . . I thought . . . but he can't have her. She's mine! I gave everything—" Sobs grabbed at her throat. "I gave everything."

Mrs. Docker's voice was soft as the sawdust on the floor. "Now, now," she said. "Why don't you come by the fire and get warm? Have a cup of ale. Jack's roasting nuts—"

"I don't want my fortune told. I want my baby!" Maggie's shout was like a dirty rag flung on Mrs. Docker's face. The woman recoiled. "He must give her back. How do I find him?"

"If you're to find Blai tonight, you'd best look to Pete Williams's or the Brewery."

It was a man who spoke, red of eye and dark of face, simmering by the fire. Mrs. Docker turned to him and said, "Can't you see—"

"I see plain. But the girl wants Blai Orrit, not you. So let her try and find him." The man lifted his chin to Maggie. "Go you there, to Mulberry Bend. You know it?"

She did, of course, everyone did. Pete Williams owned a dance hall on Orange called Almack's, a wild place where Ethiopes mixed with Irish. The Old Brewery, not far, was a tenement, hemmed in by a lane called Murderer's Alley. It was the lowest building of its kind in New York, seething with rats and misery.

"Blai Orrit, and the rest like him, that's where they be," the man said. He jerked his chin. "Now go away and take that Thing with you. You shouldn't be carrying it on a night like this."

"I don't want to," Maggie said.

She didn't want to go to Mulberry Bend, either. But she turned in the doorway and limped into the night, leaving the warmth of Mrs. Docker's face at her back.

The air had grown colder and more drear. As she walked through shadows, figures flickered in and out of sight. Maggie tried to keep her head down, lest she catch sight of something from the Other Side. But dropping her gaze meant staring at the changeling, whose white eyes glimmered in the dark. So Maggie stared ahead, trying not to mind how the buildings around her squirmed. She told herself, Even if I wander into the World-Behind, it matters not, for that is where Bride has been taken and where I must go.

Maggie's shoulders softened. She let everything blur around her. Figures scuttled here and there. The grinning teeth and black eye of a horse skull capered. Some Scots children carried lanterns with fiery faces burning inside. Maggie kept walking, and her feet found the way.

The Old Brewery hulked in the darkness, its brick walls dirty and chimneys toppling. In Paradise Square out front, a crowd warmed their hands by a bright orange fire. They were roasting nuts and telling tales, like the folk at Mrs. Docker's. But this was a different sort of crowd, and Maggie hesitated to address them. For she glimpsed giant bat wings curling out of a man's back, and a woman with a snout like a pig's. The huge hooves of a cart horse peeked from under another woman's grimy skirt hem. The child by her side twitched a fluffy tail.

"If you're looking for a toss, look elsewhere," the pig-woman said. The winged man smirked, while firelight carved holes in his face.

"I'm looking for Blai Orrit." Maggie trembled. "I'm told he might room in yon Brewery. He has a blue coat. Have you seen him?"

"And what would you be wanting with Blai?" The hoofed woman drew herself up.

"Never mind what she wants." The man's wings snapped. "If he's here, you'll find him in the basement. But I haven't seen him for some time. Could be he's moved on."

"To what?" the horse-woman guffawed.

"To her." The man grinned and billowed his wings once more.

Maggie turned on their laughter and stepped toward the tenement.

Its door looked ordinary enough, weathered wood with a few steps leading up. Splinters, a round knob, sturdy hinges. But the air felt thick and hot on the threshold. And when Maggie wrapped her hand around the knob, the earth pitched and trembled, like the sea under a boat.

She opened the door. Inside, it stank worse than the workhouse in Lansdowne—of sweat and shit and spilled gin. Maggie could feel how big the space was: like a church, with a looming ceiling, teetering stairs, and balconies climbing the walls. Light glimmered from candles, and though she could not see them, Maggie felt people everywhere. Platforms shook with pattering footsteps. Unseen hands grabbed at rails. Dust showered from above as shadowy forms clumped on the landings.

"Fresh meat." The whisper skittered around the big space like a roach in a bucket.

Maggie cleared her throat. "I've come looking for someone," she said. "A man. He took my baby."

Shuffles and whispers stirred the air. Rapid steps rattled down the stairs. Maggie thought, Here he comes, and braced herself. Blai Orrit's hands would soon snatch her shoulders; Blai Orrit's teeth would pierce her skin. He would make her his slave for a hundred years. But it was just one step from this nightmare to the next.

A foot scraped on the floorboards. Maggie clenched her fists.

"Are you looking for me?" a soft voice asked.

She whirled. She knew that voice, knew it as well as she knew her childhood prayers. "Aiden?" Her whisper was raw. "Is that you?"

The revenant didn't take breath of course, but Maggie heard a sigh all the same. "Is that what they called me?" it asked.

It shambled into view. The head hung to one side on a broken neck. The ruined fingers of its right hand dangled. Worms and grubs had made fast work of the flesh. A few dirty rags fluttered, but mostly Aiden was bones.

Maggie trembled from scalp to ankles. "Aiden. Oh, Aiden. Can you help me?"

"Help with what, love?" The jaw did not move; the listing head did not nod; but she heard him all the same. And she felt him as close to her skin as her own dirty clothes.

"Aiden, I've lost our child." The horror of it gushed through her. Maggie reeled, and the revenant grabbed with its unbroken hand. Bony fingers dug in her arm. "And I killed you too." She wept. "It was me said we should come to America. It's my fault you died. And then I left you in the gutter with your teeth scattered like penny nails. Like you were something from the midden pile. I'm so cold." She choked on words too big to fit in her throat. "Everything about me is cold. So how am I the one who is still alive?"

The revenant didn't answer. Instead, its fingers snapped and Maggie slipped to the floor. She grappled with the squirming changeling in her arms, kneeling in the filth at her dead husband's feet. "Aiden," she said. "I'm sorry."

Maggie waited for his reply. She waited for him to help her. But all that happened was a hand touched her head, warm and soft. She raised her streaming eyes. An old woman stood before her, gray hair hanging in clumps. She carried a lantern and it swung, making shadows careen around them. In the woman's skirts, Maggie glimpsed sparks of light, like stars.

"Child, are you lost?" the star-woman asked.

"I'm looking for Blai Orrit. He took my babe, and gave me this, but I want my Bride. Can you bring her? Are you the queen here?"

The star-woman bent to stare at the changeling. She looked from the monster to Maggie's wet face. "Blai Orrit's been locked in the Tombs nigh on four months," she said. "He's dead or still rotting in jail, my dear."

"But then how—"

"What is it you think you hold?"

Maggie swallowed. "Why, a changeling. One of yours, begging your pardon. And I'd like my own baby back."

The glittering woman tugged on her hand. "Come outside, child. I think I can help you there."

"But I—"

"Come outside. It will be all right."

Maggie scrambled to her feet. The star-woman opened the front door. Her legs trembled as the woman pulled her out.

The sun had risen on a gray fall day. In the cool light, Maggie could see the woman's eyes were yellow, and her teeth and lips as black as a dog's. The stars in her dress did not gleam as prettily in daylight, but unseen bells tinkled whenever she moved.

"Think you that you hold a changeling child," the lady said. Maggie nodded. "Then to get your own babe back, you must put it in the fire or throw it in the river. Or didn't your grand-mother tell you?"

Maggie blinked. "She did."

"Just so." The woman nodded. "Well. The river is not far off. And we've still a good blazing fire in front of us. Which is it to be?"

Maggie gazed about. The bonfire still burned in Paradise Square, its embers rippling with heat and color. But where fell creatures had warmed themselves the night before, people now stood in the dawn. Maggie recognized the woman with the hooves, although she wore ordinary black boots now and florid paint on her mouth. A few thin children had joined her. One poked a stick at the flames, while another hopped up and down. Neither of them had tails. The smell of wood smoke wafted, and so did sweet tobacco.

The changeling child had stopped squirming. Maggie could no longer feel its tail curling around her forearm. Her legs gave out and she sat down, right on the steps of the Old Brewery. The old woman sat beside her, and little bells chimed in the morning air.

"I bought milk for my baby," Maggie said. "All my pennies. And the doctor called it poison."

The star-woman asked, "Was this child your first?" Maggie nodded. "Well. There will be others."

"But my husband is dead." Her throat ached so she could hardly bear it. "I begged him to come away with me, and he died fighting in the street."

"There's always another man. It won't be your husband, but it will be someone. Life goes on," the lady said.

"Must it?"

The woman didn't answer. The sun crawled higher. Hot tears on Maggie's face grew cold.

"It's not a changeling, is it?" she asked at last.

"No."

"And you're not a faery-lady."

The woman smiled her black smile. "Are you sure?"

"No." Maggie laughed, in spite of her weeping. "But I see now. It doesn't matter if you are. There's always another world. But it's never better than here." She looked at the babe in her arms. In the clear daylight she saw Bride had died and was blue and cold and stiff as a stick.

The sun inched higher in the sky. The whore by the fire left off warming her hands and crossed the square to stand before them. "I'm sorry about your baby," she said.

"I tried so hard." Maggie bent her head and kissed Bride's cold face. "I tried."

"Ah, love, love," said the whore. "We all do."

She sat on Maggie's other side, pressing her fire-warmed body to her cold one. Maggie leaned her head up against the whore's shoulder. They sat that way for a long time. And when Maggie was ready, the whore and the star-woman walked with her to the church. They stood by while she spoke to the father there about arranging another funeral. And they kept standing as she went to put flowers on Aiden's grave and light a candle for his soul.

A Kingdom of Sugar Skulls and Marigolds

Eric J. Guignard

Hey, PACHUCO.

You ever seen the lights go green in a woman's eyes when she takes the hand of a man made of bones? He's dressed like the finest of *charros* with his *greca* suit of black and gold that twinkles as stars in a moonless night, and the buckle of his *piteado* belt is carved from sacred jade. He could be the mariachi of dreams, though for all the voice of his song, he don't play no music, he just dances.

He's a badass *chingón* too; even if just a thing of bones, you wouldn't mess with him. He wears this big top hat instead of a sombrero, and it's tall as an eagle can fly, all shiny black with a silk band around its crown covered in roses and cockscomb and chrysanthemums, and it's crazy the hat never moves while he dances, and somehow you get this feeling you don't want it to move either, because if it did, it'd be bad, even though it's a skull already wearing this hat, just a skull with carnival paint and sweet candy hearts, but what's under the hat is still worse. . . .

And he don't stop dancing for nothing.

With her.

The woman whose eyes go green, the woman whose face turns a cobweb of stitches, a slash of crosshatch lips in the shape of a heart, an empty cutout of eyes surrounded by whorls of orange, surrounded by azure, surrounded by crimson, all curled-up squiggles, like a wind washing long hair down a pale-faced chasm, and they dance until she's gone.

That's how death takes you, okay?

And that woman, pachuco, she could be anyone, even you.

Órale . . .

I KNOW YOU'D ASK, wouldn't you? How I woke in the morning to realize I fucked up twice?

No *madre* around, I know you'd ask that too, if I kiss her with this mouth, but the *puta* ran off when I was three, left me and Papá and my sisters for some *wheto* bandleader. . . . I wonder what'll happen when she dies; she won't be mourned here. Where do the lonely souls go, the sad girls?

So when I wake, it's just me in the kitchen, and my aching head is lying on the table feeling like a punching bag that's overstuffed, 'cause maybe I drank too much last night . . . maybe I passed out thinking of Santi.

And like I said, I'm alone, but also there's this voice speaking in my ear.

"Hey, *vato,*" the voice says. "Hey, sleepyhead, wake up."

I crack open my eyes, and light in the kitchen burns like the sun has a grudge, and all I can do is squint. The kitchen is turned sideways too, the mezcal bottle looking knocked over, it should be pouring into my face.

"You going to sleep the day away?" It talks fast, this voice, but it's quiet too, like whispering some urgent secret.

I groan and suck in the drool that's puddled by the crack of my mouth. Inside my mouth it's dry as sand, like all the spit worked its way out and stuck the side of my face to the tabletop, you know?

"Pachuco, you won't like if I have to wake you."

I lift my head real slow, and the kitchen turns how it should. I blink, and the light gets less bright, just a yellow bulb and some rays slipping through messy curtains. Okay, better, so I look around, but there's no one else, maybe I'm imagining things. Besides the drool I left on the table are the skull, the bottle, the switchblade, and the book.

"Cojeme," I mutter. You don't get hung over with mezcal like you do tequila, but you still feel like a couple rocks go grating in your head.

I could blame Yoli I'm like this, since she left the mezcal open on the counter like a gift not just to Papá but to me as well. But then again, maybe it's my own fault. . . . Maybe I should finally grow up and shit. Yoli's mezcal knocks your ass out like a Kid Gavilan bolo punch, and I knew it would.

"There you are."

The voice again, and no one's around. It's stupid, but all I can say is, "Who's talking?"

"¡Órale!" the skull on the table answers, all excited like a dog you reward for doing a good trick.

I startled, and you'd think I should have reacted more, but my brain just doesn't get it. "How?"

"Don't you know, *vato*? You're the one made me."

That's true, I guess, out of sugar and water and meringue powder. Some paint, some icing . . . But I didn't make it to talk. "Who are you?"

"Read my name, pachuco."

Though my eyes are all bleary, I look what I'd written on its eggshell brow. The letters are carved between frosted vines, Cupid hearts, playing-card spades.

"Santi?"

"You need go back to school," the sugar skull answers. "Learn your letters."

I rub my eyes twice, each lid feeling made of cement. Focus. The skull is life-size, I'd inked some crazy work on it: red scar stitching that pulled its rictus grin up razor-sharp cheekbones, and a classy butterfly spread-winged across the cavity that would have been a nose. Above the green swirls and flames of orange are the letters I carved last night, but something's wrong with them: they don't spell what they're supposed to. My breath hisses out, *"Ay wey."*

I'd switched two letters. . . . Instead of SANTI, I carved the name SAINT. Which is how I fucked up the second time.

I turn my head away. "No, you ain't real."

"Don't disrespect me. You think I'm a dream, open your eyes."

I do. I turn back. Nothing changes.

"Happy?" Saint asks.

"No."

On my way to the faucet to dunk my head, it all comes back, revving, rushing in my mind, flashbacks of making sugar skulls with my sisters, Yoli and Li'l Chica.

See, Yoli turned the back porch into an art studio couple years ago. She's got all the marionettes and ceramic animals with stars for eyes and shit, the masks that laugh through one mouth and cry through another. You never seen skill like hers, weaving dried peppers into moon faces, painting pictures of Mayan gods and these warriors fighting under night-sky pyramids, and they don't wear no protection but for bird feathers, it's crazy.

She got us to make our own skulls for Dia de los Muertos this year instead of buying from the old ladies in market stalls on every corner in the hood. You just mix the ingredients in a mold and let dry, and yesterday they were ready. So we decorated while listening to AM radio, where Miguel Aceves Mejía sang his heart out in "Tú, Solo Tú," and no one could sound better, 'cept maybe that cowboy yodeler, Bill Haley, who came on next with "Rocket 88" that was *chinga* cranked.

Yoli made her skull for Papá, and Chica made her skull for Abuelita, and I made mine for Santi. . . .

I hack and spit into the sink, rinse my mouth, run water through my hair, until my head feels a little better. I turn back, admitting, "I don't know what I was thinking last night."

"Not strange for you, pachuco," Saint says, "and that's a problem."

"Yoli said maybe the spirits could visit, you call them right, being Day of the Dead, you know?"

"Maybe they do. Maybe there are other ways to save them."

I grab the bottle of mezcal off the table and take a gulp straight from its lip. "Who needs saving?"

"Besides you? You tried calling someone else, I think."

I did.

It's Yoli, who also inherited this big-ass book of black magick, *Brujería Magia Negra*. . . .

The autumn heat had cooled to ice when the sky broke yesterday, and Yoli started messin' around with that book, reading things, lighting candles, and her *novio,* Dante, came over, and we opened up the mezcal that was supposed to be a gift to Papá's altar, and Dante smoked out the room with joints of hash and ground-up peyote. Yoli spoke about calling back spirits, if you carve their name into the sugar skull and read this certain passage, and I started seeing things, I was fucked-up, but that was it.

I didn't read none of her book, I didn't say none of the chants, I don't mess around with that shit. . . .

Until they left, and I was alone, everyone else partying on the streets for the festival. I could have gone too, but I couldn't, if that makes sense. . . . I mean, me and Santi used to roll together every year since we were little, and me doing it without him just made me fuckin' cry.

I couldn't do nothing but sit at the kitchen table with the skull I made for him, and something in my chest grew all heavy, and I started drinkin' more, and I started talking to Santi, like why it had to go like that. . . .

And somehow Yoli's book of black magick ended up in my hands and, like I said, I don't mess around with that shit, but maybe I spoke a few words. . . . Maybe I read from some pages things I don't understand but said them anyway, out loud, like a certain passage, while I carved Santi's name with a switchblade into the skull.

"Hey, you with me, or you back in la-la land?" Saint asks.

"So what now?" My question is a shrug.

"Go say hello."

"To who?"

Sudden as Chivo's gunshot, there's a *clack-clack-clack* sound coming from the sitting room. I don't know what it is, and part of me doesn't want to find out. It's the kind of sound don't belong in a home, a sound like tap dancers moving on *American Bandstand,* their shoes make that sharp clatter on the wood floor when they step hard and fast.

"You got a visitor."

I eye Saint wearily and flick open my switchblade. "Someone like you, or I gotta cut a fool?"

"Why don't you find out."

Again: *Clack-clack-clack.*

I push through the swinging saloon doors and would've screamed right there if my voice hadn't fled for my balls.

There's a skeleton in the room, walking around as if no problem, smoking one of Papá's cigarettes we left on his remembrance altar. It isn't a corpse, not like scarecrow-ragged or anything, no blood, no dirt, no worms crawling from its eyes, but it's clean, okay, like a cartoon skeleton, pale and scrubbed, every bone in place. It's dressed to the nines too, better than I could do, like it's going dancing at the Cocoanut Grove. The skull has a real thin mustache, like how Papá had, and it wears these big steel rings on its bone fingers like Papá used to wear—his *thumpers,* is what he called them—for street brawling.

It's looking at the altar, where a photo still shows Papá's face— no smile—behind a frame of glass, decked out in brimmed *tando* as wide as his shoulders, and the starched white collar of his satin shirt flares over a fingertip coat no one could wear so well. The *R.I.P.* in lipstick is Li'l Chica's, and the collection of votive candles is from Abuelita, one for each saint she brought from Juárez, which number more than the altar can hold. Abuelita's own mourning altar is across the room; she followed Papá three years later to the underworld of Mictlan.

Eight years ago, I was twelve, Papá got beat in East L.A. by sailors with baseball bats and lead pipes. Papá got beat so bad, his head looked like a piñata busted open, and all the little candies poured out.

Those are the candies now painted over the face of this skeleton.

It turns to me, wearing those same clothes from the picture, and it says my name: *Clack-clack-clack.*

Saint's voice comes from the kitchen. "Family reunion, *ey, vato?*"

It's Papá who lifts up his big bony arms for a big Papá hug, and I don't want to touch him, but I ain't got a choice either; he's coming to me, and I have my switchblade in hand and could cut through a rib, but I'd never raise a hand to him, even if he's just a dead thing clacking my name over and over, and so we embrace.

And there's a fuckin' trickle of water coming down my eye, that's how it makes me feel, but I've been all kinds of somber emotions lately too.

"You going to leave me out?" Saint asks, like he's lonely.

When Papá lets go, he goes into the kitchen and brings the sugar skull back, held in the clattering crook of an elbow that looks like a yo-yo, the way it swings loose back and forth.

"This is all kinds of nuthouse," I tell them, shaking my head from one to the other. "I don't even know."

"This ain't nothing. You wanna see some shit? Let's roll, paint the town, get some skull *heinas.*"

Clack-clack-clack.

They don't glance back, Papá and Saint just fling open the front door and walk outside.

I follow, and the door frame creaks when I grab it for support, because my legs go to soup at what I see. I almost turn away, though it's no more crazy than talking to a skull made of sugar or of dead Papá carrying it around.

Jet-black and electric blue: that's the night sky, shimmering and buzzing like lights of an all-night diner, while agate-dusted shades zoom by, darting through alleys of a crowded universe. My eyes fight to adjust, to make sense, because the crescent moon is this sideways grin of teeth, clamping a cigar that blows puffs of firecracker flares, which drip shadows onto the hands I shoot up in reflex. The stars pulse too, like you've never seen. They're glitter pinwheels and pink hearts and lemon snow cone twirls, and the pin-striping of a Chevy hardtop runs across it all in zigzag waves like stitchwork that if you undid, everything would fall apart. . . .

Your head would spin dizzy, you tried looking too long.

All I could stutter is, "What . . . ?" and, "How . . . ?" and, "Where's the daylight . . . ?"

"It's midnight, *vato.*"

"It's only morning, like ten."

"It's Dia de los Muertos, pachuco. It's always midnight."

I nod, *okay,* and I know this is crazy, but I kinda felt I belonged too, as much as you can belong walking into the page of some dime-store comic.

"*¡Órale!*" Saint exclaims at my lowrider. "Your bomba is slick. Shotgun!"

I don't even recognize my Impala, parked curbside, it's been changed. The trunk is popped open like a casket of red silk, but instead of a corpse, it overflows with wild marigolds, bright in every hue of gold; my wheels are nothing but tribal suns, dark blue as tattoo ink, surrounded by whirling flames; and the car's paint job is of skulls, I mean every skull you could want, funny skulls with winking eyes, vicious skulls with fangs for teeth, even *mamacita* skulls lookin' sexy with emerald smoke simmering from empty sockets, and all these skulls got teeth that are clattering.

Papá gets in back right behind the driver's seat and places Saint so he'll sit next to me.

"Rev it up," the sugar skull says.

"Where we going?"

"Where you think?"

Clack-clack-clack.

And I guess I knew all along where I'm supposed to go . . .

Santi.

So we cruise, and it reminds me of the last time I was with him. . . . Fuckin' everything reminds me of Santi: the touch of his long fingers that were always crazy warm; the way his voice would drop when he whispered some shit no one else should know; even the smell of his hair, he'd mix olive oil into the pomade, and it'd just glow like you've never seen.

We'd grown up on the same block and would ride our bicycles together up Whittier Boulevard the way older cholos drove their rides low and slow. When I was nine, he took me out shooting the first time, and we'd capped glass bottles in the concrete channels of the L.A. River. He handled my business when

I got fucked with too; others disrespected me 'cause I'm a little thinner, a little smaller than most in the *varrio*, maybe I talk a little shit, too, but Santi always had my back. . . . Even when I got older, and I wanted to be hard and roll with the Eastside White Fence gang, it was Santi set me straight.

Now he was gone, like everyone else I'd loved, like Papá, like Abuelita—

"Wait, I just thought of something," I say.

"You can think?" Saint asks, like a smart-ass.

"I made your skull, and you're here, and Yoli made Papá's skull, and *he's* here. But Abuelita . . . Li'l Chica made her. How come she's not around?"

"It takes longer coming up here from Juárez."

Oh. I nod, like I should know.

Clack-clack-clack. Papá wants to reminisce about Abuelita the way I'd been on Santi.

Clack-clack-clack, he says again as I turn a steering wheel that's made of peppermint through our *varrio,* down 4th to Lorena, past Fresno Street, past Concord.

Clack-clack-clack, he goes on, and there's all kinds of people out tonight, people who don't belong, ghosts of people. I can see through them, like the stories always tell, these ghosts that are half-mist, half-solid, only their faces are all painted slick for Day of the Dead, and their eyes glow green as molten jade.

There's other things too, skeletons like Papá, and there's headless conquistadors on steeds of papier-mâché, there's a marching band of big brass instruments, like I mean, it's the instruments themselves marching, with little key feet, just blowing crazy tunes. There's banners that fly like Arabic carpets, there's wolves made of agave, even dogs and cats saunter around on two legs like they own the streets, and their eyes are huge and round as shiny gold wheels.

Clack-clack-clack, Papá says, and Saint nods along, a sort of roll back and forth on the seat, since he's without a neck.

"Your *abuelita* don't like the life you're leading," Saint adds, like he's all concerned. "You need to make something of yourself, go to school or some shit."

I blow air, shrug him off. "The fuck you know?"

Papá's hand is quick when he slaps the back of my head. *Clack-clack-clack.*

"*¡Chingados!*" That hurt; a skeleton whack, especially when it's wearing thumpers, leaves a mark.

"Abuelita and I go back," Saint says, all nonchalant. "Maybe she came up through a different school, but I've been hangin' with our people of the sun since the Mexica fled to Tenochtitlán."

I don't even sweat him to explain, I don't need to. That big-ass book of black magick Yoli inherited—*Brujería Magia Negra*—was Abuelita's, and don't ask where she got it. Abuelita sacrificed so we could have a better life, and not just in America.

Abuelita was a witch doctor in Mexico, conjure, maybe you call hoodoo. She'd go off on these spiritual journeys to Mictlan and do some shit. Abuelita was the only person ever scared Papá.

She died five years ago, only when Dia de los Muertos came around a few months later, she thought maybe she'd come back. The next morning they found the sailors accused of beating Papá to death. Those sailors looked like red candy apples after you take a big bite, and their heads were skulls with black holes for eyes, each plugged by a marigold that spun on pinwheel stems.

All I know is, you don't fuck with Abuelita.

Meanwhile, Saint is still talking. "Abuelita says, you don't change your ways, you're gonna dance soon with Mictlan-tecuhtli, the top hat man. His dance, *vato,* it takes only a bullet to do. You'll see soon, like your friend. And he was the smart one."

"What you know about Santi?"

"More than you think. Like I said, I've been around. He's down there in Mictlan, kingdom of the underworld. There it's sugar skulls and marigolds forever. And not in a good way."

I shake my head. "What'd you come here for? To lecture me from Abuelita or cut me with Santi?"

"I didn't come here for your sparkling conversation, that's for sure. I help people. Give them what they need."

"You do?"

"Don't you know? You called me."

"I didn't call you."

"What's my name, pachuco?"

Again, that misspelling. I nod, okay.

"So think. What you need?"

I know what it is when we arrive at Evergreen cemetery. It's how I fucked up the first time. . . . Only what do I call it now: Closure? Atonement? Forgiveness?

It's Santi, and I don't deserve nothing from him but his hatred.

Truth is, I'm not a fighter, I'm not tough, I ain't shit, and Santi always saw through my bluffs, my doubts. He *knew* me like brothers do, knew more about me than even myself, and he accepted it all.

It's hard to repeat what took place, to even admit . . . But listen, okay, it happened I wasn't thinking. Two months ago . . .

We were back in the concrete channels of L.A., laying low in the shade of ducts that crisscross the dry river, just chillin' from late summer heat. I was downin' a bottle of Four Roses whiskey, and I didn't even care.

"*Carnal,* you need to kick back some," Santi said. "You're going to drink yourself to a grave young."

"Who the fuck cares," I said, and I meant it.

"I do, *carnal.*"

I blew out air, shrugged him off.

"You don't believe?" And out of nowhere, he turns to me like he's going to say something else, and there's this fire in his eyes as he leans in, like now it's one of those secrets he's got to say, only there's no one around, so why's he need to whisper, and then his lips were on mine . . .

I froze, there's this warmth I never felt before. His chest pressed lightly to my own, his hands circled my wrists, pulling me closer, and I dropped the whiskey bottle.

The explosion of glass, it was loud, okay, especially in those channels, it echoed. It made me jerk back, I yanked my arms free, but my mouth hesitated, like it acted on its own, didn't want to give up.

Then we were apart.

"Fuck was that?" Santi asked, like I was the one did it to him.

And I flushed, got all hot under the collar he was calling me a queer in my mind. My heart was confused, it was excited, it was scared, angry, embarrassed . . .

"I didn't do shit," was all I could say, this flat denial.

But now I think back, what Santi really said was, "Fuck was that?" in a voice that's only joyful, like a weight had lifted off. . . . It was me took his words the wrong way.

And there wasn't nothing more than what happened anyway, just a kiss. My homie kissed me, is all.

But turned out, we weren't alone. Chivo was passing through on the embankment above us with some of his White Fence cholos. The whiskey bottle exploding, it must have drawn his attention. He *saw* us, if even for a moment.

And they were at us like that, running down the cement slope, all kinds of curses and shouts. I knew it was trouble when I heard the words, "Fuckin' *hotos*!"

Nobody does that here, what Santi and me did, nobody who doesn't want to get jumped by every dude looking to make a name about how badass they are, how *vigilant,* protecting the streets from cocksucking homos.

So I knew what was going down: someone tries putting a gay jacket on you, and you don't deny it with fists, you'll be wearing that jacket the rest of your life, no matter what else.

"Butt bandit *pendejos*!" It was a blur of faces, my head rocked left, knocked right, I saw stars fly overhead. I swung back, connecting with I don't know who or what, I just hit and ducked at the same time, shouting that I didn't do nothing.

"*¡Hotos!*" I heard again, and I couldn't believe I once wanted to run with those guys.

So by then I'd already said it, I'd thought it, I believed it: when I broke free from the fight, tumbling away, I swore it wasn't my fault. I turned and pointed at Santi. "He's the fag, not me!"

Like I said, it's hard to admit. . . . There's Santi, blood leaking from his mouth, an eye all swelled, and I called him out like that. I was dazed, afraid, there was no time to think; I just didn't want to have been seen doing that . . . I was thinking my family would hate on me, though now I find out no one could hate on me more than myself.

And it didn't matter anyway what I said, the White Fence crew was just lookin' to brawl, to hurt anyone for any reason, 'cause that's how they earn fuckin' street cred.

They advanced on me, I remembered the switchblade I carry around, and I pulled it out.

Chivo paused, then from his own pocket he pulled this zip gun, handmade from piping and a block of wood, the firing pin nothing more than a rubber band, but it puts a .22 hole in your head all the same. He'd used it on a rival from the Maravilla street gang the month before.

"You want to play, *puto*?" he asked.

I trembled, my switchblade went away. I raised my hands. Santi launched himself at Chivo, hit him dead-on, and he said, "Run, *carnal*!"

And I did.

Behind me came the crack of Chivo's gunshot, louder than anything. . . .

And now here we are.

I lead Saint and Papá through the cemetery, its bright colors nothing like a cemetery should look, with lawns of rose petals and vaults of starburst. We pass gravestones of sweetbread emblazoned with crossbones on the crust, each topped by La Madonna candles that flicker flames of red, of pink, of blue.

Saint says, "The flames are made of sugar, *vato*. You know that?"

I shake my head slow, while a sweet scent of clay and icing skims across the wind.

Green-eyed ghosts are everywhere too, prosperous or poor, old or young, boxers, brides, priests, and monsters, they've all had that last dance, all had their faces painted. They ignore us, smoking cigarettes with loved ones, toasting shots to old times upon their burial mounds of flowers and fruit, and we ignore them in turn.

My heart's for only one grave. And I could get there with my eyes closed, I've been here almost every day.

"Over the next rise," I say, my chin pointing the way up while my hands wring at each other.

We pass a crypt decked in lucky charms and flaming-heart tattoos, and only then I see too late, a clique of gang members—seven of them—from the La Purissima Crowd, Eastside Varrio White Fence.

It's crazy twisted they're here too, but I guess even cholos got loved ones to visit.

I recognize them all: Big Shadow, Spider, Puppet, Javi, Huero, Scrappy, and their leader, fuckin' Chivo, passing a bottle with dead homies.

My heart goes cold with hatred.

Puppet sees me, elbows Javi. They point, throw their *W.F.*

signs. The others stare me down, and Chivo sticks a finger in and out of his mouth, I know what it's supposed to mean. I step quicker. They got better shit to do at least, they return to their own affairs, though their laughs echo.

"Fuck those punks," Saint says.

"Yeah," I reply, hoping they don't hear.

We crest that last rise and follow a slope down. Around us señoritas dance and musicians play and even little boy and girl ghosts go chasing each other with hoops and sticks.

And then we're at Santi's grave. It looks fresh, the dirt turned over, moist. Here, whorling wet vines slink across, and tall-stemmed cherries fan out like swirls of smoke. The flower wreaths I laid for him are still in bloom of precious scents, even if they're two months old.

A figure is sitting on the headstone, looking down at the earth, looking all solemn too, nobody's here to mourn him.

"Santi?"

He glances up, and the faintest of smiles pulls at the stitching of his lips. I could think he's wearing makeup, only no makeup can cause eyes to glow green like this. Besides the smoldering light and the cobwebbed forehead, the corkscrew brows, the crucifix chin and carved spade nose, Santi might appear as I seen him last.

"What's up, *carnal,*" he says.

"I—I . . ." And it's all stutters from me.

"You need a moment alone?" Saint asks.

I shrug, and he knows that's a *yes.* Papá carries the sugar skull away, I see them last turning behind a mausoleum. And by *last* I mean I don't see nothing else for a minute after, because my eyes are a well of tears, everything's a blur.

I break down, "I'm sorry, man, I'm so damned sorry—"

"It's okay, *carnal,* I shouldn't have done that."

Which makes me feel worse, him apologizing, when it's me

done all the wrong. That moment between us, what we did, I didn't expect it, but it felt like it's supposed to, and I can't think of nothing else, except how I left him, and here's Santi taking the blame.

"No . . ." I want to tell him more, but it's hard to get the words out.

I reach to touch him, and my hand passes through.

"It's too late for me, *carnal*. The top hat man already came, we did the dance."

"It should've been me, Santi, I shouldn't have left you. I'd have fucked those bitches up for what they did."

A voice snaps from behind. "What'd you say about us, *ese*?"

The world freezes, everything silent but for that voice. . . . When I turn, there's Chivo and his White Fence crew.

Big Shadow taunts, "You come here tonight to suck some ghost chorizo, *hoto*?"

They laugh while spreading in a circle around me, I think of a hangman's noose set to tighten.

I look to Santi for help, his eyes meet mine then fall. His head is a sad shake when he says, "I'm only a ghost, *carnal*, I haven't been called forth. The name on the skull, you know it's not mine. I can't step through."

The old defense rears up as their noose constricts. "I didn't do anything!"

"Then why're you here?" Chivo asks. "And why'd you run from us, *puto*? That was guilt."

I go to my second defense, flick out the switchblade from my pocket.

"You got stones to use it now, *hoto*?" Spider says, and the White Fencers move in even closer.

I slash at the air, but it's no good, the effect like a child throwing his rubber ball at a pack of wolves, and my heart's pounding enough to break ribs. I know what's next, they start whistling, shadow-punching the air around me, taking warm-up swings with crude weapons.

"You're gonna wish you stayed last time," Javi promises.

I close my eyes: all I want is to be a child again, me and Santi riding our bicycles up Whittier Boulevard together, only I know it's too late, and now I just want this over. . . .

A clatter erupts, a sound like tap dancers moving on the wood floor of *American Bandstand,* and I open my eyes to Papá! He doesn't give warning, just launches himself at the nearest one with a deafening *clack-clack-clack!*

Papá hits the dude with his thumpers; it takes a couple moments for me to recognize it's Scrappy he hit, because Scrappy's face goes sliding to the left, while a couple teeth go flying to the right.

Now it's on. . . .

I lash out with my blade fast at Chivo, but he dances backward, I miss by inches. My arm's extended when I slice at him, and Big Shadow has a big baseball bat. . . . He swings down, and my forearm cracks. The knife goes flying, and I scream in pain and anger, and all else while I trip to my knees.

I was never a fighter like Papá—even if just his skeleton— who goes after Huero next. At least my screams don't sound like Huero's, once Papá hooks a frightening punch to the cholo's kidney, and follows with a cross that caves in Huero's nose.

I'm not even a threat anymore, holding my arm and groaning, but Chivo makes sure I feel the kick of his steel toe across the side of my face. I go from kneeling to sprawling while he laughs.

Papá roars, *Clack-clack-clack!*

Javi goes down next under Papá's thumpers, I think Javi's face will be scarred as Frankenstein once he's out of the hospital.

And all the time, Saint is shouting from the ground where Papá dropped him, "Kick 'em in the *huevos,* gouge out their eyes!"

It's three down, but then Big Shadow uses that bat to the back of Papá's skull, and Papá stumbles. And Spider has a lead pipe, and Puppet has iron-link chains wrapped around each fist. . . . They take turns pounding at Papá, one after the other, and with each blow, pieces of bone break away in dust and splinters, cometing across the night sky.

There's just too many of them, and it's like Papá getting beat to death all over, only I'm here to witness it; his skeleton arms snap away, his spine comes apart, his bones fall to pieces, like Tinkertoys you toss across the floor. There's nothing but pegs and rods, connectors and slots.

Saint's not a smart-ass anymore when he says, "Oh, damn."

And all the while, Chivo's still laughing.

Santi's ghost says to him, "Haven't you done enough, asshole? Just get out, leave us alone!"

"You're the one talking about assholes, you must like them so much, huh?" Chivo mock-thrusts his hips with grunts.

"Always a punk, only tough with a gun and a gang. I'll see you in Mictlan, you'll be sorry."

"If that's where *hotos* go, you won't see me ever." But Chivo stops laughing.

He scans his crew, realizing half of them are out. Suddenly he pulls that zip gun, points it at me, his dark eyes glinting flames.

"Look what happened to Scrappy, Huero," he says like it's my fault. His voice drops, it's even worse than his shouts, his taunts, when he speaks real quiet to the others. "Get him."

I'm curled up in a protective ball until they grab me, pulling each of my arms and legs so I'm spread-eagle, facedown, straining. I can barely cry out 'cause I can barely breathe.

And I don't see what's going to happen, but I feel it: Chivo's gun pushing deep in my ass, and all this because of a kiss. . . .

"You like it going in, don't you?" Chivo asks.

"He didn't do nothing, it was me!" I hear Santi's voice. I want to scream, *It's not true,* but neither will it matter.

"You should thank me," Chivo answers. "I'm sending him to you, you can pork each other in hell."

More laughs. More jeers.

A thud sounds like a dump truck smacking into a wall, and my right arm is freed. I look up to see Puppet sailing twenty feet through the air. He shatters two headstones when he lands, and he don't get back up that night.

The others let me go, I roll over. There's a new skeleton standing beside Papá's bones, a short, squat skeleton wearing a handmade Campeche dress trimmed with lace and mourning crepe. Its skull is draped by a black mantilla veil, held in place by a tortoiseshell *peineta* I recognize as having been passed down from its own grandmother's grandmother.

Abuelita has arrived from Juárez, and her hair is of marigolds. She's holding that book of black magick, *Brujería Magia Negra*. She says, *Clack-clack-clack*.

Spider's head is knocked sideways like a crowbar tried to pry it off his body. He spins a full circle from the blow and lands in a heap.

Big Shadow gapes, and his eyes fill with the fright of your last dance, when she says again, *Clack-clack-clack*.

And something sorta collapses under his T-shirt when he gets hit, I don't know how many ribs it is, only his feet fly up while his head goes down, and then he's curled in a ball like I was, gasping for breath with sobs I never heard before.

"Fuckin' *puta* witch!" Chivo shouts, turning the gun from me to her, that gun he thinks makes him so tough.

He fires, and the shot is thunderous; there's a gasp when the bullet hits Abuelita's head, only I half realize the gasp is from me.

The tortoiseshell *peineta* that had been her grandmother's grandmother's falls away, smashed to bits by the bullet. There's a smoking hole in the front of her skull too, but a spray of marigolds blossoms instantly from it. I don't think she cares about the bullet hole anyway; it's the tortoiseshell *peineta*—since that was a family heirloom and all—that's going to be the thing to set her off.

And I won't joke, at this moment I almost feel bad for the *cabron*. He don't even know what he's done. . . .

Like I said before, you don't fuck with Abuelita.

Her skull eyes seem to widen, or maybe it's the barbed wire thorns that circle them, causing the effect of those sockets to stretch and spin, and she raises both her arms like she's holding up the night sky, and when the sleeves of her dress slide down, I can see the ink still there, tattooed runes along thin bone arms.

Clack-clack-clack, she says.

Clack-clack-clack!

Clack-clack-clack!

The air in the cemetery just goes still, like it's been sucked out, and this red light glows around Chivo, and then he fuckin' explodes.

There's no other way to put it, but it's like he had a stick of dynamite inside; Chivo is dead as dinosaurs.

I gulp, wiping splatter off my face. Blink a couple times.

And Chivo returns. . . .

He rises from the muck that was himself, this version that's half-mist, half-solid. His eyes are all cartoon-huge, like he can't believe it either. He pats himself over while we watch. There's no blood, no mud, nothing wrong, his khakis still got their tight crease.

He glares at us one by one, last at me. "I'm gonna make you pay, *hoto.*"

"No, *vato,* you forget," Saint tells him. "It's time for your last dance."

And maybe Chivo was half-mist already, he looked so pale, but now any color left in his face goes to milk.

There's a sorta swirl like a whirlwind of fog and leaves, and the big whooshing sound of a waterfall, and this painted skeleton of a giant steps from the air as if coming through an invisible doorway.

He's larger than anyone and dressed sharp in *charro regalia,* with a *greca* suit sparkling to the sheen of ten thousand gems, and if you don't know already who he is, the top hat on his skull is tall as an eagle can fly. . . .

It's King Mictlantecuhtli, the top hat man, and when his great gold teeth clatter, the ground shakes.

The king of Mictlan glances to each of us with a smile you could drive a car through, and he makes a grand bow, and that top hat brushes along the ground, and everywhere it touches, marigolds sprout.

He turns to Chivo and holds out a long bone hand, inviting the dance to begin, and I see the appliqués at his jacket cuff are webs of crystal.

Chivo don't accept the hand.

The leader of the White Fence gang looks to piss himself, if ghosts could do such a thing, and he turns and bolts like his shoes are on fire.

Only there's no running from the underworld.

Chivo's run turns into a twirl, and he spins and spins backward to the King's hand, and with each spin, Chivo's face has a bit more marking to it, a dab of violet, a swirl of orange, a dash of teal.

Mictlantecuhtli clicks his boots together and circles Chivo, their fingers touching so dainty, one foot skimming forward, while the other slides back, then a reverse, and the toe and heel click together in this hop-and-stomp style I recognize from *ballet folklórico,* the kind of folk dancing I seen Abuelita do when I was a little boy.

And the mariachi ghosts of the graveyard emerge around us playing from their shadows, a roar of trumpeters and guitarists, a sweet racket of violins, a jangle of spurs and bells, and there's even a bass *guitarrón* that's almost as big as Mictlantecuhtli himself.

The King does a triple-step turn, and his knees are flexed just right, so he leaps and lands so silent, you could hear his shadow applaud.

I move back to Saint and Abuelita, who are whistling along.

Chivo screams as brilliant rosebuds stipple his brow, he flails his arms while curlicue stitches cross his cheeks, his foot skips forward, crosses behind the left, and he whirls graceful as a ballerina while his eyes spill green fumes. Mictlantecuhtli dips him, leaning in close to the cholo's face.

Chivo screams again, curses some string of insults, then swings a wild haymaker punch. Mictlantecuhtli was lifting Chivo back up while leaning to the music, and in such a way Chivo's punch knocked off the tall top hat.

That top hat, you know, you don't want to see what's beneath. . . .

It isn't no crown of a skull under there, no inside of a bleached bone cranium or nothin'; it's a door, this crumbling hole in an ageless wall, and we glimpsed through to Mictlan itself— Mictlan, where the skulls and marigolds don't ever dance; Mictlan, where the flames are made of sugar . . .

Chivo's screams dry up, I think right there he just quits. Mictlantecuhtli is done with him anyway. The King lifts Chivo in that big bone hand and lobs him like an underhand baseball through the opening in his skull.

Then the top hat goes back on, and Mictlantecuhtli makes a final bow to us before spiraling away in a cloud of fog and leaves.

And I stop holding my breath.

Abuelita makes a *clack-clack-clack* sound like she don't care no more, and Papá's shattered bones knit back together, and he stands up.

Papá clacks back to her, his eye sockets cast down, all sheepish and shit.

Abuelita clacks to Saint next. He winks and tells me, "Adios, *vato,* it's been swell, but the swelling's gone down."

Then he's gone, the sugar skull fallen still.

Abuelita last shakes a single bony finger at me. *Clack-clack-clack.*

And I'm like Papá, my eyes cast to the ground. "Yes, ma'am," and, "I'll be good, ma'am."

She gives one more *clack-clack-clack,* it's almost affectionate, and hands me the book of black magick.

Abuelita looks around, throws some gang sign of the underworld, and she and Papá vanish. Around me, other ghosts start fading too, and the moon above is normal again, I know there's not much time.

I turn to Santi, he's already growing dim, but I haven't made my peace. . . .

"Wait!" I say, only he just shakes his head all sad like I failed a test, and he dissolves.

I stare at his headstone, a slab of cold marble stabbing up from dark earth. There's only the echo of my name drifting on a breeze along with a sound could be clacking to remind why I'm here. . . .

"Wait for me, wait for me," I start praying. I didn't go through all this just to lose him again.

I find my switchblade lying on the ground, and though my arm's still throbbing, I scratch out the name of *Saint* from the sugar skull.

Maybe it's no good, maybe nothing happens. Maybe it's too late, the magick breaks at dawn, or all this ain't worth it, but I have to try, what I got brought here for. I don't want to start a new day all alone but for a mold of sugar inside a cemetery.

And even if it *does* work, I don't know how long he can stay, how strong is Abuelita's witchcraft, but I hope it's a lifetime, I hope he can hear me say every day what I should've told him for so long. . . .

I open the *Brujería Magia Negra* to a certain passage, and I read out loud while carving a new name into the skull's brow, and this time I make sure to get every letter right.

The Turn

Paul Kane

I T'S ALWAYS THE SAME. They can't help themselves.

When they hear it, when they hear *me,* they turn. That's the key. It's what leads to their downfall. You can't blame them, of course. It's natural; it's instinct. Something which, for generations, has kept them safe. A need to look, to see who might be behind them. Who or what might be following. It has kept people alive, in fact, which is ironic when you think about it. Because the same action now, tonight, is what will ensure their death.

The footsteps are all they can hear, nothing else. From a distance, then closer. Soft, then loud; so loud, they cannot ignore them. The one sign they are being trailed. No breath on their neck, no hand on the shoulder. Merely the footfalls, the staccato tapping on the pavement behind, keeping pace with them. Walking or running, it doesn't matter which.

At first, they might think it's an echo, as some have done before. In underpasses, beneath bridges, or even in alleyways where sound can bounce off the walls. They might stop, cock an ear to make sure. And, of course, the footsteps will pause at the same time . . . because I'm right behind them. They stop, *I* stop. I can't do anything until they look. It's the way it works. Don't ask me how or why.

Then they begin walking again, noticing the difference between the two sets of noises. That they're not at exactly the same time, they're out of . . . step a fraction. Another clue they are not alone. They might not be, even before I find them—target them. Though I prefer the more solitary soul, I have been known to make my presence known to couples from time to time. Holding hands, believing they are safe; the very notion of that tonight! Safe. No one is safe on this date. Not from me. Not if they turn, anyway.

It's the reason I take so many, because I can only operate one night out of every year. Again, it's the way things are—they are the rules. Like Santa coming at Christmas, except I take instead of give.

There are legends about me, if you care to look. If you can be bothered to do the research. Some say I'm one of the dead, but I don't count myself amongst their number. I am not a shade, waiting for the line to blur between this world and the next, although we do appear at the same time. The ones I select join their ranks, certainly, but I am not from them. Some have speculated I am Death itself, and perhaps there's a grain of truth to that one. Yet Death comes to everyone, and it can come at any time. Bound by its own rules, of course, but very different ones. Maybe, in my own way, I lighten Death's load for one night? It's not for me to comment. Some have said I am the spirit, the very embodiment of what this night is really about. That one I like, but again I cannot lay claim to the crown.

The simple truth is, I am none of these things. I am something else.

Bound by what I must do, what I have done for such a long

time now, I cannot remember anything else. I have no pity, show no compassion. I'm incapable of feeling love, remorse, or fear. I have no emotions whatsoever, just a purpose. A calling. And it calls, oh *how* it calls.

Some might say I am playing a game, toying with humanity. It's one way of looking at things, I suppose. If that is the case, then I am one of the few remaining who knows how to play it.

Take this person, for example. Dressed, as so many are tonight, as a monster—but a fictional one. Something from a culture I cannot possibly begin to understand. The garb is ludicrous, made as it is from rubber, as is the mask with its fangs and horns. This man has no idea what a *real* monster is. Has no idea why the tradition of hiding one's face even began: to hide from the monsters, from evil on this night. To disguise yourself so the dead will not recognize you. He has no idea of its heritage; all he cares about is having a good time—no doubt on his way to some gathering or another, already weaving as if he's been drinking.

I slot myself in behind him, mirroring his actions, though I am a straight line. An unerring manifestation of determination, never wavering in my chosen course of action. It takes him a little while to even realize I'm there, his senses dulled by the alcohol. He knows something isn't right but can't quite work out what. Wait for it. Yes, *there.* He looks down at those oversize feet, claws at the ends of each toe; realizes it cannot possibly be his own footsteps he's hearing. That it's someone else here with him, on the relatively quiet stretch of road.

Then a shake of the head; it's his imagination. Nothing more. Continue on, rush off to where the lights and music await. But he can't quite shift that nagging feeling, the *clack-clack-clack* like a fly buzzing round his head. Not him: someone else.

Someone behind him.

He stops suddenly, and I stop too. The man looks down again, then left and right. I wait, it won't take long. Not now. He'll look, he'll succumb any minute now. They always do. Up until then, I cannot lay a finger on him. But afterward ... oh, afterward ...

There it is. The turn. First of the head, glancing over his shoulder; then the whole body, facing me. Though I cannot see it, there is an expression of terror beneath his mask.

If only he'd known. If only he'd remembered the old ways, the ancient traditions. But then, nobody ever seems to these days; sad but true.

Oh well. Time for another turn now.

My turn.

TIM NOLAN KNEW about the old ways, the ancient traditions.

He should do, he'd been hearing about them since he was small. Ever since he could remember, he'd been taught the lessons, the rules. What to do, what not to do. What *never* to do. On this day, this night. Schooled in them by a grandmother who'd been more of a parent to him than anything, after his own had both died in a car accident—around this time of year, as a matter of fact. Off on a weekend break when a freak storm had caused the roads to become treacherous, caused Tim's father to skid and hit a tree.

"They never listened," his grandmother used to say. "I told them not to go. Oh, my sweet baby girl."

Perhaps it was why she focussed on the bad things that could happen during this particular holiday, fuelled by the fact she herself was originally from the old country. Whatever the reason, she'd passed her paranoia on. Told him curses were real, that ghouls and goblins and ghosts actually did walk the earth on October 31. Taught him the best way to ward off such evil, as well.

Fire was one of the most effective weapons, and for many

years in their garden a bonfire had burned brightly which he would help Gran to build. "That's right, nice and big. They won't dare come anywhere near us now, Timothy," she'd say. "Let them try!"

Turnips and potatoes with coals or candles inside them would also protect the front and rear of the property, a defensive ring. And as his grandmother prepared them, she would mutter spells, incantations handed down through the family line and which she would eventually pass on to him. More protection, while they would hole up inside as if under siege. Waiting out the night, ignoring any knocks at the door—which were more than likely children trick-or-treating, but you couldn't be too careful—waiting until dawn's early light when they would be safe again. And because he didn't know any different, it was simply normal to him.

Tim no longer built a bonfire in the garden, because for one thing he now lived in a much smaller property, outside of town. But he would fill the place with candles, the vast majority around the windows and doors. He'd utter the words his grandmother had taught him; it was no different to people saying their prayers at night ("Now I lay me down to sleep . . ."), though God had no part in this.

Tim would also stay inside no matter what, to be on the safe side. No parties or answering the door, he'd sit by an electric fire and wait, smoking one cigarette after the other. The rest of the year, he wasn't particularly superstitious. He didn't go out of his way to walk under ladders or break mirrors, but he wouldn't have lost any sleep over doing so either. No, this date was the focal point, and if he could get through unscathed, then it was almost as if he'd be protected for the rest of the year, like evil would leave him alone if it hadn't been able to find him then.

It was one of the reasons he'd remained alone all these years, especially after his gran had been diagnosed with dementia and had to go into a home. Tim had done his best to look after her as long as he could, but when she was becoming a danger not simply to herself, but to him and their neighbors . . . That time she'd turned the kettle on without filling it, for example, and almost burned the whole place to the ground; well, Tim had been given no choice. It had meant downsizing, but with his job as IT support for a small family firm, he'd more or less managed. Yet another reason he wasn't able to splash the cash and impress a potential partner.

Not that they would have understood this . . . whatever it was. Would sure as hell never join him when he hid away every year. People these days just wanted to celebrate, go out and get drunk dressed up as all sorts; it had made his grandmother so mad. "They've forgotten what it's all about," she would wail. "But that's what *they* want us to do. There are even toys in the supermarkets! Toys, Timothy! Singing devils, pitchforks, plastic pumpkins!"

It would not be the ideal environment for—thinking ahead, as he always did—a child. To have to explain why they couldn't go and join their friends out there having fun. What if something should happen to them? What then?

A child who existed in Tim's imagination. A family which could be snatched away as easily as his own had been. Cursed. Tricked.

Dead.

It was better to only have to look out for himself, as selfish as that sounded. As lonely as it sounded. Best not to drag anyone else into this, real or imaginary. He could control what happened in his life on that date, could please himself. Nothing, absolutely nothing, would ever get him to set foot out through the door and leave his protection behind.

Except this year there had been a call. Tim hadn't answered it, obviously, because those things out there that could do you harm were cunning. The more the world had changed, the more they changed with it, utilizing the technology that gave him his living every day (apart from this one, which he always took off work if it was a weekday).

He let the call ring off, used to ignoring the outside world. Arms folded and sitting next to the fire; it was probably those telemarketing people again, or a prankster who'd giggle down the line. But the answer phone had picked up, the caller leaving a message he couldn't fail to hear. A female voice, but deep.

"Hello, I'm trying to get through to a Mr. Timothy Nolan. Pick up if you're there." Tim twitched in the seat, took a drag on his cigarette, but didn't get up. "It's . . . This is Saint August's calling, by the way. I've . . . well, I'm afraid it's bad news."

Saint August's: where *she* was.

He leaned forward now, stubbing out the smoke, his other hand going to his chin and rubbing it frantically.

"It's about your grandmother," said the voice. "Look, if you're there, please answer. You need to get here as soon as possible.

"I'm afraid she's taken a turn for the worse."

NOW, I'M NOT saying they don't struggle, even after they've seen me.

It's instinct again, human nature. The need to protect oneself; I understand that. But ultimately it's pointless. Take this one, the jogger who didn't seem to care either way what night it was. Making her way through the park, colorful outfit so she could be seen—cap on her head with her blond hair fed through the gap at the back, swaying from side to side as she ran.

I waited until she slowed, taking a drink from the flask she had on her hip, before setting off again. I made sure she heard the footsteps though, before she put her earphones back on, otherwise she would have been lost to me. If you don't hear them, you don't get the urge to turn, and my chance is gone. Fortunately, she figured out someone was there quite quickly, spinning around and jogging backward, as if she didn't have a care in the world.

She did, however, not long afterward. More than she could cope with . . .

That was when the struggle began, but it didn't last very long. Never does. In the end, you can't fight the inevitable. And in the same way people have to turn, they also have to submit to me. To my attentions.

You can call what I do "killing," but there's a crudeness about the word which leaves a bad taste in the mouth. It's so much more than the ending of a life. *So much* more. In my own way, I turn them as well: from flesh to spirit. Relieving them of the burden of their self, free to be with those who have passed, to go to a place of eternal rest. No more worry, once the end has come. The woman had her cares, especially when she encountered me, but then—once it was over—she really did have none in this world. Nor the next.

I changed her, turned her. It's what I do best. It's the *only* thing I do, actually. At least today.

Is there a quota? you're probably wondering. A certain amount of people I need to fit in? Not as such, but I like to get to as many as I can. Some slip away from me, of course, whether by accident or sheer fate. One, I recall, heard me, but as he was about to turn, as I was about to take him, someone called to him from across the road—spoiling the moment. Thoughts of whoever might be behind vanished as he rushed to meet his friend, hand raised, no thought for what he missed out on by mere seconds. The turn, then the turn.

Another I remember tripped and fell headlong onto the ground in front of her before she could look. After that, she was obviously more concerned about how she might have injured herself than anything else, phone out and calling for assistance. My cue to leave. Quite apart from anything else, if she couldn't walk, how could I follow? How could I *make* my footsteps in the first place? When they are still, so am I.

It happens. You get used to it. But oh, the frustration. I'll admit to reaching out sometimes, even before they've looked back, even before they see me. Reaching, preempting the moment, though it leads to sorrow if they get away. The longing, the sense of what might have been.

Of missing out on the feeling that overwhelms me afterward: the heat, the glow filling me up. Not a feeding on the soul as such, but a by-product of it. Some kind of reward? I don't know. All I know is how good it feels. Better than any drink or drugs you people have ever experienced. A euphoria the likes of which—

But what's the point of trying to explain; you'll never understand. It is a process we're both a part of, *playing* our parts in, to be precise. Cause and effect, one thing leading to the next.

And there he is, another. My eye falling inevitably upon him as I silently move from one place to the next. There, wandering around out here, looking like a lost soul already. Looking like prey.

You. Yes, you! It's your time.

It's your turn now.

IT WASN'T A PRANK; it wasn't fairies or demons or anything else tormenting him.

Tim had rung Saint August's back and they'd confirmed the truth of it. His gran was dying.

"She's not been taking much food for a while now, as you know," the nurse on duty told him. Not the same woman who'd left the message, this one had a lighter tone. A bit too light, given the nature of the information she was imparting, like she was on the verge of laughter. "We've been trying her with fluids, and she did perk up a bit. But tonight . . ."

Tonight she was dying. On this day of all days, on this *date*. She was dying and she was alone—or at least in any way that counted. There were staff present, clearly, but not family; and that was the important thing. The woman, who had brought him up, fed and clothed him for so many years, kept him safe, was slipping away, and he wasn't there to even hold her hand as she did so.

"Are you sure?" Tim asked, and realized he sounded like the most heartless person ever. Do I have to come? Can't someone else deal with it? But it wasn't that, and if anyone would have understood, it was his gran. It was because of her he was the way he was, for Christ's sake!

There was a sigh at the other end of the line, then that laughing voice again: "Yes, we're sure, Mr. Nolan. *If* you're going to come, though, time is a factor."

Tim lowered the phone, looked around, as if waiting for someone to make the decision for him. But there was no one else; there hadn't been for a long time. Just him and—

If *you're going to come* . . .

He held the receiver to his ear again. "I'm on my way," he told the nurse.

What choice did he have?

Quickly Tim went around blowing out the candles and switched off his fire—he didn't want another disaster like the kettle incident—then grabbed his keys. Upon opening the door, he stood there for a moment or two, unable to move, not wanting to cross the threshold. Then he thought again of his gran, sucked up a breath, and ventured out. He almost forgot to close the front door behind him and lock it, in his haste to reach the relative safety of his car. It was only then he let out the breath he'd been holding.

His hands were shaking as he started the engine; almost pulled out and hit another vehicle, the driver blaring his horn at Tim. *Get it together,* he told himself. *Get it together. You need to do this, for Gran.*

Looking over his shoulder now, checking his blind spot instead of relying on his mirrors, he filtered into the traffic, thankful at least for the fact it wasn't raining.

By the time he was approaching town, however, it was clear that was the only thing he could be thankful for. The traffic had practically ground to a halt, a consequence of some kind of carnival going on up ahead; more of those celebrations his grandmother never approved of. After he'd moved about an inch in twenty minutes, Tim decided the best course of action might be to pull over and leave the car by the side of the road, make for the underground, which would take him more or less to the door of Saint August's.

. . . time is a factor.

So, locking up his car, he headed off in the direction he thought the station lay. But everything looked so different at night, especially tonight. Like the landscape was suddenly shifting around him. He was panicking, which didn't help: about the fact he was out here in the first place, the first time in as long as he could remember on this date; about the fact he needed to get to his gran. It would be safer there with her; it always had been by her side.

People dressed in all kinds of outfits, from cheesy movie monsters to media personalities and cartoon characters (what exactly did Marilyn Monroe or Daffy Duck have to do with anything?), kept bumping into him. Tim wanted to get away from them, get to somewhere quiet where he could think—because the noise was incredible! Too much to bear.

He ended up ducking into a side street he wasn't familiar with, emerging out the other end in an equally strange location, the lamps covered in bunting, the same bunting covering the street names everywhere, apparently. Tim raced across that road and up another. None of it looked right. And the more he searched for some kind of landmark he recognized, the more lost he became, the more his wish appeared to have been granted. To be away from the crowds, away from everything.

Tim lit up a cigarette, but even that didn't taste right, and he soon stamped it out again.

Station, he needed to be heading toward the nearest station. Tim took out his phone to check his location but promptly dropped it on the ground. He heard the crack of the screen even before he scooped it back up. Pressing the buttons did little good, nor did shaking it as a last resort.

Tim looked around again, as he had in his home. For someone to help him. But what few people there seemed to be around now were otherwise engaged: laughing, drinking, some brawling, which he steered clear of.

It was as he floundered around, looking either for a station or someone of sound mind to aid him in his quest, that he heard the sound. Maybe he'd been aware of it a little earlier but hadn't properly noticed it. Either way, he certainly did now.

Footsteps.

He could have sworn that in his bumbling search he'd just looked up the street he was heading down. That there had been no sign of anybody. So how—

Tim froze, a chill running through him which had nothing to do with the October weather. The sound of the footsteps stopped as well. He closed his eyes, then opened them again, swallowing dryly.

His mind flashed back to his grandmother, but it wasn't because he was afraid he'd reach her too late. No, this was a memory of something she'd said a long time ago: one of the things she'd told him when she'd been arming her Timothy against the evil.

"If, and I do mean if," she'd said to him, holding up one of her already wizened fingers, "you find yourself outside and alone on that night—for whatever reason—and you hear someone behind you, you hear footsteps, whatever you do, don't turn."

"Why?" the younger version of himself had asked.

"Because," his grandmother had said, moistening her lips, something the nurses had had to do for her later on in her life, "because you really don't want to see what's behind you."

"I don't?"

"No, you don't. And if you happen to do such a thing, young Timothy, death will soon follow."

He'd swallowed back then as well, throat as dry as his grandmother's lips. As dry as it was right now. Tim took a tentative step, then another and another.

The sound was echoed back at him twofold. A darker twin. *But don't look for a shadow,* he reminded himself. That was almost as dangerous. *Don't look* at all! *Keep your head fixed, looking forward. Keep looking for the station. Remember Gran.*

Fire, that's what he needed. Protection. And then he remembered his lighter, the one in his pocket. Tim dug into his jeans again and fished it out, flicking it open and sparking a flame. He held it out to the side of him, a warning. Hoping the footsteps, which were getting closer by the meter, would die off. Hoping the thing following him would leave him alone.

It's just another reveler, he told himself. Tim knew he was being silly, and at any other time of year he might have believed it. But if he did, he would have to admit that everything he'd done all these years had been a waste of time as well. That there had been no need to barricade himself in; no such thing as tricks, as curses. As monsters.

Things you couldn't explain. Things like whatever was behind him, whatever he felt sure was stalking him.

But it can't do anything, Tim reminded himself. *It can't do a thing unless you—*

TURN, DAMMIT!

This is getting old. It had been a novelty at first, the lost soul, the wanderer I'd taken for an easy mark, who had actually turned out to be more clued up than I thought. Imagine that.

He'd resisted, even *after* he realized I was there. The man in the jacket and jeans, short brown hair; unremarkable in every way. Except one. He knew the traditions, knew what they meant. Even if he didn't fully believe in them, he was prepared to give them the benefit of the doubt. It's what has saved him so far, because I cannot act unless he looks. He knows that.

The lighter had been a nice touch. Fire, to ward away the ghosts, the spirits. Would have worked if I were one of those, which I think we've firmly established I'm not. I'm not afraid of fire. The people I hunt could be *on* fire for all I care. It wouldn't stop me from doing what I do. What I've always done.

I'm beginning to think this lost soul has always done what *he's* doing as well: protected himself. I've certainly never seen him out and about on my travels. I wonder.

Doesn't matter. What does it matter? All that matters is he sees me. I don't exist until he does.

But it doesn't look like he's going to bite, however long I follow him. However close I get. No, he has to. He *has* to. Unless they're interrupted, they always—

Come on, come on.

Bastard! A little peek, that's all I'm asking. It's human nature; it's instinct.

Well, now it's become a matter of pride. A principle at stake.

A . . . challenge. That's right, this is a challenge—and it's been a long time since that's happened, let me tell you!

Right. Get in nice and tight, match those movements, those footfalls of his. As close as I can possibly get without being right on top of him, without actually touching him, as if I can.

Come on, come on. Just—

TURN.

It was killing him. Knowing what was there, what he would never be able to escape this night once it had a fix on him. Even if Tim reached a station, even if he made it to his grandmother's side, wouldn't he simply be leading the evil to her?

He didn't know what to do.

. . . time is a factor.

The lighter hadn't achieved anything, apart from burning his fingers, so he'd snapped it closed again. He didn't need protection from anything else when he had this thing on his tail. Nothing would dare come near him.

Tim began to imagine what it might look like, the creature, the being his gran wouldn't even name let alone describe. Fangs, horns? No, too clichéd. Too human, if that made sense. It would be something nobody would be able to imagine, something that came out once a year to . . . what, feed? Was that what it would do? Eat him, like the wolf in that fairy tale?

Or something else? Was it going to do another unimaginable thing if he simply—

No. Don't focus on that, because it wasn't going to happen. Tim wasn't stupid, could keep this up forever if need be.

However, part of him was desperate to know. Not only what it was, this thing—but also whether all he'd ever been taught, all he'd ever done on this night and the rest of it, had been worthwhile. Had been worth it. The loneliness, keeping people at arm's length (and what kind of life had that been, when you thought about it?).

He gritted his teeth as the footsteps grew louder and louder. So loud, he wasn't even sure if they were real anymore, or in his head. More tricks, another curse.

Please, no ... he said to himself. It was too much. He couldn't—

And then, suddenly, as if it was out of his control, it was happening.

He was looking over his shoulder. He had turned, like he was always going to do. Like he was destined to do, apparently. The same as everyone else.

Tim let out a whimper when he saw what was behind him. A whimper that soon became a laugh. More of a laugh than the nurse's breathy tones on the phone: a chuckle even when confronted with his stalker.

Because there, behind him, was a man. Just a man.

He had his hood up against the cold, head tilted downward, but Tim could see clearly it was a man's face underneath. Laughing again, and turning fully around, he let out a sigh of relief. "Oh, thank God!" he said. All that worry, that concern and it had only been—

Tim paused when he saw the man's expression. There was something odd about it, something dangerous. More dangerous than imagined terrors, because he was here and they weren't. But before he could do anything else, like run or defend himself, *protect* himself, the blade was out and up, into him at a point where the man knew it would do the most damage, and quickly. Two more stabs followed, and his attacker stepped back, leaving Tim confused, clutching his wounds, hands coming away wet and black with blood.

Tim's vision was blurring as he too stepped backward, staggering actually as he felt the life draining out of him. And he could have sworn as he did so that he saw something . . . something else.

Then he was falling, dropping. Dying. This man had turned him, just as he had turned for the man. Transformed him into . . .

Yes, there, now he could see it. More clearly than he had ever seen anything with his old eyes, now practically useless and closing. He saw the streets filled again with people, but these weren't revelers; they were those who had passed. Those who had been allowed to "visit," if only for one night. Tim smiled, or at least he thought he did. Because there, not too far away, was his gran—and she wasn't alone. Two figures stood with her, by her side, beckoning.

His family.

Tim moved, though he had no idea how. Toward the shapes, the glowing shapes that had been indistinct at first but were becoming more solid by the second—certainly more solid than anything else around him in what he used to call the real world. Tim beamed again, not frightened anymore. No longer a lost soul.

He thought briefly about what had happened to him, about what he was leaving behind back there. What he'd seen. But he didn't look, didn't actually care anymore. What was in front of him was more important than everything he was leaving behind, so he wouldn't do that no matter what.

Tim wasn't about to turn.

I TURN AWAY from the body.

He will be the last one tonight. Time . . . time to leave; my cue. But as I hurry on my way, tucking my weapon out of sight, head down to avoid being seen by any cameras, I suddenly have regrets. Not about what I've done tonight, because that's what I always do. What I have been doing for so many years, ever since childhood. Ever since I was taught it by my grandfather. No, not that . . .

I suddenly regret the act. Pretending to be something I'm not. Something powerful, when I'm far from that. Then I think about the look on the man's face. Not the fear I usually see in my victims' eyes as they're murdered (another crude word, but then, we're not pretending anymore, are we?), but something else.

Frightened of something else he'd seen.

Something I'm curious about, but now terrified of myself. That and the footsteps I can hear behind. And I know I have to look, can't help myself. I *must* see whatever he saw. It's human nature; it's instinct.

We always have to turn.

Jack

Pat Cadigan

"DARK TIMES DRAW dark spirits," my mother says, looking at me significantly. "That's one of the solid truths in this world."

"Maybe in all worlds," my grandmother adds, with the same look.

Being the dutiful seventh daughter of a seventh daughter, I nod patiently, as if I haven't heard this a hundred times a day for the last two months. I'm trying to cut them some slack—they're both mothers, and mothers always worry. But they're like I've never gone solo on All Souls' Day till now. Granted, I've never done *this* job before, but for crying out loud, I'm not a kid in the first flush of talent; I'm thirty-one. Both my mother and grandmother were younger when they did this for the first time—ten years younger, in Mother's case. I've taken over a lot of the family business so Grandma can retire. This is what I signed up for. I'm ready; I've got this.

.   .   .

BY THREE THIRTY in the afternoon, I'm in the cemetery dressed in groundskeeper drag pretending to look for leaves to rake. I hadn't planned to get there so early, but I had to get away from all the last-minute fussing and instructions before they attracted a jinx.

It's such a nice day for all the souls that I'm glad I came early. The sky's clear, and the afternoon is still alive and well, too early for the shadows to lengthen. The air's got a chilly bite, but it's not windy, so there's not a whole lot to rake. I saunter around in my jacket and overalls, my hat pulled low, rake over my shoulder.

All Souls' Day isn't a busy time here the way it is in more traditional areas. Cemetery traffic is practically nonexistent on the natural world side of the veil. There's more on the supernatural side, of course—in spots where the trees still have enough leaves to give shade, I catch movement in my peripheral vision, souls flitting from one place to another. They know I'm not a real groundskeeper, but I feign complete unawareness of spirits abroad, partly to show them my business here doesn't concern them and partly to get well into character. I'm no method actor, but it takes more than five minutes to be credible.

Eventually I make my way to the area where monuments tend to be ostentatious, if not downright ridiculous. This is also where the crypts are located, including the Perlmutters', which has seen a great deal of activity on the part of Anna May Perlmutter, the latest late Perlmutter to be interred there. According to signs and portents as interpreted by Grandma, it's also going to see some serious trouble, drawn there by Anna May's inability to rest in peace.

It's still early, but what the hell, I'm here, so I check all three crypts and several of the showier monuments. Everything's okay—no vandalism, no leftover occult detritus and/or beer cans the real maintenance staff missed, no sign anyone's tried breaking in. But it's not so much people breaking *in* I'm concerned about.

It's pretty tidy around the Perlmutter crypt, but ruffling the grass with the charmed rake reveals traces of Anna May as far as thirty feet from the crypt. Although they're not that recent—from what I can tell, she hasn't been outside in several hours, which is kind of strange for a spirit who's been acting up so much.

Maybe it was the daylight—some of the newly dead find it overwhelming after a while. Or maybe the saints intimidated her. A lot of them get pretty puffed up, especially the martyrs. Although, who can blame them? All Saints' Day is for those who don't have their own commemorative day of the year, and hardly anyone other than theology scholars know who they are.

My mind is still wandering when I spot a car moving slowly along the road about a hundred feet down from where I am. I saw it cruising around earlier, slowing down, speeding up slightly, slowing down again. The two people in the front seat were looking for something, maybe an interesting gravestone to take a rubbing on. Or they could be looking for a particular grave.

You would think what with the Internet and websites and practically everything being online, no one would ever drive around a cemetery looking for someone's grave. And you would be *so* wrong. It never occurs to some people they can actually call the cemetery office and ask. Like they don't even know cemeteries *have* offices, with live people working there. Do they think when someone dies, a grave magically digs itself and it'll be waiting for them after the funeral, complete with headstone?

Maybe they do, for all I know. People can be so damned strange, and just when you think you've seen everything, someone'll show you a whole new level of bizarre. But nothing weirds the human animal out like death. Even the steadiest, most down-to-earth hardheads can totally lose their compos mentis where death is concerned.

And that's just the living. The dead are worse.

Especially the recently deceased, "recently" being less than a full calendar year, usually a lot less. In general, the longer people have been dead, the less they crave life. How long varies with the individual, but eventually even the most stubborn haunts will accept that the realm of the living is out of their reach.

The problem is, this isn't *always* true.

Every year, there are a few days when the border between the natural and the supernatural worlds gets less solid, less real, less . . . *there,* and nobody knows why. There are all kinds of theories but no genuine information. It's kind of like what we have instead of quantum mechanics. The natural world has spooky action at a distance; the supernatural set has border theory.

Personally, I think it really *is* quantum mechanics—there's some kind of wave function that's supposed to collapse but doesn't—it just stops. Only temporarily, but the repercussions go beyond the level of single photons all the way up to the world humans experience so that something that's usually real becomes not so real.

Hey, does that really sound *less* plausible than "just because it's Samhain"?

NIGHTFALL TAKES ME BY SURPRISE. I know it's getting dark earlier every day now, but something seems off. I consult my phone; the almanac says sunset's at 17:36, full dark by 18:00, give or take, so it shouldn't look like the middle of the night now, at 17:45. Which makes this one hell of a gigantic glamour. It must have taken him ages to build up that much juice. Well, time is the one thing he's not short on. Time and darkness.

My mother phones at 17:46. "What does it look like where you are?"

"Midnight," I whisper. "You?"

"We're right on the edge of the illusion—looks *very* weird, like a Norway night in June. Of course, nobody on the natural side's noticed. Where are you?"

"Right by the Perlmutter necro-mansion. Nothing'll get by me."

"Don't call it that, it's a crypt. Is there—"

"Something's happening—gotta go." I hang up before she starts telling me more stuff she told me a thousand million times already. Then I see I didn't tell a white lie after all.

The tiny, round, yellow-orange light bobbing along in the dark is normally imperceptible to the living, but I have a charm—or maybe I should call it an app, since I keep it on my phone with the non-magical software. The charm/app can also detect the siren song emanating from the light. I don't really hear that so much as feel it; if I had fillings in my teeth, they'd be vibrating. *I'm* vibrating, all over, with the sensation that something really, really wonderful is about to happen, and if I can get near it, I'll get the one thing I want most.

Or rather, what I'd want most if I were dead and unhappy about it: life. But not *ordinary* life, not the kind with mortality preinstalled. The siren song says this is ceaseless life, uninterrupted and unending. Continual life, incessant life, enduring and abiding life. Nonstop, perennial, perpetual life with no death at all, none whatsoever, just 100 percent life. Life and only life. Life, life, and more life. All life, all the time.

Everybody thinks that would be the most wonderful thing, and for all I know, that might even be true. What if you never had to worry about running out of time? You could do everything you ever wanted to do, and if it didn't work out or if you simply got bored, you wouldn't have wasted your best years going down a dead end. You could just move on to something else without worrying about time's winged chariot hurrying near.

But that's not how things work here. On this plane of existence, all life spans are finite, and death is mandatory. No matter what side of the veil you're on, natural or supernatural, each life owes a death. Even inanimate objects meet entropy. It's science—the laws of thermodynamics. It's also a big philosophy thing, with people spending their whole finite lives studying it.

But really, what it all comes down to is, you can't get something for nothing. For the same reason things don't pop into existence from nowhere or vanish without a trace, you can't live forever. Period.

Except for the loopholes. There are *always* loopholes.

The only place you'd find loopholes for the first two things, however, is in the heart of a black hole. You'd have to be fast, though—they don't last but a zillionth of a second.

The loophole for living forever is worse.

Actually, it's not even so much a loophole as it is an extremely nasty bit of legerdemain. If you fell for it, you'd regret it for all eternity and hate yourself for just as long. I wouldn't call that living, but maybe it doesn't look so bad if you're desperate and dead.

I ONCE OVERHEARD a woman who'd just been to a funeral say something to the effect that the dead person's troubles were over. I didn't even have to look at her to know she lived only in the natural world.

Natural world people have it easy—they only have to make sure the physical remains of dead people end up where they're supposed to. They have a wide variety of ceremonies and rituals, but all of them, without exception, are for the living. I don't mean that disparagingly. Bereaved people deserve to be comforted. But *we're* the ones who have to deal with the spirits of the dead, and it's not easy.

Say, for instance, Anna May Perlmutter's family and friends remember her in their prayers (those that say them), and her grandchildren ask God to bless her every night when they kneel beside their beds under the approving eye of Mommy and/or Daddy. That's all very nice, even admirable, but none of those prayers, no matter how pure and sincere, would keep Anna May from being swindled out of her afterlife.

That's *my* job. It's part of the family business, which has been operating for centuries.

Anna May Perlmutter died a week and a half ago at eighty, and according to the profile my mother put together from her obit and information gleaned from various other sources, she's definitely not happy about it. Anna May Perlmutter didn't just let life happen to her, she participated. Twenty years ago, she beat breast cancer and never looked back. When she developed high blood pressure, she always took her medication, although there was still too much salt in her diet. She probably didn't expect the stroke that took her out in one fell swoop (no one ever does).

No doubt she had felt it immediately when the boundary separating natural and supernatural started to thin out. The newly dead feel its decrease in *there-ness* most keenly. The process starts at the official end of All Saints', one second after midnight, and it continues all day. Souls that wander before the sun comes up are usually the lost ones—nobody knows where they go or what they do when they're not roaming around in the predawn dark, not even them. It's all very weird and creepy. I've only been in a graveyard before sunrise on All Souls' Day a few times, helping Grandma gather magical items to replenish the pantry, and it left a bad taste in my head for days afterward.

If Anna May Perlmutter went out among the predawn spirits, it wasn't for long. Maybe she thought she was saving her energy by staying in the crypt while the boundary between life and death grew progressively less substantial. Maybe she was hoping it would disappear altogether or at least that it would get weak enough locally for her to force her way all the way through to life again.

There's an old story about how someone who'd died far too young actually managed to break through the boundary and reenter the living world. Supposedly the living air spontaneously regenerated the original physical body, and the person went home to be reunited with loved ones and lived to be a hundred.

Needless to say, this is an urban legend. It probably arose from stories about people who'd been mistakenly pronounced dead suddenly sitting up and asking for food or drink (something that happened often enough in the days before modern medicine to make people justifiably nervous about being buried alive). That isn't the same as genuine resurrection, but the distinction is lost on the desperate dead, who seize on the story like it was on the *CBS Evening News* a minute before they died.

There are creatures who home in on that kind of desperation, like a shark knowing when there's blood in the water. The natural world has con artists and phishers, bastards who have a talent for finding the most vulnerable and picking them clean. On the supernatural side, we've got all kinds of nasty creatures, from stingers and biters, more nuisance than anything, to genuine dangers like poison vessels and soul suckers. Not to mention wannabe tricksters, who are really just losers with a mean streak.

And then there's Jack.

Jack is the guy who knows where the line is and never considers *not* crossing it. He's like that one friend who doesn't simply have to win all the time, he—or she—has to win ugly, even if it backfires. Jack is never *not* in trouble, and he's always on the lookout for someone, anyone, he can off-load his problems onto.

And just like Grandma foresaw in the signs and portents,

he's coming this way. Anna May Perlmutter isn't the only desperate dead person wanting to beat the Reaper, but for some reason, Jack seems to think she's the most promising.

THE ROUND LIGHT is close enough now that it looks more like a lantern—the light shines out from top and bottom and both sides. Jack carved it himself and very skillfully, too. He's had centuries of practice, but what's really impressive is, it's a turnip. It's a *big* turnip, easily the size of a small pumpkin or gourd, but recognizable, with a handle woven from green turnip tops.

The turnip was what they used to carve way back in the day and across the sea. The pumpkin was a New World vegetable, and it had yet to be introduced to the land whose misfortune it was to produce Jack. Some say that was Ireland, some say Scotland or England. At various times, Jack has claimed each of those in turn as well as others. He can produce authentic-sounding accents from anywhere in Europe. Grandma said the first time she met him, he pulled off a convincing Magyar.

The lantern stops twenty feet from the front of the crypt. Jack is only a vague shape behind the bright light. Bright and warm—I can feel heat cutting through the cold of the November night. Then the lantern starts moving slowly to the right. I can hear Jack's feet in the grass. The warmth recedes, but only a little. The burning ember in Jack's turnip (how deceptively silly that sounds!) never abates; the longer it remains in one place, the warmer everything becomes. If Jack stayed here long enough, the air itself would catch fire.

Fortunately, he's not allowed to do that. He has to keep moving, him and his turnip, always following nightfall, never staying anywhere long enough to become familiar, to be remembered, or to see a sunrise.

I know, you're thinking of *The Flying Dutchman,* right? Same idea, different details. *The Flying Dutchman* is actually a sailing ship, complete with captain and crew. I don't know what their deal is, but it probably involves hubris. There are lots of stories about immortal travelers, most of them very romantic.

But not Jack's. Nobody ever found his story at all romantic back when it was widely known. Nowadays, it's pretty obscure, but he's still one of the Top Ten Dangers Before *and* After Death, and it would be a mistake to underestimate him.

I definitely won't make that mistake. I've been preparing for my first encounter with Jack for the last year. My mother and my grandmother have been coaching me. I've studied the lore. I know this guy, backward and forward. Jack is a clever little bastard who outsmarted himself and got what he deserved, and he's *still* trying to wiggle out of it. But I won't let that happen. Even though I'm starting to feel so anxious, my nerves are turning into holy rollers.

The light starts coming back toward me. It's getting really warm now. I want to take off my jacket except I'd probably rattle every bush and tree within fifty feet. Then suddenly, he says, "Oh, *there* you are!"

For a second, I think he's talking to me. But then I see a woman by the side of the Perlmutter crypt. She's wearing an evening dress that's mostly black sequins, accented with lines of silver beads. Her short, curly hair keeps changing from red to brown to white; she apparently can't decide how old she is now. Definitely not eighty, though.

"You can see me?" she says warily.

"And hear you. You've been calling to me since last night, Anna May."

She starts to move toward him, then catches herself. "How? I don't even know who you are."

"We're family. I'm your many-many-times-great-uncle Jack. So sorry you're dead."

Well, that explains why he's going for Anna May instead of any of the other desperate souls in the vicinity. Jack's so completely focused on Anna May, they can't get closer than the farthest reach of the light coming from the lantern. Not an enormous distance—far enough to keep anyone from interfering, close enough to find another sucker if Anna May won't bite. But he seems pretty sure that the family connection will make her more receptive. And I just have to wait—by law, I can't intervene unless or until he actually starts trying to talk her into something.

Anna May leans forward but still doesn't move toward him. "You're the first, uh, the first one I've been able to communicate with. Everyone else around here sounds like—well, I don't know what. Like they're all speaking in tongues."

This can happen with the newly dead, especially if they're actively resisting the idea of being dead, like Anna May. It probably wouldn't make her feel any better to know they don't understand her, either.

"So maybe you can tell me," she goes on. "Is this *it*? Does it ever get more interesting? Does it ever get interesting at all? What am I doing wrong?"

Jack holds the turnip lantern to one side and raises it a little higher to give her a good look at his handsome smile. "I'm afraid I couldn't say. You see, I'm *not* dead."

Anna May actually draws back a little.

"Really. No lie. Come closer and see for yourself." Jack stamps his feet to show her he's mashing down the grass and making footprints, something souls can't do, at least not those only ten days dead. He's wearing an expensive Edwardian-style suit. Somewhere, someone's mortal vessel is decomposing in the nude.

Anna May hesitates, then approaches slowly, gliding, more

like ice-skating than walking. Her age is still fluctuating, but Jack keeps on giving her the old I'm-*such*-a-handsome-rascal smile and never bats an eye. Three feet away from him, she stops short and says, "I can *smell* you!"

Whatever Jack was expecting her to do or say next, this wasn't it. I'm thrown off balance myself. The dead can be unpredictable, but Anna May just won the Never-Heard-That-One Award.

Jack's mouth opens and closes a few times before he finally finds his voice. "I do hope I'm not giving offense."

"It's your suit. I can smell the wool. That's strongest. I can also smell the polish on your shoes. And something else."

"Waterproofing treatment," Jack says confidently.

"No, you stepped in something."

I can't see her expression too well, but Jack's isn't very happy. I'm wondering if I'll have to intervene at all. Anna May might be too smart for him.

Early on in his career as an itinerant bastard, Jack had a much harder time finding anyone who'd even listen because so many people knew about him. Several generations passed before he could get any takers. Whenever he did, the devil himself had to put things right again, and quickly, before Jack managed to sneak into heaven or hell. That would have sealed the deal so it could never be undone—Jack would be free and clear and whoever he'd conned into taking the turnip lantern would be screwed.

Anna May looks up from Jack's shiny, smelly shoes to the lantern in his hand, to his face, and then suddenly back to the lantern.

"Is that a—a *turnip*?" she asks incredulously.

"At one time, that's all people had." He sounds smooth, but there's a little nervous undertone in his voice. Or maybe that's my wishful thinking. "Back in the old country, that is."

"And which old country would that be?" Anna May asks.

Jack oozes some more charm. Is it working on her? I don't see how anyone would buy it, but I'm not desperate and dead. "I lost my accent ages ago. You couldn't possibly guess."

Is the son of a bitch flashing her an aura? I use another charm app on my phone; sure enough, he's glowing emerald green. Anna May doesn't see it, but she can feel the suggestion.

"I'm tempted to say Ireland," she says finally, "but I don't know why. And I don't think that's right."

"How many folks from the auld sod have ye met, darlin'?"

"You sound like someone in a musical comedy," Anna May says, laughing a little. "I don't believe you."

He drops the lilt. "Then tell me—what *do* you believe?"

Anna May gives another small laugh. "Can you be more specific?"

"Do you believe in eternal life? As in being able to live forever?"

"I don't think it matters one way or the other, seeing as how I'm *dead* forever."

"What if you're wrong about that? What if life could be yours just for the asking?"

"You mean resurrection?" Anna May is skeptical. "I thought that was just at the end of the world." Then she whirls around, peering through the darkness. "Is *that* why it got dark so early— it's the end of the world?" She looks up at the sky. "I thought it would be a lot noisier. Or is this just the preliminary? How long before things really get going?"

"Calm down, dear, it's *not* the apocalypse. Not that one, anyway," Jack says. "In fact, this could be the beginning—the beginning of something amazing, more wonderful than anyone ever dreamed of—for *you*. And *only* you—"

That's my cue. I stroll out of the shadows holding up my own lantern—my cell phone, with the flashlight app. "You're busted,

Jack. Take your turnip and hit the road before you overstay your welcome."

Anna May Perlmutter goes pale, and I mean all over so that for a few moments, she's barely visible before fading back in again, looking like *she's* seen a ghost.

Jack blinks at me, genuinely astonished. "How old are *you*— twelve? Kid, you've got lousy parents, turning you to witchery before you're old enough to marry."

Witchery? He's really dating himself with that one. "I'd be flattered," I say, "except at your age, everybody looks twelve. Ms. Perlmutter, you need to move away from him."

Anna May Perlmutter's appearance suddenly settles at what could be her late forties or early fifties. "Why?" she asks, suspicious.

"He means you harm. I only want to protect you."

She laughs at me, in a hard, unkind way. "You're a little late, honey. I'm *dead*."

"Actually, you're not all *that* dead. Not as dead as *she* wants you to be." Jack gestures with the lantern. "Not yet."

Anna May looks from him to me and back again. "What's *that* supposed to mean?" She turns to me with a troubled frown. "Were you *spying* on me? What kind of person spies on *dead people?*"

"I wasn't *spying*." I can't help feeling a little impatient, even though I know it's just Jack's influence. Family is family, no matter how many generations separate them. "I don't want you to get talked into something you'll regret forever."

"I. Am. *Dead*," the woman says, enunciating like I'm an idiot. "What's *he* gonna do—kill me?"

"I'll explain, but I'd rather there be more space between you and him," I tell her. "Even just two feet."

"Or two miles," Jack says.

"Or ten miles. I vote for ten miles," I say.

Jack looks at Anna May, who hasn't budged. "Sorry, kid, you're outvoted," he says, breezy and dismissive. "Now, go play with a poppet or something, the grown-ups are trying to have a conversation."

Anna May hasn't moved away, but she hasn't moved toward him, either. Or toward me. If she were alive, she'd think we were both lunatics. But she's not alive.

And Jack is family. It's extremely difficult to obstruct a family connection when one relative is desperate, dead, and looking for a way out of the grave, and the other one seems to be offering just that very thing. Anna May is not a naïf; she knows if something's too good to be true, it probably is. But that's a fact of life, and she's dead. She's dead and he's Uncle Jack, and all bets are off.

"I've lived so long, you wouldn't believe it," Jack is saying.

"Tell me how long, and I'll decide if I believe it or not."

"Go ahead, tell her," I say carelessly. "She's family, she has a right to know."

But that's the last thing Jack wants to do, and I know why—it might sound so utterly absurd to her, it'll snap her right out of his influence. It won't matter how much he swears and promises and pleads it's the truth, she'll be done with him and he'll have to hit the road. If he stays too long in one place, the ember will burn through the turnip and he'll have to carry the fiery thing in his pocket. It won't kill him, or even do much damage, but it'll be a serious pain till he can find a farmers' market open at night (he can't shop indoors; they always throw him out for smoking).

"Really you won't believe it," he says after a bit.

"Give me a ballpark figure," Anna May says. "Half a century? A whole one?"

"Much, *much* longer than that," I say, enjoying this. I can't wait to write it up after I get home. Too bad I didn't get it all on video. Although it's not too late; I take out my phone, hoping I can catch her reaction when Jack tells her he's 1,537 years old. It should be priceless. Normally the dead don't show up on video, but I have a charm app for that, too. Sometimes it's hard to believe smartphones are actually tech from the natural world side of the veil; you can cram in all kinds of charms and spells as software. What a great time to be alive.

"Suppose I said I'm a little over fifteen?" Jack says coyly.

"Fifteen what?" Anna May says. "Leap years?"

Jack just smiles. After fifteen centuries, the bastard figured out how to forestall giving her a straight answer. He's starting to make the devil seem like a lovable old rogue. Hell, he makes *Richard Nixon* seem like a lovable old rogue.

"Forget it," Anna May tells him, sounding really annoyed now. "I can do the math—leap years would make you a lot younger than I am. Or was."

"All right, it isn't leap years," Jack purrs, trying to come off as mischievous.

Anna May's not having any. "Then what is it?" she demands. "Fifteen *what*? I insist you tell me right now, or this conversation is over."

No getting around that one; Jack has to answer truthfully. "Centuries," he sighs.

Just because Jack has to tell the truth on request, however, doesn't mean *I* can't call him a liar. "*Centuries?*" I laugh. "You expect anyone to believe that? The lady's *dead,* not stupid."

"Shush, both of you!" Anna May snaps. "I'm trying to think."

Jack has the nerve to smirk at me. If Anna May's trying to think after his ridiculous-sounding claim, it means he's still in with a chance.

"Fifteen-plus centuries," Anna May says finally. "If that's true, why quit now? Who's after you?"

"I haven't an enemy in the world," he says smoothly. It's true, but not the whole truth. He doesn't have any friends, either. He's nothing to anyone. "And while I could easily go on living for another fifteen hundred years, lately I've been thinking that's rather . . . well, selfish."

"Really." Anna May sounds completely neutral.

"Really. Then I just happened to hear of your passing, and I thought, why not keep it in the family?" That smile is a thousand watts. I'd like to punch it, but I'm magically restrained from committing physical violence in the absence of physical danger, even though it would be in the service of good. It's something about might corrupting right.

"So just hypothetically," Anna May says, "how would it work? How do you transfer your . . . uh . . ."

"Extended life span," Jack says helpfully.

"How do you transfer that to me? And what will happen to you? Will you suddenly crumble into dust? Or do I get your body while your soul goes somewhere else?"

"Oh, you get your own body back," Jack tells her.

"I should have known there was a catch!" Anna May draws back. "Being eighty forever? Forget it!"

"You *won't* be eighty," Jack says quickly. "When you live forever, there's no old age. And no illness. People who live forever don't get sick. They don't even catch colds. No allergies, either."

I can see that sounds a lot better to her. "I suppose I'll have to move every few years so people won't notice I'm not getting older," she says. I doubt she even knows she said *I'll,* like it's no longer hypothetical.

"Who knows, you might even decide you'd rather be on the move," Jack says. "Most people never get to travel as much as they want to. All the interesting places you could see, the people you could meet—I can't even begin to tell you."

"I always did want to see the world," Anna May says, more to herself.

"Not like that you don't," I tell her.

"Are you still here?" Jack says to me. "If you really want to argue with someone, go find a bar and pick a fight with a stranger. This is private family business."

"No, it's a con," I say to Anna May. "If you go for it, you'll be in a world of more hurt than you ever imagined."

"Ever had chemotherapy and radiation?" she asks me evenly. "Didn't think so. Check back with me if you ever do. Then you can talk about a world of hurt."

"You're not thinking clearly," I say. "Ask him about how he's been making a living for the last fifteen-hundred-plus years, ask him how many places he's lived—"

She tells me to shush. To Jack, she says, "Why are you *really* offering this to me?"

"I told you. I felt—"

"Selfish, yeah, yeah, heard you the first time. It's gotta be more than that. Is the Mob after you? Or a bunch of jealous husbands? Are you a fugitive from the law? What happened that's so bad you'd rather die?"

"It's not that I'd rather *die,*" Jack says carefully. "I just have a feeling deep in my heart that it's time—long past time—to pass the torch. Or in this case, the lantern. And as I said, I want to keep it in the family."

"You still haven't told me what'll happen to you. Don't you know?"

"Not for certain." He practically simpers. "If I don't move on to the afterlife immediately, I'll live out a normal life span as a mortal."

"You won't find some way to come after me in a couple of years because you changed your mind?"

"I swear to you, by all that is, ever has been, or ever will be that I'll never try to take the lantern back," he says cheerfully. "Now come here and stand in front of me—no, facing away—"

She's going for it. In seven times seven generations, nobody in our family business has ever failed to prevent Jack's tricking someone living or dead into taking the lantern from him. If it happens on my watch, I'll be making it up to the devil for decades, even if he manages to catch Jack before he can sneak into the afterlife. And if he doesn't—

If Jack somehow slips past all the safeguards and alarms and sentinels and whatever else they have to keep trespassers out, I won't be the only one who pays for it, it'll be my entire family, past, present, and future. They'll yank my forebears out of their afterlives like mad dentists on a teeth-pulling binge. Future generations will find themselves born into disgrace and futility; most will probably never know why, and when death comes, it will be no respite, just more misery.

Don't think for a moment I'm exaggerating. The devil is still as mad at Orpheus for trying to break Eurydice out as he was the day it happened. And Orpheus didn't even get away with it. Or how about "Prometheus"—does that name ring any bells? You know, the guy who can't hang onto his own liver because *a frickin' eagle eats it every day*? Which I happen to know is no picnic for the eagle, either.

Any of those things could happen to me and my family, and being dead won't save any of them. I have to do something. What do I do?

"—put your hands right where mine are," Jack is saying.

"But they'll go right through yours," Anna May says. "We can't touch."

"Don't worry about that," Jack says. "Just keep your hands curled around the handle as if you were holding it. Concentrate on your intention to take it while I concentrate on my intention to—"

I dart forward, and before she can get her hands into place, I push Jack backward. It's just a little push, nothing that could be called violent, but it catches him off balance and he moves out of position. Anna May yells as I pass through her, a faux pas made worse for my doing it on purpose.

Automatically I start to turn toward her to apologize, then think better of it. Too late—Jack's reflexes are fifteen hundred years ahead of mine. The handle of the goddamn turnip lantern is in my hands before I know it, and Jack is sidling away, both hands empty.

"Isn't *this* an exciting development!" Jack says, practically squealing. "Not what I originally had in mind, but screw it. Plan B works just as well."

For a few moments, Anna May can only make outraged noises. "That's supposed to be *mine*!" she says finally. "Give it back!"

"No, thank you!" Jack's actually dancing with joy.

"Then *you* give it to me." Anna May tries to move into position in front of me, and I dodge her.

"Sorry to tell you, she won't," Jack says. "She's not nasty enough. Not right now—maybe in fifteen hundred years. Or maybe it won't take that long before she's trying to play *Let's Make A Deal* with dead relatives."

"What the *hell*?" Anna May is so emotional, she produces a chill both Jack and I can feel.

But an otherworldly chill is the least of what I'm feeling. The life that I saved Anna May from is sinking into me, and it's worse than I ever could have imagined. To know that I can never have a place to call my own and where I belong; to know that no matter where I go, I'll be out of place. To be among people but never of them; to pass by, to be passed by; to exist always in a neutral state, without influence or effect or even acknowledgment; to always be unattached to anyone or anything, not unwanted, just unthought-of and unremembered. Alive only because I am unwelcome in either heaven or hell, and easily spotted by the gatekeepers in both those places because I'm carrying the only thing I own—an ember of hellfire Old Nick tossed at me when he refused me entrance, so I could find my way in the unending nighttime where I live my useless life.

No, that wasn't me, that was Jack. *Was* Jack, but now it *is* me. And it's only what I deserve for being such an idiot. Anna May will never thank me. She has no idea what I saved her from. Grandma and Mom—

"So how's martyrdom?" Jack asks me. "Is it everything you ever hoped for? Hey, heaven called—they were trying to get in touch with someone who matters."

And all at once, I have this crazy idea. I must have lost my mind, I think, but what the hell—I've lost everything else.

"Well, Jack, if you're already getting calls, you might as well take my phone." I toss my cell at him, and he snatches it right out of the air so easily, I can't help admiring his skill. After fifteen hundred years of having things thrown at him, he could probably field for the Yankees.

I move so Anna May is directly between us. "Oh, and Anna May, if you still want to live forever, here—catch!"

She automatically puts her hands out, but she's a ghost; there's no way she can catch anything. The turnip goes right through her, straight at Jack's midsection. I'm really gambling that since he just caught my phone, his reaction will be equally automatic; if the lantern hits the ground, the ember will burn through the turnip, and I'll have to carry it in my pocket till I can make a new one.

Merciful fortune smiles on me. Jack drops my phone and catches the lantern before he gets a chunk of hellfire in the belly, which in his now-mortal state would be a terribly painful way to die.

He lets out a long stream of profanity in a register I wouldn't have imagined he could reach and at twice the volume I'd have thought was humanly possible. It's a while before he runs down; when he does, he collapses in a heap on the grass. Careful to keep hold of the lantern, of course.

"Okay, I think we know how you feel," I say after a bit. "Now if that's all, I think you'd better pick your sorry, no-good, not-welcome-even-in-hell ass up off the ground and get outa here before you wear out your welcome."

For a second, he doesn't move. Then he slowly pulls himself to his feet and walks off without another word.

"What just happened?" Anna May asks me.

"We both just dodged the biggest, most horrible poison bullet there ever was," I reply. I'm so relieved I don't even care that Mom and Grandma are gonna kick my ass when I get home for almost screwing up.

"Yes, but *what just happened*?" Anna May says again.

"Jack happened," I tell her. But I can see she's not going to let it go at that. "Jack, who really is part of your family tree, I'm sorry to say—"

"But not a direct ancestor," she puts in. "An uncle."

"Your Jack was not a very nice guy. If he didn't invent the seven deadly sins, he improved on them. He also messed around with black magic. It's not supposed to work for you people, but—"

"'You people'?" Anna May says archly.

"Do you wanna hear this or not?" I say, and she nods. "Black magic isn't supposed to work for *you people in the natural world*." I pause to see if that's all right with her; it is. "But sometimes, something dangerous gets lost and ends up where it shouldn't, and someone's stupid or evil enough to use it. Which Jack did. He summoned the devil and sold his soul for riches and good looks and a big schwanzstucker and who knows what else."

"Did people even know to do that in the year six hundred?" Anna May says doubtfully. "I'm not sure 'the devil' was a term used before—"

"Ms. Perlmutter," I say, feeling very, very tired. "Deals with the devil are as old as mankind, and there's always been some genius who thinks they can pull a fast one on the devil and get away with it. Your uncle Jack sold his soul to the devil for whatever they had back then that would be like wealth and fame and lots of gratuitous porn-style sex. But eventually the party was over, and the devil came to take Jack to hell."

Anna May almost asks a question, then thinks better of it. "Go on."

"On the way to hell, they pass an apple orchard, and Jack tells the devil he wants an apple to eat on the way. The devil tells him to help himself. Jack goes up the nearest tree, tries to pick a nice juicy-looking fruit, and falls down. He gets up, climbs the tree again—same thing. This happens half a dozen times before the devil loses it and tells Jack to stay put, he'll get it for him.

"As soon as the devil climbs the tree, Jack whips out a knife and carves a cross on the bark, trapping the devil there."

Now Anna May looks a bit shocked. "Dirty trick."

"You have no idea. The devil's furious, but Jack won't scratch out the cross, and the devil can't make him. Jack leaves him there and goes off to live out the rest of his no-good, nasty life, and when he dies, as all people must, he heads for heaven. But heaven doesn't take people who sell their souls to the devil, not even if they manage to get out of the deal by screwing the devil over. So Jack goes off to hell. He knows the devil's long out of the tree and ready to get some payback. But if the devil fell for that dumb apple tree trick, Jack thinks he might be able to pull another fast one, even on the devil's home turf. But when Jack gets there, the demon on the door tells him he's not welcome, get lost.

"Jack raises a stink, and finally the devil himself comes out to tell him that hell doesn't have to take him just because heaven won't. Jack is out in the cold—the *real* cold, where there's nothing and nobody. There isn't even any daytime, only darkness. Jack wants to know what he's supposed to do and where he's supposed to go and how can he even find his way around when it's dark all the time. So the devil tosses him an ember of hellfire and says he can use that for a lantern, don't say I never gave you anything, now get off my lawn.

"Jack had to carry it in his pocket, which hurt like hell—real hell—but didn't kill him. After a while, he got the idea of carving a turnip and using it as a lantern. This happens to be the direct ancestor of the jack-o'-lantern. Most people don't know that."

"That's some story," Anna May says.

"And you're not mad at me anymore for cheating you out of immortality?" I can't resist teasing her a little.

"Not a bit," she says. "When you threw that thing—that lantern—through me, I felt it in a way I didn't when he was trying to get me to hold the handle. It was—I don't know how to describe it. Ghastly. A sense of unending, relentless *loss*. It was quick, only a second, but I never want to feel it again. It must have been worse for you—"

"Forget it," I say, because there's nothing I'd rather do myself. "All Souls' Day isn't over for another few hours. Wander around some more if you want. Eventually someone'll be along to take you to what comes next. Don't ask me what that is. The living never even get a hint. Okay?"

"Okay," she says. "Thanks. I owe you my, uh, afterlife."

"My pleasure," I say, and take myself down the hill and away from the Perlmutter crypt as fast as I can without actually breaking into a run. It's very foolish to run around in a graveyard in the dark, and I'm done doing anything foolish for a while.

Lost in the Dark

John Langan

Ten years ago, Sarah Fiore's *Lost in the Dark* terrified audiences. Now, on the anniversary of the movie's release, its director has revealed new information about the circumstances behind its filming. John Langan reports.

I

PETE'S CORNER PUB, in the Hudson Valley town of Huguenot, is a familiar college-town location: the student bar, at whose door aspiring underage patrons test their fake ID's against the bouncers' scrutiny and inside of which every square inch is occupied by men and women shouting to be heard over the sound system's blare. Its floor is scuffed, its wooden tables and benches scored with generations of initials and symbols. More students than you could easily count have passed their Friday and Saturday nights here, their weekend dramas fueled by surging hormones and pitchers of cheap beer.

During the day, Pete's is a different place, the patrons older, mostly there for its hamburgers, which are regarded by those in the know as the best in town. A few regulars station themselves at the bar, solitary figures there to consume their daily ration of alcohol and possibly pass a few words with the bartender. Between lunch and dinner, the place is relatively quiet. You can bring your legal pad and pen and sit and write for a couple of hours, and as long as you're a good tipper, the waitress will keep warming your cup of decaf. The bartender has the music low, so you can have a conversation if you need to.

This particular afternoon, I'm at Pete's to talk to Sarah Fiore. To be honest, it's not my first choice for an interview, but it was the one location on which we could agree, so here I am, seated in a booth at the back of the restaurant. The upper half of the rear wall is an unbroken line of windows that curves inward at the top, for a greenhouse effect. I'm guessing it was intended to give a view out over the town, but the buildings that went up behind the bar frustrated that design. Still, they provide plenty of natural light, which must save on the electric bill.

It's Halloween, which seems almost too on the nose for the interview I'm here to conduct. Already, small children dressed as characters from comic books, movies, and video games wander the sidewalks, accompanied by parents whose costumes are the same ones they wear every day. I see Gothams of Batmen, companies of Stormtroopers, palaces of Disney princesses, and MITs' worth of video game characters. There are few monsters, which saddens me, but I'm a traditionalist. In a couple of hours, the town will host its annual Halloween parade, for which they'll close the lower part of Main Street. It's quite a sight. Hundreds of costumed participants will assemble in front of the library—just up the street from Pete's—and process down toward the Svartkill River, which forms the town's western boundary. Once there, they'll turn into the parking lot of the police station, where they'll be served cider and doughnuts by members of the police and fire departments, accompanied by the mayor and other local officials. I find it quite sweet.

In the interest of full disclosure, I should add here, while we're still waiting for Sarah Fiore to arrive, that she and I know one another. Specifically, she was my student twenty-one years ago, in the first section of Freshman Composition I taught at SUNY Huguenot. She was in her midtwenties, settling down to pursue a degree after several years of working odd jobs and traveling. She was a big fan of horror movies, wrote several essays about films like *Nosferatu* (the original), the Badham *Dracula,* and *Near Dark.* We spent fifteen minutes of one class arguing the merits of *The Lost Boys,* much to the amusement of her fellow students. After the semester was over, I occasionally bumped into Sarah in the hallways of one building or another, which was how I learned that she was transferring to NYU for its film program. I told her she would have to make a horror movie.

Eleven years later, when *Lost in the Dark* was released, I remembered our exchange. I hadn't seen Sarah since that afternoon in the Humanities building, had no idea how to get in touch with her to offer my congratulations for her good reviews. "A smarter *Blair Witch Project,*" that's the one that sticks in my mind; although the only thing Sarah's film shares with Eduardo Sànchez and Daniel Myrick's is its reliance on handheld cameras for the faux-documentary effect. Otherwise, *Lost in the Dark* has a much more developed narrative, both in terms of the Bad Agatha backstory and the Isabelle Price main story. The sequels did a lot to perpetuate the brand and helped to add Bad Agatha to the pantheon of contemporary horror villains. Sarah's involvement with these films was limited, but she pushed for

J. T. Petty to direct the second, and she reached out to Sean Mickles to bring him in for the third. As a result, you have a trilogy of horror movies by three different directors that work unusually well together. Sarah's sets up the story, Petty's explores the history, and Mickles's does its weird meta-thing about the films. While her name is on the fourth and fifth movies as producer, that had more to do with the details of the contract her agent worked out for her. Recently, there's been talk of a *Lost in the Dark* television series. AMC is interested, as is Showtime. There have been a couple of tie-in novels, and a four-issue comic book published by IDW.

Truth to tell, I think a good part of the continuing success of the Lost in the Dark franchise has to do with its Halloween connections. It didn't hurt the original film to be released Halloween weekend, and whoever thought up giving away Bad Agatha masks to the first dozen ticket buyers was a promotional genius. Plastic shells with a rubber band strap, they were hardly sophisticated, but there was a crude energy to their design, all flat planes and sharp angles. An approximation of the movie's makeup, the masks captured the menace of the character. It's the eyes that do it, especially that missing left one. The bit of black fabric glued behind the opening gives the appearance of depth, as if you're seeing right into the center of Bad Agatha's skull and the darkness therein. The last I checked, one of the original masks was going for four hundred dollars on eBay. The versions that have been released with each subsequent Lost in the Dark installment have varied in execution (though a colleague said that the mask she received was the best thing about the fourth movie), but they've become part of the phenomenon.

Throughout this time, Sarah Fiore has kept herself busy with other projects. She wrote and directed two films, *Hideous Road* (2009) and *Bubblegum Confession* (2011), and was director for *Apple Core* (2012). She wrote and directed the 2014 Shirley

Jackson documentary for PBS's *American Masters,* which was nominated for an Emmy. With Phil Gelatt, she cowrote an adaptation of Laird Barron's "Hallucigenia" that John Carpenter was rumored to be considering. Yet none of these movies or scripts has attached to her name the way the Lost in the Dark series has. For the most part, she's borne this with good grace, expressing in numerous interviews her gratitude for the films' success.

While not inevitable, it's hardly surprising that, in today's short-term-memory culture, any work of art with staying power is going to be milked for all it's worth. In the case of the original *Lost in the Dark,* this means a celebration of the movie's ten-year anniversary. There's a special-edition Blu-ray with an added disc full of bonus features, screenings of the film in select theaters, and a new batch of Bad Agatha masks. Plus, the announcement that Takashi Shimizu has signed on to direct the sixth Lost in the Dark movie, which is supposed to herald a bold new direction for the franchise. None of this is especially remarkable; much lesser films receive much grander treatment.

What is of note lies buried within the fifteen hours of new footage on the Blu-ray's bonus disc. There's a forty-minute group interview during which Sarah and Kristi Nightingale, who was her director of photography, and Ben Formosa, who played Ben Rios, sit around a table with Edie Amos of *Rue Morgue* discussing the origins and shooting of the movie. It's the kind of thing film geeks love: behind the scenes of their favorite film. There's a pitcher of water on the table, a glass in front of each participant. Sarah sits with her elbows on the table, her hands clasped. She's wearing a black linen blouse, her long black hair pulled back in a ponytail. Kristi leans back in her chair, the mass of her curly brown hair springing from underneath an unmarked blue baseball cap. A black-and-white Billy Idol, circa *Rebel Yell,* sneers from the front of her white sweatshirt. Ben has shaved his head, which, combined with noticeable weight loss, gives him the appearance of having aged more than his former companions. The red dress shirt he's wearing practically glows with money, an emblem of the success he's enjoyed in his recent roles. Edie sits with a tablet in front of her. Her oversize round glasses magnify her eyes ever so slightly.

The conversation flows easily, and the first fifteen minutes are full of all sorts of minutiae. Then, in response to a question about how she arrived at the idea for the movie, Sarah looks down, exhales, and says, "Well, it was supposed to be a documentary."

At what she assumes is a joke, Edie laughs, but the glance passed between Kristi and Ben gives the lie to that. She says, "Wait—"

Sarah takes a sip from her water. "I'd known Isabelle since NYU," she says, referring to Isabelle Router, who played the ill-fated Isabelle Price. "She was from Huguenot, which was where I'd done my first two years of undergrad. We kind of bonded over that. She knew all about the area, these crazy stories. I was never sure if she was making them up, but any time I went to the trouble of fact-checking them, they turned out to be true. Or true enough. That's why she was at school, for a degree in cultural anthropology. She wanted to study the folklore of the Hudson Valley.

"Anyway, we kept in touch after we graduated. I landed a position working for Larry Fessenden, Glass Eye Pix. Isabelle went to Albany for her doctorate. There was this piece of local history Isabelle wanted to include in her dissertation. She'd heard it from her uncle, who'd been a state trooper stationed in Highland when she was growing up. Sometime around 1969 or '70, a train had made an unscheduled stop just north of Huguenot. This was when there was a rail line running up the Svartkill Valley. Even then, the trains were on their way out, but one still pulled into the station in downtown Huguenot twice a day. This was the night train, on its way north to Wilt-wyck. It wasn't very long, half a dozen cars. About five min-utes after it left town, the train slowed, and came to a halt next to an old cement mine. A couple of men were waiting there, dressed in heavy coats and hats because of the chill. (It was only mid-October, but there'd been a cold snap that week. Funny, the details you remember.) No less than five passengers said they witnessed a woman being led off the very last car on the train by one of the conductors and another woman wearing a Catholic nun's veil. None of the passengers got a good look at the woman between the conductor and the nun. All of them agreed that she had long black hair and that a man's overcoat was draped across her shoulders. Other than that, their stories varied: one said that she had been bound in a straitjacket under the coat; another that she'd been wearing a white dress; a third that she'd been in a nightgown and barefoot. The woman didn't struggle, didn't appear to notice the men there for her at all. They took her from the conductor and the nun and, guiding her by the elbows, steered her toward the mine opening. Before anyone could see anything more, the train lurched forward.

"I suppose that might've been all, except one of the passengers was so bothered by what she'd seen that she called the police the minute she walked in her front door. The cops in Huguenot didn't take her seriously, told her it was probably nothing, the engineer doing someone a favor. This was not good enough for our concerned citizen, who went on to dial the state police next. Their dispatcher said they'd send someone out to have a look. Isabelle's uncle—what was his name? John? Edward?"

"Richard," Kristi Nightingale says. She is not looking at Sarah.

"Right, Richard, Uncle Rich," Sarah says. "He was the one they sent. It was pretty late by the time he reached the old access road that led to the mine. He told Isabelle he didn't know what to expect, but it wasn't a pair of fresh corpses. He stumbled onto the men ten feet inside the mine entrance. One had been driven forward into the wall with such force, his face was unrecognizable. The other had been torn open."

"Wait," Edie says, "wait a minute. This is real? I mean, this actually took place?"

Sarah nods. "You can check the papers. It was front-page news for the *Wiltwyck Daily Freeman* and the *Poughkeepsie Journal* for days. Even the *Times* wrote a piece on it: 'Sleepy College Town Rocked by Savage Killings.'"

"Well, what happened?"

"Nobody knew," Sarah says. "The whole thing was very strange. Apparently, the dead men were the same guys who had met the woman from the train. It turned out they were brothers who came from somewhere down in Brooklyn—Greenpoint, maybe. I can't remember their name, something Polish. Neither of their families could say what they were doing upstate, much less why they'd been waiting at the mine. Nor was there any trace of the conductor or the nun. All of the convents within a three-hour radius could account for their residents' whereabouts. The conductor who had been working that section of the train was a new guy who didn't return the next day and whose hiring information turned out to be fake. Of the mysterious woman, there was no trace. The police searched the mine, the surrounding woods, knocked on the doors of the nearest houses, but came up empty-handed.

"There were all kinds of theories floating around. The most popular one involved organized crime. There used to be a lot of Mafia activity in the Hudson Valley. They had their fingers in the local sanitation businesses. Great way to dispose of your rivals, right? The story was, they also used some of the old mines and caves for the same purpose. In this version of events, the woman had been brought to the mine to disappear into it. Whoever she was, she or someone close to her was guilty of a particularly grievous trespass, and this was the punishment.

"But then what? How had she turned the tables on her captors and killed them? Not to mention, in such an ... extravagantly violent manner. You could imagine adrenaline allowing her to overpower one of the men, seize his gun, and shoot him and his partner before they had the chance to react. Crushing a man's skull against a rock wall, cracking his friend's chest open was harder to believe. Plus, neither one showed evidence of having been armed.

"Maybe the woman hadn't been there to be murdered; maybe she was there to be traded. She'd been kidnapped, and the mine was the place her abductors had selected to return her to whoever was going to pay her ransom. Or she was a high-class prostitute, being transferred from one brothel to another. Either way, the scheduled meeting went pear-shaped and the men died. It didn't explain why they had done so in such a fashion, but the cops liked it better, it felt more probable to them.

"There were other, wilder explanations offered, too. The dead guys were Polish. This was the end of the sixties, the Cold War was in full swing, and Poland was slotted into the Eastern Bloc. Were the brothers foreign agents? Was the woman a fellow spy who had failed in her duties? Had she been sent here to be liquidated? Then rescued by other spies? Or were the brothers working for the U.S. government, and the woman a captured spy who had to vanish? These weren't the craziest scenarios, either. *Rosemary's Baby* was pretty big at this time, which may explain why some people picked up on the detail of the nun who stepped off the train. Could it be that the woman had been carrying the spawn of Satan, or otherwise involved in diabolical activities? It would account for the savagery of the brothers' deaths—the devil and his followers are pretty ferocious—if not for what the men had been doing at the mine in the first place. It's been a while since the Catholic Church sanctioned anyone's murder.

"In the end, the investigation dead-ended. Officially, it was left open, but in the absence of any credible leads, the cops turned their attention elsewhere."

Sarah drinks more water. "Within a year or two, the local kids were telling stories about the woman in the mine. Some of them portrayed her as criminally insane, delivered to the place to be kept in a secret cell constructed for the sole purpose of confining her. Other accounts made her a witch, dropped at the mine for essentially the same purpose, imprisonment. Whether she was natural or supernatural, the woman escaped her bonds, slaughtered her jailors, and was now on the loose, ready to abduct any child careless enough to allow her too close. A few years later, when *The Exorcist* was released, the narrative adapted itself to the film, and the woman became demonically possessed, transported upstate for an exorcism, which obviously had failed. It was one of the peculiarities of the story, the way it shaped itself to the current cultural landscape. The woman morphed into a teen with dangerous psychic abilities, an alien masquerading as a human, even a vampire. For older kids, venturing into the mine, especially at night, and especially at Halloween, became a rite of passage. After the railroad stopped running in the seventies, high school and college kids would drive to the access road and hike to the entrance to build bonfires and drink.

"A similar process happens all over the country—all over the world. Something bad happens, and it hardens into the seed for stories about a monstrous character. This was what Isabelle's dissertation director said. There was nothing unusual about the woman in the mine, as the local kids called her. Isabelle disagreed, said she had additional information that distinguished this narrative from the rest. Once again, it involved her uncle, Rich, the cop.

"Ten years to the date after he answered his first call about the mine, he received a second. A group of high school seniors had been partying outside the entrance, and one of them had gone into it on a dare. That was three hours ago, and there had been no sign of him since. A couple of the other kids started in after their missing friend but could find no trace of him as far as they dared to go. Everybody panicked, and eventually someone who was sober enough drove home and phoned the police. The Huguenot cops were busy with a costume party at one of the university's dorms that had gotten out of hand when someone spiked the punch with acid, so the call was booted to the state troopers. Rich suspected a Halloween prank, probably by the missing kid on his friends, possibly by all the kids on the cops. Despite that, he drove to the access road and made his way on foot to the spot.

"There, he encountered a dozen teenagers, all of them more or less sober, so sick with worry, he decided they must be telling the truth. Flashlight in hand, he set off into the mine to search for their friend. He wasn't nervous, he told Isabelle. Sure, he remembered the bodies of the men he'd discovered a decade before, but he'd seen a lot of dead bodies in the meantime, and if none was quite as bad as those two, a few had come close. The dark had never bothered him, nor did the thought of being underground. He was more concerned about the debris littering the floor: rocks of varying sizes, dusty boxes, rusted bits of old machines, the occasional tool. His feet crushed fast-food containers, kicked the bones of small animals, clanged on an empty metal lunch box. There was one good thing about the clutter—it allowed him to track the missing student without much difficulty.

"He came across graffiti farther inside the mine than he would have expected. He read names of people, sports teams, bands. He saw hearts encasing the names of lovers, peace symbols, even the anarchist A. He stumbled through a heap of beer cans, whose musical clatter wasn't as comforting as he would have liked. Finally, he came upon the portrait."

"Portrait?" Edie says.

"A woman's face," Sarah says, "done in charcoal on a patch of rock about head level. Whoever she was, Rich said, she was striking. Long black hair, high, strong cheekbones, full lips. Her left eye had been smeared, which made it look like a hole into her skull. The artist had given the picture a force, a vitality Rich struggled to define. He said it was as if she were two seconds away from stepping right out of the rock.

"By this point, he was pretty far in. Any sounds of the high school students had long since ceased. He was grudgingly impressed that the kid had traveled this distance. On the right, the tunnel he'd been walking opened on a shallow chamber. He swept his light across it and stopped. There was a bed in there, its metal frame spotted orange with rust from the damp, its mattress black with mold. Lying half on the bed was a long piece of clothing—a straitjacket. He entered the room, lifted the restraint to check it. Mold blotched the material. What wasn't mold was covered in writing, in symbols. He saw rows of crosses, Stars of David, crescent moons, other figures he didn't recognize but assumed were religious, too. He held up the straitjacket, passed the light over it. The right front side and sleeve were stained with what he was certain was blood. He replaced the garment on the bed and heard a footstep behind him.

"It was some kind of miracle, Rich said, he didn't spin around gun in hand and shoot whoever was there, or at least brain them with his flashlight. Of course it was the missing student, who'd gotten himself good and lost in the mine's recesses and had only come upon Rich through dumb luck. 'Why didn't you call for help?' he asked the kid. Because there was someone else down there, the kid said. A woman. He'd seen her at the other end of one of the tunnels, right before the torch he was carrying guttered out. There was something wrong with her face, and when she saw him, her expression made him turn and run as fast as he could. The student couldn't say how long he'd been hiding, listening. He'd thought Rich was *her* and had debated fleeing farther into the mine before she saw him. Now that he'd found Rich, it was imperative the two of them exit this place without delay.

"Had he heard the kid's story outside, Rich told Isabelle, beside the fire he and his friends had built, he would have taken the tale with a block of salt. This far into the mine, the only source of light his flashlight, facing the stone cell with the weird straitjacket, the tale sounded less incredible. The student was all for bolting for the entrance, which Rich nixed. They needed to pay attention to their surroundings, he said, or the kid would find himself lost again, and he didn't want that, did he? 'No way,' the kid said.

"The walk back to the surface took a long time. Rich did his best to remain calm, not let the student's hysteria affect him, but there was a stretch of tunnel, about halfway to the exit, in which he was suddenly certain he and the kid were not alone. The hair on the back of his neck lifted, and his mouth went dry. For fear of spooking the student, he didn't want to stop, but the echo of their feet on the walls made it difficult to decide if the sound he thought he was hearing, a whispering noise, like fabric swishing over rock, was more than his imagination. He didn't want to put his hand on his gun, either, though the spot between his shoulders itched, as if something was stalking him and the kid, just a handful of footsteps behind them in the dark. The kid picked up on it, too, and asked him if there was someone else there with them, if *she* had found them. Rich heard the panic rising in the student's voice and said no, it was only the two of them. If the kid suspected him of lying, he didn't say anything.

"At last—at long last, Rich walked the student out of the mine and into the waiting arms of his friends, who were overjoyed at their reappearance. It was all he could do, Rich said, not to look back into the mine. He was afraid he'd see a woman standing inside it, something terribly wrong with her face."

There's a moment of silence, during which both Kristi and Ben fidget. Finally, Edie says, "That's . . . incredible."

"Isabelle thought so," Sarah says. "A couple of years after that, the stories about the woman in the mine gained a new detail: the left side of her face was scarred. Whether the student Rich had retrieved told his story, or other kids ventured into the mine and discovered the drawing he'd seen, that became part of the description. It didn't hurt that the first *Nightmare on Elm Street* was released around then, with its disfigured villain. The point is, there was something interesting going on, and Isabelle already had enough information to justify further research and analysis. She told me she was planning to make the woman in the mine the center of her dissertation, an instance of the way traditional folk story was affected by the presence and pressure of newer narrative forms. The professor overseeing the project disagreed. She more than disagreed; she told Isabelle her idea was a nonstarter. Instead, she wanted Isabelle to go south, to Kentucky, where there were reports of a lizard monster that had been spotted during a local disturbance at the end of the sixties. It wasn't that Isabelle wasn't interested in the lizard monster, but she had done a lot of work on the other topic, and she didn't want to drop it. Her professor's attitude left her unsure what to do, scrap what she had and start over, or look for another director who would be more agreeable to her plans. Either way, she was watching the completion of her dissertation recede into the future. Which happens, but is still a bummer.

"Enter me. Through five years of busting my ass, I had convinced Larry that I could and should be trusted with a camera and a small crew. We were searching for the right project. I read a lot of scripts; nothing clicked. I tried writing a couple of screenplays, myself, but they weren't any better. Then one night, I'm talking to Isabelle on the phone. We spoke every couple of weeks, caught up on what each of us was doing. She'd been telling me about the woman in the mine forever, since undergrad. I must have heard the story a thousand times. This particular night, the thousand and first time, things fell into place, and I realized I had my movie right in front of me. I would take Isabelle's research project, and I would put it on-screen. I would make a documentary about the woman from the mine, about the whole weird thing. Isabelle had assembled a huge archive. There were audio interviews with twenty people. There were hundreds of photographs. There were maps. There were police reports, train schedules, articles about mining. Before I even started, I figured I had a good portion of what I needed for my movie. Production costs would be relatively low, which is never a bad thing for a beginning filmmaker. Sure, a documentary wasn't exactly the most exciting debut, but I planned to jazz it up by filming an excursion to the mine. We'd take a look around inside, see if we couldn't find the drawing Isabelle's uncle had described. If we did—or better, if we located the straitjacket—it would give the film an added *oomph*.

"Isabelle didn't need much convincing. She saw the documentary as a middle finger to her professor, a way of demonstrating exactly how wrong the woman was. I doubted it would matter to her; her head sounded as if it was pretty tightly wedged up her own ass. But the idea led Isabelle to sign on with me, so I didn't argue."

"Hold on," Edie says, "hold on. Did you make this? Are you telling me *Lost in the Dark* is a documentary?"

"No," Sarah says, "no, it's—it's more complicated than that." For the first time in the interview, she is flustered. Both Kristi and Ben appear to be barely containing the impulse to bolt. "We went to the mine—this was after Isabelle and I had put together a rough introduction, twenty minutes laying out the story of the mysterious woman. Her uncle Rich was retired in Tampa, but we interviewed him via phone, and he repeated everything he'd told Isabelle. I had arranged for a professor from SUNY Huguenot who specialized in folklore to sit down for a conversation with Isabelle about the woman.

"First, though, I wanted to shoot our trip. I planned it for Halloween, because how could I not? That was when everything had started, when kids built their bonfires outside the entrance, when Rich had ventured into its tunnels. I had my crew: Kristi on camera, George Maltmore on sound, a couple of film students who'd agreed to do whatever we needed them to. The barest of bones. And Isabelle, who was our guide. I gave George and Isabelle handheld cameras, and Priya and Chad a camera to split between them. I wasn't expecting anyone to catch anything remarkable; I liked the idea of having shots from other perspectives.

"At dusk on Halloween, we entered the mine. I was certain we'd run into kids partying there. In fact, I was counting on it. I wanted it as an illustration of an annual event, a local ritual. But there was no one there. As far as setbacks go, it wasn't bad. After filming the mine's exterior, we walked into it."

Edie waits a beat, then says, "And . . . ?"

"And we came out again," Sarah says. "Eventually."

II

A SYNOPSIS OF *Lost in the Dark* is simple enough: An academic leads a film crew into an abandoned mine in search of a mysterious woman who disappeared there decades ago. While in the mine, the crew is plagued by strange and frightening incidents, culminating in a confrontation with the missing woman, who is revealed to be a supernatural creature. After she brutally murders most of the crew, the others flee deeper into the mine. The movie ends with the survivors proceeding into the dark, pursued by the woman.

The devil lives in the details, though, doesn't he? After all, you could make a terrible film from such a plot. There are three scenes, I think, on which the movie's success depends. It seems to me a good idea to pause here a moment and consider them. The IMDb listing for *Lost in the Dark* features what has to be one of the most thorough descriptions of any film listed on the site. At twenty-three thousand words, it's clearly a labor of love. In the interest of not reinventing the wheel, I'd like to quote its summaries of the scenes I'm interested in. This is how the movie begins:

Synopsis of *Lost in the Dark* (2006)

The content of this page was created directly by users and has not been screened or verified by IMDb staff.

Warning! This synopsis may contain spoilers.

See plot summary for non-spoiler summarized description.

Professor Isabelle Price (Isabelle Router) is being interviewed in her office. Thirty-five years ago, she says, on Halloween night, a woman was brought by train from Hoboken, New Jersey, to a spot north of the upstate New York town of Huguenot. As she speaks, the screen cuts to a shot of a 1960s-era passenger train speeding across farmland, then back to her. The woman's name, she says, was Agatha Merryweather. The screen shows a graduation-style portrait of a young woman with dark eyes and long black hair. The image switches to a large blue-and-white two-story house. In a voice-over, the professor says that for the previous four years, Agatha Merryweather had been confined to the basement of her parents' home in Weehawken, New Jersey. During that time, neighbors reported frequent shouts, screams, and crashes coming from the house. The photograph of the house is replaced by one of police reports fanned out over a desktop. The Weehawken police, the voice-over continues, responded to 108 separate noise complaints; although only at the very end did they actually enter the house. The camera zeroes in on the report on top of the pile. When the Merryweathers opened the front door to their house, Professor Price says, the police saw the living room in shambles, furniture upended, lamps smashed, a bookcase tipped over. They also saw Agatha Merryweather, age twenty-one, crouched in one corner of the living room, wearing a filthy nightdress. The screen shows a photograph of a middle-aged man and woman, him in a brown suit, her in a green dress. Agatha's parents, the voice-over says, assured the officers that things were not as they appeared. Their daughter was not well, and every now and again, she had fits. The police thought the couple was acting strangely, so they entered the house. One of them approached the girl. The screen shows an open door, its interior dark. The other officer, Professor Price says, was drawn to the door to the basement. As the camera focuses on the darkness within the doorway, she says, he noticed that the door had been bolted and padlocked, but that the bolt and the lock had been torn loose when the door was thrown open, apparently with great force. There were no working lights in the basement, but the officer had his flashlight. He went downstairs and discovered a bare, empty space, with a pile of blankets for a bed and a pair of buckets for a toilet. The walls were covered in writing, row after row of crosses, six-pointed stars, crescent moons, other symbols the cop didn't recognize. The smell was terrible.

The screen returns to Professor Price, sitting at her desk. From behind the camera, the interviewer (Gillian Bernheimer) asks what happened next. The answer to that question, the professor says, is very interesting. While the police were going about their business, Mrs. Merryweather was on the phone. As you can imagine, the officers were certain they had stumbled onto a case of child abuse. Before they had finished questioning Mr. Merryweather, a black car pulled up in front of the house. Out steps Harrison Law, the archbishop of Newark, with a couple of assistants. The film shifts to a clip of a heavyset man wearing a bishop's miter and robes and holding a bishop's crozier, greeting a crowd outside a church. The officers were surprised, the professor says, and even more surprised by what the archbishop said to them: This woman is under the care of the Church. She is suffering from a terrible spiritual affliction, and her parents are working with me to see that she returns to health.

The screen returns to the professor. The interviewer asks how the police reacted. Professor Price says, They were very impressed. This was when the Church still commanded considerable respect. For an archbishop to intervene personally in a situation was unusual. The cops were willing to give him a lot more leeway than they would in a similar situation today. Although, she adds, to his credit, one of the officers still wrote a fairly extensive report on the incident, which is how we know about it.

The interviewer asks if there was any follow-up. The professor shakes her head. She says, The report was filed and forgotten. However, she was able to track down one of the Merryweathers' former neighbors. This person, who did not want to be identified, said that the morning after the police made their incursion, they watched Agatha Merryweather be led down the front steps of her house by a priest and a nun. She appeared to be wearing a straitjacket. The priest and nun helped her into the backseat of a black car. The black car drove off, and that was the last the neighbor saw of Agatha. Professor Price says she asked the neighbor if they remembered the date of Agatha's departure. As a matter of fact, the neighbor said, they did. It was Halloween.

What were the priest and nun doing there? the interviewer asks. The professor says she can only guess. She's been in touch with the archdiocese of Newark, not to mention Harrison Law, who currently holds a position at the Vatican. Neither was any help. The archdiocese claims to have no record of contact between the former archbishop and the Merryweathers. Harrison Law says that the assistance he offers those under his pastoral care comes with a guarantee of utter discretion.

The interviewer says, It sounds like the Church was a dead end. Which leads me to ask, How did you learn about Agatha Merryweather in the first place? And what led you to connect her to the woman who left the train outside Huguenot?

Professor Price says, Bear with me. She holds up a photocopy of a drawing. It shows the face of a young woman with dark eyes and long black hair, and bears a strong resemblance to the photograph of Agatha Merryweather. She says, This was made by a police sketch artist in Wiltwyck, New York, after several of the passengers who were on that train called the police to express their concern. All of their reports agreed that the woman was wearing a straitjacket and was accompanied by a priest and a nun. The professor lowers the piece of paper. She says, The passengers also agreed that Agatha and her companions were met by another pair of men, also priests, outside the entrance to the mine formerly run by the Joppenburgh Cement Company. The police might have passed off the reports as not worth more than a call to Saint John's in Joppenburgh to ask if their priests had met someone off the Wiltwyck train. However, one of the reports came from a local judge, who insisted on a more thorough investigation. This, Professor Price says, is how they found the bodies.

Bodies? the interviewer asks. The professor is replaced by a series of black-and-white crime-scene photographs. They show a pair of naked men lying side by side next to the wall of a cave. Their legs are together, their arms are at their sides, and their eyes are shut. Their throats have been torn open, down to the bone. There are long scratches on their faces and their arms. The wall beside them is splashed with blood, as is the floor near them. In voice-over, Professor Price says, These two were found by the officers who were sent to check the site. As you can see, their clothes, any jewelry they might have been wearing, whatever might have identified them, has been removed. The evidence was that they were killed after a brief, fierce struggle. Obviously, the cause of death was the wound to each man's throat. The medical examiner said their throats had been ripped apart by a set of teeth, most likely human, though he noted irregularities in the bite marks upon which he failed to elaborate. After their deaths, the men were stripped and positioned together. Whoever had tended to the corpses had been careful to leave no traces of themselves. As for the assailant: a scattering of bloody hand- and footprints were found near the top of the tunnel wall, nearly twelve feet up. They retreated into the mine for twenty-five feet, and stopped.

The professor returns to the screen. The interviewer asks her what exactly she's saying. Professor Price says she doesn't know. For eight days, the police conducted a substantial investigation. The murders were front-page news in papers up and down the Hudson Valley. They were the lead story on all the local TV news broadcasts. There was a lot of concern that a homicidal maniac or maniacs was on the loose. One of the local papers speculated that the killings might be the work of a Manson-style cult. Huguenot was quite the counterculture mecca at this time. After a few days, the story moved from the front page to page two or three, but it was still very much news. A couple of the passengers on the train thought the dead men were the priests who had helped Agatha Merryweather off the train, but none of the local clergy admitted to knowing them. The sketch I showed you was published in the paper, shown on TV. This was how Agatha Merryweather was identified as the woman on the train. A couple of her former neighbors saw the sketch and called the local police to say they recognized her. The police went to the Merryweathers' house, but it was empty, the couple nowhere to be found. None of the neighbors had seen them leave. Apparently, the police did some kind of follow-up with the Church, but they don't appear to have had any more success than I did.

The professor says, In Huguenot, the police searched for Agatha in surrounding homes and buildings and turned up nothing. They brought in dogs in hopes they might discover something. Two of the dogs pissed themselves, then started fighting with such ferocity, their handlers needed help separating them. A third dog went into the mine a hundred yards, sat, and started to howl. The police had dismissed the bloody hand- and footprints on the wall as some kind of red herring; although they hadn't been able to explain why the false lead had been placed in such an outlandish place. Now they decided to search the mine. They broke out the flashlights and set off into its tunnels in pairs.

The interviewer asks if they found anything. Professor Price says, They did. In one of the mine's side passages, the police came across what was left of a straitjacket. It was stiff with dried blood and had been ripped open by its wearer. More officers were brought in to assist in the effort. Several reported hearing sounds ahead of or behind them, footsteps, mostly, though one pair of officers described something growling close to them. The police said they were concentrating their efforts on the mine, which was where they were reasonably certain their suspect was hiding. And then . . . nothing. The search was called off.

Called off? the interviewer asks. The professor nods. Why? the interviewer asks. The professor says, No one knows. The mine remained the best lead. There was no trace of Agatha Merryweather anywhere else. When they heard about it, the local papers tried to get to the bottom of what had happened, but the police stonewalled them. It didn't take the papers long to move on to other stories. Since that time, no more has been done to determine Agatha Merryweather's fate.

Really? the interviewer asks. The professor says, I've made a pretty thorough search. There are stories the local kids tell, legends, but nothing in the way of formal investigation. Oh, Professor Price says, but I did learn one more odd fact in the course of my research. The bodies of the murdered men that were left at the mine's entrance? Three days after they arrived at the county morgue, they were claimed, by a John Smith, of Manhattan. The interviewer says, An alias? Professor Price nods. She says, I haven't talked to every John Smith who was living in the city at that time, but I'm pretty confident whoever came for those corpses did so under a fairly blatant pseudonym. Why? the interviewer asks. The professor says, That question comes up a great deal, doesn't it? If we're going to answer it, then I think we need to start with the place where Agatha Merryweather was last seen. We have to go to the mine.

· · ·

The second scene occurs two-thirds of the way through the movie. By this point, we're well into the mine. In addition to Isabelle Price, we've met Carmen Meloy, the director; Kristi Fairbairn, the cameraperson; George Slatsky, the sound person; and Ben Rios and Megan Hwang, the interns. We've passed the entrance, with its remnants of parties past, its scattered garbage, beer cans, and bottles, random articles of clothing, and graffiti, including the warning about "Bad Agatha," a name everyone in the film crew, with the exception of Isabelle, picks up. Following the old map of the mine Isabelle has folded into her knapsack, we've descended the main tunnels, running across strange, rusted pieces of machinery, shovels and other tools, a dusty copy of *Playboy* that's been a source of temporary amusement. Along the way, we've had snippets of Isabelle recounting the story of Agatha Merryweather, as well as moments of the crew reacting to the tale. We've encountered the portrait of Agatha's face, split between a normal right and a cadaverous left half; we've flinched when Ben touches it and jumped in our seats when he starts screaming, only to laugh with nervous relief as his outburst dissolves into laughter, and Megan calls him an asshat.

We've worked out some of the relationships among the crew, as well. Ben and Megan are involved; she's worried about how her parents will react to her dating someone who isn't Korean. We catch the tail end of a couple of heated, whispered exchanges between them. George is short-tempered, preoccupied with his ten-year-old daughter, for full custody of whom he's locked in legal combat with his ex-wife. Kristi is unhappy from the start with this project, a sentiment exacerbated by a mild case of claustrophobia. Carmen spends much of her time checking in with the others, consulting on technical matters, touching base on personal ones. Isabelle is focused on searching the mine with an intensity that's unnerving; she gives the strong impression of being in possession of additional information she has not shared with her companions.

(A pause here to say that Isabelle Router deserves credit for a remarkable job of acting. Granted, her part is based to a large extent on her actual background; she nonetheless delivers an exceptional portrait of a woman struggling to maintain her composure in the face of pressures external and internal.)

On the soundtrack, sounds that started as background noise, barely distinguishable from the clamor of the crew proceeding, have increased in volume substantially. Some are identifiable: a low, weak sobbing, the kind that comes at the end of hours' crying; the rattle and click of a small rock being knocked across the floor into another rock. Some are harder to place: a metallic ping and a sudden, deafening roar that sends the film crew into wide-eyed panic, racing headlong through the tunnels as the sound goes on and on.

This is what brings them to a low opening on their left, into a small cave where they spend a solid minute shouting, cursing, and screaming, until the noise drains away and we're left with their mingled panting. Only now do they notice the chamber they've entered. Overhead, the ceiling slopes down into darkness. To either side, walls that are marked with rows of unfamiliar symbols stretch to join it. Directly in front of the crew, a narrow trench bisects the floor, running away into blackness. The bottom of the trench is streaked with blackish-red liquid. Despite the warnings of the others, Ben Rios kneels and extends a hand to the substance. When he raises his fingertips to his nostrils, he pulls his head back, lips wrinkling in disgust. "Blood," he says, as we knew he would.

While the others digest this news, Isabelle Price is on the move, sweeping her flashlight over the weird figures on the walls. Geometric shapes—mostly circles within circles—punctuate long lines of characters that appear almost hieroglyphic. She directs her light to the floor and picks out something scratched on the rock, a rectangle the size of a dinner tray. YES is incised in its upper left-hand corner, NO in its upper right-hand corner. The letters of the alphabet line the inside of the rectangle, beginning with A below the YES and Z under the NO. A series of lines, some more recent than others, loop from letter to letter to the flat stone positioned at the rectangle's center. The lines seem to have been drawn in blood. Isabelle lifts the flat stone and turns it over, revealing its underside smeared with shades of red. Rock in hand, she crosses to the trench, where she kneels to dip the rock in the blood there. As the crew members exclaim and ask her what she's doing, Isabelle returns to the primitive Ouija board and replaces the stone within it. She beckons Ben and Megan to join her, but Ben refuses. After a brief debate, George says he'll take part in the professor's little séance. Passing his equipment to Ben, he lowers to his knees to Isabelle's right; Megan is on the left. There's a whispered exchange off camera, Kristi asking Carmen what the fuck is going on, Carmen telling her to keep shooting.

Here's how the IMDb entry describes what happens next:

Professor Price says, Rest your fingers on the stone lightly, like this. She places the tips of her fingers on the stone. Megan and George do the same. The professor says, Good. Now clear your minds.

Megan asks, How are we supposed to do that? Have you seen where we are?

Just do the best you can, Professor Price says. You can close your eyes, if it helps.

Megan shakes her head no, but George shuts his eyes. He says, All right, what next?

The professor closes her eyes. She asks, Is anyone there?

Nothing happens.

Professor Price says, Is anyone there?

Slowly, the stone scrapes across the floor. Megan screams, but keeps her fingers on it. George says, What the hell? The professor says, Easy. Stay calm. Keep your hands on the planchette.

Megan says, The what?

George says, The stone.

Right, Professor Price says, the stone. Her eyes are open. The stone settles on YES. The professor nods. She asks, Who is there?

The stone slides from YES to the letter A beneath it. Then to G, back to A, to T, to H, and back to A. Professor Price says, Agatha.

Kristi's voice says, Holy shit. Ben Rios crosses himself.

The professor asks, What happened to you, Agatha?

The stone spells out T-R-A-P-P-E-D.

Professor Price says, Trapped? You were trapped here, in the mine?

The stone moves to YES.

The professor asks, Why?

The stone spells B-A-D.

Professor Price says, You were bad.

The stone spells B-A-D.

The professor frowns. She asks, How were you bad?

The stone does not move.

Professor Price says, How were you bad, Agatha?

The stone spells out B-L-O-O-D.

The professor says, I don't understand. How were you bad, Agatha?

George says, Seems pretty obvious to me. She was doing something with blood. Ben says, Maybe she was drinking it.

The stone slides to YES.

Professor Price says, Please, let me do the talking. What were you doing with blood, Agatha?

The stone moves to NO.

The professor says, All right. Who trapped you here, in the mine?

The stone spells K-L-E-R-O-S.

Megan asks, Who is Kleros? George shakes his head. Professor Price says nothing. Ben says, I think it's Greek. Carmen asks, Greek? Ben says, Yeah. It's like the root of clergy.

The professor asks, Where are you from, Agatha?

The stone moves to NO.

Professor Price repeats the question.

The stone does not move.

The professor exhales. She asks, Can we help you, Agatha?

The stone does not move.

Professor Price waits for an answer. None comes. She asks, Are you still there, Agatha?

The stone does not move.

Megan asks, What happened? George says, We lost her. He sits back, lifting his hands from the stone. Megan does the same. The professor maintains contact for a few seconds more, then she sits back, too.

Kristi says, What the fuck was that? Carmen says, Yeah, Isabelle, what's going on?

Isabelle Price starts to speak, but her answer is interrupted by George shouting, Shit! and scrambling backward. Megan screams and stumbles to her feet. The professor raises her hands, startled.

The planchette stone is bleeding. All over its surface drops of blood appear, swell, and collapse into streams that trickle to the edges of the stone and spill onto the floor. Kristi shouts, Fuck! Megan turns and collides with Ben. Blood pools around the planchette stone. Professor Price stares at it. Carmen says, Isabelle, what the fuck is happening? Blood spreads over the words and letters of the Ouija board. Ben mumbles something.

George is praying, Our Father, Who art in Heaven. Blood flows
to the edges of the trench in the center of the cave and slides
into it. Kristi says, What is this? What is this? What are we seeing? What? Carmen tells everyone to move away from the
blood, to come over beside her. The crew does, except for the
professor. Carmen says, Isabelle. Come here, Isabelle.

Professor Price turns around. Her face is blank. Her left eye
is red, blood pouring from it down her cheek.

The third and final scene is, of course, the movie's climax. By
now, the movie's title has been realized, as the film crew has
emerged from the cave to discover that their panicked flight
has carried them off Isabelle's map. Despite following several
seemingly familiar paths, they have remained lost. Their complaints have grown more hysterical.

In the meantime, Carmen has succeeded in coaxing Isabelle out of the trancelike state into which she fell. The sclera
of her left eye is still stained red with hemorrhages, but it's no
longer actively bleeding. Prompted by Carmen and Kristi, she
has revealed some of the secrets we've suspected her of harbor-
ing. Her research on Agatha Merryweather, she says, led her
to a website that's kind of a clearinghouse of weird information. There was an entry for the Bound Woman of the Mine that
sounded as if it might connect to the information she'd already
gathered. The site kept crashing her computer, so she wasn't
able to read all of the listing, but the portion she finished was
intriguing. It concerned a fourteen-year-old girl who had been
responsible for a series of terrible murders in northwestern New
Jersey during the early nineteen sixties. This was farm country,
near the Pennsylvania line. For some reason, after her appre-
hension by the sheriff, the local Catholic priest was brought in
to consult on the case. This led to another pair of priests being
summoned, an older man and a younger one, whose accents no

one recognized. They said they were members of a small order, the Perilaimio. Eventually, the girl was released into their custody on the condition she remain confined to her house. At some point thereafter, she, her parents, and the priests were discovered to have fled for an unknown destination. There was talk of a search for her, but it came to nothing.

When Kristi asks what any of this has to do with anything, Isabelle reveals that the website gave a name for the girl: Agatha Merryweather. Obviously, with the assistance of the Church, she and her family fled east, where they were resettled in Weehawken. The question was, why?

This Agatha was possessed, George says. That's where the story is heading, isn't it?

That is what she thought, Isabelle says, until she looked into the order to which the priests belonged, the Perilaimio. It's an old, old group, maybe older than the Church itself.

What is she talking about? Megan wants to know. How can there be a part of the Church that came before it?

Like Christmas trees, Ben says, or Yule logs. Pagan things the Church folded into it.

That's it exactly, Isabelle says. The Perilaimio were charged with managing the *Keres*.

Which means what? Kristi asks.

Death-spirits, Ben says.

Death-spirits? Megan says. How does he know this stuff?

He took Greek in high school, Ben says.

Does he mean ghosts? Megan says.

Sounds more like devils, George says.

No, Isabelle says. These are beings of the primordial dark, beyond the Church's sway. They depend on blood to maintain their presence in this world. They can't be cast out, or destroyed, only contained.

Which is what happened here, George says. Agatha Merry-weather was brought to this place to imprison her.

That's the theory, Isabelle says. At first, she read this entire story as a case of a mentally ill girl subjected to a prolonged victimization by religious maniacs. The mine, she assumed, was intended as a jail, primitive but low profile. Most likely, the men who transported her to upstate New York planned for her to die in these tunnels, of malnutrition or disease.

Why would they have thought this? Kristi says. Didn't Isabelle just say the death-spirits couldn't be killed?

It's complicated, Isabelle says. The *Keres* are fundamentally violent; they can't be killed by violent means. However, if their host dies of natural causes, they lose their hold on it.

This makes no sense, Kristi says. How does any of this make sense?

The point is, Carmen says, Isabelle thought they were dealing with a crazy person.

Honestly, Isabelle says, she was sure Agatha had been dead for years. The most she expected was to find her remains.

Instead, Kristi says, they have . . . this. What they have.

"Us," George says, "lost. In the dark. With a monster."

Their wandering has brought the crew to another unfamiliar location, a small chamber whose rough walls recede at regular intervals to what appear to be doorways.

This is the IMDb summary of what ensues:

Ben shines his flashlight on the recess farthest to the right. It shows solid rock. He swings the light to the left. The next recess opens on a passageway. He swings the light to the left, to the recess directly across from him. It is solid, too, but there is something on the rock at approximately head level. It is the same portrait the film crew saw at the beginning of the expedition, a woman's face, the left half a skull. Megan shrieks. Kristi says, What the fuck? Ben says, It's only another drawing, and crosses to it. He reaches out his free hand to touch it. He says, See?

His flashlight goes out. Megan shrieks again. Carmen says, Ben? George says, Now is not the time for screwing around, kid. He aims his flashlight at the recess.

There is a flurry of motion. Ben screams. George's flashlight beam swings from side to side, trying to keep up with the action. Kristi shouts. Carmen points her flashlight in Ben's direction. She says, There! There! Ben continues screaming. There is someone grabbing him from behind. White arms wrap around his neck and chest. White legs encircle his waist. A head with long black hair presses against his neck. Ben grabs at the arms. He slaps at the head. He stumbles back into the wall. Megan screams, Someone do something! Professor Price shouts, Agatha! Agatha, stop!

Agatha growls and tugs her head back. There is the sound of flesh tearing, followed by a hiss as blood sprays from Ben's open throat. He drops to his knees, slaps at Agatha's hands, and falls forward, Agatha still clinging to him. She drops her head to his neck. There is the sound of her slurping his blood. Kristi says, Holy shit. Megan screams, You fucking bitch! and runs at Agatha, raising her flashlight as a club. Agatha ducks her swing and leaps onto her. She knocks Megan onto her back, and rips her throat out. Kristi says, Jesus Christ.

George says, We have to get out of here. He runs from the chamber. Agatha jumps off Megan onto the wall. She hangs on it like a spider. Professor Price shouts, Agatha! Please! Agatha! Agatha scrambles up the wall and out of the light. Carmen sweeps her flashlight around the ceiling. Kristi shouts, Where did she go? Where is she? The professor shouts, Agatha! Please!

Agatha drops onto Carmen. Her flashlight spins away. She screams. Agatha growls. Kristi and Professor Price scramble out of the way. There is the sound of Carmen struggling. Kristi shouts, Come on! Let's go! Now! Carmen shouts, Wait! Help me! Kristi says, I'm sorry, and runs through the passageway Ben discovered. Carmen shouts, Kristi! Agatha snarls. The professor says, Agatha, please, then follows Kristi. Carmen screams.

The screen goes black.

After five seconds, there is a clatter, and the screen fills with Kristi's face, illuminated by the camera light. She says, I don't know why I'm doing this. There's no way either of us is getting out of here. I can hear her—Agatha. She's coming closer. Kristi begins to cry. She says, I just wanted to say, I'm sorry about Carmen. I couldn't do anything about Ben and Megan. Maybe I couldn't have helped Carmen, either, but I'm sorry. She wipes her eyes with the back of her hand. She says, And George, if you make it out of this place, and somehow see this, fuck you, you chickenshit piece of shit.

The camera turns to show Isabelle Price's face. Kristi says, You never told us everything, did you? Professor Price shakes her head. Kristi asks, Anything you want to say now? Isabelle shakes her head. Kristi says, You know this is all your fault. The professor nods. Kristi says, We're going to leave this camera here, in hopes that someone will find it. Which is about as stupid as all the rest of this, but hey, why stop now? She sets the camera down, turned to light the tunnel she and Professor Price are headed down. She says, We still have a flashlight. We'll hold off using it as long as we can, to save the batteries. Professor Price starts along the tunnel. Kristi follows. When she is almost out of view, Kristi stops and turns. She says, I can hear her. Hurry.

The women disappear into the darkness. For the next three minutes, the credits roll over the scene. Once the credits are finished, the camera light dims. There is the sound of bare feet slapping stone. Agatha's face fills the screen. Her features are those of a young woman, covered in blood. Her eyes are wide.

Blood plasters her hair to her forehead and cheeks. The screen flickers. Agatha's left eye is an empty socket, her left cheek sunken, her lips on this side drawn back from jagged teeth. The screen flickers again, goes to static, then goes dark.

III

IT'S THE TEACHER in me: I can't help wanting to discuss all the things *Lost in the Dark* does right. The opening, for example, which imparts a substantial amount of background information to the viewer without sacrificing interest, as well as the Agatha Merryweather narrative, itself, which taps into the enduring fascination with the Catholic Church and its secrets (which, if I felt like being truly pedantic, I would point out is one of the ribs of the larger umbrella of the Gothic under which the movie shelters). Or the way the film suggests there's even more to the Agatha narrative than we've been told, than anyone's been told. Only Isabelle Price knows the full story, and to the end, she keeps back some portion of it. By making her the model for the portraits of Agatha the crew encounter, a similarity no one mentions, the movie visually suggests a connection between the women, which contributes to the audience's growing sense that the characters are in a situation that's much worse than they understand. (It's one of the enduring conceits of the film that the identity of the actress who portrays Bad Agatha has never been revealed. The credits assign the part to Agatha Merryweather. I'm of the camp that would wager money Isabelle Router played the monster; it fits too well with the portrait ploy not to be the case.)

Were it not for Sarah Fiore's interview in the Blu-ray extras, this article might address itself to exactly such a critical analysis. That interview, though, changed everything. According to

Sarah, the trip into the mine to shoot footage for Isabelle Router's documentary lasted much longer than they had planned, almost twenty hours. During that time, the crew became lost, wandering out of the mine into a series of natural tunnels and caves. While underground, they had a number of strange experiences, about half of which at least one member of the crew caught on film. They returned to the surface with a couple of hours of decent footage that was not what they had been planning on. After a rough edit, Sarah sat down with Larry Fessenden to watch the film. He loved it. He also thought she had abandoned her plan for a documentary in favor of an outright horror movie. Thinking quickly, Sarah responded to his enthusiasm by saying that yes, she had decided to go a different route. Fessenden offered to produce a feature-length version of what he'd seen, on the condition that Sarah revise the script to give it a more substantial narrative. Since there was no actual script at that moment, his request was both easier and harder to fulfill; nonetheless, she agreed to it. She also agreed that she should keep as much of what she'd shown him as they could in the longer film. This turned out to be about forty minutes of an hour-and-forty-minute movie. Isabelle Router was willing essentially to play herself, as were Kristi Nightingale and George Maltmore. The interns, Priya and Chad, had no interest in taking part in another expedition to the mine, so they were replaced by a pair of actors, Ben Formosa and Megan Park. Rather than juggle the roles of director, scriptwriter, and actor, Sarah hired Carmen Fuentes to play her. The rest is cinema history.

If we're to believe Sarah, *Lost in the Dark* was built from another film, a piece of fiction constructed using a significant portion of nonfiction. I use the "if" because as soon as word of her interview got out, the question of its authenticity was raised. After all, this was a filmmaker who had started her career with a faux documentary. What better way to mark the ten-year anniversary of that production than with another instance of the form, one designed to send audiences back to pore over the original movie? By those who took this view of Sarah's revelations, she was variously praised for her cleverness and decried for her cynicism. I've swung back and forth on the matter. I did my due diligence. The narrative Sarah relates, of the mysterious woman who stepped down from the train to Wiltwyck, the murdered men at the entrance to the mine, is true. You can read about it online, in the archives of the *Wiltwyck Daily Freeman* and the *Poughkeepsie Journal.* Confirming Isabelle Router's uncle's story proved more difficult. Richard Higgins died in Tampa three years ago. I located one of his former colleagues, Henry Ellison, who confirmed that Rich had gone into the mine to retrieve that dumbass high school kid. Of any more than that, Rich never spoke to him.

Still, there's sufficient evidence that Sarah Fiore was telling at least some of the truth. This doesn't mean there was a documentary shot between her discovery of this information and *Lost in the Dark.* Once again, I did some digging and came up with contact information for all but one of the members of the (supposed) original crew. Wherever Chad Singer currently resides, it's beyond my rudimentary sleuthing abilities to locate. Of the remainder of those involved, Priya Subramani listened to my introduction, then hung up and blocked my number. Kristi Nightingale told me to go fuck myself; I'm not sure if she also blocked me, since there didn't seem much point in calling back. George Maltmore instantly was angry, demanding to know who the hell I thought I was and what the hell I thought I was playing at. Despite my best efforts to reassure him, he became increasingly incensed, threatening to find out where I lived and show up at my front door with his shotgun. Finally, I hung up on him. Somewhat to my surprise, Larry Fessenden spoke to me for almost half an hour; although he did so without answering my question in a definitive way. Sure, he said, he remembered the film that Sarah had brought to him. It was a terrific piece of work. Was what he saw a documentary? I asked. Ah, he said, yeah, that was the story making the rounds, wasn't it? He couldn't remember Sarah saying that to him at the time, but it would be something if it turned out to be true, wouldn't it?

Yes, I said, it would.

Even more unexpectedly, Isabelle Router agreed to talk. Once *Lost in the Dark* was done shooting, she and Sarah had an argument, which resulted in a falling-out that has lasted to this day. Isabelle returned to Albany, to work on her PhD at the state university, only to leave after a single semester. For the next few years, she said, she was kind of messed up. She moved around a lot, did . . . things. Eventually, she pulled herself together, settled in Boulder, where she became a yoga instructor. She asked me if I had spoken with anyone else, and what they had said. Isabelle was particularly interested to know if I'd talked to Sarah. That I had been her teacher was of great interest; she wanted to know what Sarah had been like as a student. When it came to the question of the documentary, her answers grew vague. Yes, they had done some preliminary filming in the mine. In fact, they'd gotten kind of lost down there. Did I know that the idea for the movie, for all of the supernatural stuff, was hers? It came out of the research she'd been doing for her dissertation. You did shoot a documentary first, I said.

"I don't know that I'd go that far," Isabelle said. "We were just lost in the dark. Sarah got that much right."

Nor could I coax any more definitive statement from her. There was enough in Isabelle's words for me to take them as supporting Sarah's claims but not enough to settle the matter. Not to mention, the more I paged through the notes I'd taken from all of the interviews, the less certain I was that I wasn't being played for a sucker. The extremity of Priya's, Kristi's, and

George's reactions—their theatricality—added to Fessenden's bland non-answers, and Isabelle's ambiguous replies seemed intended, *scripted*, to give the impression that not only had the documentary been filmed, it had recorded an experience singularly unpleasant. On the other hand, quite often, the truth looks glaringly untrue; as Tolstoy said, God is a lousy novelist.

In the end, I would need to speak with my former student. Rather than a phone conversation or email exchange, Sarah suggested we meet in person. Halloween, she was scheduled to attend a special late-night screening of *Lost in the Dark* at the Joppenburgh Community Theater. Why didn't we get together before that? She'd bring her laptop; there were clips she could show me that would prove interesting. I agreed, which has brought me here, seated at the back of Pete's Corner Pub, while trick-or-treaters make their annual pilgrimage.

IV

SARAH FIORE ENTERS the bar as she used to enter my classroom—walking briskly, head down, oversize bag clutched to her side. The heels of her boots knock on the wood floor. She's wearing a hip-length black leather coat over a white blouse and black jeans. With her head tilted forward, her long black hair curtains her face. Before the hostess on duty can approach her, she's crossed to where I'm sitting and slid into the bench across from me. Since I didn't meet her until she was in her midtwenties, I don't see as dramatic a change in her as I often do with my former students. That said, time has passed, which I've no doubt she notices in the tide of white hairs that has swept both sides of my beard and is washing through what brown remains on my chin. We exchange greetings, Sarah orders a martini from the waitress who's hurried to the booth, and she slides a gray laptop from her bag. She places it on the table in front of her, unopened. Hands flat on either side of it, she asks me if I've talked to the other members of the original crew.

With the exception of Chad Singer, I say, I have, and relay to her abbreviated versions of our conversations. She smirks at Kristi Nightingale's cursing, drops her head in an attempt to conceal a laugh at George Maltmore's furious show. Larry Fessenden's noncommittal response receives a nod, as does Isabelle Router's remark about them being lost in the dark. "She was intrigued to learn that I had been your teacher," I add, but it draws no further response from Sarah.

The server returns with Sarah's drink, asks me if I'd like more coffee. I decline. "If you need anything," she says, and leaves.

"All right," Sarah says after tasting her drink. "How should we do this?"

"Why don't we start with a question: Why now? Why wait ten years to reveal this new information? Wouldn't it have been simpler to do so back when the movie was first released?"

"Possibly," Sarah says. "I don't know. At the time, Isabelle and I weren't on speaking terms. We still aren't, but then, it was new. We'd had this massive fight—things didn't just turn ugly, they turned hideous. Everything felt pretty raw. Part of me did want to go public with the documentary stuff, but it was mostly because I thought it would hurt Isabelle. She was back at graduate school, trying to pull together a dissertation. If word got out that she'd been part of this crazy documentary project, I figured it would make her study less pleasant.

"For once in my life, though, I listened to my inner Jiminy Cricket and did the right thing. For a long time after that, I was so busy, I didn't have time to think about the footage. Really, when I sat down for the interview with *Rue Morgue*, I had no intention of mentioning any of that stuff. It just . . . came out. I don't see the harm in it, now. I mean, Isabelle left her doctoral program, didn't she? Isn't she a massage therapist or something?"

"Yoga instructor," I say. "But you have to admit—"

"The timing is highly suspicious, yes. I can't blame anyone who thinks that. It's what I would say."

"You, however, have the original documentary."

Sarah nods. "I do." She raises the laptop's screen. "The problem is, we're living in an age where it's easy to fake stuff like this. If you have the resources, you can put together something that would fool everyone up to and maybe including the experts. Although, why would you want to?" She lifts a hand to forestall my answer. "Yeah, publicity, I know. It's a case of diminishing returns. If all I was after was to generate interest in the movie, I would have ended my story saying that the original footage was lost, wiped when my computer crashed. It wouldn't be worth whatever meager spike in sales you might project for me to go to the trouble of creating a new fake film."

"Which is exactly the sort of thing I'd expect you to say, if you were trying to pass off a fake movie as authentic."

"Yeah," she says, sweeping her fingers over the computer's touch pad to bring it to life. "The thing is, if you want to believe something's a conspiracy, you will. No matter what I say, one way or the other, it'll be evidence of what you're looking for."

"Fair enough."

"Okay." She taps keys and turns the computer ninety degrees, allowing me a view of the screen. The window open shows a woman's head and shoulders foreground right, the entrance to the mine background left. It's Isabelle Router, her face burnished by the same late-afternoon sunlight that paints the rock face behind her bronze. "This is how we began," Sarah says. "Isabelle standing in front of the mine, reciting the history of the mystery woman. We could watch it, but you already know the story, right?"

"Right."

"Let's . . ." She fast-forwards ten minutes. We're inside the mine, rough rock walls and ceiling, scattered trash on the floor. To anyone who's seen *Lost in the Dark,* it's a familiar shot, although the voices are different. Somewhere off screen to the right, Chad Singer is saying, "Am I going to have to carry this for very long? Because it is *heavy.*" From what sounds as if it might be behind the camera, George Maltmore is muttering about the acoustics of this damn place. Much closer, Kristi Nightingale says, "Eww," at the desiccated carcass of a small animal, likely a mouse. "We had to swap out the soundtrack for something more atmospheric," Sarah says to me. "Plus, Chad had left, so we couldn't use his voice." She pauses the video. "There's plenty more of this kind of thing I can show you, if that's what you want." She advances five minutes, to the crew encountering a piece of Jack Kirby–esque machinery the approximate dimensions of a refrigerator, its yellow paint faded and flaked away in patches, the large round openings in its sides strung with cobwebs. A leap of another six minutes brings us to the comic relief of the ancient *Playboy,* its cover and interior pages crumpled. The crew's jokes approximate those in the later film. Ten minutes more down the dark tunnel brings the first surprise of the interview, the portrait of a woman's face on the rock wall. It's exactly as it appears in *Lost in the Dark.* Despite myself, I flinch, say, "Jesus. This is for real?"

"It's what we found," Sarah says.

I stare at the waves of the woman's hair, the lines of her cheekbones and nose, the weird smearing on the right-hand side of the drawing, which gives the left half of the face a roughly skeletal appearance. I fight the urge to reach my fingers to the screen. "I assumed—I mean, I know Isabelle's uncle mentioned it in his story, but I figured he invented it."

"Me too," Sarah says. "It seemed hard to believe, didn't it? Like something out of a horror movie."

"Who did it?" I can't stop looking at the portrait, which is in some ways no different from what I've seen previously, and in other ways has been fundamentally changed. Stranger still, the portrait's resemblance to Isabelle remains as strong as ever. "I mean, did Isabelle have any friends who were artists?"

"She swore it wasn't her," Sarah says. She lets the movie play. The camera pans from the tunnel wall to Isabelle, who is not pleased. "Very funny," she says.

"What do you mean?" Kristi says.

"You think I don't know who this is?"

"Isabelle," Sarah says, "we didn't do this."

"Yeah, right," Isabelle says.

"Seriously," Kristi says.

"You think we had something to do with this?" Priya Subramani says.

"Obviously," Isabelle says. "How else do you explain it?"

"Um, someone drew it," Chad says. "Someone who isn't one of us."

"Are you sure?" Isabelle says.

"Yeah," Chad says. "When my friends say they didn't do something, I believe them."

"What would be the point?" Sarah says. "Why would we do this, and then lie to you about it?"

Doubt softens Isabelle's features, but already, she's invested too much in the argument to yield the point. Plus, she doesn't want to contemplate the implications of the crew telling the truth. She says, "Whatever," and turns away.

The camera swings to Sarah, who blows out through pursed lips while rolling her eyes.

"Probably should have omitted that last bit," she says, tapping the touch pad and freezing the screen. "After we returned from the mine and were going through the footage, Kristi suggested that maybe Isabelle was responsible for the drawing. I told her there was no way, she was being ridiculous. Had she not seen Isabelle's reaction to the thing? When the group of us met to screen what Kristi and I had put together, she asked Isabelle about the portrait point-blank. I didn't stop her. I'll admit: I was curious. Isabelle acted genuinely surprised at the accusation, enough for me to believe her. Although, when I think about her performance in *Lost in the Dark,* how well she acted, I wonder."

"Why would she have done that?"

"To back up the story that had brought us there in the first place," Sarah says.

"I don't know," I say. "That seems like a little far to go."

"Well." Sarah brings the movie ahead another ten minutes, hurrying the crew through a pair of large spaces whose flat ceilings rest on rock columns the girth of large trees. In the second chamber, their flashlights pick out a shape to the right, a dark mound like a heap of rugs. Flashlights trained on the thing, they cross the space toward it. As they approach, the mound gains definition, resolving into the carcass of a large animal. When they reach it, Sarah returns the film to normal speed.

"—is it?" Chad is saying.

"I think it's a bear," Sarah says.

"No way," Kristi says.

"There are bears here?" Priya says.

"Yes," George says, "black bears." He steps away from the group to circle the remains.

"Be careful," Priya says.

"Yeah, George," Chad says, "watch yourself."

"Relax," George says. "This fellow's been dead a long time." He crouches next to the bear's blunt head, playing his light back and forth over it. His eyes narrow. "What the hell?"

"What?" Sarah says.

"What is it?" Priya says.

"From the looks of things," George says, "something tore out Gentle Ben here's throat."

"Is that strange?" Chad says.

"What could do that?" Kristi says.

"I have no idea," George says. "Another bear, maybe. A mountain lion, I guess."

"Hang on—I want to see this," Kristi says. The camera moves around the animal's prostrate form to where George sits on his heels, his flashlight directed at the bear's head. Its eyes are sunken, shriveled, its teeth bared in a final snarl. The right canine is missing, the socket ragged, black with blood long crusted. What should be the animal's thick neck is a mess of skin torn into leathery ribbon and flaps, laying bare dried muscle and dull bone. "Jesus," Kristi says.

"Should be more blood," George says. He sweeps his flashlight over the floor around them, whose dust and rock are unstained. "Huh."

"What does that mean?" Priya says.

"Could it be, I don't know, poachers?" Chad says.

"Black bear isn't protected like that," George says. "You're supposed to have a license, but if you shot one by mistake, you wouldn't need to go to this amount of trouble to hide it. Not to mention, I don't know what gun would inflict this type of wound."

"Maybe it was shot," Chad says, "came in here to escape, and another bear got it."

George shrugs. "Anything's possible. Doesn't explain the lack of blood, though."

"I do not like this," Kristi says.

"Hey," Priya says, "where's Isabelle?"

Sarah pauses the movie.

"What happened to Isabelle?" I say.

"She . . . wandered off," Sarah says.

"In a mine?"

"Yeah," Sarah says, "that was what the rest of us thought."

"Where did she go?"

"All the way to the end of the mine, and then farther. There's a network of caves the mine connects to. We spent most of the shoot searching for her—about fifteen hours." The next twenty minutes of the film advance in a succession of scenes, each of which leaps ahead another half hour to hour and a half. The expression on the crew's faces oscillate between irritation and worry, with intermittent stops at fatigue and unease. Sarah says, "We hadn't brought much in the way of food or drink; we hadn't expected to be down there for more than a couple of hours. We ran out of both pretty quickly. Not long after, Chad floated the idea of turning around, heading for the surface, where we could call for help, bring in some professionals to find Isabelle. Kristi was aghast at the thought of abandoning her here. The others agreed. We kept on moving farther underground. Isabelle had left enough of a trail for us to follow; although there were a couple of times we really had to search for it. Finally, we arrived at this spot."

She taps the touch pad. The screen shows the tunnel dead-ending in a shallow chamber filled with junk: rows of rusted barrels, any identifying marks long flaked off; cardboard boxes in various stages of mildewed collapse; shovels and pickaxes, mummified in dusty cobwebs; a stack of eight or nine safety helmets leaning to one side.

"Shit," Sarah says.

"What do we do now?" Chad says.

"Go back," George says, "see if we can pick up the trail again at that last fork."

"Hang on," Kristi says. The view moves behind the row of barrels closest to the wall. As the camera's light shifts, so do the barrels' shadows, swinging away from the rock to reveal a short opening in it. "Guys," Kristi says, bringing the camera level with her discovery. Manhole-sized and -shaped, the aperture admits to a brief passage, which ends in darkness.

"What is it?" Sarah says.

"Some kind of tunnel," Kristi says. The opening swims closer.

"What are you doing?" Sarah says.

"Wait," Kristi says. The screen rocks wildly as she crawls through the passage.

"Hey!" George calls.

Kristi emerges into a larger space. Curved walls expand to a wider exit. The camera scans the floor, which is strewn with an assortment of stones. A rough path pushes through them. "Guys!" Kristi shouts.

The film jumps to Priya scrambling out of the tunnel. Chad helps her to her feet. To the left, George says, "Is everyone sure about this?"

"No," Chad says.

"I don't know," Priya says.

"Do you want to abandon Isabelle down here," Kristi says, "in the dark?"

"It's worth checking out," Sarah says. "We'll go a little way. If we don't see any sign of her, we'll turn around."

"What the fuck is she doing here?" Priya says.

"When we find Isabelle," Sarah says, "we'll ask her."

Another cut, and the crew is standing in blackness that extends beyond the limits of their flashlights. Ceiling, walls are out of view; only the rock on which they're standing is visible. Chad and Kristi shout, "Hello!" and, "Isabelle!" but any echo is at best faint. "Where are we?" Priya says. No one answers.

In the following scene, an object shines in the distance, on the very right edge of the screen. "Hey," Kristi says, turning the camera to center the thing, "look." The rest of the crew's lights converge on it.

"What . . . ?" Priya says.

"It looks like a tooth," Sarah says.

"It's a stalagmite," George says. "Or stalactite. I get the two confused. Either way, it isn't a tooth."

"It's not a stalagmite," Chad says. "The surface texture's wrong. Besides, you usually find stalagmites and stalactites in pairs, groups, even. Where are the others?"

"So what is it, Mr. Geologist?" George says.

"It's a rock," Kristi says.

It is, though both Sarah's and George's identifications are understandable. Composed of some type of white, pearlescent mineral, it stands upright, three and a half, four feet tall, tapering from a narrow base to a flattened top the width of a tea saucer. Halfway down it, there's a decoration, which, when the camera zooms in on it, resolves into a picture. Executed in what might be charcoal, it's a face, the features rendered simply, crudely. In the scribble of black hair, the black hole of the left eye, it isn't hard to recognize the repetition of the portrait near the mine's entrance. "What the fuck?" Kristi says.

"What is this?" Priya says. "What is happening here?"

"Um," Chad says. The view draws back from the face to show Chad standing beside the stone, in the process of picking up something from its flattened top. Frowning, he raises a thin, shriveled item to view. "I think this is a finger."

"Jesus Christ," Kristi says. "Are you sure?"

"No," he says, replacing the digit gingerly, as if it might shatter.

"What the hell is this?" George says.

"We need to leave," Priya says. "Right now, we need to leave."

"I think she might be right," Kristi says.

"Just a little farther," Sarah says. "Please. I know this is— this is scary, I know. But please . . . We can't leave Isabelle here. Please."

"What makes you think she's even in this place?" George says.

"I do not want to be here anymore," Priya says. "We have to *leave*."

"Sarah," Kristi says.

Without another word, Sarah walks past the strange rock in the direction the crew was heading, her flashlight spreading its beam across the floor in front of her.

"Hey!" Kristi says.

"What is she doing?" Chad says.

"Making a command decision," George says.

"Are we going to follow her?" Chad says.

"What choice do we have?" Kristi says. "We already lost Isabelle." The camera moves after Sarah.

From behind, Priya says, "This is so unfair."

After the next cut, the screen shows Sarah a half-dozen steps in front of the crew, trailing her light through blackness. "Sarah," Kristi says. "Wait up." The others join her in calling Sarah's name, urging her to slow down. "Come on!" Priya says.

When Sarah stops, it isn't because of the requests directed at her. Her light slides over the cave floor to her left, illuminating a low line of dark rocks. As she changes direction toward it, so do the others, aiming their lights at her destination. "What now?" George says.

Less than a foot tall, the line is composed of stones fist sized and smaller. They're black, porous, distinct from the rock on which they're arranged. At either end, the row connects to a shorter line of the same rock, each of which joins another longer row of rocks, forming a rectangle the dimensions of a large door. The space within it sparkles and flashes in the lights. Chad kneels and reaches into the rectangle, toward the nearest piece of dazzle, only to snatch his hand back with a "Shit!"

"What is it?" Priya says.

"Glass," Chad says, holding his fingers to display the blood welling from their tips. "It's filled with broken glass." He sticks his fingers into his mouth.

"Fuck," Kristi says.

"What does this mean?" Priya says.

"Yeah, Sarah," Kristi says, "what the fuck is this?"

"I—" Sarah starts, but George interrupts her: "Shh! Hear that?"

"What?" Kristi says.

"I do," Priya says.

"What?" Chad says.

"Over here," George says, waving his light at the blackness on the far side of the stone rectangle. "Listen."

Everyone falls silent. From what seems a long way away, a faint groan is audible.

"Is that Isabelle?" Chad says.

"Who else would it be?" Kristi says. "Come on." Now she takes the lead, skirting the edges of the stone design as she heads in the direction of the moaning. "Isabelle!" Kristi shouts. "We're here!"

In the middle distance, the cave floor shimmers white. This is not the crystalline fracture of broken glass; rather, it's the flat glow of light on liquid. "What the hell?" Kristi says. She is approaching the shore of a body of water, a lake, judging by the stillness of its surface. Given the limited range of the camera's light, the lake's margins are difficult to discern, which gives it the impression of size. This close to the water, the groaning has a curiously hollow quality. The camera swings right, left, and right again. "Isabelle!" Kristi shouts.

The rest of the crew catches up to her. Exclamations of surprise at the lake combine with calls to Isabelle. Flashlight beams chase one another across the water, roam the shore to either side. "Where . . . ?" Kristi says.

"There," Sarah says, pointing her flashlight to the right. At the very limit of the light's reach, a pale figure stands in the water, a few feet out. Camera bouncing, the crew runs toward it.

Arms wrapped around herself, Isabelle Router stands in water ankle-deep. Her eyes are closed, her mouth open to emit a wavering moan. Priya splashes into the lake, at Isabelle's side in half a dozen high steps. When Priya touches her, Isabelle convulses, her groans breaking off. Her eyes remain closed. "It's all right," Priya says. "Isabelle, it's all right. It's me. It's Priya. We're here."

"Priya?" Isabelle's voice is a hoarse whisper.

"Yeah," Priya says, "it's me. Everyone's here. We found you. It's all right."

Isabelle opens her eyes, lifts her hands against the lights.

"Isabelle," Sarah says, "are you okay?"

"You're here," Isabelle says.

"We are," Sarah says.

"What happened to you?" Kristi says.

"You're all right," Priya says.

Isabelle drops her eyes, mumbles something.

"What?" Priya says.

Her gait stiff-legged, Isabelle sloshes toward the shore. She does not stop once she's on dry land; rather, she continues barefoot past the crew, the camera tracking her. "Wait a minute," Kristi says, "where are you going?"

Without looking back, Isabelle says, "Out."

"That's it?" Kristi says. "We go to all this trouble and ... that's it? 'Out'? Really?"

"Kristi," Sarah says.

"No, she's right," Chad says.

Priya steps out of the water. "She's obviously freaked-out," she says.

"She's obviously a pain in my ass," Kristi says.

"Guys," Sarah says, "could we have this discussion while we're keeping up with Isabelle?"

"Yeah," Chad says, "it'd suck to lose her a second time."

"Shut up, Chad," Kristi says.

Three quick scenes show the crew traversing the darkness that lies between the subterranean lake and the tunnel to the mine. Even after she cuts her right foot on a rock, leaving a bloody footprint until the others catch up to her and insist on bandaging it, which George does, Isabelle maintains a brisk pace. She does not let up after they have reentered the mine, though the comments from the others shift from complaint to relief. Throughout, Kristi continues to return to the question of what happened to Isabelle, asking it at sufficient volume for her to hear; Isabelle, however, does not answer.

Not until they have reached the portrait of the woman nearer the mine's entrance does Isabelle stop. Immobile, she stares at the artwork as the rest of the crew gathers around her.

"What now?" Kristi says.

In reply, Isabelle screams, a loud, high-pitched shriek that startles everyone into stepping back. The scream goes on and on and on, doubling Isabelle over, breaking into static as it exceeds the limits of the recording equipment. While Isabelle staggers from foot to foot, bent in half, her mouth stretched too wide, the soundtrack cuts in and out, alternating her screaming with an electronic hum. The members of the crew stand stunned, their expressions shocked. Tears stream from Isabelle's eyes, snot pours from her nostrils, flakes of blood spray onto her lips and chin. The audio gives up the fight, yielding to the empty hum. Finally, Priya runs to Isabelle, puts her arms around her, and steers her away from the drawing, toward the exit. While she remains doubled over, Isabelle goes with her. Chad and George follow. For a moment, Sarah studies the portrait, then she, too, turns to leave.

The camera remains focused on the wall, at the weird image that so strikingly resembles Isabelle Router. It zooms in, until the half-skeletal portion of the face fills the screen. As it does, the soundtrack recovers. Isabelle is still screaming, the sound echoing down the mine's tunnels. The picture goes black. "Directed by Sarah Fiore" flashes onto the screen in white letters.

"And that's it," Sarah says, freezing the film.

"Huh," I say. I'm suddenly aware that in the time I've spent viewing Sarah's video, the sun has dropped behind Frenchman Mountain, hauling night down after it. The autumn light has slid from the windows at the back of the bar, leaving a tide of blackness pressed against them. I can hear the shouts and shrieks of the trick-or-treaters, somewhere in that darkness. It's absurd, but after spending the last hour immersed in the film's subterranean setting, I have the impression that the blackness of the mine has escaped into the night. I swallow, say, "That's something."

"Larry was worried it was too oblique," Sarah says. "He liked it, but he thought the film needed developing. I was—it was surreal, you know? I had this documentary I'd put together that showed . . . I don't know what, and here was this filmmaker I respected treating it as if it was fiction, and I realized, *Yeah, you could watch it that way,* and then I thought, *Wait, was that what it was?*" She shakes her head.

"Did you ever think of telling him the truth?"

"For about half a second, until he started throwing around budget numbers, talking about possible distributors. All of it was extremely modest, but compared to what I was used to— that, and the chance it represented for me as a director—well, it wasn't much of a decision.

"My biggest concern was Isabelle. She was in pretty rough shape after we exited the mine. Priya drove her to the ER in Wiltwyck right away. She had stopped screaming not long after

Priya took her away from the portrait, but her throat was a mess. She was exhausted, dehydrated, and there was something wrong with her blood: the white blood cell count was too high, or too low; I can't remember. Anyway, she was in the hospital for a couple of days. I assumed she'd have no interest in a return trip to the mine, to put it mildly, but I felt I owed it to her to fill her in on the new plan."

"And?"

"And she was completely into it, which was a surprise. She offered to help me with the screenplay, and she had some great ideas. A lot of the Bad Agatha stuff came from her." Seeing me opening my mouth, Sarah holds up a hand to forestall the inevitable question. "Yes, I asked her what had happened while she was on her own down there. She shrugged off the question, said she'd gotten lost and freaked out. Okay, I said, but what made her leave us in the first place?

"She heard something, what sounded like someone calling her name. She already thought the rest of us were pranking her with the woman's portrait; she assumed this was more of the same. Her intent was to find whoever was saying her name and kick them in the ass. Instead, she lost track of where she was, and then she had a little bit of a breakdown, and that was all she could remember clearly until she was in the hospital."

"Did you believe her?"

"Yes," Sarah says, drawing out the word, "but I was pretty sure there was more she wasn't telling me. I couldn't figure out how to persuade her to let me in on it. She told me she was fine with returning to the mine, but I was pretty nervous about it. Honestly, I would have been happier if she'd refused. The problem was, Priya and Chad had already bowed out, which meant we couldn't use as much of the documentary footage as I wanted. If Isabelle hadn't agreed, then we would have had to shoot an entirely new film, which might have exceeded our meager budget. So I went with her, and I have to admit, she did a terrific job. For all the years I'd known her, I had no idea she was such a convincing actress."

"What caused the two of you to fall out?"

Sarah frowns. "Creative differences."

"Over?"

"A lot of things." As if she's just noticed the night outside, Sarah says, "Holy shit. What time is it?" She closes the window on the laptop and squints at the corner clock. "I better go," she says, folding the computer shut. While she slides it off the table into her bag, I say, "Anything else you'd like to add?"

"It's funny," she says, easing out of the booth, "there have been moments when I've thought about posting the video online, putting it up on YouTube with no fanfare, letting whoever discovers it make of it what they will. Except, I knew people would view it as a publicity stunt, some old footage I'd stitched together to generate new interest in my movie. I had no plans to mention it during the interview for the anniversary edition, until there I was, talking about it. Once I started, I figured, why not?"

"And people still thought it was a hoax."

"Yeah. What are you gonna do?"

The walk from the booth to the bar to pay the bill is no more than twelve or fifteen feet, yet it seems to take us an hour to make it. My thoughts are racing, trying to fit what I've heard and seen this afternoon with everything else I know about Sarah and the film. After all, I'm the horror writer; it's why the editors of this publication have asked me to conduct this interview. I'm supposed to judge the veracity of Sarah's footage and, assuming I accept it as true, trace its connections to *Lost in the Dark*, explain the ways in which the fiction refracts the facts. It's a favorite critical activity, isn't it? Especially when it comes to the fantastic, demonstrating how it's only the stuff of daily life, after all. The vampire is our repressed eroticism, the werewolf our unreasoning rage. The film Sarah has shown me, though, isn't the material of daily life. I don't know what it is, because to tell you the truth, I'm more of a skeptic than a believer these days. Strange as it sounds, it's one of the reasons I love to write about the supernatural. The stories I tell offer me the opportunity to indulge a sense of the numinous I find all too lacking in the world around me. But this movie . . . I can't help inventing a story to explain it, something to do with an ancient power captured, brought to a remote location, and imprisoned there. Those dead men at the entrance, maybe they were there as a sacrifice, a way to bind whatever was in that nameless woman to the mine. The stuff inside the tunnels, the caves beyond, was that evidence of someone or someones tending to the woman, worshipping her? And Isabelle Router, her experience underground—was the movie she cowrote an act of devotion to something that found her in the dark? I half remember the line from Yeats about entertaining a drowsy emperor.

None of it makes any sense; it's all constructed with playing cards, waiting for a sneeze to collapse it. I pay the bill, and we walk out of Pete's. The sidewalks have filled with a mass of children and parents making their slow way up Main Street to the library to assemble for the Halloween parade. Zombies stagger along next to Clone troopers, while Batman brings up the rear. Clown parents carry ladybug children. Frankenstein's bride towers over the hobbits surrounding her. Witches whose pointed green chins are visible beneath the broad brims of their black hats talk to fairies sporting flower crowns and wings dusted with sparkles. There's a kid costumed as a hairy dog, an adult dressed as a boxy robot. The grim reaper swings a mean-looking scythe; Hermione Granger flourishes her wand. Vampires in evening dress walk beside superheroes in gaudier colors. A few old-fashioned ghosts flutter like sheets escaped from the clothesline.

A number of Bad Agathas are part of the procession, one of them quite small. This diminutive form darts through the crowd to where Sarah and I are standing. The mask the girl tilts at us is too big for her. It's an older design, the features angular, the left eye socket a black cavern. Sarah's eyebrows lift at the sight. The girl raises her right hand. She's holding a Bad Agatha mask, which she offers to Sarah.

Sarah hesitates, then accepts the mask. Apparently released by her act, the girl sprints away into the costumed ranks. Sarah considers Bad Agatha's stylized face, as if studying a photograph of an old acquaintance. She turns the mask over, tilts her head forward, and slides Bad Agatha's face over hers. She straightens, turns to me. Whatever witty remark I was preparing dies on my tongue. Without another word, Sarah turns and joins the parade.

For Fiona

The First Lunar Halloween

John R. Little

October 1, 2204

THE DISCUSSION TOPIC was buried in the last part of the
Tranquility City Council monthly agenda: Halloween
Celebration.

It was brought forward by Susan Sauble, after she'd been
inundated by requests from her students. Susan was the 149th
Cohort Group Leader and had been in that position through all
their school years, since they were five. Now the fifteen kids in
the cohort were all twelve Earthies old (or nearly so).

The mayor read the agenda item out loud and called on
Susan to speak.

"Thank you, Mr. Mayor.

"Here in Tranquility, we've always encouraged our kids
to research their heritage on Earth. Nobody remembers all
the details, of course, but we all feel the ties we have to our
homeland."

She paused so that everyone could use their own imagination however they wished. She herself had only ever seen Earth directly twice. It was a bright, shining white sphere hanging above the moon's surface, totally wiped of life but a constant reminder on video screens of their original homeland.

"This year, one of our students found a reference to an ancient holiday tradition called Halloween. It is full of fun, laughter, delightful costumes, mock fear, and other attributes. The holiday seems quaint, while allowing our cultural roots to shine through. I'd like our cohort to be the first annual class to re-create Halloween here on the Moon."

She paused before adding the tough part. "And, I'd like it to be on the surface. The kids are ready to go out and see the face of Earth above them. Of course, I'll supervise, and we have a surface leader who will be with me, Jonathan Petty, to ensure all safety precautions are followed."

At first there was stunned silence in the chamber. There'd never been a situation where that many kids ventured up to the surface at one time.

The mayor broke the silence. "You know the risks."

"Yes, of course."

"The surface is so harsh . . . and . . ."

He looked to the other council members for help, but they all seemed to be busy staring at their desks.

Susan decided to finish his sentence. "The Aliens?"

He stared at her.

"We all know the rumors," she said. "Jonathan assures me the trip will be totally safe."

In the end, though, Susan convinced them that this was a perfect opportunity. In her mind, she had the perfect field trip planned, and she wanted it to be the most memorable event the kids would ever experience during their school years.

The motion passed seven to two.

October 31, 2204

SUSAN HAD SPENT much of her spare time the past couple of weeks researching information about Halloween, and she was fascinated with what she found. She and Jonathan worked together to plan the field trip.

The documents she could find were few, though. When the Earth was destroyed, so too was the vast repository of data that Tranquility relied on. Now, the Internet seemed like a vague myth. All that survived was the random pieces that happened to be downloaded when the Earth-Link was severed, and memoirs and journals from the original Tranquility residents. These were the ones she pored over.

"Susan?"

She looked up from her monitor. Jonathan. She smiled at him.

Jonathan was forty-two Earthies old, compared to her own thirty-nine. Tall, even for a Moonie, wide infectious smile, full of confidence. She liked him.

"Ready?" he asked.

"I'm not sure, but I suppose I'm as ready as I'm going to be."

She could feel herself getting anxious, and she took some deep breaths to try to calm herself. Going up to the surface was still a big deal to her.

Jonathan took her hand and half pulled her along. "It's going to be fine. They're going to have a blast."

"I know."

She didn't know any such thing.

Over the past few weeks, the pair had planned the trip. He was the surface expert and took Susan's ideas and made them practical.

The kids were all waiting for them at Groundport. Their parents were helping them into suits. Most of the kids were taller than Susan, and it was sometimes a challenge to find a suit that fit each person perfectly, but after a while, everyone seemed happy.

First step: decorations.

"Okay, parents, you can leave now. Kids, you need to decorate each other's suits with your markers. Remember, the costumes used to be scary. Monsters, aliens, ghosts, whatever you like."

The decorations took about an hour. Susan decorated the front of Jonathan's suit with a big mouth with two legs sticking out. She remembered seeing pictures of long-extinct giant fish when she was going to school herself, and she tried to remember what they might look like.

"I love this idea," Jonathan said to her. "I *get* this thing. Halloween. It's a chance to pretend to be somebody else for a little while. You can use the occasion to become somebody frightening or someone who aspires to greatness. It's a temporary do-over, a break from the boredom of our everyday lives."

Boredom? Susan knew Jonathan spent several hours every week up on the surface. Hard to imagine that being boring.

The decorations would all disappear from the suits when they came back, cleansed with the normal re-entrance routine.

She stared at the PETTY marked at the top of Jonathan's suit. It was bright green, as was everybody else's name. Once outside, there would be no other way to tell everyone apart.

"Okay, it's time," she called to the class. The suits were starting to get warm, but they couldn't activate the cooling system until their helmets were in place.

"Can I ask a question?"

Susan looked over and wasn't surprised to see it was Matt Wiley. He was always asking questions. "Of course," she answered.

"What about the Aliens? Aren't they up on the surface?"

She hesitated and looked to Jonathan. He nodded and

answered, "There's no reason to believe the Aliens are on the Moon. That's an old myth with no facts to back it up."

"Are you sure?"

"I've been topside at least fifty times, and although there's a lot we don't know, we've never seen a single sign of any Aliens here. As far as we know, they're all on Earth."

A tiny voice carried from the back of the class, a voice Susan recognized immediately as belonging to her own daughter, Selene.

"What if you're wrong?"

Susan said, "Nobody is wrong. This is totally safe, so you just need to enjoy your first Halloween!"

They finished up and started to gather around the tube. Only five people at a time would fit, so Jonathan went first with four kids. The next two trips took four kids each, while Susan waited for the last trip with the final two teens, including Selene.

As they rose up the two hundred meters to the surface, Susan felt like she was leaving her life behind. Going upside never felt normal to her. It was leaving the safety of the underground city for the vast expanse of the surface.

Nobody liked it. People belonged underground.

When she left the tube, the Earth was almost full, and it blasted enough light to cast shadows.

She tried to ignore it. She had to watch the kids.

"Testing. Can everybody hear me? Raise your hand if you can."

Everyone raised an arm, some slower than others, but that was normal kid behavior. She knew they wanted to run and jump and explore, as she had the first time she herself visited the surface all those Earthies ago.

Soon enough.

There were surprises ahead, and she wanted them to enjoy them.

"So, remember, this is Halloween! It's intended to be scary and fun and thrilling and . . . well, mysterious. I know you all want to go run around and jump, but we're here to follow the Halloween Path."

Even though most of their helmets had darkened due to the bright Earth-shine, she could see the kids staring at her in wonderment.

"Look at Earth," she said. "That was where our ancestors came from. Humans lived there for thousands of years."

She didn't add, "Before they were all killed in a single day."

She stared up, too. Earth was an extraordinary mystical globe high above, a brilliant gem stretching out above them, four times wider than the sun.

Jonathan added, "It used to be blue. The Aliens killed everyone and the planet ended up covered in bright white clouds. Nobody knows if it'll stay that way forever."

"When we get back," said Susan, "you need to write a report, so pay attention."

Jonathan took the lead and started half walking, half hopping ahead. Everyone else followed, with Susan at the end. She didn't mind. It was Jonathan who'd come out the day before to set up the Path. She was just happy to see the kids on the surface, not freaking out, and being part of the day.

It was time.

Jonathan led the way to Station One, as they had planned. Everyone except him was skittish and had difficulty controlling their movements, but they were all having fun. Susan knew the suits were completely safe, so even if somebody fell onto a sharp rock, no damage would happen. If it was her, all she would feel would be embarrassment.

The Halloween Path was set up in the shape of a diamond with three stops before they would head back to Tranquility.

Altogether, the trip should take an hour. Everyone had enough air for three hours.

The group hopped and skidded their way to the first stop. Jonathan had planned the route to navigate around any large rocks or craters. His footprints were still there from when he'd set everything up. All their footprints would be there the next time anybody took the same route. Nothing changed on the Moon.

When everybody arrived at the first stop, Susan checked the time. All good.

The kids formed a semicircle around a flat rock that had a holo-projector set up. When they crowded around, the projector started automatically using a technology nobody understood. They could hear the narration clearly in their suits.

Susan lost interest, having seen the show a dozen times already. The visuals showed an old-fashioned home as it might have existed on Earth, with kids showing up shouting "Trick or treat!" before a witch answered, screamed at them, and sprinkled candy into their bags. She hoped it was close to being accurate, but they'd never know for sure.

Instead, she looked back to the sky, to the amazing Earth.

Even though the sun was below the horizon, it barely mattered. Earth was the Moon's bigger sun now.

Looking away from the homeland, the sky was pitch-black, sprinkled with a million tiny stars. She felt an urge to reach up and scoop the stars in her hand, like she imagined humans scooping grains of sand from a beach.

A sense of nostalgia grew in her, the loss of humanity's roots, and she wondered about the most common mystery in Tranquility: Were the Aliens still on Earth, and if so, what were they doing?

The Halloween show finished with a loud clap, and the kids

all jumped. So did Susan. Even though she knew it was coming, she'd been lost in thought.

"Time to go to Station Two," said Jonathan. "Susan will be leading this time, so get in line behind her."

As she led the way, Susan remembered some of the things that she'd found out about Halloween that she hadn't managed to incorporate into the three projection shows. There just wasn't time to include bobbing for apples, Halloween kisses, razor blades in candy, pumpkin pie, orange and black, egging houses (whatever that was), theme parks, and a hundred other topics that she'd dug up. Who knew how many were real and how many were myths? That was part of the fun.

Besides, she needed to leave some things for the class to research on their own.

She glanced back to be sure everyone was following her.

It took another ten minutes to get to the second stop, and Susan was starting to feel a bit winded. She wasn't used to traveling this way.

When she got to the stop, the kids gathered around and started watching the second holo-cast. This one talked about traditions related to fortune tellers and diviners as well as people telling ghost stories to scare younger children.

Her favorite was how unmarried women sitting in a darkened room on Halloween night could look into a mirror to see the face of her future husband. If she saw a skull instead, she would die before marriage.

She could remember the script word for word, since she'd written it, with Jonathan's help, of course.

Suddenly she looked around and realized Jonathan was not there. She blinked and looked again, sure her mind must be deceiving her.

But, no.

The tension that had been building up inside her made Susan

feel like she was going to explode. She gulped and tried to not react, so that she wouldn't scare the kids.

"Jonathan?"

No reply. Matt Wiley turned to look at her and then joined her as she hopped a bit in the direction they'd come.

"Jonathan!" Susan knew that there was panic in her voice, but she couldn't help it.

"Miss Sauble?"

Matt was beside her and had put a gloved hand on her shoulder.

"It's okay, Matt. I think he just went to get something."

"I know," Matt said. "He's the expert."

The other kids were staring at them. Susan subconsciously looked for the girl with SAUBLE in bright green letters on her helmet. After another minute of no response from Jonathan, she said, "Let's backtrack a bit. Maybe he's nearby."

They all started following along the messy footprints they had left. As they did so, Susan changed her frequency and asked Tranquility Central Communication if they'd heard from Jonathan. They had not.

It was a stretch to call Tranquility a city. Only two thousand people lived there, all the people left alive in the solar system. The outpost had started as a mining camp before the invasion, pulling out a surprising amount of raw diamonds. Every woman on Earth had wanted an engagement ring with a diamond from the Moon.

Now Tranquility did no mining. Its sole purpose was survival of the remaining humans.

About two hundred meters back, they found where he'd left the path. Two grooves led off to one side. They hadn't been there earlier. Susan felt dread, knowing with a weird certainty that the parallel grooves were from Jonathan's boots as he had been dragged.

"Stay here," she said to the kids. Matt wanted to go with her, but she held out her arm to him, too. "I won't go far."

The grooves curved back behind a crater that rose high above her head. She shuffled along slowly, and her heart jumped when she saw a helmet ripped apart, lying on the ground.

On the faceplate, she could see PETTY in the now-familiar bright green color.

Blood covered the whole area, a giant splatter of darkness. It had flash frozen in the frigid temperatures.

The helmet itself had a giant jagged rip in it, like a ridiculous monster had taken a bite from it.

Aliens.

She wanted to scream, but she couldn't. She wanted to run, but it felt like her feet were nailed to the Moon's surface.

"Jonathan . . . ?"

Whatever she said, the kids would hear.

There was no sign of the rest of Jonathan's space suit, or of his body. There was a wide path that she could see continued to move around the crater into the emptiness beyond.

She had to get the kids to safety without panicking them.

Susan moved back to the front of the path, where the kids stared silently at her.

"It's okay," she said. "Mr. Petty needed to go back because of a minor problem with his suit. We're going to go back now, too."

One of the kids asked, "Why did he just leave without telling us?"

Susan didn't know for sure who asked, but she just snapped, "Because he didn't. Let's go."

But where?

She knew the general direction to get to Station Three on the Halloween Path. They would have to go there, and then she could figure out the direction back to Tranquility.

"This way," she said.

Susan started walking and realized she needed somebody she trusted to bring up the rear. Not Selene, though. She needed her up front, close to her.

"Matt, you make sure everyone follows. Okay?"

"Sure."

Susan had never felt so alone in her life. She knew only a general way to the third stop, and she worked to get there. Every few minutes she stopped and hopped around to face the kids to be sure they were all following.

It took twenty minutes to get to the third stop.

When she got there, the holo started playing, but she just ignored it. The Halloween trip was the very last thing on her mind.

It'd been an hour since they'd left the city. Two hours of air left.

She counted the cohort members in her head . . . twelve, thirteen, fourteen . . .

Fourteen.

"Oh no."

Matt Wiley was missing.

"Matt?" She waited a beat and then yelled, "MATT!" She knew the yelling would do no good. If he was alive, he would have answered the first call. Safety was drilled into every Moonie as soon as they could crawl.

Aliens.

No, it couldn't be. They weren't really on the Moon.

Were they?

Nobody knew for sure, but the old stories that had been passed down for a half-dozen generations told of how the Aliens destroyed Earth and then left an outpost on the Moon, not realizing that humanity's only remaining habitat was there.

Maybe they found out today.

She looked up at the blazing Earth, shining brightly in the

sky, and wondered as so many others did before her, what exactly happened up there?

They would never know. She looked back at her fourteen remaining kids.

"Stay here. Move closer together so you can watch each other. I'll be right back."

She hopped back along the way they'd come, pursing her lips from fear. If something happened to her, what would happen to the kids?

She had to get them back.

There was no sign of Matt as she tracked back for several minutes.

If he was hurt somewhere and she left him, he would likely be dead before a rescue team would find him. Time was their enemy now as much as anything else.

If she didn't leave him, who knew what would happen to the other kids?

She stopped and tried to think, but her mind didn't seem to want to work. She didn't know what to do.

"Mom?"

Selene's voice shocked her back to reality. "I'm coming back," she said.

"We're scared."

"I know. I'm almost there."

THE TRIP BACK to Groundport was the longest walk of Susan's life. She kept imagining Matt calling to her, but she knew it was never real. None of the remaining kids heard anything.

She took the trailing position this time, and she kept constantly chatting about which direction to go, so the kids would know she was still there.

When they got back to the Port, she once again counted the kids. Fourteen.

Oh, God, how can I tell Matt's parents that I left him out there?

She blinked away tears and forced herself to just work on the task at hand. She waited for the shaft to open and she loaded the first five kids inside. She made sure Selene was in that first group.

Shortly everyone was back inside in pressurized rooms. As per normal protocol, they were scanned and cleansed, and then they waited in a holding area.

Susan thought about Aliens.

All the kids were chattering to each other, now that they were safely home. She knew they'd all been terrified on the surface, and she wondered if they'd ever feel comfortable going back again.

As the mandatory hour-long quarantine period ended, a door slid open and they were free to leave.

Standing in the doorway was Jonathan Petty.

She thought she was hallucinating, or maybe that Aliens had somehow entered his brain and were controlling his body.

"Hi, everybody!" he called. He was grinning widely, and two techies that walked into the room with him laughed along with him.

"What the hell?" Susan stared but didn't know what to say.

"It's Halloween, remember?"

The kids all stared at him, as confused as Susan.

"Remember what I said about Halloween? It's a chance to be somebody you're not. Sometimes that's a scary person, and this year I wanted to make you all feel like you were experiencing a real Halloween up on Earth. I wanted to be an Alien for you, and scare you a bit."

"You mean . . . your helmet? The blood?"

"All fake. Prepared ahead of time. I thought the blood was a nice touch."

It still wasn't sinking in to Susan. "It wasn't real?"

She looked at the kids, and she could see them all starting to smile and grin, mostly at her own discomfort. After all, they hadn't seen the site where Jonathan's helmet and spilled blood were.

Fake blood, she corrected herself.

"I really think this is what Halloween was like," Jonathan said. "Kids going out trick-or-treating and the people in their homes scaring them. Isn't that right?"

Susan couldn't help but nod. That sounded right to her, too. She just hadn't expected to live through a real Halloween.

Why had the people on Earth done this year after year?

"Halloween must have been awful," said Selene.

Jonathan smiled. "We'll never understand, but the good points must have outweighed the bad."

In spite of herself, Susan ran to Jonathan and hugged him. She'd never done that before, but she still needed to be convinced he was real.

"Where's Matt?" she asked.

"Matt?"

Susan looked through the door Jonathan had come through. "Isn't he with you? He'd want to . . ."

She snapped her head back.

"Tell me he was part of the trick."

Jonathan shook his head. "I don't know what you're talking about."

He looked at the kids, scanning them all, and then he said, "Oh, God, what happened?"

"He was there one minute and then he wasn't."

"He's still out there?"

Susan couldn't reply. She felt sick and frozen.

. . .

THE RESCUE TEAM suited up quickly. Susan and Jonathan went with them. She led them to the last place she knew for sure Matt had been with them, and then to the third leg of the Halloween Path, the first place she noticed he was missing.

They never found a trace of him. A week later, they held a remembrance service for him.

In her heart, Susan blamed herself. She should have been the one at the end of the line, not Matt.

When she was back in her cabin that evening, she cried.

She never wanted to think about Halloween again.

About the Authors

Kelley Armstrong is the author of the Cainsville modern gothic series and the Casey Butler crime thrillers. Past works include the Otherworld urban fantasy series, the Darkest Powers & Darkness Rising teen paranormal trilogies, the Age of Legends fantasy YA series, and the Nadia Stafford crime trilogy. Armstrong lives in Ontario, Canada, with her family.

Pat Cadigan sold her first professional science fiction story in 1980 and became a full-time writer in 1987. She is the author of fifteen books, including two nonfiction books on the making of *Lost in Space* and *The Mummy,* one young adult novel, and the two Arthur C. Clarke Award–winning novels *Synners* and *Fools.* She has also won the Locus Award three times and the Hugo Award for her novelette, "The Girl-Thing Who Went Out for Sushi," which also won the Seiun Award in Japan.

She can be found on Facebook and Pinterest, tweets as @cadigan, and lives in North London with her husband, the

Original Chris Fowler, where she is stomping the hell out of terminal cancer. Most of her books are available electronically via SF Gateway, the ambitious electronic publishing program from Gollancz.

Elise Forier Edie is an award-winning author and playwright based in Los Angeles. Recent publications include horror and fairy stories in *Cast of Wonders, Disturbed Digest,* and *Enchanted Conversation.* Her hit play *The Pink Unicorn,* about a transgender teenager, has been seen throughout the United States and Canada, most recently in Minneapolis and Pittsburgh. Elise is a member of the Horror Writers Association, the Society of Children's Book Writers and Illustrators, and the Authors Guild.

She has taught writing and arts classes at Central Washington University, Northland Pioneer College, West Los Angeles College, and the Arizona Commission on the Arts. She is a proud graduate of the Odyssey Writing Workshop. You can find out more about her at www.eliseforieredie.com.

Brian Evenson is the author of a dozen books of fiction, most recently the story collection *A Collapse of Horses* and the novella *The Warren.* His novel *Last Days* won the American Library Association's award for Best Horror Novel, and his collection *The Wavering Knife* won the International Horror Guild Award. He has been a finalist for an Edgar Award and the Shirley Jackson Award. His work has been translated into French, Greek, Italian, Japanese, Persian, Spanish, and Slovenian. He lives in Valencia, California, and teaches in the School of Critical Studies at the California Institute of the Arts.

Jeffrey Ford is the author of the novels *The Physiognomy, Memoranda, The Beyond, The Portrait of Mrs. Charbuque, The Girl in the Glass, The Cosmology of the Wider World,* and *The Shadow Year.* His short story collections are *The Fantasy Writer's Assistant, The Empire of Ice Cream, The Drowned Life, Crackpot Palace,* and *A Natural History of Hell.* Ford's short fiction has appeared in a wide variety of magazines and anthologies. Both books and stories have been translated into nearly twenty languages worldwide. Ford is the recipient of the World Fantasy Award, the Nebula Award, the Edgar Allan Poe Award, the Shirley Jackson Award, the Hayakawa Award, and the Grand Prix de l'Imaginaire. He lives in Ohio in a 120-year-old farmhouse surrounded by corn and soybean fields and teaches part-time at Ohio Wesleyan University.

Eric J. Guignard is a writer and editor of dark and speculative fiction, operating from the shadowy outskirts of Los Angeles. His work has appeared in publications such as *Nightmare* magazine, *Black Static, Shock Totem, Buzzy Mag,* and *Dark Discoveries* magazine. He won the Bram Stoker Award, was a finalist for the International Thriller Writers Award, and was a multinominee of the Pushcart Prize. Outside the glamorous and jet-setting world of indie fiction, Eric's a technical writer and college professor, and he stumbles home each day to a wife, children, cats, and a terrarium filled with mischievous beetles. Visit Eric at www.ericjguignard.com; his blog, ericjguignard .blogspot.com; or Twitter: @ericjguignard.

Stephen Graham Jones is the author of sixteen novels, six story collections, and more than 250 stories and has some comic books in the works. His current book is *Mapping the Interior.* Stephen's been the recipient of an NEA Fellowship in Fiction, the Texas Institute of Letters Jesse H. Jones Award for Fiction, the Independent Publishers Award for Multicultural Fiction, and three This Is Horror Awards, and he's made Bloody Disgusting's Top

Ten Horror Novels of the Year. Stephen teaches in the MFA programs at the University of Colorado at Boulder and the University of California, Riverside (Palm Desert). He lives in Boulder, Colorado, with his wife, two children, and too many old trucks. Visit him at Twitter: @SGJ72.

Dark fantasy and horror author Kate Jonez has twice been nominated for the Bram Stoker Award and once for the Shirley Jackson Award. Her short fiction has appeared or is forthcoming in *The Best Horror of the Year, Volume Eight*; *Black Static*; *Pseudopod*; and many anthologies. She is also the chief editor at Omnium Gatherum, a multiple-award-nominated press dedicated to publishing unique dark fantasy, weird fiction, and horror. Kate is a student of all things scary, and when she isn't writing, she loves to collect objects for her cabinet of curiosities, research obscure and strange historical figures, and photograph Southern California, where she lives with a very nice man and two little dogs who are also very nice but could behave a little bit better.

Paul Kane is the award-winning, bestselling author and editor of more than seventy books—including the Hooded Man trilogy (revolving around a postapocalyptic version of Robin Hood), *Hellbound Hearts,* and *Monsters.*

His nonfiction books include *The Hellraiser Films and Their Legacy* and *Voices in the Dark,* and his genre journalism has appeared in the likes of *SFX, Rue Morgue,* and *Death Ray.* His latest novels are *Lunar* (set to be turned into a feature film), *The Rainbow Man* (as P. B. Kane), *Blood RED, Sherlock Holmes and the Servants of Hell,* and *Before.* His work has been optioned and adapted for the big and small screen, including for U.S. network television.

He lives in Derbyshire, United Kingdom, with his wife Marie O'Regan, his family, and a black cat called Mina. Find out more at www.shadow-writer.co.uk.

John Langan is the author of two novels, *The Fisherman* and *House of Windows.* He has published two collections of stories, *The Wide, Carnivorous Sky and Other Monstrous Geographies* and *Mr. Gaunt and Other Uneasy Encounters.*

With Paul Tremblay, he coedited *Creatures: Thirty Years of Monsters.* He is one of the founders of the Shirley Jackson Awards, for which he served as a juror during its first three years. He reviews horror and dark fantasy for *Locus* magazine and lives in New York's Hudson Valley with his wife and son. His newest collection of stories, *Sefira and Other Betrayals,* will be published in 2017.

John R. Little's first novel, *The Memory Tree,* was nominated for a Bram Stoker Award in 2008. Since then, three of his other books have also been nominated for the Stoker, with *Miranda* winning. His most recent novels are *Soul Mates* and *DarkNet.*

His short fiction has been published in the magazines *The Twilight Zone, Cavalier,* and *Weird Tales* and in anthologies, including *Shivers IV, Blood Lite II, Dark Delicacies III: Haunted, Qualia Nous,* and others.

You can connect with John at his website, www.johnrlittle .com, or on Facebook. He'd love to hear from you.

Jonathan Maberry is a *New York Times* bestselling author, five-time Bram Stoker Award winner, and comic book writer. He writes in multiple genres, including suspense, thriller, horror, science fiction, fantasy, action, and steampunk, for adults, teens, and middle grade. His works include the Joe Ledger thrillers,

Rot & Ruin, Mars One (now in development for film), the Pine Deep Trilogy (in development for television), *Captain America,* and many others. He is the editor of high-profile anthologies, including *The X-Files, V-Wars, Scary Out There, Out of Tune, Baker Street Irregulars,* and *Nights of the Living Dead.* The popular V-Wars: A Game of Blood and Betrayal board game is based on his novels and comics. He lives in Del Mar, California. Find him online at www.jonathanmaberry.com.

Seanan McGuire lives, works, and watches way too many horror movies in the Pacific Northwest, where she shares her home with her two enormous blue cats, a ridiculous number of books, and a large collection of creepy dolls. Seanan does not sleep much, publishing an average of four books a year under both her own name and the pen name Mira Grant. Her first book, *Rosemary and Rue,* was released in September 2009, and she hasn't stopped running since. When not writing, Seanan enjoys Disney Parks, horror movies, and looking winsomely at Marvel editorials as she tries to convince them to let her write for the X-Men. Keep up with Seanan at www.seananmcguire .com, on Twitter as @seananmcguire, or by walking into a cornfield at night and calling the secret, hidden name of the Great Pumpkin to the moon. When you turn, she will be there. She will always have been there.

S. P. Miskowski's novel *Knock Knock* and novella *Delphine Dodd* were finalists for the Shirley Jackson Award. She is a recipient of two National Endowment for the Arts Fellowships. Her short stories have been published in the anthologies *October Dreams II, The Hyde Hotel, Cassilda's Song, Autumn Cthulhu, The Madness of Dr. Caligari,* and *Darker Companions: Celebrating 50 Years of Ramsey Campbell* and have appeared or will soon appear in *Black Static, Supernatural Tales,* and *Strange Aeons.* With Kate Jonez she edited the anthology *Little Visible Delight.*

A full-time writer for many years, Garth Nix has also worked as a literary agent, a marketing consultant, a book editor, a book publicist, a book sales representative, a bookseller, and a part-time soldier in the Australian Army Reserve. Garth's books include the award-winning and bestselling Old Kingdom series *Sabriel, Lirael, Abhorsen, Clariel,* and *Goldenhand*; the science fiction novels *Shade's Children* and *A Confusion of Princes*; many fantasy novels for children, including *The Ragwitch*; the six books of the Seventh Tower sequence; the Keys to the Kingdom series; and the recently published *Frogkisser!,* which is being developed by Fox Animation and Blue Sky Studios as an animated musical. He is also the author of *Newt's Emerald,* a "Regency romance with magic," and with Sean Williams has cowritten *Spirit Animals: Blood Ties,* the Troubletwisters series, and the Have Sword, Will Travel series. More than five million copies of Garth's books have been sold around the world; they have appeared on the bestseller lists of *The New York Times, Publishers Weekly, USA Today, The Sunday Times,* and *The Australian,* and his work has been translated into forty-one languages. He lives in Sydney, Australia. To find him on social media, please visit www.garthnix.com, www.facebook.com/garthnix, and Twitter @garthnix.

Joanna Parypinski is a college English instructor by day and a writer of the dark and strange by night. Her fiction and poetry have appeared at NewMyths.com and in *The Burning Maiden, Volume 2*; *Dark Moon Digest*; *Arcane II*; *The Literati Quarterly*; and elsewhere.

When she isn't grading or concocting tales and verse, she may be found playing the cello, wandering around local cemeteries, or dreaming of October. She loves Halloween so much that she is even having a Halloween-themed wedding! For more, visit her website at joannaparypinski.com.

About the Editors

Ellen Datlow has been editing science fiction, fantasy, and horror short fiction for more than thirty-five years. She currently acquires short fiction for Tor.com. In addition, she has edited more than fifty anthologies, including The Best Horror of the Year series, *Fearful Symmetries, The Doll Collection, The Monstrous,* and *Black Feathers.*

A multiple award winner for her work, Datlow is a recipient of the Karl Edward Wagner Award, given at the British Fantasy Convention for "outstanding contribution to the genre," and has been honored with Life Achievement Awards by both the Horror Writers Association and the World Fantasy Convention.

She lives in New York and cohosts the monthly Fantastic Fiction Reading Series at KGB Bar. More information can be found at www.datlow.com, on Facebook, and on Twitter as @EllenDatlow.

Lisa Morton is a screenwriter, an author of nonfiction books, a Bram Stoker Award–winning prose writer, an editor, and a

Halloween expert whose work was described by the American Library Association's *Readers' Advisory Guide to Horror* as "consistently dark, unsettling, and frightening." As a Halloween expert, she has appeared on the History Channel and BBC Radio and in the pages of *Real Simple* magazine and *The Wall Street Journal,* and she served as consultant on the first official U.S. Postal Service Halloween stamps. Her most recent releases include *Ghosts: A Haunted History* and *Cemetery Dance Select: Lisa Morton*. She lives in the San Fernando Valley and can be found online at www.lisamorton.com.

Permissions

THE BLUMHOUSE BOOK OF NIGHTMARES
The Haunted City

Original and terrifying fiction presented by Jason Blum, the award-winning producer behind the groundbreaking *Paranormal Activity*, *The Purge*, *Insidious*, and *Sinister* franchises. Jason Blum invited sixteen cutting-edge writers, collaborators, and filmmakers to envision a city of their choosing and let their demons run wild. *The Blumhouse Book of Nightmares: The Haunted City* brings together all-new, boundary-breaking stories from such artists as Ethan Hawke (*Boyhood*), Eli Roth (*Hostel*), Scott Derrickson (*Sinister*), C. Robert Cargill (*Sinister*), James DeMonaco (*The Purge*), and many others.

Horror

THE APARTMENT

Mark and Steph have a relatively happy family with their young daughter in sunny Cape Town until one day when armed men in balaclavas break in to their home. Left traumatized but physically unharmed, Mark and Steph are unable to return to normal and live in constant fear. When a friend suggests a restorative vacation abroad via a popular house-swapping website, it sounds like the perfect plan. They find a genial, artistic couple with a charming apartment in Paris who would love to come to Cape Town. Mark and Steph can't resist the idyllic, light-strewn pictures and the promise of a romantic getaway. But once they arrive in Paris, they quickly realize that nothing is as advertised. When their perfect holiday takes a violent turn, the cracks in their marriage grow ever wider, and dark secrets from Mark's past begin to emerge.

Horror

FERAL

Allie Hilts was still in high school when a fire at a top secret research facility released an airborne pathogen that rapidly spread to every male on the planet, killing most. Allie witnessed every man she ever knew be consumed by fearsome symptoms: scorching fevers and internal bleeding, madness and uncontrollable violence. The world crumbled around her. No man was spared, and the few survivors were irrevocably changed. They became disturbingly strong, aggressive, and ferocious. Feral. Three years later, Allie has joined a group of hardened survivors in an isolated, walled-in encampment. Outside the guarded walls the ferals roam free and hunt. Allie has been noticing troubling patterns in the ferals' movements and a disturbing number of new faces in the wild. Something catastrophic is brewing on the horizon, and time is running out. The ferals are coming, and there is no stopping them.

Horror

BLUM**H**OUSE
BOOKS

ANCHOR BOOKS

Available wherever books are sold.

www.blumhousebooks.com